WIN

Harlan Coben

WIN

CENTURY

1 3 5 7 9 10 8 6 4 2

Century
20 Vauxhall Bridge Road
London SW1V 2SA

Century is part of the Penguin Random House group of companies
whose addresses can be found at global.penguinrandomhouse.com.

Penguin
Random House
UK

First published in Great Britain by Century in 2021
First published in the USA by Grand Central Publishing in 2021

www.penguin.co.uk

A CIP catalogue record for this book is available from the British Library.

Hardback ISBN 9781529123845
Trade paperback ISBN 9781529123852

Printed and bound in India by Thomson Press India Ltd.

The authorised representative in the EEA is Penguin Random House Ireland,
Morrison Chambers, 32 Nassau Street, Dublin D02 YH68.

Penguin Random House is committed to a sustainable future
for our business, our readers and our planet. This book is
made from Forest Stewardship Council® certified paper.

MIX
Paper from
responsible sources
FSC® C018179

To Diane and Michael Discepolo
With love and gratitude

CHAPTER 1

The shot that will decide the championship is slowly arching its way toward the basket.

I do not care.

Everyone else in Indianapolis's Lucas Oil Stadium stares at the ball with mouth open.

I do not.

I stare across the court. At him.

My seat is courtside, of course, near the center line. An A-list Marvel-Superhero actor sporting a tourniquet-tight, show-biceps black tee sits on my left, you know him, and the celebrated rapper-mogul Swagg Daddy, whose private jet I bought three years ago, dons his own brand of sunglasses to my right. I like Sheldon (that's Swagg Daddy's real name), both the man and his music, but he cheers and glad-hands past the point of sycophantic, and it makes me cringe.

As for me, I sport a Savile Row hand-tailored suit of pinstripe azure, a pair of Bedfordshire bespoke Bordeaux-hued shoes created by Basil, the master craftsman at G. J. Cleverley's, a limited-edition Lilly Pulitzer silk tie of pink and green, and a specially created Hermès pocket square, which flares out from the left breast pocket with celestial precision.

I am quite the rake.

I am also, for those missing the subtext, rich.

The ball traveling in the air will decide the outcome of the college basketball phenomenon known as March Madness. Odd that, when you think about it. All the blood and sweat and tears, all the strategizing and scouting and coaching, all the countless hours of shooting alone in your driveway, of dribbling drills, of the three-man weave, of lifting weights, of doing wind sprints until you hurl, all those years in stale gyms on every level— Biddy basketball, CYO travel all-stars, AAU tournaments, high school, you get the point—all of that boils down to the simple physics of a rudimentary orange sphere back-spinning toward a metallic cylinder at this exact moment.

Either the shot will miss and Duke University will win— or it will go in and South State University and their fans will rush the court in celebration. The A-list Marvel hero attended South State. Swagg Daddy, like yours truly, attended Duke. They both tense up. The raucous crowd falls into a hush. Time has slowed.

Again, even though it's my alma mater, I don't care. I don't get fandom in general. I never care who wins a contest in which I (or someone dear to me) am not an active participant. Why, I often wonder, would anyone?

I use the time to focus on him.

His name is Teddy Lyons. He is one of the too-many assistant coaches on the South State bench. He is six foot eight and beefy, a big slab of aw-shucks farm boy. Big T—that's what he likes to be called—is thirty-three years old, and this is his fourth college coaching job. From what I understand, he is a decent tactician but excels at recruiting talent.

I hear the buzzer go off. Time is out, though the outcome of the contest is still very much in doubt.

The arena is so hushed that I can actually hear the ball hit the rim.

Swagg grabs my leg. Mr. Marvel A-List swings a muscled tricep across my chest as he spreads his arms in anticipation. The ball hits the rim once, twice, then a third time, as though this inanimate object is teasing the crowd before deciding for itself who lives and who dies.

I still watch Big T.

When the ball rolls all the way off the rim and then drops toward the ground—a definite miss—the Blue Devil section in the arena explodes. In my periphery, I see everyone on the South State bench deflate. I don't care for the word "crestfallen"—it's an odd word—but here it is apropos. They deflate and appear crestfallen. Several collapse in devastation and tears as the reality of the loss sinks in.

But not Big T.

Marvel A-Lister drops his handsome face into his hands. Swagg Daddy throws his arms around me.

"We won, Win!" Swagg shouts. Then, thinking better of it: "Or should I say, 'We win, Win!'"

I frown at him. My frown tells him I expect better.

"Yeah, you're right," Swagg says.

I barely hear him. The roar is beyond deafening. He leans in closer.

"My party is going to be lit!"

He runs out and joins the celebration. En masse, the crowd charges the court with him, exuberant, rejoicing. They swallow

Swagg from my view. Several slap me on the back as they pass. They encourage me to join, but I do not.

I look again for Teddy Lyons, but he is gone.

Not for long though.

———————

Two hours later, I see Teddy Lyons again. He is strutting toward me.

Here is my dilemma.

I am going to "put a hurting," as they say, on Big T. There is no way around that. I'm still not sure how much of one, but the damage to his physical health will be severe.

That's not my dilemma.

My dilemma involves the how.

No, I'm not worried about getting caught. This part has been planned out. Big T received an invitation to Swagg Daddy's blowout. He is entering through what he believes is a VIP entrance. It is not. In fact, it is not even the location of the party. Loud music blasts from down the corridor, but it is just for show.

It is only Big T and I in this warehouse.

I wear gloves. I have weaponry on me—I always do—though it will not be needed.

Big T is drawing closer to me, so let's get back to my dilemma:

Do I strike him without warning—or do I give him what some might consider a sporting chance?

This isn't about morality or fair play or any of that. It matters to me none what the general populace would label this. I have been in many scrapes in my day. When you do battle, rules rapidly become null and void. Bite, kick, throw sand, use a

4

weapon, whatever it takes. Real fights are about survival. There are no prizes or praise for sportsmanship. There is a victor. There is a loser. The end. It doesn't matter whether you "cheat."

In short, I have no qualms about simply striking this odious creature when he's not ready. I am not afraid to take—again to use common vernacular—a "cheap shot." In fact, that had been my plan all along: Jump him when he's not ready. Use a bat or a knife or the butt of my gun. Finish it.

So why the dilemma now?

Because I don't think breaking bones is enough here. I want to break the man's spirit too. If tough-guy Big T were to lose a purportedly fair fight to little ol' me—I am older, much slighter, far prettier (it's true), the very visual dictionary definition of "effete"—it would be humiliating.

I want that for Big T.

He is only a few steps away. I make my decision and step out to block his path. Big T pulls up and scowls. He stares at me a moment. I smile at him. He smiles back.

"I know you," he says.

"Do tell."

"You were at the game tonight. Sitting courtside."

"Guilty," I say.

He sticks out his huge mitt of a hand for me to shake. "Teddy Lyons. Everyone calls me Big T."

I don't shake the hand. I stare at it, as though it plopped out of a dog's anus. Big T waits a second, standing there frozen, before he takes the hand back as though it's a small child that needs comforting.

I smile at him again. He clears his throat.

"If you'll excuse me," he begins.

"I won't, no."

"What?"

"You're a little slow, aren't you, Teddy?" I sigh. "No, I won't excuse you. There is no excuse for you. Are you with me now?"

The scowl slowly returns to his face. "You got a problem?"

"Hmm. Which comeback to go with?"

"Huh?"

"I could say, 'No, YOU got a problem' or 'Me? Not a care in the world'—something like that—but really, none of those snappy rejoinders are calling to me."

Big T looks perplexed. Part of him wants to simply shove me aside. Part of him remembers that I was sitting in Celebrity Row and thus I might be someone important.

"Uh," Big T says, "I'm going to the party now."

"No, you're not."

"Pardon?"

"There's no party here."

"When you say there's no party—"

"The party is two blocks away," I say.

He puts his mitts on his hips. Coach pose. "What the hell is this?"

"I had them send you the wrong address. The music? It's just for show. The security guard who let you in by the VIP entrance? He works for me and vanished the moment you walked through that door."

Big T blinks twice. Then he steps closer to me. I don't back up even an inch.

"What's going on?" he asks me.

"I'm going to kick your ass, Teddy."

Oh, how his smile widens now. "You?" His chest is the approximate size of a squash court's front wall. He moves in closer now, looming over me, staring down with the confidence of a big, powerful man who, because of his size, has never experienced combat or even been challenged. This is Big T's amateurish, go-to move—crowd his opponent with his bulk and then watch them wither.

I don't wither, of course. I crane my neck and meet his gaze. And now, for the first time, I see doubt start to cloud his expression.

I don't wait.

Crowding me like this was a mistake. It makes my first move short and easy. I place all five of my fingertips on my right hand together, forming something of an arrowhead, and dart-strike his throat. A gurgling sound emerges. At the same time, I sidekick low, leading with my instep, connecting directly on the side of his right knee which, I know from research, has undergone two ACL surgeries.

I hear a crack.

Big T goes down like an oak.

I lift my leg and strike him hard with my heel.

He cries out.

I strike him again.

He cries out.

I strike him again.

Silence.

I will spare you the rest.

Twenty minutes later, I arrive at Swagg Daddy's party. Security whisks me to the back room. Only three types of people get in here—beautiful women, famous faces, fat wallets.

We party hard until five a.m. Then a black limo takes Swagg and yours truly to the airport. The private jet is gassed up and waiting.

Swagg sleeps the entire flight back to New York City. I

shower—yes, my jet has a shower—shave, and change into a Kiton K50 business suit of herringbone gray.

When we land, two black limos are waiting. Swagg involves me in some kind of complicated handshake-embrace as a way of saying goodbye. He takes one limo to his estate in Alpine. I take the other directly to my office in a forty-eight-story sky-scraper on Park Avenue in midtown. My family has owned the Lock-Horne Building since it was completed in 1967.

On the way up in the elevator, I stop on the fourth floor. This space used to be home to a sports agency run by my closest friend, but he closed it down a few years back. I then left the office empty for too long because hope springs eternal. I was sure that my friend would change his mind and return.

He didn't. And so we move on.

The new tenant is Fisher and Friedman, which advertises itself as a "Victims' Rights Law Firm." Their website, which won me over, is somewhat more specific:

We help you knee the abusers, the stalkers,
the douchebags, the trolls, the pervs, and
the psychos right in the balls.

Irresistible. As with the sports agency that used to lease this space, I am a silent partner-investor in the firm.

I knock on the door. When Sadie Fisher says, "Come in," I open it and lean my head inside.

"Busy?" I ask.

"Sociopaths are very much in season," Sadie says, not look-ing up from the computer.

She is right, of course. It's why I invested. I feel good about the work they do, advocating for the bullied and battered, but I also see insecure-cum-violent men (it's almost always men) as a growth industry.

Sadie finally glances in my direction. "I thought you were going to the game in Indianapolis."

"I did."

"Oh, right, the private jet. Sometimes I forget how rich you are."

"No, you don't."

"True. So what's up?"

Sadie wears hot-librarian glasses and a pink pantsuit that clings and reveals. This is intentional, she explained to me. When Sadie first started representing women who'd been sexually harassed and assaulted, she was told to dress conservatively, garments that were shapeless and drab and hence "innocent," which Sadie saw as more victim blaming.

Her response? Do the opposite.

I am not sure how to broach the subject, so I just say, "I heard one of your clients was hospitalized."

That gets her attention.

"Do you think it would be appropriate to send her something?" I ask.

"Like what, Win?"

"Flowers, chocolates..."

"She's in intensive care."

"A stuffed animal. Balloons."

"Balloons?"

"Just something to let her know we are thinking about her."

Sadie's eyes turn back to the computer screen. "The only thing our client wants is something we don't seem to be able to give her: Justice."

I open my mouth to say something, but in the end, I

stay silent, opting for discretion and wisdom over comfort and bravado. I turn to leave, when I spot two people—one woman, one man—walking toward me with purpose.

"Windsor Horne Lockwood?" the woman says.

Even before they whip out their badges, I know that they are in law enforcement.

Sadie can tell too. She rises automatically and starts toward me. I have a slew of attorneys, of course, but I use those for business reasons. For personal affairs, my best friend, the sports agent/lawyer who used to inhabit this office, always stepped in because he had my full trust. Now, with him on the sidelines, it seems that Sadie has instinctively slid into the role.

"Windsor Horne Lockwood?" the woman says again.

That is my name. To be technically correct, my full name is Windsor Horne Lockwood III. I am, as the name suggests, old money, and I look the part, what with the ruddy complexion, the blond-turning-gray hair, the delicate patrician features, the somewhat regal bearing. I don't hide what I am. I don't know whether I could.

How, I wonder, had I messed up with Big T? I am good. I am very good. But I am not infallible.

So where had I made a mistake?

Sadie is almost by my side now. I wait. Instead of responding, I let her say, "Who wants to know?"

"I'm Special Agent Karen Young with the FBI," the woman says.

Young is Black. She wears an Oxford blue button-down shirt under a fitted cognac-hued leather jacket. Très fashionable for a federal agent.

"And this is my partner, Special Agent Jorge Lopez."

Lopez is more central stock. His suit is wet-pavement gray, his tie a sad and stained red.

They show us their badges.

"What's this about?" Sadie asks.

"We'd like to talk to Mr. Lockwood."

"So I gathered," Sadie replies with a bit of bite. "What about?"

Young smiles and puts her badge back in her pocket. "It's about a murder."

CHAPTER 2

We hit a little bit of a wall. Young and Lopez want to take me someplace without further explanation. Sadie will have none of that. Eventually I intervene, and we come to an agreement of sorts. I will go with them. I will not be interrogated or questioned without an attorney present.

Sadie, who is wise beyond her thirty years, doesn't like this. She pulls me aside and says, "They'll question you anyway."

"I'm aware. This isn't my first run-in with the authorities." Nor my second or third or . . . but Sadie does not need to know this. I don't want to continue stalling or being "lawyered up" for three reasons: One, Sadie has a court appearance, and I don't want to hold her up. Two, if this does involve Teddy "Big T" Lyons, I would prefer that Sadie not hear about it in this rather head-on manner for obvious reasons. Three, I'm curious about this murder and preternaturally overconfident. Sue me.

Once in the car, we travel uptown. Lopez drives, Young sits next to him. I am in the backseat. Oddly enough, anxiety is coming off them like tangible sonar. They are both trying to be professional—and they are—but under that, I can sense the undercurrent. This murder is something different, something out of the ordinary. They are trying to hide that, but their excitement is a pheromone I cannot fail to smell.

Lopez and Young start off by giving me the customary silent treatment. The theory is a rather simple one: Most people hate silence and will do anything to break it, including saying something incriminating.

I'm almost insulted that they are trying this tactic on me.

I don't engage, of course. I settle into the backseat, steeple my fingers, and stare out the car window as though I'm a tourist on my first visit to the big bad city.

Finally, Young says, "We know about you."

I reach into my jacket pocket and press down on my phone. The conversation is now being recorded. It will go straight to the cloud in case one of my new FBI friends discovers that I'm recording and opts for deletion or phone breakage.

I am nothing if not prepared.

Young turns to face me. "I said, we know about you."

Silence from me.

"You used to do some stuff for the Bureau," she says.

That they know anything about my relationship with the Federal Bureau of Investigation surprises me, though I don't show it. I did work for the FBI immediately after I graduated from Duke University, but my work was highly classified. The fact that someone told them—it had to be someone on top— again informs me that this murder case is out of the ordinary.

"Heard you were good," Lopez says, catching my eye in the rearview mirror.

Moving quickly now from the silent treatment to flattery. Still I give them nothing.

We drive up Central Park West, my home street. The odds now seem slim that this murder has to do with Big T. For one thing, I know that Big T survived, albeit not intact. Second, if the feds wanted to question me for anything related to that, we would be headed downtown toward their headquarters at 26 Federal Plaza; instead, here we are, traveling in the opposite direction, toward my own abode in the Dakota, on the corner of Central Park West and Seventy-Second Street.

I consider this fact. I live alone now, so it is not as though the victim could be a loved one. It could be that the courts had issued some sort of search warrant for my residence and found something incriminating that they wish to spring on me, but this too seems unlikely. One of the Dakota doormen would have warned me of such an invasion. One of my hidden alarms would have buzzed my phone. I'm also not careless enough to leave around anything that might implicate me for authorities to locate.

To my surprise, Lopez drives us past the Dakota without a pause. We continue uptown. Six blocks later, as we reach the Museum of Natural History, I spot two NYPD squad cars parked in front of the Beresford, another esteemed prewar apartment building, at Eighty-First Street.

Lopez is now studying me in the rearview mirror. I look at him and frown.

The Beresford doormen wear uniforms seemingly inspired by Soviet generals from the late seventies. As Lopez pulls to a stop, Young turns to me and asks, "Do you know anybody in this building?"

My reply is a smile and silence.

She shakes her head. "Fine, let's go."

With Lopez on my right and Young on my left, they escort me straight through the marble lobby and into an already-waiting wood-paneled elevator. When Young presses the button for the top floor, I realize that we are heading into rarefied air—

figuratively, literally, and mostly monetarily. One of my employees, a vice president at Lock-Horne Securities, owns a "classic six" apartment on the fourth floor of the Beresford with limited views of the park. He paid over five million dollars for it.

Young turns to me and says, "Any clue where we are headed?"

"Up?" I say.

"Funny."

I bat my eyes in modesty.

"The top floor," she says. "Been there before?"

"I don't believe so."

"Do you know who lives there?"

"I don't believe so."

"I figured all you rich guys know each other."

"Stereotyping is wrong," I say.

"But you've been to this building before, right?"

The elevator door opens with a ding before I bother not replying. I figured that we would be let out into a grand apartment—elevators often open directly into penthouse suites—but we are in a dark corridor. The wallpaper is a heavy maroon fabric. The open door on the right leads to a corkscrew staircase of wrought iron. Lopez goes up first. Young signals for me to follow. I do so.

There is junk everywhere.

Six-foot stacks of old magazines, newspapers, and books line both sides of the stairs. We need to go up single file—I spot a *Time* magazine from 1998—and even then we have to turn our bodies to the side to slip through the narrow opening.

The stench is suffocating.

It is a cliché, but it is a cliché with merit: Nothing smells like a decaying human body. Young and Lopez both cover their noses and mouths. I do not.

The Beresford has four turrets, one atop each corner of the edifice. We reach the landing of the northeastern one. Whoever lives here (or perhaps more accurately, lived), up high on the top level of one of the most prestigious buildings in Manhattan, was a full-fledged hoarder. We can barely move. Four crime technicians in full garb with the shower caps are attempting to comb and climb through the clutter.

The corpse has already been zipped up. I'm surprised that they haven't moved it out of here yet, but everything about this is odd.

I still have no idea why I'm here.

Young shows me a photograph of what I assume is the dead man—eyes closed, white sheet pulled up high on the body, right up to the chin. He was an older man with white-to-gray skin. I would venture to say in his early seventies. He is bald on top with a gray hair ring that's overgrown by the ears. His beard is big and thick and curly and dirty-white, so that it looks as though he were eating a sheep when the photograph was taken.

"Do you know him?" Young asks.

I opt for the truth. "No." I hand the photograph back. "Who is he?"

"The victim."

"Yes, I figured that, thank you. His name, I mean."

The agents exchange a glance. "We don't know."

"Did you ask the tenant?"

"It is our belief," Young says, "that he is the tenant."

I wait.

"This tower room was purchased almost thirty years ago by an LLC using an untraceable shell company."

Untraceable. I know this all too well. I use similar financial instruments often, not so much to avoid taxation, though that is often a fringe benefit. In my case—as it appears was the case for our late hoarder—such actions are more about anonymity.

"No identification?" I say.

"We haven't found one yet."

"The building employees—"

"He lived alone. Deliveries were left at the bottom of the steps. The building has no security cameras in the upstairs corridors, or if they do, they aren't admitting it. Co-op fees were paid on time from the LLC. According to the doormen, Hermit—that was their nickname for him—was a big-time recluse. He went out rarely and when he did, he would wrap his face in a scarf and leave via a secret basement exit. The manager just found him this morning after the smell started wafting down to the floor below."

"And no one in the building knows who he is?"

"Not so far," Young says, "but we're still going door-to-door."

"So the obvious question," I say.

"That being?"

"Why am I here?"

"The bedroom."

Young seems to expect me to reply. I don't.

"Come with us."

As we start to the right, I can see the view of the Natural History Museum's giant round planetarium across the street, and to the left, Central Park in all its glory. My apartment too has a rather enviable view of the park, though the Dakota is only nine stories high while here we are somewhere above the twentieth floor.

I am not easily surprised, but when I enter the bedroom—when I see the reason why they brought me here—I pull up. I do not move. I just stare. I fall into the past, as though the image in front of me is a time portal. I am an eight-year-old boy sneaking my way into Granddad's parlor at Lockwood Manor. The rest of my extended family are still out in the garden. I wear a black suit and stand by myself on the ornate parquet floor. This is before the family destruction or perhaps, looking back on it now, this is the very moment of the first fissure. It is Granddad's funeral. This parlor, his favorite room, has been over-sprayed with some kind of cloying disinfectant, but the familiar, comforting smell of Granddad's pipe still dominates. I relish it. I reach out with a tentative hand and touch the leather of his favorite chair, almost expecting him to materialize in it, cardigan sweater, slippers, pipe, and all. Eventually, my eight-year-old self works up the courage to hoist myself up to sit in the wingback chair. When I do, I look up at the wall above the fireplace, just as Granddad so often did.

I know that Young and Lopez are watching me for a reaction.

"At first," Young says, "we thought it had to be a forgery."

I continue to stare, just as I did as an eight-year-old in that leather chair.

"So we grabbed an art curator from the Met across the park," Young continues. The Met being shorthand for the Metropolitan Museum of Art. "She wants to get this off this wall and run some tests, just to be positive, but she's pretty certain—this is the real deal."

The hoarder's bedroom, as opposed to the rest of the tower, is neat, tidy, spare, utilitarian. The bed against the wall is made. There is no headboard. The side table is bare except for a pair of reading glasses and a leather-bound book. I now know why I was brought here—to see the only thing hanging on the wall.

The oil painting simply called *The Girl at the Piano* by Johannes Vermeer.

Yes, that Vermeer. Yes, that painting.

This masterpiece, like most of the only thirty-four Vermeer

paintings in existence, is small, a foot and a half tall by a foot and four inches wide, though it packs an undeniable punch in its simplicity and beauty. This *Girl*, purchased nearly a hundred years ago by my great-grandfather, used to hang in the parlor of Lockwood Manor. Twenty-plus years ago, my family loaned this painting, valued in excess of $200 million by today's standards, along with the only other masterpiece we owned, Picasso's *The Reader*, to the Lockwood Gallery in Founders Hall on the campus of Haverford College. You may have read about the nighttime burglary. Over the years, there have been constant false sightings of both masterpieces—most recently, the Vermeer on a yacht belonging to a Middle Eastern prince. None of these leads (and I've checked several personally) panned out. Some theorized that the theft was the work of the same crime syndicate who stole thirteen works of art, including works by Rembrandt, Manet, Degas, and yes, a Vermeer, from the Isabella Stewart Gardner Museum in Boston.

None of the stolen works from either robbery has ever been recovered.

Until now.

"Any thoughts?" Young asks.

I had put up two empty frames in Granddad's parlor, both as a homage to what was taken and a promise that his master-pieces would someday be returned.

Now that promise, it seems, will be at least half fulfilled.

"The Picasso?" I ask.

"No sign of it," Young says, "but as you can see, we still have a lot to look through."

The Picasso is far larger—over five feet tall and four feet wide. If it was here, chances seem strong that it would have been found already.

"Any other thoughts?" Young asks.

I gesture toward the wall. "When can I bring it home?"

"That'll take some time. You know the drill."

"I know a renowned art curator and restorer at NYU. His name is Pierre-Emmanuel Claux. I would like him to handle the piece."

"We have our own people."

"No, Special Agent, you do not. In fact, per your own admission, you grabbed a random person from the Met this morning—"

"Hardly a random—"

"This is not a big ask," I continue. "My person is educated in how to authenticate, handle, and if necessary, restore a masterpiece like few people in the world."

"We can look into it," Young says, trying to move us past this topic. "Any other thoughts?"

"Was the victim strangled or was his throat cut?"

They exchange another glance. Then Lopez clears his throat and says, "How do—?"

"The sheet was covering his neck," I say. "In the photograph you showed me. That was done, I surmise, to cover trauma."

"Let's not get into that, okay?" Young says.

"Do you have a time of death?" I ask.

"Let's not get into that either."

Shorter version: I'm a suspect.

I'm not sure why. Surely, if I had done this deed, I would have taken the painting with me. Or perhaps not. Perhaps I was clever enough to have murdered him and left the painting so it would be found and returned to my family.

"Do you have any other thoughts that might help us?" Young asks.

I don't bother with the obvious theory: The hermit was an art thief. He liquidated most of what he pilfered, used the profits to hide his identity, set up an anonymous shell company, purchased the apartment. For some reason—most likely because he either loved it or it was too hot to unload—he kept the Vermeer for himself.

"So," Young continues, "you've never been here before, right?"

Her tone is too casual.

"Mr. Lockwood?"

Interesting. They clearly believe they have evidence that I have been in this turret. I haven't been. It is also clear that they took the unusual step of bringing me to the murder scene to knock me off my game. If they had followed the normal protocol of a murder investigation and taken me to an interrogation room, I would be on my guard and defensive. I might have brought a criminal attorney.

What, pray tell, do they think they have on me?

"On behalf of my family, I'm grateful the Vermeer has been found. I hope this leads to the speedy recovery of the Picasso. I'm now ready to return to my office."

Young and Lopez don't like this. Young looks at Lopez and nods. Lopez slips into the other room.

"One moment," Young says. She reaches into her binder and pulls out another photograph. When she shows it to me, I am yet again puzzled.

"Do you recognize this, Mr. Lockwood?"

To buy time, I say, "Call me Win."

"Do you recognize this, Win?"

"You know that I do."

"It's your family crest, is that correct?"

"It is, yes."

"It will obviously take us a long time to go through the victim's apartment," Young continues.

"So you said."

"But we found one item in the closet of this bedroom." Young smiles. She has, I notice, a nice smile. "Only one."

I wait.

Lopez reenters the room. Behind him, a crime scene technician carries an alligator-leather suitcase with burnished metal hardware. I recognize the piece, but I can't believe it. It makes no sense.

"Do you recognize this suitcase?" Young asks.

"Should I?"

But of course, I do. Years ago, Aunt Plum had one made up for every male member of the family. They are all adorned with the family crest and our initials. When she gave it to me—I was fourteen at the time—I tried very hard not to frown. I don't mind expensive and luxurious. I do mind vulgar and wasteful.

"The bag has your initials on it."

The technician tipped the luggage so I could see the tacky baroque monogram:

WHL3.

"That's you, right? WHL3—Windsor Horne Lockwood the Third?"

I don't move, don't speak, don't give anything away. But, without sounding overly melodramatic, this discovery has given my world a shove off its axis.

"So, Mr. Lockwood, do you want to tell us why your luggage is here?"

CHAPTER 3

Young and Lopez want an explanation. I start with the complete truth: I had not seen the suitcase in many years. How many years? Here my memory becomes foggier. Many, I say. More than ten? Yes. More than twenty? I shrug. Could I at least confirm that the suitcase had belonged to me? No, I would need a closer look, to be able to open it and look at its contents. Young doesn't like that. I didn't think she would. But can't I at least confirm the suitcase is mine just by looking at it? I couldn't for certain, sorry, I tell them. But those are your initials and your family crest, Lopez reminds me. They are, I say, but that doesn't mean someone didn't make up a duplicate suitcase. Why would someone do that? I have no idea.

And so it goes.

I make my way down the spiral staircase and move into a corner. I text Kabir, my assistant, to send a car right away to the Beresford—no need to get a return ride from my federal escorts. I also have him prepare the helicopter for an immediate trip to Lockwood, the family estate on the Main Line in Philadelphia. Traffic between Manhattan and Philadelphia is unpredictable. It would probably be a two-and-a-half-hour car ride at this hour. The helicopter takes forty-five minutes.

I am in a rush.

The black car is waiting for me on Eighty-First Street. As we head toward the helipad on Thirtieth Street and the Hudson River, I call Cousin Patricia's mobile.

"Articulate," she says when she answers.

I can't help but smile. "Wiseass."

"Sorry, Cuz. All okay?"

"Yes."

"I haven't heard from you in a while."

"And I you."

"So to what do I owe the pleasure?"

"I'm about to take a copter into Lockwood."

Patricia doesn't reply.

"Could you meet me there?"

"At Lockwood?"

"Yes."

"When?"

"In an hour."

She hesitates, which is understandable. "I haven't been to Lockwood in . . ."

"I know," I say.

"I have an important meeting."

"Cancel it."

"Just like that?"

I wait.

"What's going on, Win?"

I wait some more.

"Right," she says. "If you wanted to tell me on the phone, you'd do so."

"See you in an hour," I say, and disconnect the call.

We fly over the Benjamin Franklin Bridge, which traverses the Delaware River separating New Jersey from Pennsylvania. Three minutes later, Lockwood Manor rises into view, as though it deserves a soundtrack. The copter, an AgustaWestland AW169, passes over the old stone walls, hovers in the clearing, and lands in the lawns by what we still call the "new stables." It is coming on a quarter century since I razed the original stable, a building dating back to the nineteenth century. The symbolic move was uncharacteristically mawkish on my part. I had convinced myself that a tear-down-and-rebuild might hurl the memory in the mind's debris.

It did not.

When I first brought my friend Myron to Lockwood—we were college freshmen on a midterm break—he shook his head and said, "It looks like Wayne Manor." He was referencing Batman, of course—the original television show starring Adam West and Burt Ward, the only Batman that counted to us. I understood his point. The manor has an aura, a magnificence, a boldness, but "stately Wayne Manor" is reddish brick while Lockwood is made of gray stone. There have been additions over the years, two tasteful albeit huge renovations on either side. These new wings are comfortable and air-conditioned, brighter and airier, yet they try too hard. They are facsimiles. I need to be in the original stone of Lockwood. I need to experience the damp, the must, the drafts.

But then again, I only visit nowadays.

Nigel Duncan, the longtime family butler/attorney—yes, it's a bizarre mix—is there to greet me. Nigel is bald with a three-wisps comb-over and double chin. He sports gray-on-gray sweats—gray sweatpants with a Villanova logo and a tie-string waist around the protruding gut, and an equally gray hoodie with the word "Penn" across the front.

I frown at him. "Nice groufit."

Nigel gives me an elaborate bow. "Would Master Win prefer me in tails?"

Nigel thinks he's funny.

"Are those Chuck Taylor Cons?" I ask, pointing to his sneakers.

"They're very chic," he tells me.

"If you're in eighth grade."

"Ouch." Then he adds, "We weren't expecting you, Master Win."

He is teasing with the Master stuff. I let him. "I wasn't expecting to come."

"Is everything okay?"

"Groovy," I tell him.

Nigel's sometimes-English accent is fake. He was born on this estate. His father worked for my grandfather, just as Nigel works for my father. Nigel has taken a slightly different path. My father paid for him to go to the University of Penn undergrad and law school in order to give Nigel "more" than the life of a butler and yet handcuff him via obligation to stay on at Lockwood permanently, per his family tradition.

PSA: The rich are very good at using generosity to get what they want.

"Will you be staying the night?" Nigel asks.

"No," I say.

"Your father is sleeping."

"Don't wake him," I say.

We start toward the main house. Nigel wants to know the purpose of my visit, but he would never ask.

"You know," I say, "your outfit matches the manor's stone."

"It's why I wear it. Camouflage."

I give the horse stables no more than a quick glance. Nigel sees me do it, but he pretends otherwise.

"Patricia will be here soon," I say.

Nigel stops and turns toward me. "Patricia, as in your cousin Patricia?"

"The very one," I tell him.

"Oh my."

"Will you show her into the parlor?"

I head up the stone steps and into the parlor. I still get the faint whiff of pipe tobacco. I know that's not possible, that no one has smoked a pipe in this room in almost four decades, that the brain not only conjures up false sights and sounds but, more often, scents. Still the smell is real to me. Maybe aromas do indeed linger, especially the ones we find most comforting.

I walk over to the fireplace and stare up at the empty frame where the Vermeer once hung. The Picasso took up residence on the opposite wall. That was the sum total of the "Lockwood Collection"—three hundred million dollars of value in only two works of art. Behind me I hear the clatter of heel against marble. The sound, I know, is not being made by Chuck Taylors.

Nigel clears his throat. My back stays toward them.

"You don't really want me to announce her, do you?"

I turn, and there she is. My cousin Patricia.

Patricia's eyes roam the room before settling on me. "It's weird to be back," she says.

"It's been too long," I say.

"I concur," Nigel adds.

We both look at him. He gets the message.

"I'll be upstairs should anyone need me."

He closes the massive doors to the parlor as he departs. They shut with an ominous thud. Patricia and I say nothing for the moment. She is, like yours truly, in her forties. We are first cousins; our fathers were brothers. Both men, Windsor the Second and Aldrich, were fair in complexion and blond, again like yours truly, but Patricia takes after her mother, Aline, a Brazilian native from the city of Fortaleza. Uncle Aldrich scandalized the family when he brought back the twenty-year-old beauty to Lockwood after his extended charity-work journey through South America. Patricia's dark hair is short and stylishly cut. She wears a blue dress that manages to be both chic and casual. Her eyes are shiny almond. Her resting face, rather than the cliché "bitch," is grippingly melancholy and startlingly beautiful. Cousin Patricia cuts something of a captivating and telegenic figure.

"So what's wrong?" Patricia asks me.

"They found the Vermeer."

She is stunned. "For real?"

I explain about the hoarder, the Beresford turret, the murder. I am not known for possessing subtlety or tact, but I'm trying my best to build up to the reveal. Cousin Patricia watches me with those inquisitive eyes, and again I fall back into a time portal. As children, we roamed this acreage for hours on end. We played hide-and-seek. We rode horses. We swam in the pool and the lake. We played chess and backgammon and worked on our golf and tennis. When the estate became too pompous or grim, as was Lockwood's wont, Patricia would look at me and roll her eyes and make me smile.

I have only told one person in my life that I love them. Just one.

No, I did not say it to a special woman who, say, eventually broke my heart—my heart has never been broken or even tweaked, really—but to my platonic male friend Myron Bolitar. In short, there has been no great love in my life, only a great friendship. Relatives have been the same. We are bonded in blood. I have cordial, important, and even compelling relationships with my father, my siblings, aunts, uncles, cousins. I had virtually no relationship with my mother—I didn't see or speak to her from the time I was eight years old until I watched her die when I was in my thirties.

This is a long way of telling you that Patricia has always been my favorite relative. Even after the big rift between our fathers, which is why she hasn't been at Lockwood since her teens. Even after the devastating tragedy that made that rift both unfixable and, alas, eternal.

When I finish my explanation, Patricia says, "You could have told me all this on the phone."

"Yes."

"So what else is there?"

I hesitate.

"Oh shit," she says.

"Pardon?"

"You're stalling, Win, which really isn't like you...oh damn, it's bad, right?" Cousin Patricia takes a step closer to me. "What is it?"

I just say it: "The Aunt Plum suitcase."

"What about it?"

"The hoarder didn't just have the Vermeer. He had the suitcase."

———

29

We stand in silence. Cousin Patricia needs a moment. I give it to her.

"What do you mean, he had the suitcase?"

"Just that," I say. "The suitcase was there. In the hoarder's possessions."

"You saw it?"

"I did."

"And they don't know who this hoarder is?"

"Correct. They haven't made an identification."

"Did you see the body?"

"I saw a photograph of his face."

"Describe him."

I do as she asks.

"That could be anyone," she says when I'm done.

"I know."

"It doesn't matter," Patricia says. "He always wore a ski mask. Or... or he blindfolded me."

"I know," I say again, this time more somberly.

The grandfather clock in the corner begins to chime. We stay silent until it finishes.

"But there's a chance, I mean, even a likelihood..." Patricia moves toward me. We had been standing on opposite ends of the parlor. Now we are only a yard or two apart. "The same man who stole the paintings also...?"

"I wouldn't jump to conclusions," I say.

"What does the FBI know about the suitcase?"

"Nothing. With the monogram and crest, they've concluded that it's mine."

"You didn't tell them—?"

I make a face. "Of course not."

"So, wait, are you a suspect?"

I shrug.

"When they figure out the suitcase's real significance," Patricia begins.

"We will both be suspects, yes."

———————

My cousin, for those who haven't already guessed, is *the* Patricia Lockwood.

You've probably seen her story on *60 Minutes* or the like, but for those somehow not in the know, Patricia Lockwood runs the Abeona Shelters for abused and homeless girls or teens or young women or whatever the current correct terminology may be. She is the heart, the soul, the drive, and the telegenic face of one of the country's highest-graded charities. She has deservedly won dozens of humanitarian awards.

So where to start?

I won't go into the family split, how her father and mine had a falling-out, how the two brothers battled, how my father, Windsor the Second, won and vanquished his sibling, because, in truth, I think my father and my uncle would have eventually reconciled. Our family, like many both rich and poor, has a history of fissure and repair.

There is no bond like blood, but there is no compound as volatile either.

What stopped the potential repair was the great finalizer— death.

I will state what happened as unemotionally as possible:

Twenty-four years ago, two men in ski masks murdered my uncle Aldrich Powers Lockwood and kidnapped my eighteen-year-old cousin Patricia. For a while, there were sightings of her—a bit like with the paintings, now that I think about it—but they all led to dead ends. There was one ransom note, but it was quickly exposed as a money scam.

It was as though the earth had swallowed my cousin whole.

Five months after the kidnapping, campers near the Glen Onoko Falls heard the hysterical screams of a young woman. A few moments later, Patricia sprinted out of the woods and toward their tent.

She was naked and covered in filth.

Five. Months.

It took law enforcement a week to locate the small resin storage shed, the sort you'd buy at a chain hardware store, where Patricia had been held prisoner. The shattered manacle she'd managed to break with a rock was still on the dirt floor. So too a bucket for her waste. That was all. The shed was seven feet by seven feet, the door secured with a padlock. The exterior was forest green and thus nearly impossible to spot—a dog from the FBI's canine unit found it.

The storage shed earned the headline "Hut of Horrors," especially after the crime lab located DNA for nine more young women/teens/girls, ranging in age from sixteen to twenty. Only six of the bodies have been found to this day, all buried nearby.

The perpetrators were never caught. They were never identified. They simply disappeared.

Physically, Patricia seemed as okay as one could hope. Her nose and ribs had shown signs of past breakage—the abduction had been violent—but those had healed well enough. Still, it took time to recuperate. When Patricia re-engaged with the world, she did so with a vengeance. She channeled that trauma into a cause. Her passion for her fellow females, those who'd been abused and abandoned with no hope, became a living, breathing, palpable thing.

Cousin Patricia and I have never spoken about those five months.

She has never raised it, and I'm not the kind of person who invites people to open up to them.

Patricia begins to pace the parlor. "Let's step back and try to look at this rationally."

I wait, let her gather herself.

"When exactly was the painting stolen?"

I tell her September eighteenth and the year.

"That's, what, seven months before..." She still paces. "Before Dad was murdered."

"Closer to eight."

I had done the math on the helicopter.

She stops pacing and throws up her hands. "What the hell, Win?"

I shrug.

"Are you saying the same guys who stole the paintings came back, murdered Dad, and kidnapped me?"

I shrug again. I shrug a lot, but I shrug with a certain panache.

"Win?"

"Walk me through it," I say.

"Are you serious?"

"As a heart attack."

"I don't want to," Patricia says in a small voice that is so unlike her. "I've spent the last twenty-four years avoiding it."

I say nothing.

"Do you understand?"

I still say nothing.

"Don't give me the silent man-of-mystery act, okay?"

"The FBI will want to see whether you can identify the murdered hoarder."

"I can't. I told you. And what's the difference now? He's dead, right? Let's say he was this old bald guy. He's gone. It's over."

"How many men broke in, the night of your abduction?" I ask.

She closes her eyes. "Two."

When Patricia opens her eyes again, I offer up another shrug.

"Shit," she says.

CHAPTER 4

We decide to do nothing for the moment. In truth, Cousin Patricia decides—it is her life that will be turned upside down, not mine—but I concur. She wants to think about it and see what else we can learn first. Once we open this particular door, there is no way to close it again.

I look in on my father, but he is still resting. I don't disturb him. Most days he is lucid. Some he is not. I climb back into the helicopter and leave Lockwood. I set up a rendezvous with a woman on my app. We decide to meet at nine p.m. She uses the code name Amanda. I use the code name Myron because he finds this app so repulsive. I asked him to explain why. Myron started with the deeper meaning of love, of connection, of being as one, of waking up and making someone else a part of your life.

My eyes glazed over.

Myron shook his head. "Explaining romantic love to you is like teaching a lion to read: It isn't going to happen, and someone might get hurt."

I like that.

You don't have this app, by the way. You can't get this app.

An hour later, I enter my office. Kabir, my assistant, is there. Kabir is a twenty-eight-year-old Sikh American. He has a long beard. He wears a turban. I probably should not mention any of this because he was born in this country and acts more like a stereotypical American than anyone I know, but as Kabir puts it, "The turban. You always gotta explain the turban."

"Messages?" I ask him.

"A ton."

"Any pressing?"

"Yes."

"Give me an hour then."

Kabir nods and hands me a water bottle. It is a cold beverage with the latest NAD molecules, which help slow down aging. I am provided the latest compound from a longevity doctor at Harvard. The elevator takes me down to the private workout room in the basement. There are free weights, a boxing heavy bag, a speed bag, a grappling dummy, wooden practice swords (bokkens), rubber handguns, a Wing Chun dummy with hardwood arms and legs, you get the idea.

I train every day.

I have worked with some of the best fighting instructors in the world. I have practiced all the fighting techniques you know—karate, kung fu, taekwondo, krav maga, jujitsu of various stripes—and many you don't. I spent a year in Siem Reap studying the Khmer fighting technique of Bokator, which roughly though aptly translated means "pounding a lion." I spent two college summers outside of Jinhae in South Korea with a reclusive Soo Bahk Do master. I study strikes, takedowns, submissions, joint locks (though I don't like them), pressure points (not really useful in a true battle), one-on-one combat, group attacks, weaponry of all kinds. I am an expert marksman with a handgun (I am proficient with a rifle, but I rarely find a need for it). I've worked with knives, swords, and blades of all sorts, and while I greatly admire the Filipino form of Kali Eskrima, I've learned more from our Delta Force's elite blend of styles.

I am alone in my gym, so I take off everything but my underwear—a boxer-brief hybrid for those who must know—and start running through a few traditional katas. I move fast. Between sets, I work three-minute rounds with the punching bag. Best cardio conditioner in the world. In my youth, I trained five hours a day. Now I still go a minimum of an hour. Most days, I work with an instructor because I still thirst to learn. Today, obviously, I do not.

Money, of course, makes all this possible. I can travel anywhere—or I can fly in any expert for any length of time. Money gives you time, access, cutting-edge technology and equipment.

Don't I sound a bit like Batman?

If you think about it, Bruce Wayne's only superpower was tremendous wealth.

Mine too. And yes, it's good to be me.

Sweat coats my skin. I feel the rush of that. I push harder. I've always pushed myself. I've never needed to be pushed by anything external. The only training partner I ever worked with was Myron, but that was because he needed to learn, not because I needed motivation.

I do this for survival. I do it to keep fit. I do it because I enjoy it. Not all of it, mind you. I enjoy the physical. I don't enjoy the obsequious "yes, sensei" patriarchal nonsense that certain martial arts thrust upon their students, because I bow to no man. Respect, yes. Bow, no. I also don't use these techniques, per the platitude, "only for self-defense," an obvious untruth on the level of "the check is in the mail" or "don't worry, I'll pull out." I use what I learn to defeat my enemies, no matter who the aggressor happens to be (usually: me).

I like violence.

I like it a lot. I don't condone it for others. I condone it for me. I don't fight as a last resort. I fight whenever I can. I don't try to avoid trouble. I actively seek it out.

After I finish with the bag, I bench-press, powerlift, squat. When I was younger, I'd have various lifting days—arm days, chest days, leg days. When I reached my forties, I found it paid to lift less often and with more variety.

I hit the steam room, sauna, and then, when my body temperature is raised, I jump into a freezing cold shower. Putting the body through certain controlled stresses like this activates dormant hormones. It's good for you. When I exit the shower, three suits wait for me. I choose the solid blue one and head back to my office.

Kabir holds up his phone. "The story's hit Twitter."

"What are they saying?"

"Just that the Vermeer was found at a murder scene. I'm also getting a ton of calls from the press interested in a quote."

"Any porn magazines?" I ask.

Kabir frowns. "What's a porn magazine?"

Today's youth.

I close the door. My office has an enviable view and oak wood paneling. There is an antique wooden globe and a painting of a fox hunt. I look at the painting and wonder how the Vermeer might look there instead. My mobile rings. I look at the number.

I should be surprised—I haven't heard from him in a decade, not since he told me he was retiring—but I'm not.

I put the phone to my ear. "Articulate."

"I can't believe you still answer the phone that way."

"Times change," I say. "I do not."

"You change," he says. "I bet you don't 'night tour' anymore, do you?"

Night tour. Back in the day, I used to put on my dandiest suit and stroll through the most crime-ridden streets in the thick of the night. I would whistle. I would make sure all could see my blond locks and alabaster-to-ruddy complexion. I am rather small boned and, from a distance, appear frail—a bully's irresistibly tasty morsel. It is only when you get close to me that you sense there is considerable coil under the clothes. But by then, it is usually too late. You've seen the easy mark, you've laughed about me with your friends, you can't back out.

I wouldn't let you even if you tried.

"I do not," I tell him.

"See? Change."

I stopped night touring years ago. It was oddly discriminatory and all too random. I am now more selective with my targets.

"How are you doing, Win?"

"I'm fine, PT."

PT has to be in his mid-seventies by now. He recruited me for my brief stint with the Federal Bureau of Investigation. He was also my handler. Very few agents know about him, but every FBI chief and president has met with him their first day on the job. Some people in our government are considered shadowy. PT is shadowy to the point of nonexistence. He barely makes a blip on anyone's radar. He lives somewhere near Quantico, but even I don't know where. I also don't know his real name.

I could probably find out, but while I enjoy violence, I don't relish playing with fire.

"How was the basketball game last night?" PT asks.

I stay silent.

"The NCAA finals," he says.

I still say nothing.

"Oh, relax," he says with a chuckle. "I watched the game on TV. That's all. I saw you sitting courtside next to Swagg Daddy."

I wonder whether this is true.

"I love his stuff, by the way."

"Whose stuff?"

"Swagg Daddy's. Who else are we talking about? That song where he juxtaposes bitches ripping out a man's heart to bitches ripping off a man's balls? I feel that. It's poetic."

"I'll let him know," I say.

"That would be great."

"Last time I heard from you," I say, "you told me you retired."

"I did," PT says. "I am."

"And yet."

"And yet," he repeats. "Is your line secure, Win?"

"Do we ever know for certain?"

"With today's technology, we do not. I understand the FBI located your property today."

"For which I'm grateful."

"There is more to it, however."

"Isn't there always?"

"Always," he agrees with a sigh.

"Enough to get you out of retirement?"

"Tells you something, doesn't it? I assume there is a reason you aren't fully cooperating."

"I'm just being careful," I say.

"Can you stop being careful by the morning? Let me rephrase." His tone did not change—nothing you could hear anyway—and yet. "Stop being careful by the morning."

I do not reply.

"I'll have a plane meet you at Teterboro at eight a.m. Be there."

"PT?"

"Yes?"

"Have you identified the victim?"

I hear a muffled female voice through the line. PT tells me to hold on and calls to the woman that he'll only be a moment more. A wife maybe? It's shocking how little I know about this man. When he comes back on the line, he says, "Do you know the expression 'this one's personal'?"

"When you trained us," I say, "you stressed that it was never personal."

"I was wrong, Win. Very wrong. Tomorrow, eight a.m."

He hangs up.

I lean back, throw my feet on the desk, and replay the conversation in my head. I am looking for nuance or hidden meanings. None come to me other than the obvious. There is a knock-pause-double knock on my office door. Kabir sticks his head through it.

"Sadie wants to see you," he tells me. "She sounds . . . unhappy."

"Gasp oh gasp," I say.

I take the elevator back down to Sadie's law office, where I'm greeted by the receptionist-cum-paralegal, a recent college graduate named Taft Buckington III. Taft's father—he is known to all as Taffy—is a fellow member of Merion Golf Club. We play a lot of golf, Taffy and I. Young Taft meets my eye when I enter and shakes his head in warning. There are four attorneys in total at Fisher and Friedman, all female. I told Sadie once that perhaps she should hire one man to make it look good. Her response, which I loved, was simple:

"Shit no."

Instead the sole male is the receptionist-cum-paralegal. Make of that what you will.

When Sadie spots me standing next to Taft's desk, she beckons me to her office and closes the door once we are both inside. I sit. She stands. This was Myron's old office. Sadie kept Myron's desk. It was still here when she took over the lease and so she asked whether she could purchase it. I called Myron to see what he'd charge, but as I expected, he said to give it to her. Still, it's disconcerting to be in here because nothing else is the same. The small refrigerator where Myron kept his stash of Yoo-hoos has been replaced by a printer stand. The posters from Broadway shows—there is no straight male in North America, with the possible exception of Lin-Manuel Miranda, who loves musicals more than Myron—are gone now. Myron's office was eclectic and nostalgic and colorful. Sadie's is minimalist and white and generic. She wants no distractions. It's all about the client, she once told me, not the attorney.

"I have permission to tell you this," Sadie begins. "Just so we are clear. It's no longer attorney-client privilege because, well, you'll see."

I say nothing.

"You know about my hospitalized client?"

"Just that."

"Just what?"

"That you have a client who was hospitalized."

This isn't true, by the way. I know more.

"How did you find out?" Sadie asks.

"I overheard someone in the office talking about it," I say. This is also a lie.

"Her name is Sharyn," Sadie continues. "No last name for now. It doesn't matter. Names don't matter. Anyway, her case is textbook. Or it starts out textbook. Sharyn is doing a graduate degree at a large university. She meets a man who works at the same university in a somewhat prestigious job. It starts off great. So many of these do. The man is charming. He flatters her. He's super attentive. He talks about their grand future."

"They always do that, don't they?" I say.

"Pretty much, yeah. It's not fair to label every guy who starts sending you flowers and showering you with tons of attention as a psycho—but, I mean, there is something to it."

I nod. "Not all overly attentive boyfriends are psychos—but all psychos are overly attentive boyfriends."

"Well put, Win."

I try to look modest.

"So anyway, the romance starts off great. Like so many of these do. But then it starts to grow weird. Sharyn is in a study group that includes both men and women. The boyfriend—I'm going to call him Teddy, because that's the asshole's name—doesn't like that."

"He gets jealous?"

"To the nth degree. Teddy starts asking Sharyn a lot of questions about her guy friends. Interrogating her, really. One day, she checks the search history on her laptop. Someone—well, Teddy—has been looking up her guy friends. Teddy shows up at the library unannounced. To surprise her, he says. One time he brings a bottle of wine and two glasses."

"As cover," I say. "A faux romantic gesture."

"Exactly. The behavior escalates, as again it always does. Teddy gets upset if her study sessions run too late. She's a student. She wants to go to a campus party or two with her friends. Teddy, who works as an assistant coach, insists on going. Sharyn starts to feel the walls closing in. Teddy is everywhere. If she doesn't respond to his texts fast enough, Teddy throws a fit. He starts accusing her of cheating. One night, Teddy grabs Sharyn's arm so hard he bruises her. That's when she breaks up with him. And that's when his psycho stalking starts."

I am not a good sympathetic ear, but I try very hard to appear like one. I try to nod in all the right places. I try to look concerned and mortified. My resting face, if you will allow me to use that annoying colloquialism again, is either disinterested or haughty. I struggle thus to engage and look caring. It takes some effort, but I believe that I'm pulling it off.

"Teddy shows up unannounced begging her to take him back. On three separate occasions, Sharyn has to call 911 because Teddy's pounding on her door after midnight. He's pleading with her to talk to him, says she's being unfair and cruel not to hear him out. Teddy actually cries, he misses her so bad, and eventually he convinces her that she"—here Sadie makes quote marks with her fingers—"'owes' him the chance to explain."

"And she agrees to meet?" I ask, mostly because I worry I've been silent too long.

"Yes."

"This," I say. "This is the part I never get."

Sadie leans forward and tilts her head to the side. "That's because while you're trying, Win, you're still too male to get it. Women have been conditioned to please. We are responsible not just for ourselves but everyone in our orbit. We think it is our job to comfort the man. We think we can make things better by sacrificing a bit of ourselves. But you're also right to ask. It's the first thing I tell my clients: If you're ready to end it, end it. Make a clean break and don't look back. You don't owe him anything."

"Did Sharyn go back to him?" I ask.

"For a little while. Don't shake your head like that, Win. Just listen, okay? That's what these psychos do. They manipulate and gaslight. They make you feel guilty, like it's your fault. They sucker you back in."

I still don't get it, but that's not important, is it?

"Anyway, it didn't last. Sharyn saw the light fast. She ended it again. She stopped replying to his calls and texts. And that's when Teddy upped his assholery to the fully psychotic. Unbeknownst to her, he bugged her apartment. He put keyloggers on her computers. Teddy has a tracker on her phone. Then he starts texting her anonymous threats. He stole all her contacts, so he floods mailboxes with malicious lies about her—to her friends, her family. He writes emails and pretends he's Sharyn and he trashes her professors and friends. On one occasion, he contacts Sharyn's best friend's fiancé—as Sharyn—and says she cheated on him. Makes up a whole story about some incident in a bar that never happened."

"Imaginative," I say.

"You don't know the half of it. He starts sending Sharyn messages, pretending to be her friends saying what a fool she is to let a sweet guy like Teddy go."

I frown. "Imaginative albeit pathetic."

"Beyond pathetic. These men—sorry, I don't want to sound sexist, but they are almost always men—are insecure losers of biblical proportions."

"Does Sharyn go to the police?"

"Yes."

"But that doesn't prove helpful, does it?"

Her eyes light up. Sadie is in her element now. "This is why we exist, Win. The law as it is now can't really help the Sharyns of the world. It hasn't yet caught up to technology, for one thing. Teddy hides himself using VPNs and burner phones and fake email addresses. It's impossible for anyone to prove who is stalking her. That's why the work we do, it's so important."

I nod for her to continue.

"So now that he's been dumped again, Teddy doesn't let up. He sends a naked picture of Sharyn to her ninety-one-year-old grandmother. He makes up a video filled with lies about Sharyn—that she hates Jews, that she's into all kinds of weird sex, that she's a white nationalist, you can't imagine. And get this. When Teddy is confronted with what he's done, he claims that Sharyn is setting him up. That he dumped her and she can't move on and this is her way of getting back at him."

I shake my head.

"Anyway, that's when Sharyn finally learned about us."

"How long ago?"

"February."

I wait.

Sadie swallows. "Yes. I know, I know, it's a long time."

"And?"

"And we were trying, Win. We dug in deep and found out Teddy has done this before to at least three other women—it's one reason why he keeps moving from college to college."

"The colleges know?"

"Institutions protect their own. So he agrees to resign quietly and they agree not to say anything. On at least one occasion, money exchanged hands, and the victim signed a nondisclosure agreement."

I frown some more.

"So anyway, we do what we can for Sharyn. We get her a temporary order of protection against Teddy. I told her to write down everything she remembers—everything Teddy did—and to keep a diary of everything he does from here on out. This is key—to keep a record from the get-go if you can. We go to law enforcement, just so we are on record, but like I said, this is why our work is so important. Police aren't really trained in digital forensics."

I lean back and cross my legs. "So far, this sounds like a classic case for your firm."

"You're right." She smiles sadly. "Teddy is textbook. He sounds like my ex."

Sadie's stalker had taken it to the next level too, but this is not the time to bring that up. I sit back and wait. I already know the bare bones of this story, but she is filling in the details. I am also not sure where she is going with it.

"Sharyn ends up dropping out before she gets her degree because Teddy keeps harassing her. She moves up north, starts at another school. But Teddy finds her again. Like I said, we dig up other victims, but no one wants to come forward. They're scared of him. And then Teddy turns up the harassing by proxy."

She stops and looks at me. I figure she is waiting for my prompt, so I repeat: "Harassing by proxy?"

"You know what that is?"

I do, but I shake my head no.

"In his case, Teddy sets up profiles on Tinder and Whiplr and rougher sex apps, ones that deal with BDSM and whatever, as Sharyn. He posts her photos. He carries on conversations as Sharyn, sets up hookup rendezvous. Strange men start showing up at Sharyn's apartment at all hours expecting sex or role play or whatever. Some get mad when she turns them away. Call her a cocktease and worse. Teddy works it hard. And then..."

Sadie stops. I wait.

"Then Teddy begins a flirtation with one guy on an underground site. As Sharyn. It lasts for six weeks. Six weeks, Win. I mean, that's devotion, right? 'Sharyn'"—again with the finger quotes—"tells the guy all about her violent rape fantasies. 'Sharyn' tells the guy she wants to be attacked and handcuffed and gagged—Teddy even gives the guy the place to purchase this stuff—and then Teddy sets up a time for the guy to role-play raping her."

I sit perfectly still.

"This guy, he thinks he's talking to Sharyn. He's been told for weeks to be violent, to hit Sharyn and punch her and tie her up, to use a knife. He's even been given a safe word. 'Purple.' Don't stop, he says as Sharyn, unless you hear me say 'purple.'"

Sadie looks away and blinks. My hands tighten into fists of rage.

"Anyway, that's how Sharyn ended up in the hospital. Her condition...it's not good."

Again: I already know all this. I wonder how to proceed because I still don't understand the panic. So I make my voice tentative. "I assume Teddy still hid his identity?"

Sadie nods.

"Ergo the police couldn't touch him," I continue.

"That's correct."

"He got away with it?"

"So it seemed."

"Seemed?"

"Teddy's full name is Teddy Lyons. Do you know the name?"

I tap my chin with my index finger. "The name rings a bell."

"He's an assistant basketball coach for South State."

"Really?" I say, trying not to oversell it.

"We just got word. Last night, after the big game, Teddy was attacked. They beat the hell out of him, did some serious damage."

They. She said "they." Conclusion: I am still in the clear.

"Broken bones," she continues. "Internal bleeding. Some kind of serious liver damage. They say he'll never be the same."

I try very hard not to smile. I am not completely successful. "Ah, that's a shame," I say.

"Yeah, I can see you're all broken up about it."

"Should I be?"

"We had him, Win." Her gaze through her glasses is an inferno. I see the passion that drew me to her and her cause in the first place. Sadie is a doer, not a talker. We are similar in that way.

"What do you mean, 'had him'? You just said he was getting away with it."

"After what happened to Sharyn, I reached out to Teddy's other victims again. They finally agreed to come forward. Sharyn was ready to go public too. That would be traumatic, of course. Teddy had taken so much from them already."

"Hmm." I lean back and cross my legs. I hadn't really considered the repercussions. I rarely do. But...no, no, at the end of the day, she's wrong. I say, "Then it seems Teddy's beating helped them."

"No, Win, it didn't. Once you change your mind...It's cathartic in the end, fighting back, standing up to your abuser.

But more than that, we had a big press conference lined up for when Sharyn got out of the hospital. Imagine it—four victims on the steps of the State Capitol, telling the world their stories. We had two state assemblymen ready to appear with us. It would have ruined Teddy's reputation—but more important, those compelling stories would help us pass a bill— a bill this office"—Sadie taps her desk—"had drawn up. The two assemblymen were going to present it to the governor."

I wait.

"And now," Sadie says, "poof, that's all gone."

"Why?" I ask.

"Why what?"

"Why can't you still tell the stories?"

"It won't have the same impact."

"Pish. Of course it will."

"Someone attacked Teddy last night."

"So?"

"So now he's the victim of a vigilante."

"You don't know that," I say. "It could be that he tried again, this time with the wrong woman."

"And she beat him to a pulp?"

"Or her family did, I don't know." I snap my fingers. "Or it could have been an unrelated mugging."

"Come on."

"What?"

"It's over, Win. The war is still to be fought, but this battle is lost. We needed public sympathy. But our monster is in a coma. Someone on Twitter will claim the victims beat him. Teddy's mother will say that these scorned women lied about her baby boy—that they made him a target. It isn't just about facts, Win. We need to win the narrative."

I think about it. Then I say, "I'm sorry," with perhaps too little enthusiasm.

Just to clarify: I'm not sorry about what I did to Teddy. I'm sorry I didn't wait until after the press conference. Sadie has to be an optimist. I sadly am not. The law would never have caught up to Teddy. He would have been embarrassed, perhaps lost his job, but he also would have fought back in terrible ways. He would have trashed Sharyn and the other women. He would have claimed to be the victim of their harassment, not the other way around, and too many people would have believed him. That was what Sadie was fighting against here.

I believe in Sadie Fisher. She may eventually prevail. But not today.

It is eight thirty p.m. I have my own appointment in half an hour, but it is easy enough to cancel. "We could all go out for a drink," I say to her.

"Are you serious?"

"We can commiserate."

Sadie shakes her head. "I know you're trying to be kind, Win."

"But?"

"But you're clueless."

"Colleagues don't get out for drinks?"

"Not tonight, Win. Tonight I have to go to the hospital and tell Sharyn what happened."

"Perhaps she'll be relieved," I say. "Teddy can't hurt her anymore. That should offer her some comfort, no?"

Sadie opens her mouth, thinks about it, closes it. I can see she's disappointed in me. She pats my shoulder as she walks out the door.

I check my app. My rich-people dating program is so far

down the Dark Web that there is no way anyone could set up a Teddy-like fake profile. Even if they could, they'd never get past the other security. The message reads:

Username Amanda is waiting for you.

So my partner for the evening has arrived at the suite already. No need to keep her waiting.

CHAPTER 5

The app offers several secret entrances.

Tonight, we will use the one at Saks Fifth Avenue department store. The venerable Saks, located between Forty-Ninth and Fiftieth Street on Fifth Avenue, has a high-end jewelry department called the Vault. It's located in the basement. Behind that, you'll find a door that used to lead to a dressing room. It is locked, but we with the app can open it with a key fob. You enter through the door and take the steps down a level to an underground passage. The passage leads to an elevator under a high-rise on Forty-Ninth Street near Madison Avenue. The elevator only stops on the eighth floor. At this point it takes an eye scan. If your eye doesn't pass the scan, the elevator doors do not open into the private suite.

It's good to be rich.

To be approved for this app you must have a net worth of over $100 million. The monthly costs are exorbitant, especially for someone like me who uses this service frequently. The app's service is simple: Match rich people with other rich people for sex. No strings attached. It is high end. It is boutique. But mostly, it is sex.

The app has no name. Most of the clients are married and crave the ultimate in confidentiality. Some are public figures. Some are gay or otherwise LGBTQ+ and fear exposure. Some, like me, are simply wealthy and seek sex with no attachments or repercussions. For years, I picked up women at bars or night-clubs or galas. I still do on occasion, but when you get past the age of thirty-five, this behavior feels somewhat desperate. In my somewhat dubious past, I hired prostitutes. There was a time when, every Tuesday, I would order both dim sum and a woman from a place on the Lower East Side called Noble House— my own version of Chinese Night. I believed at the time that prostitution was the oldest and a (per the House) Noble profession. It is not. When I worked a case overseas, I learned about human trafficking and the like. Once I did, I stopped.

Like with the martial arts, we learn, we evolve, we improve.

With that option gone, I tried working the once-fashionable "friends with benefits" angle, but the problem is, friends by definition come with strings. Friends come with attachments. I don't want that.

Now for the most part I use this app.

Username Amanda sits on the bed wearing nothing but the provided satin-trim Turkish terry-cloth robe. Veuve Clic-quot La Grande Dame, a rosé champagne, is poured. There are chocolate-dipped strawberries in a silver bowl. A first-rate sound system can play whatever musical stylings suit your taste. I usually leave that to the woman, but I'd prefer no soundtrack.

I like to listen to her.

Username Amanda rises, smiles, and saunters toward me

with a flute of champagne. Myron always says that a woman looks sexiest in a terry-cloth robe with wet hair. I used to pooh-pooh said sentiment in favor of a specific black corset and matching garter belt, but now I think Myron may be onto something.

We learn, we evolve, we improve.

The sex tonight is great. It usually is. And when it's not, it is still sex. There is an old joke about a man wearing a toupee—it may be a good toupee, it may be a bad toupee, but it is still a toupee. The same with sex. I've heard often that sex with a stranger is awkward. I've rarely found this to be the case. Part of this might be my expertise—the techniques I traveled the world to learn involve more than fighting—but the secret is simple: Be present. I make every woman feel as though she is the only one in the world. It is not an act. A woman will sense if you lack authenticity. While we are together, this woman and I, it is just us two. The world is gone. My focus is total.

I love sex. I have lots of it.

Myron waxes philosophical on how sex must be more than what it is—that love or romantic entanglement enhances the physical experience. I listen and wonder whether he is trying to convince me or himself. I don't like love or romantic entanglements. I like sharing certain physical acts with another consensual adult. The other stuff doesn't "enhance" sex for me. It sullies it. The act itself is pure. Why muddy that with the extraneous? Sex may be the greatest shared experience in the world. Yes, I enjoy going out for a gourmet meal or a good show or the company of dear friends. I appreciate golf and music and art.

But do any of those compare to an evening of sex?

Methinks not.

This is one reason I liked prostitution. It was a straight transaction—I got something, she got something. No one owed anybody anything at the end of it. I still crave that, to leave the room knowing that my partner got out of it as much as I did. Perhaps that's why I am good at it. The more she enjoys it, the less I feel in her debt. I also have a tremendous ego. I don't do things that I'm not good at. I'm a very good golfer, a very good financial consultant, a very good fighter, and a very good lover. If I do something, I want to be the best.

When we finish—ladies first—we both lie back on the cream-colored Mulberry silk sheets and down pillows. We take deep breaths. I close my eyes for a moment. She pours more of the sparkling rosé and hands me a flute. I let her feed me a chocolate strawberry.

"We've met before," she says to me.

"I know."

This isn't uncommon. Her real name is Bitsy Cabot. The superrich travel in rarefied albeit similar circles. It would be strange if I didn't know most of the women. Bitsy is probably a few years older than I am. I know she splits her time between New York City, the Hamptons, and Palm Beach. I know that she is married to a rich hedge fund manager, but I can't remember his first name. I don't know why she's doing this. I also don't care.

"At the Radcliffes'," I say.

"Yes. Their gala last summer was wonderful."

"It's for a good cause."

"It is, yes."

"Cordelia throws a good party," I say.

You probably think that I can't wait to get dressed and leave—that I don't ever spend the night so as to avoid any attachment issues. But you'd be wrong. If she wants me to stay, I stay. If she doesn't, I leave. Sometimes she is the one to leave. It doesn't really matter to me. I sleep the same whether she is here or not. This bed is quite comfortable. That's all that really matters.

She isn't going to reach me by staying. She isn't going to repel me either.

One major point in favor of the overnight: If we do stay, I often get a spectacular morning encore without the hassle of finding another partner. That's a nice bonus.

"Do you go to the gala every year?" she asks.

"When I'm in the Hamptons," I say. "Are you on any of the committees?"

"The food one, yes."

"Who does the catering?" I ask.

"Rashida. Do you know her?"

I shake my head.

"She's divine. I can message you her contact."

"Thank you."

Bitsy leans over and kisses me. I smile and hold her gaze.

She slips out of bed. I watch her every move. She likes that.

"I really enjoyed tonight," she says.

"As did I."

Another thing that may surprise you: I don't have a problem with repeat engagements because in truth there are only so many fish in this particular sea. I am honest about my intentions. If I feel that they want more from me, I end it. Does this always work as cleanly as I'm making it sound? No, of course not. But this is as clean as it gets and maintains what I require.

For a few more moments I don't move. I bathe in this

afterglow. It's two a.m. As much as I've enjoyed tonight, as much as I am certain I would relish an encore or two with her, I try to imagine spending the rest of my life only making love to Bitsy Cabot. To any one person, really. I shiver at the thought. I'm sorry—I don't get it. Myron is married now to a stunning, vibrant woman named Terese. They are in love. If it works out as Myron hopes, he will never know the flesh of another.

I don't get it.

Bitsy heads to the bathroom. When she comes out, she is dressed. I am still in the bed, my head propped in my hands.

"I better head back," she says, as though I know where back is. I sit up as she says, "Goodbye, Win."

"Goodbye, Bitsy."

And then, like all good things, it's over.

———————

The next morning, I have a car service take me to the airport to visit my old FBI boss, PT.

I used to love to drive. I am a big fan of Jaguars and still keep two at Lockwood—a 2014 XKR-S GT that I use when I'm out there and a 1954 XK120 Alloy Roadster, which my father gave me for my thirtieth birthday. But when you reside in Manhattan, driving is out of the question. The borough is basically a parking lot that sways forward. One of the great things that money can buy is time. I don't fly private or have a driver because I crave more comfort in my life. I spend the money on those items because at the end of your life, you will crave more of what the annoying experts coin "quality time." That's what private jets and chauffeur-driven cars allow you to do. I have the ability to buy time—and that, when you think about it, is the closest thing to buying happiness and longevity.

The driver today is a Polish woman from the city of Wrocław named Magda. We talk for the first few minutes of the journey. Magda is reluctant at first to engage—exclusive drivers are often schooled on not bothering the upscale clientele—but I find every human being is a tale if you ask the right questions. So I probe a bit. I can see her eyes in the rearview mirror. They are a deep blue. Blonde hair peeks out of her chauffeur cap. I wonder about what the rest of her looks like, because I'm a man, and at heart, all men are pigs. It doesn't mean I would do anything about it.

Today's vehicle is a Mercedes-Maybach S650. The Maybach brand gives you a wheelbase stretch of eight inches, so that your chair can tilt back forty-three degrees. The plush seat has a power footrest, a hot-stone massage setting, and heated armrests. There is also a folding tray/desk so as to get work done, a small refrigerator, and cupholders that can cool or heat, depending on your preference.

Come to think of it, perhaps I do crave the comfort.

Teterboro is the closest airport from Manhattan for private aircraft. I flew into Teterboro with Swagg Daddy after our night of quasi debauchery in Indianapolis. When we reach the well-guarded gate on the south end, Magda is waved through straight to the tarmac. We pull up next to a Gulfstream G700, a plane that hasn't really hit the market yet. I'm surprised. The G700 is expensive—close to $80 million—and government officials, even top-echelon, clandestine ones like PT, are not usually that extravagant. Middle Eastern sheiks use the G700, not FBI agents.

I have no idea where we are going or when we will be back.

I assume that I am to be flown to Washington or Quantico for my meeting with PT, but I really do not know for certain. Magda has been instructed to wait for me. She gets out of the car and comes around to open my door. I would insist on doing it myself, but that might be patronizing. I thank her, climb the plane steps, and step inside.

"Hello, Win."

PT sits up front with a wide smile. I haven't seen him in nearly two decades. He looks old, but then again, I guess he is. He doesn't rise from his seat to greet me, and I notice the cane next to him. He is big and bald with huge gnarled hands. I bend toward him and stretch out my hand. His grip is firm, his eyes clear. He gestures for me to sit across from him. The G700 can hold nineteen passengers. I know this because someone is trying to sell me one. The seats are, as you might expect, wide and comfortable. We sit facing one another.

"Are we going anywhere?" I ask.

PT shakes his head. "I figured this would be a good spot to meet privately."

"I didn't know the G700 had been released yet."

"It hasn't been," he says. "I didn't fly in on this."

"Oh?"

"I use a government-issue Hawker 400."

The Hawker 400 is a far smaller and older jet.

"I'm borrowing this for our meeting because it's more comfortable than the Hawker."

"That it is."

"And because the Hawker probably has listening devices on board."

"I see," I say.

He looks me over. "It's really good to see you, Win."

"You too, PT."

"I hear Myron got married."

"He invited you to the wedding."

"Yeah, I know."

PT doesn't elaborate, and I won't push it. Instead, I try to take the lead.

"Do you know who the dead hoarder is, PT?"

"Do you?"

"No."

"You're sure, Win?"

I don't like the glint in his eye. "I only saw a corpse photo of his face," I say. "If you want to show me more—"

"No need," he says. As I said, PT is a tall man. You can see that even as he sits. He rests his palms on his high knees, as though posing for a statue. "Tell me about the suitcase."

"You're not going to tell me who the victim is," I ask, "or do you not know?"

"Win?"

I wait.

"Tell me about the suitcase."

His voice has an edge. It is meant, I assume, to intimidate, but directed at me it comes across as something more worrisome.

It comes across as fear.

"I'm waiting," PT says.

"I know."

"Why won't you tell us about your suitcase?"

"I am protecting someone," I tell him.

"Noble," PT says. "But I need to know."

I hesitate, though in truth I knew that we would get to this point.

"Whatever you tell me stays between us. You know that."

PT leans back and gestures for me to go ahead.

"My aunt gave me the suitcase when I was fourteen," I begin. "It was a Christmas present. She made one up for all the males in the Lockwood family. Only the males. She gave the females a small makeup bag instead."

"Sexist," PT says.

"We thought so too," I say.

"We?"

I ignore him. "I also detested the bag, the whole idea of leather monogrammed luggage, really. What's the point? I didn't want it, so a female relative and I traded pieces. I took the makeup bag with her initials on it. She took my suitcase. Oddly enough, I still use the makeup bag as my travel toiletry bag. Like an inside joke."

"Wow," PT says.

"What?"

"You're dancing, Win."

"Pardon?"

"I've never heard you overexplain like this. I assume it's because you don't want to tell me who the female relative was?"

He is correct, but there is no point in stalling. "My cousin Patricia."

He looks confused for a moment. Then he sees it. "Wait. Patricia Lockwood?"

"Yes."

"Dear Lord."

"Indeed."

He tries to take this in. "So how did her suitcase end up in that closet at the Beresford?"

The FBI would have figured out about the suitcase

eventually. It's in their files. That is one of the three reasons I decided to come clean. Reason One: I trust PT as much as you can trust someone in this situation. Reason Two: If I gave PT this information, he would probably share what he knows with me. And Reason Three: The FBI will sooner or later put it together without my help and then, alas, Cousin Patricia and I will appear as though we had something to hide.

"Win?"

"After the two men murdered my uncle," I begin, "they made Patricia pack a suitcase."

My words take a few seconds to register. When they do, PT's eyes go wide. "You mean...good Lord, are you talking about the Hut of Horrors?"

"Yes."

He rubs his face. "I remember...that's right. After they murdered your uncle, they made her take some clothes. To distract or something, right?"

I say nothing.

"So what did they do with the suitcase?"

"Patricia doesn't know."

"She never saw the suitcase?"

"Never." I clear my throat and speak dispassionately. From my tone of voice, I might have been talking about office equipment or bathroom tile. "Patricia was blindfolded and gagged. Her hands were bound behind her back. They threw her and the suitcase in the trunk and drove off. When they stopped, they made her walk through the woods. She doesn't know how long, but she thinks for at least a full day. They never spoke to her. Not the whole time they walked. When they got to the shed, they locked her inside. She finally took off the blindfold. It was dark. Another day passed. Perhaps two. She isn't sure.

Someone left granola bars and water. Eventually, one of the men came back. He used a box cutter to slice off her clothes. He raped her. Then he took her clothes, threw down a few more granola bars, and locked her up again."

PT just shakes his head.

"He did this," I continue, "for five months."

"Your cousin," he says. "She wasn't the first victim."

"That's correct."

"I forget how many others."

"We know of nine others. There may have been more."

His jowls hang slacker now. "The Hut of Horrors," he says again.

"Yes."

"And they never caught the perpetrator."

I don't know whether he is asking or merely stating what we both know. Either way, his words hang in the air between us for too long.

"Or perpetrators plural," PT adds. "That was the odd part, right? Two men kidnap her. But only one keeps her captive, is that right?"

I correct him. "Only one raped her. That is her belief, yes."

In the distance, I can hear the whir of a plane taking off.

"So most likely..." PT begins, but then his voice sputters. He looks up at the cabin ceiling, and I think I see something watery in his eyes. "Most likely," he tries again, "the hoarder was one of those two men."

"Most likely," I say.

PT closes his eyes. He rubs his face again, this time with both hands.

"Does what I've told you clarify things?" I ask.

He rubs his face some more.

"PT?"

"No, Win, it doesn't clarify a goddamn thing."

"But you know who the hoarder is, right?"

"Yes. It's why I'm back. It's the case I could never let go."

"You aren't talking about the Hut of Horrors, are you?"

"I'm not," PT says. He leans forward. "But I've been search-ing for that hoarder for nearly fifty years."

CHAPTER 6

P T rubs his jaw. "What I'm about to tell you is strictly confidential."

This statement bothers me because PT knows giving me a warning like this is both superfluous and insulting.

"Okay," I say.

"You can't tell anyone."

"Well, yes," I reply, and I can hear the irritation in my voice, "that's strongly implied with the use of the phrase 'strictly confidential.'"

"Anyone," he repeats. Then he adds, "Not even Myron."

"No," I say.

"No what?"

"I tell Myron everything."

He stares at me a moment. Normally, PT displays all the emotional range of a file cabinet. Ask 'Siri, show me unflappable,' and a photograph of PT pops up on your screen. Today, though, on this Gulfstream G700, the agitation comes off him in waves.

I sit back, cross my legs, and gesture with both hands for him to bring it on. PT reaches into the briefcase by his side. He pulls out a manila folder and hands it to me. He glances out the window as I open the envelope and pull out the photograph.

"You recognize it, I assume."

I do. You would too. It is one of those iconic photographs that define the anti-war, flower-power, feminist-civil-rights counter-culture sixties or perhaps (I can't remember exactly) the very early 1970s. Along with other defining images of the era—the Chicago Seven trial, Mary Ann Vecchio kneeling over the dead body of Jeffrey Miller at Kent State, the Merry Pranksters atop their psychedelic bus, a female demonstrator offering a flower to a National Guardsman, the packed crowd at Woodstock, the Black student sit-in at the Woolworth's lunch counter—this notorious shot of six New York City college students had been plastered across the front page of every newspaper and had entered the annals of the unforgettable.

"It was taken the day before the attack," PT says.

I remember that. "How many died again?"

"Seven dead, a dozen injured."

The photograph was taken in the basement of a town house on Jane Street in Greenwich Village. There are six people in the photograph—four straggly men, two straggly women, all with long hair and garbed in Early American Hippie. All six look elated with huge smiles and bulging eyes; if I blew up the photograph, I'm sure I would see pupils dilated from something in the psychedelic family. All six hold wine bottles high in the air in some kind of bizarre victory salute. Wicks jut out of the top. The bottles, the world would soon learn, are loaded with kerosene. The next night, those wicks would be lit, the bottles thrown, and people would die.

"Do you remember their names?" PT asks me.

I point at the two men in the middle. "Ry Strauss, of course. And Arlo Sugarman."

The two leaders are household names. In most famous photographs, people search for some kind of extra meaning in the placement of subjects, almost as you would, to stay on subject, with a great painting. You can see that all here. The two men in the middle seem larger, bathed in a more distinct light. Like Rembrandt's *Night Watch*, for example, there is a ton going on in the photograph. You would first view it as a whole and then notice the individual figures. Strauss has long blond hair, like Thor or Fabio, while Sugarman has a loose Art-Garfunkel-esque Afro. Strauss holds the Molotov cocktail in his right hand, Sugarman in his left, and their free arms are draped around each other's necks. They both stare straight into the lens, prepared to take on the world, which they will soon do—and fail miserably.

"How about her?" PT asks, leaning forward and tapping the face of the young woman to Ry Strauss's right. The woman is petite and looks less sure. Her eyes are on Strauss, as though trying to follow his lead. Her bottle is only half-raised, her gesture more tentative.

"Lark Something?"

"Lake," PT corrects. "Lake Davies."

"She was the only one caught?"

"More than two years later. She turned herself in."

"There was controversy around her sentence."

"She served only eighteen months. Her defense attorney made a compelling case that her part had been relatively minor—supposedly, the men wouldn't let the women throw an explosive—and that she'd been young and stupid and in the thralls of her boyfriend Ry Strauss. Ry was the charismatic leader, the Charles Manson so to speak, of the group. Arlo Sugarman was more the nuts-and-bolts guy. Lake Davies also cooperated with us."

"Cooperated how?"

"Okay, let's go back." PT leans forward and points at the various faces as he speaks. "Ry Strauss and Arlo Sugarman were the leaders. They were both twenty-one. Lake Davies was nineteen years old, a freshman at Columbia University. The other woman, the redhead, was Edie Parker from New Jersey. The final two guys are Billy Rowan, a junior from Holyoke, Massachusetts—also Edie Parker's boyfriend—and the Black guy is Lionel Underwood. Underwood was also a junior at NYU. With me?"

"Yes."

"This photograph was taken the night before they attacked the Freedom Hall on the Lower East Side. The Freedom Hall was going to hold a USO dance with soldiers and local girls, so their plan was to burn down the hall before the dance."

I frown. "Attacking a dance."

"Right? Heroes."

"Or they were high."

"These groups believed that the United States was on the precipice of real political change and that violence would speed it up."

I frown. "Or they were high."

"Do you remember what happened that night?"

"I've read about it," I say, "but it was a little before my time."

"The group claimed they never wanted to hurt anyone. It was just going to be property damage. That's why they threw the Molotovs late at night when they knew the Freedom Hall would be empty. But one of their throws went astray and hit a telephone pole. The wires go down, sparks fly up—and all that distracts a Port Authority bus driver, who's on the ramp to the Williamsburg Bridge. In a panic, the driver swerves hard to the right. The bus hits a stone wall, flips over the overpass, and plunges into the East River. The deaths were all by drowning."

His voice trails off.

"So two-plus years later, Lake Davies walks into the FBI office in Detroit and turns herself in. But the fate of the others—Strauss, Sugarman, Rowan, Parker, Underwood—that's still a mystery."

I know all this. There have been countless documentaries, podcasts, movies, novels written about them. There was a hit folk ballad that still got radio time called "The Disappearance of the Jane Street Six."

"Why did she turn herself in?" I ask.

"She'd been on the run with Ry Strauss. That's what she told us, at least. She said a secret network of radicals had been keeping wanted militants hidden from the law. This wasn't news to us. Members of the Weather Underground, the Black Panthers, the Symbionese Liberation Army, the FALN, whatever—they were all on the run and getting help in one way or another. At one point, Davies said, Ry Strauss had cosmetic surgery to alter his appearance, using the same doctor who later worked on Abbie Hoffman. She and Strauss kept on the move, staying a step ahead of law enforcement. They ended up on a fishing boat in the Upper Peninsula. The boat capsized, and Strauss drowned. That's when she decided to surrender."

"Strauss drowned," I repeat.

"Yes."

"Like his victims?"

"Yes."

I point to the Afroed Arlo Sugarman. "Wasn't Sugarman almost captured?"

A shadow crosses PT's face. I see his fingers start to flex and unflex. "Four days after the attack, the FBI got a tip that Arlo Sugarman was hiding in a derelict brownstone in the Bronx. As you can imagine, the Bureau was being stretched pretty thin. We had a lot of agents investigating, but with six suspects to find and with a lot of tips coming in..."

He stops and takes a deep breath. He rubs his face again.

"We only sent two agents to the brownstone."

"No backup?"

"No."

"Should have waited," I say. I remember this. "Sugarman shot one of them, right?"

"A decorated agent named Patrick O'Malley. His rookie partner screwed up, let him go in through the back door on his own. O'Malley got ambushed. He died on the way to the hospital. Left six kids without a father."

"And Sugarman escaped," I say.

PT nods. "There's been no sign of him since."

"No sign of any of them."

"Yeah, the great mystery."

"Did you have a theory?"

"I did."

"And?"

"I figured they were all dead."

"Why?"

"Because I love folklore as much as the next guy, but the truth is, it's hard to stay hidden for fifty years. All those militants who went underground? They'd either surrendered or been caught by the early 1980s. The idea that all of the Jane Street Six could still be alive this whole time without being discovered—it just didn't make sense."

I stare at the photograph.

"PT?"

"Yes?"

"I assume the hoarder is one of the Jane Street Six."

PT nods.

"Which one?"

"Ry Strauss," he says.

I arch my eyebrow. "Lake Davies lied then."

"It would seem so, yes."

I consider this. "And Ry Strauss, the charismatic face of the Jane Street Six, ends up a reclusive hoarder living atop a high-rise on Central Park West."

"With a priceless Vermeer hanging over his bed," PT continues.

"That he stole from my family."

"Before kidnapping and assaulting your cousin. Not to mention, murdering your uncle."

We let that sit a moment.

Then I say, "You don't expect to keep Strauss's identity a secret, do you?"

"No, that would be impossible. We have a day, maybe two tops, before this story truly explodes."

I steeple my fingers. "So what do you want from me?"

"Isn't it obvious? I want you to investigate."

"What about the Bureau?"

"This revelation is going to bring up a lot of embarrassing memories for the FBI. You probably don't remember the Church Committee in 1975, but it revealed a whole host of illegal surveillance activities by us—on civil rights groups, feminists, anti-wars, the whole of what we called back then the New Left."

"I don't see what that has to do with me."

"The FBI will have to play this strictly by the rules," he says, giving me a meaningful glance. "Do I need to add, 'You don't'?"

"Seems you just did."

"If you'll pardon the pun," PT says, "it's win-win, Win."

"I won't."

"Won't?"

"Pardon the pun."

That gets a smile out of him. "Yeah, fair enough, though it's accurate. For your part, you get to stay involved and protect the interest of your family and more specifically your cousin."

"And for your part?"

"It's a big case to solve."

I consider that and say, "I don't buy it."

He doesn't reply.

"The last thing you need," I continue, "is another notch in your retired-undefeated championship belt." There are a lot of questions, but one keeps bubbling to the surface. So I ask it: "Why is this so important to you?"

PT answers in two words: "Patrick O'Malley."

"The agent Sugarman shot?"

"I was the rookie partner who screwed up."

CHAPTER 7

My plane is fueling up as PT walks me through the telephone-book-thick file. There is a lot for me to digest, but time is also of the essence. We both agree the first person I should speak to is Lake Davies.

"She changed her identity after being released," PT says.

"Not unusual," I reply.

"Not unusual, but in this case, suspicious. At first, she just got an official name change. Okay, fine. But two years later, after she figured that we stopped keeping tabs on her, she set up with an entirely fake ID."

But of course, PT had never stopped keeping tabs.

"Her name now is Jane Dorchester. She owns a dog-boarding business on the outskirts of Lewisburg, West Virginia, with her husband, a local real estate developer named Ross Dorchester. No biological kids, but then again, they got married twenty years ago, so she would have been mid-forties. Ross has two grown girls from his first marriage."

"Does the husband know her real identity?"

"Can't say."

There is no reason to waste time. We are already at Teterboro Airport. Kabir quickly arranges for my plane to take me to Greenbrier Valley Airport. Less than two hours after I say goodbye to PT, the jet's wheels are touching down in West Virginia. I keep sets of clothes on board, so I change into the closest thing I own to local garb—slim-fit Adriano Goldschmied faded blue jeans, a Saint Laurent plaid flannel shirt, and Moncler Berenice hiking boots.

Blending in.

A vehicle awaits my arrival on the tarmac—a chauffeur-driven Chevy Silverado pickup truck. More blending in.

Fifteen minutes after the plane has slowed to a stop, the Chevy Silverado pulls up to a long ranch house on the end of a cul-de-sac. A depressingly cheerful sign in the yard—one where every letter is a different color—reads:

Welcome to the RITZ SNARL-FUN
Hotel & Resort

I sigh out loud.

And under that, in smaller lettering:

West Virginia's Top-Rated Doggie Spa,
Hounds Down!

I sigh again and wonder about state-mandated justification for discharging my firearm.

The website, which I scanned through on the flight, touts the "Rated Five Paws" pet hotel and all its merit. The facility is a "cage-free canine establishment" for both "day care" and "overnight stays" for the "posh pup." There was an oversaturation of appropriate buzz words/phrases—pampering, grooming, positively-reinforcing, and, I'm not making this up, Zen wellness.

For a dog.

The "hotel" (as it were) is a generic ranch-style suburban home with extended eaves and low-pitched roofs. Barking dogs serenade me up the walk and through an open front door. A young woman behind the desk offers up a toothy smile and too much enthusiasm:

"Welcome to the Ritz Snarl-Fun!"

"How many times a day do you have to say that?" I ask.

"Huh?"

"Does a sliver of your soul leave your body every time?"

The young woman does maintenance on the toothy smile, but there is nothing behind it anymore. "Uh, can I help you with something?" She leans over the desk and looks down by my feet. "Where's your dog?"

"I'm here to see Jane Dorchester," I say.

"I can take care of you." She hands me a clipboard. "If you can just fill out—"

"No, no, I need to see Jane first," I protest. "I was told by my good friend Billy Bob"—more blending in—"to ask specifically for Jane Dorchester before I fill out any paperwork."

She slowly puts the clipboard back on the desk and rises. "Uh, okay. Let me see if she's available. Your name?"

"They call me Win."

She looks at me. I give her a reassuring smile. She leaves.

My phone rings. It's Cousin Patricia. I don't answer, instead text-replying:

I'll fill you in later.

I don't yet know how much of what PT told me I should share with Patricia, but it can wait. Do one thing at a time, as my father, who rarely did even that much, always told us. I prefer the way Myron's mother said the same thing with a delivery that rivaled the greatest of the Borscht Belt: "You can't ride two horses with one behind." At the time, she was talking to me about my womanizing, so her point didn't really take root with me, but I adore Ellen Bolitar and her wisdom just the same.

On my right, I see a multihued playroom of sorts—slides, tunnels, ramps, chew toys. There are rainbows painted on the walls. The floor is made of large rubber tiles that snap together in green, yellow, red, and orange. The place is bursting with more color than a preschool.

A big man comes out led by his big gut. He frowns at me. "Can I help you?"

I point to the playroom. "Aren't dogs color-blind?"

He looks confused. Then he asks again, this time allowing a little more irritation into his cadence, "Can I help you?"

"Are you Jane Dorchester?" I ask.

Big Gut doesn't like that. "Do I look like a Jane Dorchester?"

"Maybe in the boob area."

He doesn't like that either. "If you want to sign up your dog for a stay—"

"I don't," I say.

"Then I think you better leave."

"No, thank you. I'm here to see Jane Dorchester."

"She isn't available."

"Tell her I was sent here by a Miss Davies. Miss Lake Davies."

His reaction would have been about the same if I'd landed a roundhouse kick on the gut. No doubt. He knows Jane Dorchester's true identity. I'm thinking that this man must be her husband, Ross.

"Debbie," he says to the toothy young woman at the desk, "go out back and help with the spa baths."

"But Dad—"

"Just go, honey."

Merely from her use of the word "Dad," I infer that Debbie of the Desk must be one of Ross's daughters. Don't be too impressed. It's bad form to toot your own horn, but I'm pretty adept at deductive reasoning. My phone buzzes. Three short beeps. Surprising. Three short beeps indicate an incoming request from my no-name rendezvous app. I'm tempted to glance at it now. Requests don't come in that often without the male being the instigator. I am intrigued.

But the Ellen Bolitar wisdom comes to me again: One horse, one behind.

"You should leave," Big Gut says when Debbie is out of earshot.

"No, Ross, that's not going to happen."

"Just get in your car—"

"It's a truck, not a car. Very manly, don't you think?"

"We don't know anyone named Lake Davies."

I offer him my patented skeptical eyebrow arch. When applied correctly, words like "Oh please" become superfluous.

"We don't," Ross insists.

"Fine, then you won't mind if I go to the media and tell them that Lake Davies, famed flamethrower from the Jane Street Six, is now hiding in West Virginia under the pseudonym Jane Dorchester."

He steps toward me, the big gut swinging. "Look," he says in movie-tough-guy sotto voce, "she served her time."

"So she did."

"And this is still the United States of America."

"So it is."

"We don't have to talk to you."

"You don't, Ross. Your wife does."

"I know the law, pal, okay? My wife doesn't have to say a word to you or anyone else. She has rights, including the right to remain silent. We are going to exercise that right."

His belly is so close I'm tempted to pat it. "And you don't exercise that often, do you, Ross?"

He doesn't like that, but to be fair, it isn't my best work. He inches closer. The belly is almost touching me now. He looks down on me. Big men so often make this mistake, don't they?

"Do you have a warrant?" he asks me.

"I do not."

"Then you're on a private property. We have rights."

"You keep saying that."

"Saying what?"

"About having rights. Can we cut to the chase? I'm not with law enforcement. They need to follow rules. I don't."

"Don't have to..." He shakes his head in amazement. "Are you for real?"

"Let me explain. If Jane refuses to talk to me, I will go to the press and reveal her true identity as the notorious Lake Davies. I have no problem with that. But it won't end there. I will hire subordinates to hang around your home, your businesses, your upscale canine auberge, barraging her with questions wherever she goes—"

"That's harassment!"

"Shh, don't interrupt. I already spotted a one-star review for your hotel on Yelp from a woman who claims her poodle was bitten by a bichon frise whilst in your care. I'll encourage her to sue, give her my personal attorney to handle the case pro bono, perhaps locate others to join a class action lawsuit against you. I will hire investigators to look into every aspect of your personal and business life. Everyone has something to hide, and if I can't find something, I'll make it up. I will be relentless in my attempt to destroy you both, and I will be effective. Eventually, after much unnecessary suffering, you will both realize the only way to stop the hemorrhaging is to talk to me."

Ross Dorchester's face reddens. "That's ... that's blackmail."

"Hold on, let me find my line in the script." I mime flipping pages. "Here it is." I clear my throat. "'Blackmail is such an ugly word.'"

For a moment Ross looks as though he might take a swing at me. I feel that rush in my veins. I want him to, of course— to make a move so I can counter. I learned a long time ago that I cannot quiet that part of me, even as I recognize that in this instance, violence would be counterproductive to my interests.

When he speaks again, I hear pain in his voice. "You don't know what she's been through."

I give him nothing in return. This, I think to myself. This is why PT wanted me to handle this. This is why he did not want to rely on his colleagues.

"To have you barge in here like this, after all the work she's done to put the past behind her, to build a good life for us and our family..."

Part of me wants to break out one of my top-ten mime moves: playing the world's smallest violin. But again: counterproductive. "I have no intention of hurting anyone," I assure him. "I need to speak to your wife. After that, I will probably suggest you both pack a bag and take a trip for a little while."

"Why?"

"Because, like it or not, the past is coming back."

He blinks a few times and looks away. "Get out."

"No."

"I said—"

Then another voice says, "Ross?"

I turn. Her hair is short and white. She wears denim pants, an oversized brown work shirt rolled to the elbows, tired-gray sneakers. Her gloves are latex and she's carrying a bucket. Her eyes find me, perhaps hoping for mercy or understanding. When I don't give her any, I can see the resignation slowly cross her face. She turns her gaze back to her husband.

"You don't have to," Ross begins, but Jane-Lake shakes him off.

"We always knew this day would come."

Now he too has the look of surrender.

"What's your name?" she asks me.

"Call me Win."

"Let's take a walk out back, Win."

CHAPTER 8

H ow did you find me?"
We are in the backyard now. The dogs run free in
two large pens—one apparently for smaller dogs, one
for larger. A bearded collie is being groomed on a table. A bull-
mastiff is taking a bath. The sun is bright.

She waits for my answer, so I simply say, "I have my ways."

"It was a long time ago. I don't say this as an excuse. And
my role was small. I don't say that as an excuse either. But not
a day goes by that I don't think about that night."

I feign a yawn. She gives me a little laugh.

"Okay, yeah, maybe I deserve that. Maybe that was a bit
sanctimonious."

"Oh, just a bit," I reply.

She strips off the gloves, washes her hands thoroughly, dries
them with a towel. She beckons me with her head to follow her
toward a path in the woods.

"Why are you here, Win?"

I ignore the question by saying, "Tell me about the day Ry Strauss drowned in Michigan."

Her head is down as she walks. She sticks her hands in her back pockets—I'm not sure why, but I find this gesture endearing.

"Ry didn't drown," she says.

"Yet you told the police that?"

"I did."

"So you lied."

"I did."

We walk deeper into the woods.

"I'm guessing," she says, "that Ry has surfaced."

I do not reply.

"Is he dead or alive?"

Again I ignore her question. "When was the last time you saw Ry Strauss?"

"You're not an FBI agent, are you?"

"No."

"But you have a big interest in this?"

I stop. "Mrs. Dorchester?"

"Call me Lake." She has, I admit, a rather potent smile. I like it. There is a quiet strength to this woman. "Why not, right?"

"Why not," I repeat. "My interests are irrelevant, Lake. I need you to focus. Answer my questions and then I'll be out of your life. Is that clear?"

"You're something."

"I am, yes. When was the last time you saw Ry Strauss?"

"More than forty years ago."

"So that would be . . . ?"

"Three weeks before I turned myself in."

"You've had no contact with him since?"

"None."

"Any idea where he's been?"

Her voice is softer this time. "None." Then she adds, "Is Ry alive?"

Yet again I ignore her query. "Where were you the last time you saw him?"

"I can't see how it matters now."

I smile at her. My smile says, *Just answer.*

"We were in New York City. There's a pub called Malachy's on Seventy-Second Street near Columbus Avenue."

I know Malachy's. It's a legit dive bar, with harried hay-straw-haired barmaids who call you hon and laminated bar menus that make you reach for a hand sanitizer. Malachy's is not an artificially created "dive," not some Disney reproduction of what a dive bar is supposed to look like so that hipsters can feel authentic whilst remaining safe and comfy. I go to Malachy's sometimes—it is only a block from my abode—but when I do, I don't pretend I belong.

"Back in the seventies," Lake continues, "there was an underground network of supporters taking care of us. Ry and me, we moved around a lot. These people helped keep us hidden." She snags my gaze. Her eyes are an inviting gray that goes well with the hair. "I'm not going to tell you any of their names."

"I have no interest in busting old hippies," I say.

"Then what do you have an interest in?"

I wait. She sighs.

"Right, right, anyway, we moved around—communes, basements, abandoned buildings, camping grounds, no-name motels. This went on for more than two years. You have to remember, I was only nineteen years old when this started. We'd planned to blow up an empty building. That's all. No one was supposed to get hurt. And I didn't even throw one of the Molotov cocktails that night."

She is getting off track. "So you're at Malachy's in New York," I prompt.

"Yes. Stuck in a storage room in the basement. The smell was awful. Stale beer and vomit. It still haunts me, I swear. But the big thing is, Ry, he isn't stable. He never was, I guess. I can see that now. I don't know what part of me was so broken I thought only he could fix it. My upbringing was troubled, but you don't want to hear about that."

She is correct. I don't.

"But locked in that foul, tiny basement, Ry was really starting to unravel. I couldn't stay with him anymore. It was just too abusive a relationship. No, he never hit me. That's not what I mean. The woman who got us the room under Malachy's? She saw it too. That kind woman—I'll call her Sheila but that's not her real name—Sheila could see I needed help. She became a sympathetic ear. I had to leave him. No choice. But where would I go? I thought about staying underground. Sheila knew someone who could sneak me into Canada and then to Europe. But I'd been on the run for two years now. I didn't want to live the rest of my life this way. The stress, the dirt, the exhaustion, but mostly the boredom. You either travel or you hide all day. More than anything, I think wanted people turn themselves in to escape the monotony. I just craved normalcy, you know what I mean?"

"Normalcy," I repeat to keep her talking.

"So Sheila introduced me to this sympathetic lawyer who taught up at Columbia. He thought that if I turned myself in, maybe I wouldn't get that much time, you know, being so young and under Ry's influence and all that. So we came up with a plan. I made my way to Detroit. I hid out there for a few weeks. When enough time had passed, I turned myself in."

"Did you tell Ry Strauss what you were doing?"

She slowly shook her head, her face tilted toward the sky. "This was all done behind Ry's back. I left a note with Sheila trying to explain."

"How did he react to your departure?"

"I don't know," she says. "Once a plan like that goes into effect, you can't look back. It's too dangerous for anyone."

"Did you try to find out after the fact?"

"No, never. Same reason. I didn't want to put anyone in danger."

"You must have been curious."

"More like guilty," she says. "Ry was getting worse—and my answer was to abandon him. His hold on me had loosened, but...God, you can't imagine what it was like. I thought the sun rose and fell on Ry Strauss. I would literally have died for him."

Which raises the question, which I decide not to ask right now: Would you have killed for him too?

"You told the FBI he drowned in the Upper Peninsula of Michigan."

"I made that up."

"Why?"

"Why do you think? I owed him, didn't I?"

"It was a distraction?"

"Yes, of course. Get the cops off his back. I also had to explain why I chose now to turn myself in. I couldn't say it was because the great Ry Strauss was ranting at himself in a basement bar on the Upper West Side. Now we would diagnose him as bipolar or OCD or something. But back then?

Ry used to go up to the bar at night, after it closed, and line up the liquor bottles so they were equidistant from one another with the labels facing the same way. It would take him hours."

I think about the tower room at the Beresford. "Did he have any money?"

"Ry?"

"You said you were hiding in a basement below a dive bar."

"Yes."

"Did he have the money for nicer quarters?"

"No."

"Did he have an interest in art?"

"Art?"

"Painting, sculpture, art."

"I don't...Why would you ask that?"

"Did you ever commit robberies with him?"

"What? No, of course not."

"So you just relied on the kindness of strangers?"

"I don't—"

"You know other radicals held up banks, don't you? The Symbionese Liberation Army. The Brink's robbery. Did you and Strauss ever do anything like that? I don't care about prosecuting you. My guess is, the statute of limitations would be up anyway. But I need to know."

A teenage boy walks by us with three dogs on leashes. Lake Davies smiles at him and nods. He nods back. "I wanted to turn myself in right at the start. He wouldn't let me."

"Wouldn't let you?"

"Part of all worship is abuse. That's what I've learned. Those who love God the most also fear God the most too. 'God-fearing,' right? The most devout who won't shut up about God's love are always the ones raving about fire and brimstone and eternal damnation. So was I in love with Ry or was I scared of him? I don't know how thick that line is."

I'm not here to get mired down in a philosophical discussion, so I shift gears.

"Did you see on the news about a stolen Vermeer being found?"

"Yesterday, right?" It slowly hits her. "Wait. Wasn't someone found dead with the painting?"

I nod. "That was Ry Strauss."

I give her a moment to take that in.

"He'd become a hoarder and a hermit." I explain about the Beresford, the tower, the clutter, the mess, the painting on the wall. I choose not to go into my cousin's predicament quite yet. There is a bench up ahead. Lake Davies collapses onto it as if her knees have given way. I stay standing.

"So Ry was murdered."

"Yes."

"After all these years." Lake Davies shakes her head, her eyes glassy. "I still don't see why you're here."

"My family owned the Vermeer."

"So you're, what, here to find the other painting?"

I do not reply.

"I don't have it. When were the paintings stolen?"

I tell her the date.

"That was way after I turned myself in."

"Did you ever see any of the other Jane Street Six after the murders?"

She winces at the word "murders." I used it intentionally. "The underground divided us up. You can't have six people traveling together."

"That's not what I asked."

"Just one."

When she stops talking, I put my hand to my ear. "I'm listening."

"We stayed two nights with Arlo."

"Arlo Sugarman?"

She nods. "In Tulsa. He was posing as a student at Oral Roberts University, which I thought was pretty ironic."

"Why's that?"

"Arlo was raised Jewish but prided himself on his atheism."

I remember something I saw in the file. "Sugarman claimed he wasn't there that night—"

"We all did, so what?"

Fair enough. "Wasn't he a fine arts major at Columbia?"

"Yeah, maybe. Wait, you think Arlo and Ry...?"

"Do you?"

"No. I mean, I don't know for sure, but..."

I think now about Cousin Patricia and the horror of what she went through. "You mentioned Ry Strauss hurting you."

She swallows. "What about it?"

"You changed your entire identity. You pretty much went off the grid."

"Yet you found me."

I try to look modest. Then I ask, "Were you afraid Ry would try to find you?"

"Not just Ry."

"Who?"

She shakes me off, and I can see she is starting to close down.

"There is a chance," I say, "that Ry Strauss was involved in something more sinister than stolen art."

"How much more sinister?"

I see no reason to sugarcoat it. "Abducting, raping, and eventually murdering young women."

Her face loses all color.

"Perhaps with a partner," I add. Then I ask, "Do you think Ry could have been involved in something like that?"

"No," she says softly. "And I really think you should leave now."

CHAPTER 9

B ack on the plane, I start reading through the FBI file. I
call it a file, but in fact it is a three-inches-thick binder
with photocopied pages. I take out my Montblanc and
jot down the names of the Jane Street Six:

Ry Strauss
Arlo Sugarman
Lake Davies (Jane Dorchester)
Billy Rowan
Edie Parker
Lionel Underwood.

I stare at the names for a moment. When I do, when I think
of these six and the fact that only one (now two, if you include
Ry Strauss) has been seen or heard from in forty years, it
becomes apparent that PT is probably right about their fate.

Odds are strong that at least some of them, if not all,
are dead.

Then again, perhaps not. Hadn't Ry Strauss managed to survive all these years before he was brutally murdered? If Strauss could hide in the center of the largest city in the country, why couldn't the others stay underground?

Oddly enough, I am not buying my own rationale.

One could stay hidden. Two perhaps. But four?

Unlikely.

I start with the timeline and write down the following question:

Who has been seen since the night of the Molotov cocktails?

Day One, Two, and Three post-attack there were no credible sightings of any of the Jane Street Six. Pretty remarkable when you think of the manhunt. On Day Four, there was finally a break. The FBI received an anonymous tip that Arlo Sugarman was holed up in a brownstone in the Bronx. Alas, we know how that turned out—Special Agent Patrick O'Malley ends up being shot and killed on the stoop. I jot this incident down next to Sugarman's name because it is his first known sighting. The second sighting, according to what I just learned from Lake Davies, places Arlo Sugarman in Tulsa, Oklahoma, as a student at Oral Roberts University in 1975. I mark that down too.

That's it on Sugarman. No third sighting.

I move on to Billy Rowan. According to the FBI file, Rowan was spotted only once since the attack—two weeks later—by Vanessa Hogan, the mother of one of the victims, Frederick Hogan, a seventeen-year-old from Great Neck, New York. Vanessa Hogan, a devoutly religious woman, had gone on television almost immediately after her son's death to say she had forgiven those who harmed young Frederick.

"God must have wanted my Frederick for a higher purpose," she said at the press conference.

I hate this sort of justification. I hate it even more when it's reversed, if you will—when a survivor of a tragedy claims something to the effect that "God spared me because I'm special to Him," the subtle implication being that God didn't give a damn about those who perished. In this case, however, Vanessa Hogan was a young widow who had just lost her only child, so perhaps I should cut her some slack.

I digress.

According to the FBI report, two weeks after Vanessa Hogan's press conference, when the intensity of the search had waned just enough, Billy Rowan, who had also been raised in a devoutly religious home, knocked on Hogan's back door at approximately nine p.m. Vanessa Hogan was home alone in her kitchen at the time. Billy Rowan had purportedly seen her on TV and wanted to apologize in person before he went fully underground.

Okay, fine. I note this next to Rowan's name. First and only sighting.

I move on to the rest. Edie Parker, no sightings. Lionel Underwood, no sightings. And of course, when I was handed the file: Ry Strauss, no sightings.

I tap my lip with my Montblanc and mull it over. Let's suppose that they had all successfully stayed underground for all these years. Do I really believe that they never, not once, reached out to family members?

I do not.

I scan through the file and jot down the names of close

relatives I could potentially question. Ry Strauss had a quasi-famous brother, Saul, a progressive attorney who represents the downtrodden. He's a television talking head, but then again who isn't nowadays? Did Ry never contact his brother Saul, even though they lived in the same city for perhaps forty years? It's worth an ask. Saul Strauss, I know, has been on Hester Crimstein's news program, ridiculously named *Crimstein on Crime*. Perhaps Hester could offer an introduction.

The Strauss parents are deceased. In fact, of the Jane Street Six's potential twelve parents, only two are still alive—Billy Rowan's father, Edie Parker's mother. I write their names down. Next I go through surviving siblings besides Saul Strauss. That adds another nine people, though two of those belong to Lake Davies, so I won't need them. I add those names to my list. If I have more time or help, I might spread my family tree out—uncles, aunts, cousins—but I doubt that I will.

There are a lot of names here. I will need help.

My thoughts naturally gravitate to Myron.

He is down in Florida, taking care of his parents and helping his wife settle into a new job. I don't want to take him away from that. Those who know us well would note that I always came through when Myron would engage in similar quixotic quests and ask for my help—that in fact, after all the times I marched into battle for him without question or pause, Myron "owes" me.

Those folks would be wrong.

Let me clue you in on the advice Myron's father, one of the wisest men I know, gave his son and his son's best man—that would be yours truly—on Myron's wedding day:

"Relationships are never fifty-fifty. Sometimes they are sixty-forty, sometimes eighty-twenty. You'll be the eighty sometimes, you'll be the twenty others. The key is to accept and be okay with that."

I believe this simple wisdom is true for all great relationships, not just marriages, so if you add it up, how my friendship with Myron has improved and enhanced my life, no, Myron owes me nothing.

My phone pings a reminder that I have not yet responded to my rendezvous app. I doubt there will be time tonight, but it would be rude to not reply. When I click the notification and scan the request, my eyes widen. I quickly change my mind and set up a meet for eight p.m. tonight.

Let me explain why.

The rendezvous app has a rather unusual "bio" page. No, it's not like the dating apps where you spew out exaggerated nonsense about how you like piña coladas and getting caught in the rain. This page starts about akin to ratings one might give an Uber, but because most members use the app on rare occasions (unlike yours truly), the developers have supplemented personal ratings with what could crudely be called an appearance ranking. It's a far more complicated algorithm than that, scoring in many specific physical fields and on many levels. One of the app rules states that if you ask another client about your ranking—or if that client tells you—you are both immediately forced to relinquish your membership. I, for example, do not know what my rankings are.

I am confident that they are high. No need for false modesty, is there?

To give you an idea, Bitsy Cabot's aggregate ranking was an accurate 7.8 out of ten. The lowest I would go for is a 6.5. Well, okay, once I went with a 6.0, but nothing else was available. The app's scoring is very tough. A six on this app would be considered at least an eight anywhere else.

The highest ranking I've seen on the app? I was once with a 9.1. She'd been a renowned supermodel before she married a famous rock star. You know her name. That was the only woman above a nine I'd ever seen.

The woman who had currently pinged me for a rendezvous? Her ranking was a 9.85.

There is no way I was passing that up.

PT calls me. "How did it go with Lake Davies?"

I start with the obvious: "She lied about Strauss being dead." I then fill him in on the rest of our conversation.

"So what's your next step?"

"Go to Malachy's Pub."

"Forty years later?"

"Yes."

"Long shot."

"Is there any other kind?" I counter.

"What else?"

"I have compiled a list of people I may want to interrogate. I need your people to get me current addresses."

"Email me the list."

I know how PT works. He gets the information before he gives the information. Now that I've done my part, I prompt him: "Anything new on your end?"

"We got week-old CCTV footage from the Beresford. We think it's from the day of the murder but..."

I wait.

"We don't know how helpful it will be," he says.

"Is the killer on it?"

"Likely, yeah. But we can't really see much."

"I'd like to view it."

"I can email you a link in an hour."

I mull this over for a moment. "I'd rather stop by the Beresford and have one of the doormen show it to me."

"I'll set it up."

"I will go to Malachy's first."

"One more thing, Win."

I wait.

"We can't keep the ID quiet any longer. Tomorrow morning, the Director is going to announce the body belongs to Ry Strauss."

"Ain't you a good-looking fella?"

"Yes," I say. "Yes, I am."

Kathleen, the longtime barmaid at Malachy's, cackles a half laugh, half cigarette-cough at that one. She has a rye (I mean that in two ways) smile and yellow (as opposed to blonde) hair. Kathleen is comfortably north of sixty years old, but she wears it with confidence and an old-world sultry appeal that some might describe as burlesque. She is buxom and curvy and soft. I like Kathleen immediately, but I recognize that it is her occupation to be liked.

"If I was a little younger..." Kathleen begins.

"Or if I were a little luckier," I counter.

"Oh, stop."

I arch an eyebrow. It's one of my trademark moves. "Don't sell yourself short, Kathleen. The night is young."

"You're being fresh." She playfully slaps me with a dishrag

last laundered during the Eisenhower administration. "Charming. Good-looking as hell. But fresh."

On the stool to my right, Frankie Boy, who is closer to eighty, wears a tweed flat cap. Thick tufts of hair jut out of his ears like Troll dolls turned on their side. His nose couldn't be more bulbous without cosmetic surgery. I have been to Malachy's perhaps five times prior to tonight. Frankie Boy is always at this stool.

"Buy you a drink?" I say to him.

"Okay," Frankie slurs, "but just for the record, I don't think you're that good-looking."

"Sure, you do," I say.

"Yeah, maybe, but that doesn't mean I'm gonna have sex with you."

I sigh. "Dreams die hard in here."

He likes that.

As I said before, Malachy's is a legit dive bar—poor lighting, stained (and I mean that in two ways) wood paneling, dead flies in the light fixtures, patrons so regular that it's sometimes hard to see where the stool ends and their butts begin. A sign above the bar reads, LIFE IS GOOD. SO IS BEER. Wisdom. Regulars blend well with the newcomers, and pretty much anything goes but pretension. There are two televisions, one set up at either end of the bar. The New York Yankees are losing on one, the New York Rangers are losing on the other. No one in Malachy's seems to be too invested in either.

The menu is standard pub fare. Frankie Boy insists I order the chicken wings. Out comes a plate of grease with a smattering of bone. I slide it to him. We chat. Frankie tells me that he is on his fourth wife.

"I love her so much," Frankie Boy tells me.

"Congrats."

"'Course, I loved the other three so much too. Still do." A tear comes to his eye. "That's my problem. I fall hard. Then I come in here to forget. Do you know what I'm saying?"

I don't, but I tell him that I do. The song "True" by Spandau Ballet comes drifting out of the speakers. Frankie Boy starts singing along: "This is the sound of my soul, this is the sound . . ." He stops and turns to me. "You ever been married, Win?"

"No."

"Smart. Wait. You gay?"

"No."

"Not that I care. Be honest, I like a lot of the gays in here. Less competition for the ladies, you know what I'm saying?"

I ask him how long he's been coming to Malachy's.

"First time was January 12, 1966."

"Specific," I say.

"Biggest day of my life."

"Why?" I ask, genuinely curious.

Frankie Boy holds up three stubby fingers. "Three reasons."

"Go on."

He drops the ring finger. "One, that's the first day I found this place."

"Makes sense."

"Two"—Frankie Boy drops his middle finger—"I married my first wife, Esmeralda."

"You went to Malachy's for the first time on your wedding day?"

"I was getting married," he says, emphasis on the "married." "Who'd blame a man for needing a stiff drink or two beforehand?"

"Not I."

"My Esmeralda was so beautiful. Big as a barn. She wore a bright yellow wedding dress. In our wedding pictures, I look like a tiny planet orbiting a giant sun. But beautiful."

"And what's Reason Three?" I ask.

"You may be too young, but did you ever see the TV show *Batman?*"

"Oh yes." This, I think to myself, is kismet. Myron and I have watched every episode at least a million times. I nod. "Adam West, Burt Ward—"

"Exactly. The Riddler, the Penguin, oh, and don't even get me started on Julie Newmar as the Catwoman. I would have ripped off Esmeralda's right arm and slapped myself silly with it, just to sniff Julie Newmar's hair. No offense."

"None taken."

"And nowadays, we have all these"—finger quotes—"'method' actors losing a hundred pounds or whatever to play the Joker, but back then? Cesar Romero didn't even bother shaving his mustache. Just threw white makeup over it. That, my friend, was acting."

I see no reason to disagree. "And Reason Three?"

He scoffed. "I thought you were a fan."

"I am."

"So what villain appeared in the very first episode?"

"The Riddler," I say, "played by Frank Gorshin."

"Correct answer—and when did it first air?" Frankie Boy smiles and nods. "January 12, 1966."

I want to kiss this man.

"So to summarize," I say, "on your wedding day, you went for drinks at Malachy's, and then you watched *Batman* debut on TV."

Frankie Boy nods solemnly and stares down at his drink.

"Fifty years later, Malachy's is still in my life. Fifty years later, I can still watch *Batman* on my old VCR." Big shrug. "But Esmeralda? She's long gone."

We drink in silence for a moment. I need to get to the point of my visit, but I'm really enjoying this conversation. Eventually, I work my way to asking Frankie Boy whether he remembers a waitress or barmaid named Sheila or Shelly or something like that—I hope that perhaps Lake Davies slipped up and gave me the real name—and he scratches his head.

"Kathleen?" he shouts.

"What?"

"You remember a Sheila who worked here a long time ago?"

"Huh?" Kathleen is smiling, but I detect something awry in her body language. Perhaps it is the smile that suddenly seems forced. Perhaps it is the way her grip tightens on the beer tap. "Who wants to know?"

"Our good-looking friend Win here," Frankie Boy says, slapping my back.

Kathleen heads back toward us. She has the dishrag over her shoulder. "Sheila what?"

"I don't know," I say.

She shakes her head. "Don't remember a Sheila. How about you, Frankie?"

He shakes his head too, and jumps down from the stool. "Gotta take a massive wiz," he tells us.

"With your prostate?" Kathleen counters.

"Let a man dream, will ya?"

Frankie Boy hobbles off. Kathleen turns back to me. She has the kind of expression that tells you she has seen it all at least twice. Google "world weary" and her photograph pops up.

"When would this Sheila have been here?"

"1975 or thereabouts," I say.

"Seriously? That's like, what, more than forty years ago."

I wait.

"Anyway, I didn't start working here until three years later. Summer of 1978."

"I see," I say. "Anyone still here from those days?"

"Let me think." Kathleen glances up at the ceiling to make a show of thinking this over. "Old Moses in the kitchen would have been here, but he retired for Florida last year. Other than that, well, I'm the most senior employee, I guess." With that subject dismissed, she points to my empty glass and says, "Get you another, hon?"

There is a time for the subtle. There is a time for the blunt. I confess that I am far better with the blunt. With that in mind, I ask: "So what about the famous fugitives who hid in the basement?"

Kathleen rears her head back and blinks. "Huh?"

"Have you ever heard of the Jane Street Six?"

"The what?"

"How about Ry Strauss?"

Her eyes narrow. "That name rings a bell, I think. But I don't see—"

"Ry Strauss and his girlfriend Lake Davies were wanted for murder. They hid in Malachy's basement in 1975."

She doesn't reply for a few moments. Then she says, "I've heard a lot of legends about this place, but that's a new one."

But her voice is softer now. Kathleen, I've observed, usually plays for the entire bar, even in one-on-one conversations, as though the bar is a stage and she wants as big an audience as possible for every encounter.

Now suddenly she wants an audience of only one.

"It's the truth," I say.

"How do you know?"

"Lake Davies told me."

"One of the fugitives?"

"She was caught and served her time."

"And she told you she hid in this bar?"

"In the basement, yes. She told me a kind barmaid named Sheila looked after them. She said the kind barmaid saved her."

We stare at one another for a moment.

"Doubt it," Kathleen says.

"Why?"

"Ever been in our basement? I don't think anything outside the mold family could survive down there."

She cackles again, but it is far less organic now. As if on cue, a burly man on the far end of the stools slaps his hand down on the bar and gleefully shouts, "Got it!"

Kathleen yells, "What, Fred?"

"A cockroach as big as one of those park pigeons."

Kathleen smiles at me as if to say, *See what I mean?*

"I don't think Lake Davies made it up," I say.

Her reply starts with a shrug. "Well, if she's like those other crazy radicals from back then, maybe she dropped too much acid and imagined it."

"Funny," I say.

"What?"

"I never mentioned that she was a radical."

Kathleen smiles and leans a little closer. I get the cigarette smell again, though it's not entirely unpleasant. "You said the Jane Something Six or whatever, and then I remembered they

103

bombed something and killed people. Why you asking about that anyway?"

"Because Ry Strauss has never been caught."

"And you're looking for him?"

"I am."

"Almost fifty years after the fact?"

"Yes," I say. "Can you help?"

"Wish I could." She is trying too hard to act disinterested. "Be good to see a killer like that get what's coming to him."

"You think so?"

"Damn straight. You a cop?"

I arch an eyebrow. "In this suit?"

She gives another tobacco-laced laugh as Frankie Boy hops back on his stool. "Fun talking to you," Kathleen says. Then, tilting her head, she adds, "I got customers."

She saunters away.

"Man," Frankie Boy says, watching her with awe, "I could watch that caboose all day. You know what I'm saying?"

"I do."

"You a private eye, Win?"

"No."

"Like Sam Spade or Magnum, P.I.?"

"No."

"But you're cool like them, am I right?"

"As rain," I agree, watching Kathleen work the tap. "As rain."

CHAPTER 10

I have over an hour before my app rendezvous with Mrs. 9.85.

The walk from Malachy's Pub to the Beresford takes me about ten minutes. I head up Columbus Avenue and cut through the grounds of the American Museum of Natural History. When I was six years old, and my parents were still together, they took my siblings and me to this very museum. The Lockwoods, of course, got a private tour before the museum was open to the general public. One of my earliest memories (and perhaps yours) swirls around the dinosaur bones in the entrance foyer, the woolly mammoth's tusks on the fourth floor, and mostly, the huge blue whale hanging from the ceiling in the Hall of Ocean Life. I still see that blue whale from time to time. At night, the museum hosts high-end gala dinners. I sit beneath the great whale and drink excellent scotch and look up at it. I try sometimes to see that little boy and his family, but I realize that what I'm conjuring up isn't real or stored in my brain. This is true for most if not all of what we call memories. Memories aren't kept on some microchip in the skull or filed away in a cabinet somewhere deep in our cranium. Memories are something we reconstruct and piece together. They are fragments we manufacture to create what we think occurred or even simply hope to be true. In short, our memories are rarely accurate. They are biased reenactments.

Shorter still: We all see what we want to see.

The doorman at the Beresford is waiting for me. He leads me to the security monitors behind the desk. There, cued up on the screen, is a black-and-white image of two people walking single file. I can't make out much. The shot is from above, the quality not great. The person in front is likely Ry Strauss. He has a hoodie pulled over his head. The person behind him is totally bald. Both keep their heads down, walking so close together that the bald head looks to be leaning on Strauss's back.

"Do you want me to hit play?" the doorman asks.

The doorman looks young, no more than twenty-five. The military-style uniform he wears is far too big on his thin frame.

I say, "This is the basement, correct?"

"Yeah."

"Did you have any contact with"—I don't know what to call Strauss, so I point—"this tenant?"

"No," he says. "Never."

"Did anyone ever call him by a name?"

"No. I mean, we're trained to call our tenants by their last name. You know, mister or missus or doctor or whatever. If we don't know the name we use 'sir' or 'ma'am.' But with him, I mean, I never even saw the guy, and I've been here two years."

I turn my attention back to the screen. "Hit play, please."

He does. The video is short and uneventful. Strauss and assailant walk with their heads down, single file, staying close together. It looks odd. I ask him to rewind and play it again. Then a third time.

"Hit pause when I tell you."

"Okay, sure."

"Now."

The image freezes. I squint and lean closer. I still can't pick up much, but this much seems clear: Both knew that they were on a security camera and at this point—the point where I've asked the image to be frozen—the man we now know is Ry Strauss looks up into the lens.

"Can you zoom in?"

"Not really, no. The pixels get all messed up."

I doubt that I would pick up much anyway. The assumption, and I think it is a righteous one, is that the bald man behind Ry Strauss is the killer. Their manner is so off—stiff, short steps, staying so close—that I assume Strauss is being led at gunpoint.

"To your knowledge, did the deceased ever have visitors?"

"Nope. Never. We all talked about that this morning."

"We?"

"Me and the other doormen. No one remembers anyone coming to see him. Not ever. I mean, I guess they could have come with him up through the basement like this."

"I assume this visitor eventually left?"

"If he did, we don't have it on tape."

I sit back and steeple my fingers.

"We done?" the doorman asks.

"How about the footage of the tenant departing the building?"

"Huh?"

I point at the screen. "Before he met up with this visitor, I assume the deceased left the building?"

"Oh, right. Yeah."

"Could you show me?"

"Give me a second."

This video is even less eventful. Ry Strauss keeps his head down. He wears the hoodie. He walks by, though I do note that he seems in a rush. I check the time—forty-two minutes before he returns. This all adds up in my view.

"You said he never left in the daytime, correct?"

"Not that anyone remembers."

"So this"—I point to Strauss walking out during the daytime—"would be unusual?"

"I'd say, yeah. Hermit normally only went out like super late at night."

That piques my interest. "How late?"

"You'd have to ask Hormuz. He works the night shift. But really late, way after midnight."

"Will Hormuz be on tonight?"

"Yeah. Whoa, someone is coming with packages. Excuse me a moment." The young doorman departs. I take out my phone and call PT.

"Did your guys find a phone in Strauss's apartment?" I ask.

"No."

"No landline either?"

"No. Why?"

"I have a theory," I tell him.

"Go ahead."

"Someone called Strauss on a phone and told him something worrying. Perhaps that his cover was blown. We can only speculate. But someone called him and told him something so worrying that the hermit left his apartment during daylight hours. My suspicion is, it was a setup."

"How do you figure?"

"The killer placed the call to Strauss and said something on the phone they knew would get Strauss to react. When Strauss leaves the building, the killer intercepts him at gunpoint and forces Strauss to bring him back to his apartment."

"Where the killer shackles him to the bed and kills him."

"Yes."

"And leaves the Vermeer behind. Why?"

"The obvious answer," I say, "is that his murder wasn't about the stolen art."

"So what else would it be about?"

"It could be a lot of things. But I think we know the most obvious one."

"The Hut of Horrors," he says.

We are silent for a while.

"The Bureau hasn't put that part together yet, Win."

I say nothing.

"They still don't know why your suitcase is there. When they do, they'll want alibis for your cousin. And for you."

I nod to myself. His is a solid analysis.

"It seems likely," I say, "that Ry Strauss was involved in some way with the Hut of Horrors."

His voice is grave. "It does."

I feel a chill at the base of my neck. "So I'm wondering."

"Wondering what?"

"Everyone has always believed that Uncle Aldrich and Cousin Patricia were random victims of serial predators. Uncle Aldrich was killed, so as to abscond with Patricia to the hut."

"You don't think so anymore?"

I frown. "Think it through, PT. It can't be random."

"Why not?"

"Because Strauss had the Vermeer."

He takes a second. "You're right. That can't be a coincidence."

"And that means Patricia wasn't a random victim. She was targeted."

We fall into silence.

"Let me know how I can help, Win."

"I assume the Bureau will be analyzing these CCTV videos?"

"We are, but the quality is crap. And this has been a pain in my ass for years—why the hell do we keep all the cameras up high? Every criminal knows that. He just kept his head down."

"So nothing else on him?"

"They're still analyzing, but all they can tell us is he's slight, short, bald."

"It's more important that you scour the nearby buildings for CCTV," I tell him. "We need to figure out where Strauss went when he left the Beresford and who he encountered."

"On it. Where are you going now?"

I check my watch. Enough work for the moment. My mind shifts quickly to the 9.85 rating.

"Saks Fifth Avenue," I say.

———————

I am nearing Saks when the phone rings. It's Nigel calling from Lockwood.

"Your father heard about the Vermeer," Nigel tells me. "He also heard that Cousin Patricia was in the house."

I wait.

"He would like to see you. He says it's urgent."

I push the door open and enter Saks by the men's suits department. "Urgent as in tonight?"

"Urgent as in tomorrow morning."

"Done," I say.

"One favor, Win."

"Name it."

"Don't upset your father."

"Okay," I say. Then I ask, "How is he, Nigel?"

"Your father is very agitated."

"Over the Vermeer or Cousin Patricia?"

"Yes," Nigel says and hangs up.

I head into the basement of Saks and pass the Vault jewelry department.

The rendezvous app has a rather lengthy questionnaire to "discover your type in order to make the best matches." I skipped answering the questions and went straight to the comment section.

What's my type?

I wrote one word: Hot.

That's my type. I don't care whether she's blonde, brunette, redhead, or bald. I don't care whether she's short or tall, heavyset or emaciated, white, Black, Asian, young, old, whatever.

My type?

I use one type of criteria and rank them thusly:

Super Super Hot.
Super Hot.
Hot.
More Hot Than Not.

That's it. The rest, as I say, does not matter. I hold no prejudices or biases when it comes to hotness, and yet I ask you: Where are my laurels for being so open-minded?

I am first to arrive in the suite. The app tells me that my rendezvous partner is still fifteen minutes away. The shower is supplied with Kevis 8 shampoo and Maison Francis Kurkdjian Aqua Vitae scented shower cream. I take advantage of that. I strip down and close my eyes under the heavy stream of the propulsive-power-jet Speakman shower head.

I think chronologically for a moment. We have the Jane Street Six attack. We have the art heist at Haverford College. We have my uncle's murder and my cousin's abduction. Three different nights. The first two are connected by the Vermeer found in the possession of the most famous of the Jane Street Six. Then we add in the suitcase, and it becomes apparent that all three are somehow linked.

How?

Most obvious answer: By Ry Strauss.

We know Strauss was leader of the Jane Street Six. We know he was in possession of the stolen Vermeer (where is the Picasso, by the way?). We know that the suitcase, last seen when Patricia was abducted, was in his tower apartment.

Was he the mastermind behind all three?

I get out of the shower. Ms. 9.85 Rating should be here within minutes. I am about to silence my phone when Kabir calls.

"I found the security guard from the art heist."

"Go on."

"At the time of the robbery, he was an intern paying off student debts by working security at night."

I remember this. One of the criticisms leveled at both the college and our family was that we had trusted two priceless masterpieces to shoddy security. It was a criticism, of course, that proved spot-on.

"His name is Ian Cornwell. He'd only graduated from Haverford the year before."

"Where is he now?"

"Still at Haverford. In fact, he's never left. Ian Cornwell is a professor in the political science department."

"Find out if he's on campus tomorrow. Also get a copter ready. I'm flying to Lockwood first thing in the morning."

"Got it. Anything else?"

"I need some information about Malachy's."

I start telling him what I need when I hear the elevator ping.

The 9.85 rating has arrived.

I finish up quickly and say, "No calls for the next hour." Then, thinking about that rating, I add, "Perhaps the next two or three."

I disconnect the phone as she steps out of the elevator.

I had assumed the rating would be an exaggeration. It isn't.

She has always been—and remains now—at least a 9.85. For a moment, we just stare at one another. I am in my robe. She is in a crisply tailored business suit, but everything she wears always looks crisply tailored. I try to remember the last time I saw her in the flesh. When she and Myron ended their engagement, I gather, but I can't recall the specifics. Myron had loved her with all his heart. She had shattered that heart into a million pieces. Part of me found the whole thing in-comprehensible and tedious, this brokenhearted thing; part of me understood with absolute clarity why I would never let any woman leave me that way.

"Hello, Win."

"Hello, Jessica."

Jessica Culver is a fairly well-known novelist. After a decade together, she and Myron broke up because in the end, Myron wanted to settle down, marry, have children and Jessica sneered at that sort of idyllic conformity. At least, that was what she'd told Myron.

Not long after the breakup, Myron and I saw a wedding announcement in the *New York Times*. Jessica Culver had married a Wall Street tycoon named Stone Norman. I hadn't seen, heard, or thought about her since.

"This is a surprise," I say.

"Yep."

"Guess it isn't going so great with you and Rock."

Immature of me to intentionally get the name wrong, but there you go.

Jessica smiles. The smile is dazzling and beautiful, but it doesn't reach more than my eyes. I remember when that same smile used to knock poor Myron to his knees.

"It's good to see you, Win."

I tilt my head. "Is it?"

"Sure."

We stand there a few more moments.

"So are we going to do this or what?"

CHAPTER 11

The answer ends up being "what."

Jessica and I spend the next hour lying on the bed and talking. Don't ask me why, but I end up telling her about Ry Strauss and the Vermeer and the rest. She watches me closely as I speak, completely rapt. As I said, I don't get romantic relationships. During the years that Jessica and Myron were a couple, I understood that she was very attractive and immensely doable, but so are a lot of women. I never got why Myron would want only one woman or put up with her mood swings and drama. Now, as she lies alongside me and gives me that laser focus, I perhaps get a tiny sliver of the appeal.

I stop and tell her this.

"You hated me," Jessica says.

"No."

"You viewed us as rivals."

"You and I?"

"Yes."

"For?"

"For Myron, of course."

Jessica shifts on the bed. She is still clothed. I remain in my bathrobe. "You know I wrote a piece on the Jane Street Six for the *New Yorker*."

"When?"

"It was on one of the anniversaries of the attack. Twenty, maybe twenty-fifth, I don't remember. You can probably find it online." She tucked her hair behind her ear. "It's pretty fascinating stuff."

"How so?"

"It's a perfect storm of what-if tragedy. The six had originally planned to hit another USO dance hall a month earlier, but Strauss had come down with appendicitis. What if he hadn't? Several of the six were getting cold feet and threatened not to show. What if one or two had backed out? They were just stoned kids wanting to do some good. They didn't set out to hurt anyone. So what if? What if that one Molotov cocktail hadn't gone astray?"

I'm not impressed with this analysis. "Everything in life is a what-if."

"True. Can I ask a question?"

I wait.

"Why isn't Myron helping you? I mean, all the times you played Watson to Sherlock..."

"He's busy."

"With his new wife?"

I don't feel right talking about Myron with her.

Jessica sits up. "You said you need to watch the documentary on the Jane Street Six."

"I do."

"Let's watch it together and see what happens."

Jessica lies on the right side of the bed, I take the left. Our bodies are close together. I prop up the laptop between us. She puts on reading glasses and flips off the lamp. I click the play button. We start watching the documentary in surprisingly comfortable silence. I find this whole experience odd. For me, Jessica was just an annoying and inconvenient extension of Myron, never her own being. To see or experience her with no attachment to him feels somehow uneasy, not in spite of the comfort but because of it. For the first time, I am seeing her as her own entity, not just Myron's hot girlfriend.

I am not sure how I feel about that.

The documentary begins by pointing out that the group was never called the Jane Street Six. They were just six seemingly random college students, a ragtag splinter quasi-group from the Weather Underground or Students for a Democratic Society. The nickname Jane Street Six was given to them by the media after that disastrous night for the very simple reason that the famed photograph of the six of them had been taken in the basement of a town house on Jane Street in Greenwich Village. "*It was down in the dark dwelling,*" the serious narrator informed us, "*that they brewed the most deadly cocktail of all—the Molotov cocktail.*"

Dum, dum, duuuum.

The narrative then went back in time to how Ry Strauss and Arlo Sugarman originally bonded as sixth graders in the Greenpoint section of Brooklyn. They flashed up an old black-and-white classic team photo of Ry and Arlo on a Little League team, half-standing, half-kneeling, dramatically using red marker to circle the two young faces on the far right.

"Even then," Mr. Voiceover gravely intoned, *"Strauss and Sugarman stood side by side."*

The documentary mercifully skipped those poorly acted and poorly lit reenactment scenes, the ones you always see on true crime drama. They stuck to real footage and interviews with local police, with witnesses, with survivors from the bus crash, with families and friends. A tourist had snapped a photograph of Ry Strauss and Lake Davies running away. The photo was blurry, but you could see them holding hands. The rest were behind them, but you couldn't make out any faces.

The documentary did a bit on the seven victims—Craig Abel, Andrew Dressler, Frederick Hogan, Vivian Martina, Bastien Paul, Sophia Staunch, Alexander Woods.

Jessica says, "Remind me to tell you about Sophia Staunch when we're done."

The documentary focused in on five teenage boys from St. Ignatius Prep who had gone to New York that fateful night to celebrate the seventeenth birthday of Darryl Lance. Back in those days, bars and clubs were not strict about proof of age—and the drinking age had only been eighteen anyway. It came out later that the boys had gone to a strip club with the subtle moniker Sixty-Nine before hopping on the late-night bus heading back out to Garden City. Darryl Lance, who had been in his mid-forties when they filmed the documentary, spoke about the incident. He'd only suffered a broken arm, but his friend Frederick Hogan, also age seventeen, died in the crash. Lance welled up when he described the flames, the panic, the bus driver's overreaction.

"I could see the driver turn the wheel too hard. We went up on just two wheels. I could see the bus start to careen out of control and head for that stone wall. And then we plunge off the road almost in slow motion..."

They then replayed the press conference where Vanessa Hogan absolved the Six. "*I forgive them totally because it's not my place to judge, only God's. Perhaps this was God's way for Frederick to pay for his own sin.*"

I turn slightly toward Jessica. "Is she saying God executed her son for going to a strip club?"

"Apparently," she says. "I interviewed her for my story."

The doc moves on to Billy Rowan's surprise visit to Vanessa Hogan. On the screen, an older Vanessa Hogan spoke to the documentarian about it:

> "*We sat right here, right at this very kitchen table. I asked Billy if he wanted a Coke. He said yes. He drank it so fast.*"
>
> "*What did you talk about?*"
>
> "*Billy said it was an accident. He said they didn't mean to hurt anyone, that they only wanted to make a statement against the war.*"
>
> "*What did you think of this?*"
>
> "*I kept thinking how young Billy was. Frederick was seventeen. This boy was only a few years older.*"
>
> "*What else did Billy Rowan say?*"
>
> "*He saw me on the television. He said he wanted to hear me forgive him with his own ears.*"
>
> "*Did you?*"
>
> "*Yes, of course.*"
>
> "*That couldn't have been easy.*"
>
> "*The path isn't supposed to be easy. It's supposed to be righteous.*"

Jessica looks at me. "Good line."

"Indeed."

"She used it on me too."

"But?"

Jessica shrugs. "It sounded too rehearsed."

Back on the screen, Vanessa Hogan says:

> *"I tried convincing Billy to surrender, but . . ."*
>
> *"But?"*
>
> *"He was so scared. His face. Even now, I think about Billy Rowan's scared face. He just ran out my kitchen door."*

I whisper, "She's kind of hot."

"Ew."

"You don't think so?"

"You haven't changed, Win, have you?"

I smile and shrug. "What was your take when you met her?"

"Two words," Jessica says. "Batshit crazy."

"Because she's religious?"

"Because she's a nut. And a liar."

"You don't think Billy Rowan visited her?"

"No, he did. A lot of evidence proves it."

"So?"

"I don't know. Vanessa Hogan's reactions were just all off. I get the belief that your son has gone to a better place or that it's God's will, but there were no tears, no mourning. It was almost as though she expected it. Like it wasn't a surprise."

"We all grieve in different ways," I say.

"Yeah, thanks for offering up the comforting cliché, Win. But that's not it." Jessica rolls on her side to face me. I do the same. Our lips are inches apart. She smells incredibly good. "Sophia Staunch," she says.

Another Jane Street Six victim. "What about her?"

"Her uncle was Nero Staunch."

Nero Staunch was a huge name in organized crime back in the day. I roll on my back and put my hands behind my head. "Interesting," I say.

"How so?"

"Lake Davies not only changed her name, but she changed her entire identity and moved to West Virginia. I asked her if she did that because she was afraid Ry Strauss would find her."

"What did she say?"

"Her exact words were, 'Not just Ry.'"

"So she was afraid of someone else," Jessica says. "And who better than Nero Staunch?"

When we finish the documentary, Jessica asks to see my list of people to question. I show it to her. We add Vanessa Hogan. Why not? She was the last person to see Billy Rowan.

"Is Nero Staunch still alive?" she asks me.

I nod. "He's ninety-two."

"So out of the game."

"You're never really out of that game. But yes."

I add his name to the list too. We are still in the bed. Jessica meets my gaze and holds it.

"Are we going to do this, Win?"

I move to kiss her. But I stop. She smiles.

"Can't, huh?"

"It's not that," I say.

I don't quite understand what I am feeling, and that annoys me. Jessica and Myron have been over for a long time. He's happily married to another woman. She is mind-bendingly beautiful—Super Super Hot—and willing.

Jessica then reads my next thought and says it out loud: "If sex is such a casual thing to you, why can't you?"

I don't reply. She rolls out of bed.

"Maybe you should think about that," she says.

"No need."

"Oh?"

"I still think of you as Myron's girl."

She smiles at that. "Is that it?"

"Yes."

"Nothing more?"

"Like?"

"I don't know. Like something more"—Jessica looks up, fake searching for the word—"latent."

"Oh please. Could you be more obvious?"

"One of us couldn't be."

"Come back to the bed," I say. "Let me convince you otherwise."

But she is already heading to the elevator. "It really was good to see you, Win. I mean that."

And then she's gone.

CHAPTER 12

I get back to the Beresford at one a.m.

Hormuz spots me coming to the door. He hurries to open it. I flash a fake FBI identification and stick it back in my coat pocket. I realize that impersonating an officer is breaking the law, but here is the thing about being rich: You don't go to jail for crimes like this. The rich hire a bunch of attorneys who will twist reality in a thousand different ways until reality is made irrelevant. They'd claim Hormuz is a liar. They'd say I was obviously joking. They'd deny I ever flashed anything at all, or if we are on tape, they'd say I flashed a photograph of someone I was visiting. We would whisper quietly in the ears of friendly politicians, judges, prosecutors. We would make donations to their campaigns or their pet causes.

It would go away.

If by some miracle it didn't go away—if by some one-in-a-thousand chance the authorities were called in on this and stood up to the pressure and took it to trial and found a jury to convict me of impersonating an officer—the punishment would never be prison time. Rich guys like me don't go to prison. We—gasp!—pay fines. Since I have a ton of money already, a hundred times more than I could spend in a lifetime at the very least, why would that deter me?

Am I being too honest?

A similar calculation is made in my business all the time. It is why so many choose to bend the rules, break the rules, cheat. The odds of getting caught? Slim. The odds of being prosecuted? Slimmer. If you do somehow get caught, the odds of simply paying a fine that will be lower than the amount of money you stole? Great. The odds of doing any kind of real prison time? A mathematical formula constantly approaching zero.

I detest that. I don't stand for cheaters or thieves, especially those who aren't doing it to feed a starving family.

Yet here I am with my fake ID.

Do I appear the hypocrite?

"Yeah, Hermit was like a vampire," Hormuz tells me. "Only came out at night, I guess."

Hormuz has eyes so heavily lidded I don't get how he sees anything. He has a bowling-ball paunch and one of those dark faces that appear to be five-o'clock-shadowed seconds after a shave.

"You want something to drink?" he asks me. "Coffee?"

Hormuz shows me his mug, which probably began life as something in the white family but is now stained the color of a smoker's teeth.

"No, I'm good. I understand the mystery tenant used the basement exit."

"Yep. Which was weird."

"Why weird?"

"Because he'd come out over there, to the left. Then he'd circle in front of the building anyway. He'd walk right past me."

"So he took more steps this way?"

"More steps, longer elevator ride, it just didn't make sense. Except."

"Except?"

"Except the lobby has a ton of cameras. But from his elevator to the exit in the basement, there was only the one."

Made sense. "Did he ever talk to you?"

"The guy in the tower?"

"Yes."

"Not once. He'd go past me like clockwork every Wednesday night. Or, well, it was four a.m. so maybe that was Thursday morning? Still dark out though." He shakes his head. "Doesn't matter, whatever. He'd walk past me. For years this would happen. I would nod and say, 'Good evening, sir.' I'm polite like that. He's one of my tenants. I treat him with respect, no matter how he treats me. Most tenants, well, they're great. They call me by my first name, tell me to do the same with them. But I don't. I like to show respect, you know what I'm saying? I've been here eighteen years, and I would say I still haven't met half of the people who live here. They're in bed by midnight when I come on. But the tower guy? I'd nod to him every time. I would say, 'Good evening, sir.' He just kept his head down. Never said anything. Never looked up. Never acknowledged I even existed."

I say nothing.

"Look, I don't want you to get the wrong idea. I know he's dead and all, so I shouldn't speak bad about the man. I think he had issues, you know. Glenda, my wife, she watches some show on hoarders and whatnot. It's a real illness, Glenda tells me. So maybe that was it. It's not like I'm happy he's dead or anything."

"You said every Wednesday night."

"Huh?"

"You said he walked past you every Wednesday night."

"Or Thursday morning. It's weird having a midnight gig. Like tonight. I arrived Wednesday night but what time is it now?"

I check my watch. "Almost one thirty."

"Right, so it's not Wednesday night anymore. It's Thursday morning."

"Let's call it Thursday morning," I say, because this subject is irrelevant and boring me.

"Yeah, okay."

"You said you saw him walk past you every Thursday morning at four a.m."

"Yep, that's right."

"So it was a routine?"

"Yeah."

"How long had he been doing this?"

"Oh, years and years."

"Summer, fall, spring, winter?"

"Yeah, I think so. I mean, look, there were times he missed. I'm sure of it. There were months I wouldn't see him at all. Like maybe he flew to Florida for the winter, I don't know. And there were nights, well, the job is quiet. I sit. I may stick in my AirPods and stream something on Netflix, you know what I'm saying? But as soon as someone touches the door, *bam*, I'm up. We lock it after midnight. So maybe sometimes he walked by and I didn't see."

"Did you ever see him leave at other times?"

"No, I don't think so. Always four a.m. or right around then."

I think about that. "And what time did he come back?"

"He didn't stay out long. I think he just took a walk. He was back within an hour. Maybe sometimes more. I don't think it was consistent. Look, I figure he's a weirdo, wants to be alone. So he takes night walks. I've heard of stranger things, right?"

"When he walked past you heading out," I continue, "what direction was he going?"

"East."

I glance down across the street in the direction where he's pointing. "Into the park?"

"Yep."

"Every time?"

"Every time. I figured he was taking a walk. Like I said. Strange time, and I know the park is a lot safer now than it used to be, but you wouldn't see me strolling around in there at four in the morning."

I think about this. Four a.m. I wonder whether that is a clue. I think it is.

"When was the last time you saw him going out like that?" I ask.

"Recently. Last week maybe. Or the week before."

I realize that would have been the day before he was murdered. Ry Strauss goes out for his usual Thursday morning four a.m. walk. On Friday he goes out again, for the first time in forever during the daytime, and comes back with in all likelihood his killer.

I have a plan.

———

I stand in the shadows across the street from Malachy's.

The time is four a.m. By law, New York City bars must stop serving alcohol at four a.m. Coincidence? I, for one, hope not.

They say New York is the city that never sleeps. That may

be true, but right about now, her eyes are blinking closed and her head is nodding in exhaustion. My lizard brain, that survival instinct, is wary of shutting itself down. It prefers preparedness. Even as I move about my day, the lizard brain seeks out potential (or erroneously perceived) enemies and threats.

I stay hidden and watch Malachy's door. I have changed into jogging attire and a sweatshirt with a hood. No, it's not a hoodie. It's a sweatshirt with a hood. I would never wear a hoodie. I am patient. I wear earphones. I'm listening to a playlist Kabir created for me featuring Meek Mill, Big Sean, and 21 Savage. Somewhere in the past year or two, after initially scoffing at what I could not comprehend, I have to come to love what we call rap or hip-hop. I know that this music, like Malachy's Pub, was not created for me, but the underlying anger appeals. I also enjoy the humanism in the desperate posturing and bravado; they want to appear tough but their neediness and insecurity shine through so brightly I assume they must know that we are in on the joke.

Right now, as Kathleen and a male bartender lock up for the night, Meek Mill is bemoaning the fact that he can't trust women because he has issues.

I hear you, my troubled friend.

Kathleen waves goodbye to the bartender. He heads west toward Broadway, probably to the One train. Kathleen crosses Columbus Avenue and continues to walk with purpose east on Seventy-Second Street. She lives, I know from Kabir's research, on Sixty-Eighth near West End Avenue.

In short, she is not going home.

I follow from across the street. Two minutes later, she walks past the Dakota and crosses into Central Park. At this hour, the park is pretty much abandoned. I see no one else. Trailing her will be more difficult. We all possess lizard brains, don't we? And in a situation when you are a woman alone in a park and a man in a hooded sweatshirt, however tasteful that hooded sweatshirt may be, is following you, you take notice.

When she heads north on the sidewalk running along what is simply called the Lake, I take a parallel path west of her that goes through the brush. This path is dark and in some ways not the safest at night, but one, I am always armed, and two, if you are any sort of experienced mugger, you wouldn't set to pounce in an area so remote that you'd have to wait days, weeks, or months for a profitable target to happen by, would you?

I lose sight of Kathleen for seconds at a time, but so far, this appears to be working. She is making her way north toward the entrance to the wildlife thicket known as the Ramble on the north shore of the Lake. The Ramble is a nearly forty-acre protected natural reserve with winding paths and old bridges and a tremendous variety of topography and fauna and the like. There is bird-watching, yes, but in a less enlightened day, the Ramble was best known for hosting homosexual encounters. It was a spot where gay men would "cruise," as we used to say. It was supposedly the safest place to avoid being assaulted by those who meant them harm, which is to say, of course, it hadn't been very safe at all.

Kathleen stops on the bridge that crosses over the Lake and into the heart of the Ramble. The moon glistens off the water, and I can see her silhouette. A minute passes. She doesn't move. There is no reason to pretend anymore.

I come down the path. Kathleen hears my approach and turns expectantly.

"Sorry to disappoint you," I say when she sees me.

Kathleen jolts back a little. "Wait, I know you."

I don't reply.

"What the hell, are you following me?"

"Yes."

"What do you want?"

"Ry Strauss won't be coming tonight."

"Huh? Who?" But I can see the fear in her eyes. "I don't know what you're talking about."

I move closer, so she can see my disappointed frown. "You can do better than that."

"What do you want?"

"I need your help."

"With what?"

"Ry was murdered."

I just say it like that, too matter-of-factly. Breaking bad news is not my forte.

"He was…?"

"Murdered, yes."

Tears push into her eyes. Kathleen makes a fist and places the back of it against her mouth to stifle a cry. I wait, give her a moment or two. She puts the fist down and blinks into the moonlight.

"Did you kill him?" she asks me.

"No."

"Are you going to kill me?"

"If that were my plan, you'd be dead by now."

That doesn't seem to comfort her much.

"What do you want with me?"

"I need your help," I repeat.

"With what?"

"With trying to catch his killer."

CHAPTER 13

Kathleen doesn't say a word as we head back down Central Park toward Seventy-Second Street and my abode. The gate over the arch entrance of the Dakota is locked for the night. I ring the bell. Tom comes out and unlocks it for me. He's used to seeing me bring women back here at all hours, though not as many in recent years, but I think Kathleen's advanced age surprises him.

We head through a courtyard with two fountains and take the elevator up to my apartment overlooking the park. Some people are intimidated by this place. She is not one of them. She used the walk over here to regain her bearings. She moves straight toward the window and looks out. Kathleen moves with confidence, head high, eyes dry. Her clothes are wrinkled from a long night, the blouse is still working-barmaid-one-button-too-low at the neckline. I bought this apartment fully furnished from a famed composer who lived here for thirty years. You may already be conjuring up the layout in your mind's eyes—dark cherrywood, high ceilings, inlaid woodwork, antique armoires, crystal chandeliers, oversized fireplace with brass tools, ornate silk oriental carpets, red-maroon velvet chairs. If so, you are correct. Myron describes my abode as "Versailles redux," which is both spot-on in terms of impression and technically incorrect in every way, since I own nothing from that particular geography or era.

I pour Kathleen a cognac and hand it to her.

"How did you know?" she asks.

I assume that she is talking about her weekly meetings in the park with Ry Strauss. I hadn't known for certain, of course. I just followed my intuition. "For one, you have a police record for twelve arrests, all for civil disobedience at various progressive rallies."

"That's it?"

"That's 'for one.'"

"And for two?"

"You told me that you started working at Malachy's in 1978. Frankie Boy told me you were a part-timer as early as 1973."

"Frankie Boy has a big mouth." She takes a deep sip. "Is Ry really dead?"

"Yes."

"I loved him, you know. I loved him for a very long time."

I had figured this. Kathleen hadn't "rescued" Lake Davies— or if she had, only inadvertently. Her real goal in facilitating Lake's surrender was simpler: Remove the competition for Ry Strauss's affection.

"Who killed him?" she asks.

"I was hoping that perhaps you could help me with that."

"I don't see how," she says. "Do the police have any suspects?"

"Not a one."

Kathleen takes a deep sip and turns back to the window. "Poor tormented soul. All of them really. The Jane Street Six. They never meant to hurt anyone that night."

"So I keep hearing."

"Idealistic kids. We all were. We wanted to change the world for the better."

I want to get off this overly worn excuse-justification track and back on one more fertile to my investigation. "Did you know where Ry was living this whole time?"

"Yeah, of course. At the Beresford." She turns to me. "Have you seen old pictures of him? I mean, when Ry was young? God, he was so beautiful. Such charisma. Sexy as all get-out." I could see her smile in the window's reflection. "I knew he was damaged—I could see that right away—but I've always been a sucker for the dangerous type."

"Who else knew Ry lived at the Beresford?"

"No one."

"You're sure?"

"Positive."

"Did you ever visit him?"

"At the Beresford? Never. He'd never allow a guest. I know that sounds odd. Well, Ry was odd. Became odder by the day. A hermit really. He'd never let anyone else in. He was too scared."

"Scared of what?"

"Who knew? He had an illness." Then, thinking on it for a moment, she adds, "Or so I thought. But maybe, I don't know now, maybe he was right to be scared."

"How did Ry end up there?"

"In that tower, you mean?"

I nod.

"After Lake surrendered, Ry and I, we got together. He moved in with me. I had a place on Amsterdam near Seventy-Ninth. A walk-up above a Chinese restaurant. Then it became a mattress store. Then a shoe store. Then a nail salon. Now it's Asian fusion, which sounds like a fancy name for a Chinese restaurant to me. Everything that goes around comes around, am I right?"

"As rain."

"What does that mean anyway? Why would someone describe rain as being right?"

I sigh. "Anyway."

"Anyway, I shared a floor with one of those massage parlors. Not what you're thinking. They were legit. Cheap, no frills, but legit. At least I think they were legit. But who knows? All that happy-ending stuff. Who cares, I'm just babbling, sorry."

I try to sound kind as I say, "It's okay," so as to encourage her to keep talking.

"We were happy, Ry and me. I mean, sort of. Like I said, I knew what I was getting in for. It wasn't going to be forever, but I'm not big on forever. My relationships with men are like a wild buckaroo ride at a rodeo—it's exciting and crazy and I know it's going to be me who gets thrown off in the end and breaks a rib when I smack the ground."

I like her.

Kathleen turns now and gives me a well-crafted, oft-used side smile that lands.

"That ride lasted longer than I would have thought."

"How long?"

"As a couple? On and off for years. As a friend? Well, right up until today."

"I'm sorry."

"I bet the Staunch family found him."

"Nero Staunch?"

"The family always wanted revenge, you know. One of the people who died that night was a niece or something. Ry always figured they got to the others."

"The Staunches?"

"Yeah."

"Ry thought that the Staunches killed the other Jane Street Six members?"

"Something like that, yeah. The Staunch girl who got killed? I think her brother runs the family business now." She shrugs. "Ry got nuttier and more paranoid as time passed. He was erratic at best. Sometimes, for no reason, he'd start thinking the cops or Staunch was closing in on him. Maybe because he heard a funny noise or someone gave him a weird look. Maybe because Mercury was in retrograde. Who knew? So Ry would run off for a while. Sometimes he'd be gone for months. Then he'd just show up one day and want to live with me again. He'd do that—come back and stay with me—until he got the place in the Beresford."

"When was that?"

"What year? Oh, let me think. Mid-nineties maybe."

Hmm. That would be around when the paintings were stolen.

"You set up a weekly meet?" I ask.

"Yeah. Whatever was wrong with Ry, it was getting worse. You take all his issues, which are really an illness, you know, like cancer or heart diseases. Incurable maybe, I don't know. But you take all that and you take his paranoia and then you add in the fact that he really did have people after him—the FBI, the Staunches, whatever. Then pile on the guilt from that horrible night and, kaboom, like with the Molotov cocktails. So by the time Ry moved into that tower, he couldn't handle life anymore. He shut out the world."

"Except you."

"Except me." The R-rated smile again. "But I'm pretty special."

"I'm sure you are."

Are we flirting?

I move on: "When you two met for your weekly rendezvous in the park, what did you do?"

"Talked mostly."

"About?"

"Anything. He didn't make much sense in recent years."

"But you still met?"

"Sure."

"And you talked?"

"I also gave him the occasional hand job."

"Nice of you."

"He wanted more."

"Who doesn't?"

"Right? And I'd try. For old times' sake. Like I said, he used to be so damn beautiful, like you, but, I don't know, by 2000, maybe 2001, he lost his physical appeal. To me at least." Kathleen arched an eyebrow. "Still, a hand job isn't nothing."

"Truer words," I agree.

Kathleen stares me down a bit. I like that. I am, I confess, tempted. She may be on the older side, but she's got that innate sexual allure you can't teach—and I did lose out earlier tonight. Kathleen saunters now toward the crystal decanter and gestures whether it would be okay to pour herself another. I do the honors.

"To Ry," she says.

"To Ry."

We clink glasses.

"He was also afraid people would steal his stuff."

"What stuff?"

"I don't know. Whatever junk he had in his apartment."

"Did he ever tell you about his junk?"

"Huh?"

"As in, what he had in his apartment."

"No."

"Did you read about the recovered stolen Vermeer?"

Her eyes are emeralds with yellow specks. She looks at me over the amber liquor in her glass. "Are you saying...?"

"In his bedroom."

"Holy shit." She shakes her head. "That explains a lot."

"Like?"

"Like how he got the money for the apartment. There were other paintings stolen, right?"

"Yes."

"From someplace in Philadelphia?"

"Right nearby."

"Ry visited Philly a lot. When he'd run away. Had friends there, I guess, a girlfriend maybe. So yeah, Ry could have done it, sure. Maybe he fenced a painting or two, and that's how he got all that money."

It made sense.

"Did you notice any changes in him recently?" I ask.

"Not really, no." Then thinking more about it, she says, "But, well, come to think of it, yeah, but I don't think it has anything to do with this."

"Try me."

"His bank got robbed. Or at least that's what Ry told me. He was freaking out about it. I told him not to worry. Banks have to make you whole if they got robbed, I said. That's true, right?"

"Pretty much."

"But he wouldn't calm down."

I consider this. "Was he imagining it or—?"

"No, no, it was in the *Post*. Bank of Manhattan on Seventy-Fourth. He even told me—last time I saw him, come to think of it—that the bank had left a message."

"On his phone?"

"Don't know, come to think of it."

"Did he own a phone?"

"Just a burner I bought for him at Duane Reade. It lets you keep the same number for years. I don't know the details."

No phone, I knew, had been found at the murder scene. Interesting.

"He never kept it on," she continues. "He was afraid some-one could track him. He'd, like, check for messages once or twice a week."

"And the bank left him a message?"

"I guess. Or at the front desk. Whatever. They wanted him to come down to the branch or something."

"Did he?"

"I don't know."

I consider this. "Ry Strauss left the Beresford during the day on Friday. Less than an hour later, he came back with someone."

"Back to his apartment? With a guest?"

"A small bald man. They came through the basement."

"It had to be with the killer." She shakes her head. "Poor Ry. I'm going to miss him."

Kathleen throws back the rest of the drink and moves closer

to me. Very close. I don't back up. Her hand rests on my chest. Her blouse is too tight. She looks up at me with the emerald eyes. Then her hand slides slowly down my body, and she cups my balls.

"I don't think I want to be alone tonight," she whispers, giving me just a perfect little squeeze.

And so she stays.

CHAPTER 14

I sleep, though "sleep" may be the wrong word choice on this particular night, in an antique, baroque, four-poster canopy bed made of carved mahogany with an embroidered lace topper. The bed is a bit much, I confess, dominating the room in every way, the four posts nearly scraping the ceiling, but it still sets the mood.

At sunrise, Kathleen kisses my cheek and whispers, "Find the bastard who killed him."

I have no desire to avenge Ry Strauss, especially since it appears likely that he did one or more of the following (in time sequence): Stole my family's art, murdered my uncle, abducted and assaulted my cousin.

Which begs the question: What exactly am I after here?

I rise and shower. The copter awaits. When it touches down in Lockwood, my father is waiting for me. He is decked out in a blue blazer, khaki trousers, tasseled loafers, and a red ascot. He wears this outfit nearly every day with very few variations. His thinning hair is slicked back against the skull. He stands with his hands behind his back, shoulders pulled up. I see me in thirty years' time, and I don't really like that.

We greet with a firm handshake and awkward embrace. My father has piercing blue eyes that seem somehow all-knowing, even now, even when the mind has grown cloudy and erratic.

"It's good to see you, son."

"And you," I say.

We share a name—Windsor Horne Lockwood. He's the second, I'm the third. He is called Windsor. I, like my beloved grandfather, am Win. I have no son, just a biological daughter, so unless I, to quote my father, "up my game," the Windsor Horne Lockwood name will end at three. I don't really see this as any great tragedy.

We start back toward the main estate.

"I understand the Vermeer has been found," my father says.

"Yes."

"Will any of this reflect poorly on the family?"

This may seem like an odd opening question, but I'm not surprised by it. "I can't see how."

"Marvelous. Have you seen the Vermeer for yourself?"

"I have."

"And it's undamaged?" Off my nod, he continues: "This is grand news. Simply grand. No sign of the Picasso?"

"No."

"That's too bad."

The barn is up ahead on the left. My father doesn't so much as glance at it. You may be wondering why I keep making a big deal of the barn, so I will tell you plainly: I shouldn't. I was wrong. I blamed my mother, and that was a mistake on my own part. I see that now. To be fair, I was only eight years old.

How to explain this and not seem crass...?

When I was eight years old, not long after Granddad's funeral, my father and I strolled unsuspectingly into that barn. It was a setup. I know that now. I didn't then. But I didn't know a lot of things then.

Cutting to the chase: We walked in on my mother naked on all fours, with another man mounting her from behind.

Just like the horses.

I can see you nodding knowingly. This incident illuminates so much, you think with a tsk. It explains why I can't get close to a woman, why I only see them in terms of sex, why I am afraid of being hurt. Oddly enough, what I see mostly when I remember that day is not my mother on her hands and knees, her lover's hand pulling her hair, her eyes rolling back. No, what I remember most clearly is my father's ashen face, his mouth slightly agape almost as it is now from the stroke, his eyes shattered, staring out at nothing.

As I said, I was eight years old. I never forgave my mother.

That angers me.

I know that my behavior was understandable, but many years later, when I watched my mother die in her sickbed, I realized what a stupid waste it had all been. The cliché applies here—life is indeed short. I think about what she lost and what I lost, how simple forgiveness could have enhanced her short life and mine. Why couldn't I see that then? I have lived a life of few regrets. This—how I treated my own mother— is my greatest. I never considered the fact that perhaps my mother had her reasons or perhaps she didn't know better or perhaps she made, as we all do, a terrible, tragic mis- take. My mother was so young, only nineteen when she got pregnant and married my father. Perhaps she had wants that she couldn't express. Perhaps, like her oldest son, monogamy was not for her. Perhaps my father, who ended up getting married twice more, and the trappings of Lockwood Manor were stifling, suffocating, making it impossible for her to breathe. Perhaps my mother didn't want to break up a family or hurt her children and perhaps she genuinely loved this other man and in the end, who knows the truth, not me, because I never asked, never gave her the chance to explain, refused to listen until it was too late. I was only a child, but I was stubborn.

Originally, I razed that barn to rid myself of the awful memory of what my father and I had witnessed, but now I see the new edifice as more a monument to my own foolishness and stubbornness, a monument to my wasteful, judgmental blunder.

My father steadies himself by taking my arm. "When will we get the Vermeer back?" he asks.

"Soon."

"Good, and no more loaning out artwork," he grouses. "It's not like we are big collectors. Our two masterpieces should never leave Lockwood again."

I disagree with this, but I see no reason to voice that now. I love my father dearly, though objectively there is little to admire about him. He is a standard-issue, trust fund ne'er-do-well. He inherited great wealth, giving him an array of choices, and his choice has been to spend his life doing exactly what he pleases—golf and tennis, luxury clubs and travel, reading and educational experiences. He drinks too much, though I'm not sure I would call him an alcoholic. He has no interest in work, but then again, why should he? He dabbles in charities the way the wealthy often do, giving enough to appear magnanimous but not enough to cause the smallest of sacrifices. He cares very much about appearances and reputation. There is an odd psychology amongst those who inherit great wealth, because deep down inside, they realize that they did nothing to earn it, that it really was just a matter of luck, and yet how can it be that they are not special? My father suffers from this malady. "I have all this," the thinking goes, "ergo I must be somehow superior." This leads to a constant internal battle to maintain the false narrative of somehow "deserving" all these riches, of being "worthy." You push away the obvious truth—that fate and happenstance have more to do with your lot in life than your "brilliance" or "work ethic"—so as not to shatter your self-created myth.

But my father and those like him know the truth. Deep down. We all do. It haunts us. It makes us compensate. It poisons.

"On the news," my father begins, "they said the Vermeer was found in a New York City apartment."

"Yes."

"And that the thief was found dead?"

"There is probably more than one thief," I remind him. "But yes, he was murdered."

"Do you know the man's name?"

"Ry Strauss."

We don't stop short, but my father slows for a moment. His lips thin.

"Do you know him?" I ask.

"The name is familiar."

I briefly explain about the Jane Street Six. He asks a few follow-up questions. We reach the entrance to Lockwood Manor. A woman is dusting in the parlor. When we come in, she vanishes without a word as she's been trained to do. The indoor staff dress in a brown that matches the wood, the outdoor in a green that matches the lawn, both a camouflage of sorts created by my great-grandmother. The Lockwoods treat help well, but they are always just the help. When I was twelve years old, my father noticed one of our landscapers taking a break to look at the setting sun. My father pointed to the skyline and said to me, "Do you see how beautiful Lockwood is?"

"Yes, of course," young me replied.

"So do they." He gestured toward the landscaper. "That laborer gets to enjoy the same view we do. It isn't different for him, is it? He sees the exact same thing you and I do—that same sunset, that same tree line. Yet does he appreciate that?"

I don't think I realized at the time how utterly clueless my father was.

We are all masters of self-rationalization. We all seek ways to justify our narrative. We all twist that narrative to make ourselves more sympathetic. You do it too. If you are reading this, you were born in the top one percent of history's population, no question about it. You've experienced luxuries that painfully few people in the history of mankind could have even imagined. Yet instead of appreciating that, instead of doing more to help those beneath us, we attack those who got even luckier for not doing enough.

It is human nature, of course. We don't see our own faults. As Ellen Bolitar, Myron's mother, likes to say, "The humpback never sees the hump in his own back."

Nigel peeks in on us. "Do we need anything?"

"Just some privacy," my father snaps. He says "privacy" with the short *i*, as though he's suddenly British. Nigel rolls his eyes and gives my father a mock salute. To me, he glares a quick warning before closing the doors.

We sit across from one another in the red velvet chairs near the stone fireplace. My father offers me a cognac. I pass. He starts to pour his own, but his arm is slow and uncooperative. When I offer to help, he shakes me off. He can manage. It's still early in the morning. You must think he has a drinking problem, but that's not it; he just has nowhere else he needs to be.

"Your cousin Patricia was here with you," he says.

"Yes."

"Why?"

"She is a member of the family," I say.

My father lances me with the blue eyes. "Please, Win, let's not insult my intelligence. Your cousin hasn't been to Lockwood in over twenty years, correct?"

"Correct."

"And it isn't a coincidence that the day the Vermeer is found she came back, is it?"

"It is not."

"So I want to know why she was here."

This is my father, the somewhat bullying interrogator. I haven't experienced much of this side of him since his stroke. I'm glad to see his ire, even though it is aimed squarely at me. "There may be a connection," I say, "between the art heist and what happened to her family."

Dad's eyes start blinking in astonishment. "What happened to her . . . ?" His voice trails off. "You mean her abduction?"

"And Uncle Aldrich's murder," I add.

He winces at his brother's name. We stay silent. He lifts the glass and stares at the amber liquid for far too long. "I don't see how," he says.

I stay still.

"The paintings were stolen before the murder, correct?"

I nod.

"A long time before, if I recall. Months? Years?"

"Months."

"Yet you see a connection. Tell me why."

I do not want to go into details, so I switch topics. "What caused the rift between you and Uncle Aldrich?"

His eyes flare at me from over the crystal. "What does that have to do with anything?"

"You never told me."

"Our..." He takes a moment to think of the word. "Our dissolution took place years before his murder."

"I know." I stare into his face. Most people claim that they cannot see family resemblances when it comes to themselves. I can. Almost too much. "Do you ever think about that?"

"What do you mean?"

"If you and Aldrich hadn't"—I make quote marks with my fingers—"'dissolved,' do you think he would still be alive today?"

My father looks stunned, hurt. "My God, Win, what a thing to say."

I realize that I'd wanted to draw blood—and apparently, I succeeded. "Do you ever think about that possibility?"

"Never," he says too forcefully. "What has gotten into you?"

"He was my uncle."

"And my brother."

"And you threw him out of the family. I want to know why."

"It was so long ago."

He raises the glass to his lips, but now it is shaking. My father has gotten old, an obvious observation alas, but we are often told how aging is a gradual process. Perhaps that's true, but in my father's case, it was more like a plummet off a cliff. For a long time, my father clung to that beautiful edge—healthy, strong, vibrant—but once he slipped, his descent was steep and sudden.

"It was so long ago," my father says again.

The pain in his voice is a living thing. The thousand-yard stare, not all that different from the one I'd seen in that barn so many years ago, is back. I see where he is looking—another blank spot on the wall. Once upon a time, a stunning black-and-white photograph of Lockwood Manor hung in that spot. The photograph had been taken by my uncle Aldrich sometime in the late 1970s. It, like my uncle, was long gone now. I had never really thought about that until now, that even Uncle Aldrich's artistic contributions to this estate had been scrubbed away when he was hurled out of the family circle.

"You told me that it was some sort of money issue," I say. "You implied Uncle Aldrich embezzled."

He doesn't respond.

"Was that true?"

He snaps out of it with a fury. "What difference does it make? That's the trouble with your generation. You always want to unearth unpleasantness. You think dragging the ugly out in the sunlight will destroy it. It doesn't. Just the opposite. You give the ugly thing life nourishment. I never spoke of it. Your uncle never spoke of it. That's what being a Lockwood means. We both knew that many people thrive on our familial misery. They want to exploit any weakness. Do you understand that?"

I say nothing.

"Your responsibility, as a member of this family, is to protect our good name."

"Dad?"

"Do you hear me, Win? The Lockwoods don't air our dirty laundry."

"What happened?"

"Why are you suddenly in touch with Patricia?"

"Nothing sudden about it, Dad. We've always stayed in touch."

He rises. His face is red. His entire body is quaking. "I'm not discussing this any longer—"

He is too agitated. I need to calm him. "It's okay, Dad."

"—but I'm reminding you right now that you're a Lockwood. That's an obligation. You inherit the name, you inherit all that comes with it. Whatever happened with this art heist—whatever happened to my brother and Patricia—it has nothing to do with a very old rift between Aldrich and me. Do you understand?"

"I do," I say in my most tranquil tone, rising from my seat. I hold up my hands in a composed, I'm-unarmed gesture. "I didn't mean to upset you."

The door opens, and Nigel is there. "All okay in here?" He sees my father's face. "Windsor?"

"I'm fine, dammit."

But Dad doesn't look fine. His face is still flushed as though from overexertion. Nigel gives me a baleful look.

"It's time for your medication," Nigel says.

Dad grabs me by the elbow. "Remember to protect the family." Then he shuffles out of the room.

Nigel stares at me. "Thanks for not upsetting him."

"How long were you listening in?" I ask. Then I hold up

my hand. It doesn't matter. "Do you know what the rift was about?"

Nigel takes his time. "Why don't you ask your cousin?"

"Patricia?"

He says nothing.

"Patricia knows?"

Dad stands at the foot of the stairs now. "Nigel?" he shouts.

"I need to look after your father," Nigel Duncan tells me. "Have a pleasant day."

CHAPTER 15

My Jaguar XKR-S GT is waiting for me.

I slide in as my phone buzzes with a text from Kabir. It informs me that a meeting with Professor Ian Cornwell, the watchman who'd been on duty when the paintings were stolen, has been arranged for an hour from now. Kabir hadn't told Cornwell what it was about—just that a Lockwood wanted to meet. Perfect. Kabir drops a pin on the exact location of Cornwell's office at Haverford College. Roberts Hall. I know it.

As I drive through the gates of Lockwood, I call Cousin Patricia. She answers on the first ring.

"What's up?"

"No 'articulate'?" I say.

"I'm nervous. Do you have an update?"

"Where are you?"

"At the house."

"I'll be by in ten minutes."

Cousin Patricia lives in the same home from whence she

was abducted and where her father was murdered. It's a modest Cape Cod at the end of a cul-de-sac. She is divorced and shares custody of her ten-year-old son, Henry, though Henry's primary residence is, interestingly enough, with her ex, a renowned neurosurgeon appropriately named Don Quest. The cliché is that Patricia's life is her work, but clichés exist for a reason. She travels a great deal for her charity, the Abeona Shelters, making speeches and doing fundraisers the world over. Patricia was the one who suggested this somewhat unconventional custody arrangement, a fact that makes the local hoity-toity tsk-tsk over what they want to see as maternal neglect.

When I pull into her driveway, Patricia is standing outside on the gravel drive with her mother, my aunt Aline. The two women look very much alike, both stunning in similar ways, more like sisters than mother-daughter. Sometime in the seventies, Uncle Aldrich, the progressive in our rather staid family, quit college to spend three years doing charity work and photojournalism in South America. This was in the days before those soft, coddling, volunteer-abroad internship/college-essay/ vacation experiences that are all the rage for today's youth. Uncle Aldrich, who had grown up in ridiculous privilege at Lockwood, relished the opportunity to shed his past and live amongst the poorest of the poor in fairly harsh conditions. He learned and grew, so the family legend has it, and with the help of the Lockwood money, Aldrich founded a school in one of the most poverty-stricken areas of Fortaleza. The school still stands today, renamed the Aldrich Academy in his memory.

It was there, at this new school in Fortaleza, that Uncle Aldrich met a beautiful young kindergarten teacher named Aline and fell in love.

Uncle Aldrich was twenty-four years old at the time, Aline only twenty. They returned to Philadelphia a year later, having been married by a shaman of the Yanomami tribe in the Amazon. The Lockwood family was not amused by this development, but Uncle Aldrich made Aunt Aline his legal wife under American law anyway.

Not long after, Patricia was born.

Aunt Aline steps toward me as I get out of the car. Patricia shakes her head at me, a warning perhaps not to divulge anything, and I give her the slightest nod in return.

"Win," Aline says, hugging me.

"Aunt Aline."

"It's been too long."

It was Aunt Aline who found Uncle Aldrich's body in the front foyer of this very house that night. She was the one who called 911. I've heard the tape of that call, Aline distraught, hysterical, her voice occasionally breaking into Portuguese. She kept screaming Aldrich's name, as though she hoped to rouse him. At the time of the call, Aline hadn't yet realized that her eighteen-year-old daughter had been kidnapped. That realization—the realization that the nightmare of finding her husband murdered was only the beginning—would come later.

I oft wonder how Aline coped. She had no family here, no real friends, and of course, the police found her decision to go shopping by herself late suspicious. When Patricia didn't come home that night, there were those who whispered that Aline had offed her own daughter too and hidden the body. Others believed that Cousin Patricia was in on it somehow—that mother and daughter had murdered the father and now Patricia was in hiding. People want to believe these sorts of things. They want to believe that there is a reason for such tragedies, that the victim is in some way to blame, that there exists a rationale behind chaos, and thus said tragedies can't happen to them. It comforts us to think that we have control when we don't.

As Myron always quotes: Man plans, God laughs.

"I know you two need to talk," Aunt Aline says, still with a hint of a Brazilian accent, "so I'm going to take a walk."

Aline power-strides up the drive wearing running shoes, a tight Lycra top, and yoga pants. I watch her for a moment, impressed with what I see, as Patricia sidles next to me.

"Are you ogling my mother?"

"She's also my aunt," I say.

"That's not really an answer."

I kiss her cheek, and we step inside. We now stand in the foyer where her father was killed. Neither of us is superstitious, so it isn't a question of bad luck or ghosts or whatever woo-woo nonsense often sends people away from something like this, but I have always wondered about something more concrete—the memory. Patricia, who lives here alone, had watched her father get murdered in this spot. Isn't that something to avoid?

Years ago, I asked her about that.

"I like the reminder. It fuels me."

Her devotion to the cause crosses the border into obsession, but that is the case with most worthwhile endeavors. Cousin Patricia and the Abeona Shelters she has built do good. Legitimately. I know her work well and support it.

I tell her all that I've learned.

The wall in this front foyer is something of a shrine to Patricia's father. Uncle Aldrich took photography somewhat seriously, and while I don't know much about how such things are judged, his work is considered substantial. The foyer is loaded up with black-and-white prints, mostly ones he took during his long sojourn in South America. The subjects are varied—landscapes, urban squalor, indigenous tribes.

To complete the shrine effect, the framed photographs surround a single shelf that holds but one item: Uncle Aldrich's beloved camera—a rectangular-shaped Rolleiflex with twin lenses, the kind you hold at chest level rather than up to your eye. That's how I still see Aldrich clearest when I think back on him, with this camera that seemed dated even in its heyday, carefully snapping portraits of the family and, as I mentioned earlier, Lockwood Estate in general.

"What's our next step?" Patricia asks when I finish.

"I'm going to talk to the security guard at Haverford who was tied up during the art heist."

She frowns. "Why?"

"We now have a link between the Haverford heist and what happened in this very room. We have to go back and review it all."

"I guess that makes sense."

She doesn't sound convinced. I ask her why.

"I never put what happened here fully behind me, of course," she says, weighing her words before they leave her mouth, "but over the years, I think I've successfully channeled it."

I tell her she has.

"I...I just don't want anything interrupting that."

"Not even the truth?" I say, realizing how overly melodramatic that sounds.

"I'm curious, of course. And I want justice. But..." Her voice tails off.

"Interesting," I say.

"What?"

"My father wants me to drop this too."

"Whoa, Win, I'm not saying I want you to drop it." Then, thinking about it, she adds, "Is your father worried how this will all reflect on the family?"

"Always and forever."

"And that's why you're here?"

"I'm here to see you," I say, "and to find out why our fathers fell out."

"Did you ask your father?"

"He won't tell me."

"What makes you think I know?"

I look directly at her. "You're stalling for one thing."

She turns away from me, walks toward the sliding glass door, and peers out into the backyard. "I don't see how any of this is relevant."

"Oh good," I say.

"What?"

"More stalling."

"Don't be an ass."

I wait.

"Do you remember my Sweet Sixteen?"

I do. It had been a lavish albeit tasteful affair at Lockwood. I say tasteful because a number of our nouveau-riche friends tried to outdo one another with expensive cars and name rock bands and zoo safaris and celebrity appearances and "Sir, show me gauche." Patricia, on the other hand, only had her closest friends attend for a simple evening on the lawn at Lockwood.

"We did a girls' sleepover," she says. "In tents. Down by the pond. There were eight of us."

I put myself back into that moment. I'd gone to the dinner portion of the Sweet Sixteen, but the boys were then dismissed. I headed back to the main house. What I recall most about the event was that a lovely lass named Babs Stellman had attended and that someone had told me she had a crush on me. Naturally, I tried to—what's the term?—score. Babs and I did manage to sneak away for a bit and necked behind a tree. She smelled wonderfully of Pert shampoo. I remember moving my hand under her sweater, though she stopped me from going any further with the always-paradoxical line, "I really like you, Win."

"The girls all got undressed in the gazebo," Patricia continues. She lowers her head. "And your father . . . he was wrong, Win. I need you to know that. But your father accused my father of watching us through a window."

I freeze, having trouble believing what I'm hearing. "Say that again?"

Patricia almost smiles. "Now who's stalling?"

"You mean, as in my father accusing your father of being a Peeping Tom?"

"Yes, that's exactly what I mean."

"My father wouldn't make that up," I say.

"No, to be fair, he wouldn't. Do you remember Ashley Wright?"

I have a vague recollection. "She was on your field hockey team?"

Patricia nods. "Ashley was the one who got upset. She wouldn't say why. She started crying that she wanted to leave. It was all pretty weird. Anyway, her parents picked her up. When she got home, Ashley told her father that she saw my father peeking in the window when she was naked. Ashley's father went to your father. When your father confronted mine, well, fireworks. My dad denied it. Your dad pressed him. It just escalated from there. It opened up a lot of old wounds."

I mull this all over for a moment. "Ashley Wright," I say.

"What about her?"

"Was she lying?"

Patricia opens her mouth, closes it, tries again. "What difference does it make now, Win?"

She has a point.

"Do you know where she lives now?"

"Ashley Wright?" Her face blanches. "Jeez, I don't know. What, you want to talk to her? Seriously, Win? Suppose my dad was...worst-case scenario...a pervert who peeped on sixteen-year-old girls. What difference would that make now?"

Another good point. Where am I going with this? His murder and Patricia's abduction took place two years after this. I could see zero connection.

And yet.

"Win?"

I look at her. Patricia's eyes are on that wall—on that camera, on the photographs.

"I miss my father like hell. I want justice. And the fact that the man who hurt me, who did that to all those girls, could still be doing this...that's haunted me for over twenty years."

I wait.

"But it now seems pretty clear that Ry Strauss did both, right? And if that's the case, maybe we don't want this dug up."

Again she sounds like my father. I nod at her.

"What?"

"You want this to go away," I say.

"Of course I do."

"It won't."

I remind her that in a few hours, the world will know about Ry Strauss's death and the Jane Street Six and their link to the stolen Vermeer. It is only a question of time before the connection to that suitcase gets figured out by the FBI—or her connection in this is outed in some other way. I watch her deflate as I tell her all of this.

Patricia moves toward me and sits hard on the couch. I know how this is going to go. She just needs to process. Finally, she says, "I got to come home. I can never forget that."

Patricia starts to chew her thumbnail, a move I remember from our childhood.

"I got to come home," she says again. "Those other girls never did. Some . . . we still haven't found their bodies."

She looks up at me, but what can I add to that?

"I've made it my life mission to rescue kids in need—and here I am, cowering in the dark."

I realize that I've been cued up to say something comforting here, such as, "I understand" or "It's okay." Instead I check my watch, do a quick calculation of how long it will take me to get to Haverford College, and say, "I have to go."

As she walks me to the Jag, I see her working the thumbnail again.

"What is it?" I ask.

"I never thought it mattered. I still don't."

"But?" I prompt, sliding into the driver's seat.

"But you kept harping on about our fathers' rift."

"What about it?"

"You think it's relevant."

"Correction: I don't know whether it's relevant. I don't know what, if anything we are looking into, is relevant. This is how I was taught to investigate. You ask questions. You poke around and perhaps you jar something loose."

"They spoke one last time."

159

"Who spoke one last time?"

"Your dad and mine. Here. At the house."

"When?"

Patricia wills her hand to her side, so she won't bite the thumbnail again. "The night before my father was murdered."

CHAPTER 16

Founded in 1833, Haverford College is a small, elite undergraduate institution located along the tony Main Line of Philadelphia, adjacent to my two favorite exclusive clubs, the Merion Golf Club (I play a lot of golf) and Merion Cricket Club (I play no cricket but very few members do—don't ask). Fewer than 1,400 students matriculate to Haverford, yet there are over fifty buildings, most made of stone, strewn over 200 manicured acres so glorious that it is technically classified as an arboretum. The Lockwoods have been woven into the rich tapestry that is Haverford College since its conception. Windsor I and II both graduated from Haverford, both remained active, both served as chairman of the board of trustees. All of my male relatives attended (women were not admitted until the 1970s) until—hmm, now that I think of it—Uncle Aldrich was the first to break ranks by choosing New York University in the seventies. I was the second when I elected to go to Duke University in North Carolina. I loved and continue to love Haverford, but for me, it was simply too close to home, too much a known entity for what my eighteen-year-old self craved.

Professor Ian Cornwell's office in Roberts Hall faces Founders Green and, beyond that, Founders Hall, where the Vermeer and Picasso had been taking up temporary residence when they were stolen. I wonder about that, about Cornwell's office view of the building where he'd been tied up whilst the two robbers went to work. Does he think about it often or, after a while, does the view simply become the view?

Ian Cornwell tries too hard to look professorial—unruly hair, unkempt beard, tweed jacket, mustard-hued corduroy pants. His office contains half-crumbling stacks of papers on the shelves and floor. In lieu of a proper desk, Cornwell has a large square table that seats twelve, so that he can hold student seminars in an intimate setting.

"So glad you could visit," Cornwell says to me.

He has me sit in front of brochures related to the political science department. I look up at him. His face is eager, ready to pitch me to support financially some sort of study or class. Kabir has no doubt hinted that I would be interested in funding so as to expedite this appointment. Now that I'm here, I nip this hint in the bud.

"I'm here about the stolen paintings."

His smile drops from his face like a cartoon anvil. "I was under the impression you're interested—"

"I might be later," I say, cutting him off. "But right now, I have some questions about the art heist. You were the night watchman on duty."

He doesn't like my abruptness. Few people do.

"It was a long time ago."

"Yes," I reply, "I'm well versed in how time works, thank you."

"I don't see—"

"You know, of course, that one of the two paintings has been found, correct?"

"I read that in the news."

"Terrific, so there's no need to play catch-up. I've combed through the FBI file on the heist extensively. As you might imagine, I have a personal interest in this too."

Cornwell blinks as though dazed, so I continue.

"You were the only security guard on duty that night. According to your testimony, two men disguised as police officers knocked on the door to Founders Hall. They claimed there was a disturbance that needed to be investigated and so you buzzed them in. Once inside, they subdued you. They took you to the basement level, duct-taped your eyes and mouth, and hand-cuffed you to a radiator. They rummaged through your pockets, pulled out your wallet, checked your ID, and told you that they now know where you live and how to find you. A threat, I assume. Have I got all this correct?"

Ian Cornwell slumps into a chair across the table. "It was a traumatic experience."

I wait.

"I'd rather not talk about it."

"Professor Cornwell?"

"Yes."

"My family lost two priceless masterpieces on your watch."

"You're blaming me?"

"I will if you refuse to cooperate."

"I'm not refusing anything, Mr. Lockwood."

"Terrific."

"But I also won't be bullied."

I give him a moment or two so as to save face. He will capitulate. They always do.

A few seconds later, he offers up a contrite "I don't know anything that will help. I told the police everything a hundred times over."

I continue undaunted: "You estimated that one of the two men was five nineish with a medium build. The other was slightly over six feet tall and heavier set. Both were white men, and you believe that they were wearing fake mustaches."

"It was dark," he adds.

"Your point being?"

His eyes go left. "None of this was exact. The height, the weight. I mean, they could be accurate. But it all happened so fast."

"And you were young," I add, "and scared."

Ian Cornwell grabs hold of these arguments as a drowning man does a life preserver. "Yes, exactly."

"You were just an intern hoping to make a few extra dollars."

"It was part of my financial aid requirement, yes."

"Your training was minimal."

"Not to pass the buck," Cornwell says, "but the school should have provided your family with better security."

True enough, though many things about the case and the investigation bothered me. The painting had only been scheduled to be on loan for a short time, and the dates were fixed only a few weeks in advance. We had indeed added security cameras, but this was before the days of storing digital video in the cloud, and so the recordings were kept on a hard drive on the second floor behind the president's office.

"How did the thieves know where to find the hard drive?" I ask.

His eyes close. "Please don't."

"Pardon?"

"You don't think the FBI asked me all these questions a thousand times back then? They interrogated me for hours. Denied me legal counsel even."

"They thought you were in on it."

"I don't know. But they sure acted like it. So I'll tell you what I told them—I don't know. I was duct-taped and cuffed in the basement. I had no idea what they'd done. I spent eight hours down there—until someone came looking to replace me in the morning."

I know this, of course. Ian Cornwell had been cleared for a lot of reasons, the biggest being that he was only a twenty-two-year-old research intern with no record. He simply didn't have the brains or experience to pull off this heist. Still, the FBI kept surveillance on him. I, too, had Kabir go through his bank records to see whether a late windfall came into his life. I found none. He seems clean. And yet.

"I want you to take a look at these photographs."

I slide the four photographs across the table toward him. The first two are blown up from the famous photograph of the Jane Street Six. One is of Ry Strauss. The other is Arlo Sugarman. The next two are the same photographs but using a new age-progression software program, so both Strauss and Sugarman look some twenty years older—in their early forties—as they would have at the time of the art heist.

Ian Cornwell looks at the images. Then he looks up at me. "Are you kidding?"

"What?"

"That's Ry Strauss and Arlo Sugarman," he says. "You think they—"

HARLAN COBEN

"Do you?"

Ian Cornwell looks back down and seems to be studying the photographs with renewed vigor. I watch him closely. I need to gauge a reaction, and despite what you may read, no man is an open book. Still, I see something going on behind the eyes—or at least I imagine that I do.

"Hold on a second," he says.

He reaches into a cabinet near the bookshelf and pulls out a black Sharpie pen. He gestures toward the photographs. "Do you mind?"

"Be my guest."

He carefully draws mustaches on the male faces. When he's satisfied, he straightens up and then tilts his head, as though he is an artist studying his handiwork. I don't look at the photographs. I keep my focus on his face.

I don't like what I see.

"I couldn't swear one way or the other," he pronounces after he's taken some more time, "but it is certainly possible."

I say nothing.

"Is there anything else, Mr. Lockwood?"

"Just the statute of limitations," I say.

"Pardon?"

"It's up."

"I don't understand—"

"So if you had something to do with the robbery, you couldn't be prosecuted. If you, for example, gave the thieves some inside information—if you were an accessory of some sort—it's been over twenty years. The statute of limitations for this type of offense in Pennsylvania is only five years. In short, you're in the clear, Professor Cornwell."

He frowns. "Clear for what?"

"For the Lincoln assassination," I say.

"What?"

I shake my head. "Now do you see my issue with you?"

"What are you talking—?"

"You just said 'clear for what?' when it is so obvious that I am referring to the art heist." I mimic him and repeat: "'Clear for what?' It's overkill, Ian. It's suspicious behavior. Come to think of it, everything about your testimony is suspicious."

"I don't know what you're talking about."

"For example, the two robbers disguised as police officers."

"What about them?"

"That's precisely what happened in Boston during the Gardner Museum heist. Two men, same heights you describe, same build, same fake mustaches, same claim of needing to investigate a disturbance."

"You find that odd?" he counters.

"I do, yes."

"But the FBI believed that it was the same MO."

"MO?"

"Method of Operation."

"Yes, I'm aware what the term means, thank you."

"Well, that's why there are similarities, Mr. Lockwood. The theory is that the robberies were done by the same team."

"Or," I say, "that someone, perhaps you, wanted us to believe that. And a 'disturbance'? Really? Late at night in that closed building across the green? You were working there. Did you hear a disturbance?"

"Well, no."

"No," I repeat. "Did you report one? Also: no. Yet you just unlocked the door to these two men with fake mustaches. Don't you think that's odd?"

"I thought they were police officers."

"Did they have a police car?"

"Not that I saw."

"And that's another thing. There was working CCTV on the campus entrance and exits. Yet no one saw two men dressed as police officers that night."

This is a lie—the campus didn't have that kind of surveillance back then—but it's a lie that draws blood.

"I've had enough," Ian Cornwell snaps, rising to his feet. "I don't care who you are—"

"Shh."

"Excuse me? Did you just...?"

I stare him down. If you want to change someone's behavior, remember this and this only: Human beings always do what is in their self-interest. Always. That's the sole motivator. People only do the "right thing" when it suits those interests. Yes, that is cynical, but it is also true. If you want to change minds, the secret is not being thoughtful or respectful or conciliatory or presenting cogent indisputable facts to show that said mind is wrong. And for those truly in the naïve camp, the secret is not trying to appeal to our better angels or "humanity." None of that works. The only way to change someone's opinion is to make them believe that siding with you is in their best interest. Period. The end.

I know what you're thinking: I'm too lovely a creature to be this cynical. But stay with me on this.

"Here is my proposal," I say to Professor Cornwell. "You tell me the truth about what happened that night—"

"I have told—"

"Shh." I put my index finger to my lips. "Listen and save yourself. You tell me the truth. The full truth. Just me. In return,

I promise that it never leaves this room. I will tell no one. Not a soul. There will be no repercussions. I don't care whether the Picasso is hanging above your toilet or if you burned it for kindling. I don't care if you were the mastermind or a pawn. Do you see what I'm offering you, Professor? The beauty of it? The chance at freedom? You simply tell me the truth—and suddenly the burden is gone. Not only that, but you have an ally for life. A grateful, powerful ally. An ally who can get you promoted or fund whatever academic—and I mean that word in two ways— dream project you have set your heart upon."

Carrot done. Now it's stick time. I lower my voice, so he has to strain to hear. Strain he does.

"But if you choose not to accept my generous offer, I begin to dig into your life. Really dig. You probably feel confident. After all, the FBI turned up nothing twenty-four years ago. You feel secure in your lie. But that security is now an illusion. The Vermeer is back. There is at least one dead body connected to it. The FBI will revisit the theft now with vigor, yes, but more important to your world, I will do what law enforcement cannot. I will build upon what they do, and using my resources, I will raise that intensity—aimed in your direction—to the tenth power. Do you understand?"

He says nothing.

Time to toss the lifeline.

"This is your chance, Professor Cornwell—your chance to end the turmoil and deceptions that have haunted you for over twenty years. This is your chance to unburden yourself. This is your chance, Professor, and if you don't take it, I pity you and all those Cornwells who have come before and after you."

I don't bow as I finish, though I feel perhaps that I should.

As I wait for his reply, as I gaze out the window and onto the green where my father, grandfather, and great-grandfather all roamed as young men, a curious thought enters my brain, distracting me, pulling me out of this moment.

I'm thinking about Uncle Aldrich bucking family tradition by not coming here.

Why am I thinking about that? I don't know. But it's niggling at me.

I hear a chime and turn toward the sound. There is a grandfather clock in the far corner signaling the quarter hour. The door to the office bursts open, and students flow in with backpacks and expected post-lunch cacophony. Ian Cornwell says to me, "You're wrong about me. There is nothing."

He shakes off the stunned look and gives the entering students a beatific smile. I can see that he is at home here. I can see that he is happy and that he is a beloved teacher. I can see that he is good at his job.

But mostly, I can see that he is lying to me.

CHAPTER 17

My father is asleep when I get back to Lockwood.

I debate waking him—I need to ask him about his visiting his brother the night before Aldrich's murder—but Nigel Duncan warns me that he is medicated and will be unresponsive. So be it. Perhaps it is best if I learn more before I confront my father. I am also now on a tight schedule. The branch manager at the Bank of Manhattan has agreed to see me in ninety minutes.

Nigel walks me to the helicopter. "What are you trying to find?" he asks me.

"Should I dramatically pause, spin toward you, and then exclaim, 'The truth, dammit'?"

Nigel shakes his head. "You're a funny guy, Win."

The helicopter gets me back to Chelsea in time. As Magda drives me toward the Upper West Side branch of the bank, I pick up the tail. It's a black Lincoln Town Car. The same car had been following me this morning. Amateurs. I'm almost insulted that they aren't trying harder.

"Small change of plans," I tell Magda.

"Oh?"

"Kindly swing by the office on Park Avenue before we head up to the bank."

"You're the boss."

I am indeed. My next step isn't complicated. The crosstown traffic is mercifully light. When we arrive at the Lock-Horne Building, Magda moves the car to my usual drop-off point. She puts the car in park.

"Don't get out," I say.

I use the camera function on my iPhone to watch behind me. The black Lincoln Town Car is three cars back, double-parked. Such amateurs. I wait. This won't take long. I see Kabir sneaking up behind the Lincoln. He stops behind it and bends down as though to tie his shoe. He's not. He's placing a magnetic GPS under the bumper.

Like I said, this isn't complicated.

Kabir rises, nods to let me know the tracker is secure on the Lincoln's bumper, and heads back the other way.

"Okay," I tell Magda. "We can proceed."

I call Kabir as we head uptown. He will keep an eye on the car. "I'll also run the license plate," he tells me. I thank him and hang up. As we approach the bank, I add up the pros and cons of losing the tail—it wouldn't be difficult—and decide that I would rather not tip them off. Let them see me go into the branch of a bank on the Upper West Side.

So what?

Five minutes later, I am in a glass-enclosed office that looks out over the main floor. The bank itself is a lovely old building on Broadway and Seventy-Fourth Street. Way back when, this very structure was, well, a bank, from the days when banks were cathedral-like and awe-inspiring, as opposed to today's storefronts that have all the warmth of a motel-chain lobby. This branch still has the marble columns, the chandeliers, the oak wood teller stations, the giant round safe door. It is one of the few of said buildings that haven't been converted into a party space or upscale dining facility.

The bank manager's name, which is on her desk plate, is Jill Garrity. Her hair is pulled back into a bun so tight I worry her scalp might bleed. She wears horned-rim glasses. The collar of her white blouse is stiff enough to take out an eye.

"It's wonderful to meet you, Mr. Lockwood."

We do a lot of business with the bank. She hopes that my visit means more. I don't disabuse her of this notion, but time is a-wasting. I tell her I need a favor. She leans in, anxious to please. I ask her about the bank robbery.

"There isn't much to tell," she says.

"Was it a stickup? Was it armed?"

"Oh no no. It was after hours. They broke in at two in the morning."

This surprises me. "How?"

She starts fiddling with the ring on her hand. "I don't mean to be rude—"

"Then don't be."

She startles up at my interruption. I hold her gaze.

"Tell me about the robbery."

It takes a second or two, but we both know where this will go. "One of our guards was in on it. His record was clean— we did a thorough background check—but his sister's husband was somehow involved with the mob. I really don't know the details."

"How much money did they take?"

"Very little," Jill Garrity says a little too defensively. "As you are probably aware, most branches don't keep that much cash on hand. If your worry, Mr. Lockwood, involves stolen cash, none of our clients were affected in terms of their financial portfolios."

I had figured this. What I couldn't figure out was why Ry Strauss would have been upset by the robbery. It could have been his paranoia, his imagination, but it feels as though it had to be something more.

And why does Ms. Garrity still look as though she's hiding something?

"Financial portfolios," I repeat.

"Pardon?"

"You said your clients weren't affected in terms of financial portfolios."

She twists the ring some more.

"So how were they affected?"

She leans back. "I assume the robbers came for cash. I mean, that makes the most sense. But when they saw that wasn't going to happen, they went for the next best thing."

"That being?"

"This is an old building. So downstairs, in the basement? We still have safe deposit boxes."

I can almost hear something in my brain go click. "They broke into them?"

"Yes."

"All, many, or a select few?"

"Almost all."

So not specifically targeted. "Have you notified your clients?"

"It's...complicated. We are doing our best. Do you know much about safe deposit boxes?"

"I know that I would never use one," I say.

She pulls back at first, but then she settles into a nod. "We don't have them in newer branches. Truthfully, they are a headache. Expensive to build and maintain, small profit margin, they take up too much space ... and there are often problems."

"What kind of problems?"

"People store their valuables—jewelry, paperwork, birth certificates, contracts, passports, deeds, coin or stamp collections. But sometimes, well, they forget. They'll come in, they'll open their box, and suddenly they'll start yelling that a valuable diamond necklace is missing. Usually they just forgot they took it out. Sometimes it's outright fraud."

"Claim something was stolen that they never put in the box in the first place."

"Exactly. And sometimes, rarely, we mess up and it's our fault. Very rarely."

"How would you mess up?"

"If a client stops paying for their box, we have to evict them. We give many warnings, of course, but if they don't pay, we drill open the box and send the contents to our main branch downtown. One time, we drilled the wrong box. The man came in, opened his box, and all his belongings were gone."

It is starting to make sense. "And when you have a real break-in like this?"

"You can imagine," she says.

And I can.

"Suddenly, every client is claiming they had expensive Rolex watches in their boxes or rare stamps worth half a million dollars. Clients never read the fine print, of course, but the bank's liability for any loss for any reason shall not exceed ten times the cost of the annual rent for the box."

"How much do you charge to rent?"

"It's rarely more than a few hundred dollars a year."

Not very much, I think. "So now you're reaching out to clients," I continue. "Many are claiming that they lost way in excess of what you are legally obligated to pay out, correct?"

"Correct."

But alas, I think I may be putting this together. Yes, people store valuables, as she's described. But they store more than that.

They store secrets.

"What's your largest-size box?"

"In this branch? Eight by eight inches, with a two-foot depth."

No way to hide the Picasso here, then, though I didn't think Strauss would. That wasn't the point of the box. That wasn't the reason for his panic.

I take out a photo still frame from the Beresford surveillance video—the clearest shot I have of pre-murdered Ry Strauss. "Do you recognize this man?"

She studies the photograph. "I don't think so. I mean, it's hard to make out much."

"The clients you notified about the safe deposit boxes," I begin.

"What about them?"

"How did you reach them?"

"By certified mail."

"Did you call any on the phone?"

"I don't think so. That wouldn't be us anyway. We have an insurance branch in Delaware that handles that."

"So there is no chance someone from this branch would have called a client and invited them to come down here to discuss the theft?"

"None whatsoever."

I ask a few more questions, but for the first time since this mess began, I feel as though I have some clarity. As I exit, my phone rings. I'm rather surprised to see that it's Jessica.

"You busy?" she asks.

"Shouldn't we work our next rendezvous through the app?"

"You blew your chance."

"You wouldn't have gone through with it," I say.

"Guess we'll never know. But I'm not calling about that. Do you know they just announced Ry Strauss's identity?"

"I knew they were going to, yes."

"Well, I was ready for it. I pitched the *New Yorker* a follow-up story on the whole Jane Street Six. Update my previous 'Where Are They Now' piece."

"I assume they bought the pitch?"

"I can be charming when I want to be."

"Oh, I'm sure."

"So anyway, I'm going right now to interview Vanessa Hogan, the victim's mother who was the last person to see Billy Rowan. Want to come?"

Jessica says, "I can't believe Windsor Horne Lockwood the Third is taking the subway."

I hold on to the bar overhead. We are on the A train heading south. "I'm a man of the people," I tell her.

"You are anything but a man of the people."

"I'll have you know that I recently flew commercial."

Jessica frowns. "No, you didn't."

"No, I didn't. But I thought about it."

The reason for the subway ride is simpler. I don't want whoever is following me to know where we are going. I had Magda make a quick turn so that the car was out of sight for a few seconds. I used those seconds to get out and vanish into the Davenport Theatre lobby on Forty-Fifth Street, exit out the side, head into the back entrance of the Comfort Inn Times Square West, and then I reappeared on Forty-Fourth Street. I headed east toward Eighth Avenue and met up with Jessica by the subway entrance on Forty-Second Street.

You can figure out the rest of my plan, methinks.

Most likely, the black Lincoln Town Car—could you choose a more obvious vehicle?—is tailing Magda through the Lincoln Tunnel into New Jersey whilst Jessica and I take the A train to Queens where another car driver will whisk us to the home of Vanessa Hogan.

Vanessa Hogan had remarried and moved out of the modest two-family Colonial where she'd raised Frederick into a sprawling contemporary in the somewhat ritzier Kings Point village. Her son Stuart, Frederick's half brother born eight years after the Jane Street Six, opens the door and grimaces at us.

"We're here to see Vanessa," Jessica says.

"I know about you," Stuart says, giving me the fisheye. "But who's he?"

"Ms. Culver's personal assistant," I tell him. "I take wonderful dictation."

"You don't look like you take dictation."

"Flatterer."

Stuart steps onto the stoop with us and lowers his voice. "I don't know why Mom agreed to see you."

He waits for one of us to reply. We don't.

"She's not well, you know. My dad died last year."

"I'm sorry to hear that," Jessica says.

"They were married more than forty years."

Jessica tilts her head and nods and gives off waves and waves of sympathy, which when mixed with her beauty, makes Stuart go weak at the knees. I try to move out of view; this is clearly a time to let her work alone.

"That must have been hard on both of you," Jessica says with just the right amount of empathy.

"It was. And now, well, you know I never met Frederick, right?"

"Yes, of course."

"My dad met my mom after, you know, Frederick was killed in that crash. But I've heard about him my whole life. It's not like Mom just got married and moved on." He looks off and lets out a long breath. "Point is, Frederick's been dead a long time, but it still causes her tremendous pain."

Jessica says, "That must have been very hard on you, Stuart."

I try not to roll my eyes.

"Just don't upset her any more than you have to, okay?"

She nods. He looks to me. I mimic her nod. Stuart then leads us into a living room with high ceilings and skylights and blond hardwood floors. Vanessa Hogan, who is now over eighty, is a shriveled thing propped up by pillows on an armchair. Her skin is sallow. The top of her head is wrapped in a kerchief, the tell-tale sign of chemotherapy or radiation or something in that eroding vineyard. Her eyes seem huge in her shrunken skull, wide and bright and denim blue. Jessica starts toward her, hand extended, but Vanessa waves us both toward the couch across from her.

She has not taken her eyes off me.

"Who is this?" she asks.

Her voice is youthful, not so different from the one in her "I forgive them" press conference from back in the day.

"This is my friend Win," Jessica says.

Vanessa Hogan gives me a quizzical look. I expect a follow-up in my direction, but she instead shifts her attention back to Jessica. "Why did you want to see me, Ms. Culver?"

"You know about the discovery of Ry Strauss."

"Yes."

"I would like your thoughts."

"I have no thoughts."

"It must have been hard," Jessica says. "Having it all brought back."

"Having what brought back?"

"The death of your son."

Vanessa smiles. "Do you think a day goes by that I don't think about Frederick?"

That, I think, is a pretty good reply. I glance at Jessica. She tries again.

"When you heard that Ry Strauss had been found—"

"I forgave him," Vanessa Hogan interjects. "A long time ago. I forgave them all."

"I see," Jessica says. "So where do you think he is now?"

"Ry Strauss?"

"Yes."

"Burning in hell," Vanessa replies, and a mischievous smile comes to her face. "I may have forgiven him, but I don't think the Lord has." She slowly turns her eyes back to me. "What's your last name?"

"Lockwood."

"Win Lockwood?"

"Yes."

"He stole your painting."

I don't reply.

"Is that why you're here?"

"In part."

"You lost a painting to Ry Strauss. I lost a son."

"I'm not comparing," I say.

"Neither am I. Why are you here, Mr. Lockwood?"

"I'm trying to find some answers."

The skin on her hands looks like parchment paper. I can see the bruises from the intravenous needles. "There's another painting that's still missing," she says. "I saw that on the news."

"Yes."

"Is that what you're looking for?"

"In part."

"But only a small part. Am I right?"

Our eyes meet and something akin to understanding passes between us.

"Tell me what you're really after, Mr. Lockwood."

I glance at Jessica. She leaves it up to me.

"Have you ever heard of Patricia Lockwood?" I ask.

"I assume she's related to you."

"My cousin."

She sits up and gestures for me to say more. So I do.

"During the nineties, approximately ten teenage girls were kidnapped and held against their will in a storage shed in the woods outside of Philadelphia. They were brutalized for months, perhaps years, raped repeatedly, and then murdered. Many were never found."

Her eyes stay on mine. "You're talking about the Hut of Horrors."

I say nothing.

"I watch a lot of true crime on cable," Vanessa Hogan tells us. "The case was never solved, if I remember."

"That's correct."

She tries to sit up. "So you think Ry Strauss...?"

"There's evidence he was at least involved," I say. "He may not have acted alone though."

"And one girl escaped. Would that be...?"

"My cousin, yes."

"Oh my." Her hand flutters and settles down on her chest. "And that's why you're here?"

"Yes."

"But why come to me?"

"You may forgive," I say.

"But you don't?" she finishes for me.

I shrug. "Someone murdered my uncle. Someone abducted my cousin."

"You should leave it in God's hands."

"No, ma'am, I don't think I will."

"Romans 12:19."

"'Vengeance is mine, I will repay, saith the Lord.'"

"I'm impressed, Mr. Lockwood. Do you know what it means?"

"I don't care what it means," I say. "What I do know is that men who do things like that don't stop. They kill again. Always. They don't get cured or rehabilitated or, apologies, find God. They just keep killing. So tonight, when you hear on the news a young girl has gone missing? Perhaps it's those same killers."

"Unless Ry Strauss acted on his own," she says.

"That could be, but it's unlikely. My cousin said two men grabbed her."

She gives me a small smile. "You seem determined, Mr. Lockwood."

"Your son was murdered. An FBI agent named Patrick O'Malley, a father of six, was murdered. My uncle Aldrich was murdered." I pause, more for effect than anything else. "Now add in the brutality and murder of those young girls in the insufficiently dubbed 'Hut of Horrors.'"

I lean toward her, aiming for dramatic effect. "Yes, Ms. Hogan, I'm determined."

"And if you find the truth?" she asks.

I say nothing.

"What if you find the truth but you can't prove it?" Vanessa Hogan's face is animated, her tone more enthused. "Let's say you find the guilty party, but there is no way you can prove it in a court of law. What would you do then?"

I look over at Jessica. She's waiting for the answer too. I don't like lying, so I quasi divert with a question. "Are you asking me if I would let a mass murderer and rapist go free?"

Vanessa Hogan holds my gaze. I try to move us back to the subject at hand.

"Billy Rowan visited you," I say.

She blinks, sits back. "He seemed so nice when he came to my kitchen, so full of remorse." Then thinking about it more, she gives a little gasp. "Do you think Billy Rowan had something to do with that awful hut?"

"I don't know. But I do know it's all tied together somehow. The Jane Street Six. The murder of your son. The stolen paintings. The Hut of Horrors."

"And that's why you're here."

"Yes."

"I'm not well, Mr. Lockwood."

"What did Billy Rowan tell you when he came to see you?"

"He asked for my forgiveness. And I gave it to him."

183

Vanessa Hogan does not blink. She keeps her gaze steady. Her mouth barely moves, but I am convinced that she is smiling.

Then I say, "You know where Billy Rowan is, don't you?"

She doesn't move.

"Of course not," she says in a voice that's not even trying. "It's getting late. I'd like you both to leave now."

CHAPTER 18

Vanessa Hogan shuts down after that.

"Kind of blew that one," Jessica says, as we head out the door.

We hadn't, but I don't want to get into that now.

As we slip into the back of the car, my phone rings. I put it to my ear and say, "Articulate."

Jessica rolls her eyes.

Kabir says, "You want the whole story, or should I cut to the chase?"

"Oh, please draw it out and be extra verbose. You know how I love that."

"The black Lincoln tailing you belongs to Nero Staunch's crew."

I would ask him how he knows, but I'd encouraged him to cut to the chase and so he had. Kabir tells me anyway: "It was registered to a craft beer place the family uses as a front. By the way, do you know who runs the Staunch crew now?"

"I do not."

"Leo Staunch."

"Okay," I say. "And that matters because . . . ?"

"Leo Staunch is Nero's nephew. More to the point, Leo is Sophia Staunch's baby brother."

"Ah," I say. "Interesting."

"Not to mention dangerous."

"Where is this black Lincoln now?"

"Open up the map app on your iPhone. I've dropped a pin from the tracker device, so you can keep tabs on it."

"Okay, good. Anything else?"

"Remember how yesterday tons of media outlets wanted interviews because your Vermeer had been found at a murder scene?"

"Yes."

"Now imagine adding onto that the murder victim was Ry Strauss."

It would indeed be a feeding frenzy. "What are you telling them?"

"I've learned how to say 'No comment' in twelve languages."

"Thank you."

"*Ei kommenttia,*" Kabir says. "That's Finnish."

"Anything else?"

"Tomorrow morning. You have Ema for breakfast."

The one appointment I would never miss or forget.

I hang up. Jessica stares out the window.

"Would you like to go for an early dinner?" I ask her.

She considers it for a moment, and then says, "Why not?"

We arrive at the grill room at the Lotos Club, an elegant private social club whose early members include Mark Twain. It's located in a French Renaissance town house on the Upper East Side. The grill room is in the basement. It is all dark woods and rich burgundy walls. The bar is front and center. Men must wear a jacket and a tie, something you rarely find in Manhattan anymore; some consider this dress code outdated, but I relish these old-world touches.

Charles, the head waiter, recommends the sole meunière, and Jessica and I both choose it. I select a Château Haut Bailly, a Bordeaux wine from the Pessac-Léognan appellation. Their whites are underrated.

I feel my phone buzz and excuse myself. You never pull out your phone at the Lotos Club. You instead make your way into a private phone booth, the only place where you are allowed to use it. As expected, it's PT. I answer.

"Articulate."

"Sorry it took me so long to get back to you," PT says. "As you can imagine, it's been an insane day."

"Anything new on your end?"

"Nothing worth reporting. You any closer to catching my killer?"

"Killers," I say. "Plural."

"You think there's more than one?"

"You don't?"

"I'm really only interested in the one."

PT was talking about Arlo Sugarman, of course—the man he'd witnessed shoot his partner, Patrick O'Malley. "Here," I say, "our interests may differ."

"That's fine," he says. "What do you need from me?"

"There was a robbery at the Bank of Manhattan four months ago," I say.

"Okay, so?"

"I need to know everything I can about it, especially suspected perpetrators."

"Bank of Manhattan," he repeats. "I think we caught one of them."

That surprises me. "Where is he?"

"How do you know it's not a she?"

"Where is she?"

"It's a he. I just want you to be woke, Win."

I wait.

"I'll look into it."

"Also, do you have anything on the shell company Strauss set up to buy his apartment and pay his bills?"

"It's anonymous. You of all people know how hard it is to get information."

Oh, I do. "You can still find out the setup date, the state, the attorney, perhaps even the bank used to pay the bills. Someone was paying for Ry Strauss to live in the Beresford."

"On it."

I rejoin Jessica. The wine is opened. Jessica is, no surprise, delightful company. We laugh a lot. We finish one bottle and open a second. The sole is superb.

"Odd," she says.

"What's that?"

"Have we ever been alone before?"

"I don't think so."

"We always had Myron in the room."

"Feels like we still do," I say.

"Yeah, I know." Jessica blinks and reaches for the glass. "I really messed up."

I don't correct her.

"My marriage sucks," she says.

"I'm sorry to hear that."

"Are you?"

"I am now."

"Did you hate me when I left Myron?"

"Hate probably isn't the right word."

"What is?"

"Loathe."

She laughs and raises her glass. "Touché."

"I'm joking," I say. "In truth, you never mattered to me."

"That's honest."

"I never saw you as a separate entity."

"Just a part of Myron?"

"Yes."

"Like an appendage?"

"Not that relevant, frankly. Like an arm or a leg? No. Never that important."

She tries again. "Like a small satellite orbiting him?"

"Closer," I say. "In the end, you caused Myron pain. That's all I cared about. How you affected him."

"Because you love him."

"I do, yes."

"It's sweet. So maybe you understand better now."

"I don't," I say. "But go on, if you wish."

"Myron was such a big presence," Jessica says.

"Still is."

"Exactly. He sucks all the air out of the room. He dominates by just being there. When I was with him, my writing suffered. Did you know that?"

I try not to scowl. "And you're blaming him?"

"I'm blaming us. He's not a planet I'm orbiting. He's the sun. When I was with him too much—the intensity—I was afraid I would disappear into it. Like the gravity would draw me too close to his flames, overwhelm me, drown me."

Now I do scowl without reservation.

"What?" she says.

"Ignoring your mixing metaphors—are you drowning or burning up?—that's such complete and utter nonsense. He loved you. He took care of you. That intensity you felt was overwhelming? That was love, Jessica. The bona fide ideal, the rarest of the rare. When he smiled at you, you felt a warmth you'd never known before because he loved you. You were lucky. You were lucky, and you threw it away. You threw it away not because of what he did, but because you, like so many of us, are self-destructive."

Jessica leans back. "Wow. Tell me how you really feel."

"You left him for a boring rich guy named Stone. Why? Because you had true love and it terrified you. You couldn't handle the loss of control. It's why you kept breaking his heart—so you'd have the upper hand again. You had a chance at greatness, but you were too scared to grasp it."

Her eyes glisten now. She gives them a quick swipe with her index finger and thumb. "Suppose," she says, "I tried to get him back."

I shake my head.

"Why not? You don't think he still has feelings for me?"

"Won't happen. We both know that. Myron isn't built that way."

"And what about you, Win?"

"We aren't talking about me," I say.

"Well, we can change topics. You've changed, Win. I used to think you and Myron were yin and yang—opposites that complemented each other."

"And now?"

"Now I think you're more like him than you know."

I have to smile at that. "You think it's that simple?"

"No, Win. That's my point. It's never that simple."

Jessica wants to walk home alone. I don't insist otherwise. In fact, even though the car is waiting for me, I choose to do the same. She heads south. I head west and start crossing Central Park by the Sixty-Sixth Street transverse. It's a beautiful night and it's a beautiful park and the walk soothes me for perhaps three minutes—until my phone buzzes. The call is coming from Sadie Fisher's iPhone.

I have a bad feeling about this.

Before I have a chance to offer up my customary greeting, Sadie half snaps, "Where are you?"

I do not like the timbre in her voice. There is anger. And there is fear.

"I'm strolling through Central Park. Is there a problem?"

"There is. I'm at the office. Get here as soon as you can."

She disconnects the call.

I find a taxi heading south on Central Park West. Traffic is light at this hour. Ten minutes later I'm back at the Lock-Horne Building on Park Avenue. Jim is working security at the desk. I nod at him and head toward my private elevator. It's getting late now, north of ten p.m., but this building is filled mostly with financial advisors of one kind or another, many of whom need to work hours that coincide with overseas markets, many more of whom put in wastefully long hours to match the other guy vying for the same promotion. I press the button for the fourth floor, and especially tonight, with a few drinks in me, with images of Jessica Culver still swimming in my head, the memories of MB Reps—the M stood for Myron, the B for Bolitar, Myron would self-flagellate over the name's lack of ingenuity—swirl though my skull.

Sadie greets me when I get off the elevator, though "greet" may imply a temperament that is not at all apropos. "What did you do, Win?"

"Nice to see you too, Sadie."

She adjusts her glasses. It feels as though she is doing that more as a statement than a need, but whatever gets you through the night. "Do I really look in the mood?"

"Why don't you tell me what's wrong?"

Sadie steps into her office. I notice that Taft's reception desk is empty except for a box of his belongings. Sadie sees me noticing and arches an eyebrow.

"I had visitors today."

"Oh?"

"They braced me out on the street. Two huge guys."

I wait.

"What did you do, Win?"

"Who were they?"

"Teddy Lyons's brothers."

I wait.

"Win?"

"Did they threaten you?"

"Well, they didn't want to buy me a drink."

"What did they say?"

"They accused me of sending a man to hurt Teddy."

"What did you say?"

"What do you think I said?"

"That you didn't." Then I ask, "Did they believe you?"

"No, Win, they didn't believe me." She moves closer to me. "You were at that basketball game."

"So were seventy thousand other people."

"Are you really going to lie to me?"

"What exactly do you think I did, Sadie?"

"That's what I'm asking."

"It has nothing to do with you."

"No, Win, that isn't true." Sadie gestures to the empty desk. "Taft told you what Teddy Lyons did to Sharyn, didn't he?"

"As did you."

"Not until after he was hurt. You know Teddy Lyons may never walk again."

"Seems he's able to talk though," I say. "So you fired Taft?"

"I don't like spies in my office."

Fair enough.

"Do I need to find a new workspace?"

"That's up to you."

"You're going to have to do better than that, Win. What were you thinking?"

"That Sharyn deserved justice."

"Are you serious?"

I wait.

"We are law-abiding," Sadie says. "We are trying to change hearts and minds—and laws."

"Taft said Teddy was currently stalking someone else."

"Probably."

"He wasn't going to stop because you wanted to change laws," I say, realizing that I'm echoing the words I'd told Vanessa Hogan about the Hut of Horrors perpetrators.

"So you took care of it?"

I see no reason to reply.

"And now we have these goons coming after us."

"I'll handle them."

"I don't want you to handle them."

"Too bad."

"Is that the world you want to live in?" Sadie shakes her head. "Do you really want people to take the law into their own hands?"

"People? Heavens, no. Me? Yes."

"You're joking, right?"

"I trust my judgment," I say. "I don't trust the common man's."

"You hurt us. Do you realize that? We had a chance of changing—"

"A chance," I say.

"What?"

"A chance didn't help Sharyn. It probably wouldn't help Teddy's next victim either. I love what you're doing, Sadie. I believe in it. You should continue without reservation."

"And you continue to do what you do?"

I shrug. "You work on the macro level," I say. "What you do is important."

"And, what, your hope is that my work will one day make your work obsolete?"

I smile with no humor behind it. "My work will never be obsolete."

She thinks about it. "You can't spy on me."

"You're right."

"And whatever you do, it can't involve me or my clients."

"You're right."

She shakes her head. The truth is, I may indeed have messed up here. I don't care about Teddy Lyons, of course. He crossed the line and earned any and all repercussions. I don't look at it as vigilantism. I look at it as preventive offense. Think schoolyard rules. The bully hits someone. Even if the teacher is told, even if the teacher punishes the bully, the bully should expect someone to hit back.

I'd known that there was the potential for unexpected consequences, even disastrous ones, but I had added up the pros and cons and chosen to act. Perhaps I was wrong. I'm not infallible.

You need to break a few eggs to make an omelet. I don't know if that's true, but if you break the eggs, better to make an omelet than a mess.

Enough with the analogies.

"I almost called the police after the brothers threatened me," she says.

"Why didn't you?"

"And say what? You assaulted their brother."

"They could never prove it. But if I may make an observation?"

She frowns and gestures for me to go ahead.

"You didn't call the police," I say, "because you realized that the law couldn't protect you."

"And damn you for putting me in that position." Sadie squeezes her eyes shut. "Do you see what you've done? I went to law school. I swore an oath. I know that our legal system isn't perfect, but I believe in it. I follow it. And now you've forced me to abandon my integrity and principles."

She takes a deep breath.

"I'm not sure I can stay in this office, Win."

I say nothing.

"I may want out of our agreement."

"Think it over for a bit," I say. "You're right. Your anger—"

"It's not just anger, Win."

"Whatever you want to call what you're feeling. Anger, disappointment, disillusionment, compromise. It's justified. I did what I thought was best, but perhaps I was wrong. I am still learning. It's on me. I apologize."

She seems surprised by my apology. So do I.

"So what do we do now?" she asks.

"You've had a chance to chat with the brothers," I say.

"Yes."

"Do you think they are just going to leave us alone?"

Sadie's voice is soft. "No."

"So the eggs are broken," I say. "The question now is, Do we want to make an omelet or a mess?"

CHAPTER 19

I like to walk.

Most days, I walk to and from work. The route from my office to my apartment—from the Lock-Horne Building to the Dakota—is approximately two miles and takes slightly more than half an hour at a brisk pace. My routine is to head north on Fifth Avenue until I hit Central Park in front of the Plaza Hotel on Fifty-Ninth Street. I stay to the left of the Central Park Zoo, diagonally traipsing north and west until I hit Strawberry Fields and then my home in the Dakota. During my morning walk, I often stop for coffee at Le Pain Quotidien, which is located in the middle of the park. The dogs run free in this area, and I enjoy watching that. I don't know why. I've never owned a dog. Perhaps I should remedy that.

It's dark now, the park so hushed I can hear the echo of my footsteps on the pavement. Times may be better, but most people still don't stroll through Central Park at night. I recall my rather violent youth when I would "night tour" the most dangerous areas of the city. As I mentioned earlier, I no longer trawl for trouble in the so-called mean streets, craving to right some vague wrong whilst satisfying certain of my own cravings. I'm more careful with where I wreak havoc now—albeit, as I now see with Teddy "Big T" Lyons, my targeting skills are far from perfect.

I confess I'm not good about considering long-term repercussions.

I cross the *Imagine* mosaic, and up ahead I can start making out the gables of the Dakota. I am thinking about too many things at once—the Jane Street Six, the Vermeer, the Hut of Horrors, Patricia, Jessica—when my phone buzzes.

It's PT again.

I answer with "Articulate."

"I got what I could on Strauss's shell company. First off, it's called Armitage LLC."

Good name, I think. Tells you nothing. That's Rule Number One in setting up an anonymous shell—have a name that has nothing to do with you.

"What else?"

"It was filed in Delaware."

Again no surprise. If you want anonymity, there are three states you use—Nevada, Wyoming, or Delaware. Since Philadelphia is very close to Delaware, the Lockwoods have always gone that route.

"It's also not a single shell," PT says.

Yet again no surprise.

"Seems to be part of a network. You probably understand this better than I do, but LLC X owns LLC Y which owns LLC Z which owns Armitage LLC. So it's very difficult to trace back. The checks come out of someplace called Community Star Bank."

When I hear the name of the bank, I slow my pace. My grip on the phone tightens.

"Who set up the Armitage LLC?"

"It has no name. You know that."

"I mean, what attorney?"

"Hold on." I can hear him shuffle papers. "No specific lawyer, just a firm. Duncan and Associates."

I freeze.

"Win?"

Duncan and Associates, I know, is just one man.

Nigel Duncan. Butler, trusted friend, bar-admitted attorney with but one client.

In short, the shell company paying Ry Strauss's bill was set up by one of my family members.

I am about to ask PT exactly when the shell company was formed when something hard, like a tire iron, crashes into the side of my skull.

The rest happens in two or maybe three seconds.

I stagger, woozy from the blow, but I stay upright.

I hear PT's tinny voice from my phone say, "Win?"

The tire iron lands with a loud splat on the other side of my skull.

The blow jars my brain. My phone drops to the pavement. The side of my scalp splits open. Blood trickles down my ear.

I do not see stars—I see angry bolts of light.

A thick arm snakes around my neck. I am ready to make the automatic move—head butt to the nose of the man behind me—but a second man, this one with a ski mask, points a gun in my face.

"Don't fucking move."

He stands just far enough away so that even if I had all my

faculties, a move to disarm him would be precarious. Still, I would have gone for it had it not been for the blows to the skull. There are two strategies when a gun is pointed at you. One— the more obvious strategy—is surrender. Give them what they want. Don't resist in any way. This is an excellent strategy if the purpose of the gun is, for example, to rob you. To take your wallet or your watch and abscond into the night. Option Two, the one I normally prefer, is to strike fast. Train yourself to skip over the part where you are shocked into paralysis and attack immediately. It is unexpected. The gun bearer often expects you to obey and act cautiously when you first see the gun—ergo, by moving without hesitation, you can catch them unawares.

Option Two obviously has its risks, but if you suspect the gun bearer means you great harm, as I do here, it's my preferred choice out of a host of bad solutions.

But for Option Two to be effective, you need to be in full command of your skillset. I am not. My equilibrium is off. My feet are unsteady. Something dark is closing in on me—if I don't fight it, I may black out entirely.

Instead I choose not to move. To use another sports meta-phor, I take the standing eight count and hope that my head will clear.

The man with his arm around my neck is big. He pulls me tight against his chest as I hear a vehicle screeching to a halt. I am lifted in the air. I still don't resist and within seconds I am tossed in the back of what I assume is a van. I land hard. My two abductors, both wearing ski masks, jump in behind me. I hear the tires screech. The van is moving before the side door is fully slammed shut.

One chance.

Before my abductors can react, I summon whatever I have

in reserve and roll toward the partially-open-and-closing-fast sliding door. My faint hope now is to fall out of the gathering-speed van. No, this isn't a great option, but it is the best one currently available. I will protect my skull with my arms and let the rest of my body take the brunt. If I'm lucky, I will end up with a broken bone or three.

Small price to pay.

My head and shoulders are out of the van now. I can feel the wind whipping at my eyes, making them water. I close them and tuck my chin and brace for the impact of my body on New York City street asphalt.

But that doesn't happen.

A strong hand grabs me by my collar and flings me. My body goes airborne like a rag doll. I hear the van door slide shut at the exact moment my back slams against the far side of the van. The whiplash effect drives my skull into the metal side.

Another blow to the head.

I crumble to the cold floor of the van, facedown.

Someone leaps on top of me, straddling my back. I consider a move—quick spin, elbow strike—but I'm not sure I can pull it off.

Another factor: The gun is back in my face.

"Resist and I'll kill you."

Through my murky haze, I can make out the back of the driver's head. The two abductors—one straddling my back, the other pointing a gun at me—still wear their ski masks. I cling to this as a good sign. If they meant to kill me, there would be no reason to disguise their identity.

The man on top of me starts a body search. I don't move, hoping to use the time to get my bearings. The pain I can handle. The dizziness—I am undoubtedly concussed—is another matter.

He finds my Wilson Combat 1911 in the holster, pulls it out, empties it so that even if I could somehow get it back, it would be useless.

The other man, the one with the gun, says, "Check his lower legs."

He does so. It takes some time, but he finds my small gun, the Sig P365, in an ankle holster. He pulls it into my blurry view and again empties out the ammunition. Still on top of me, he leans down near my face, the wool of his mask against my cheek, and whispers harshly, "Anything else?"

A move I could make if my head was clear: Bite him. He is that close. I could bite him through that flimsy mask, rip off a part of his cheek, turn my body, throw him toward the gunman so as to block what might be an incoming bullet.

"Don't think about it," the gunman says.

He says this matter-of-factly, shifting toward the side in order to prevent the sort of attack that has crossed my mind.

Conclusion: The gunman, the one doing the talking, is good. Trained. Paramilitary perhaps. He stays far enough back, so that even if I was a hundred percent—right now I would guesstimate that I'm at best forty to fifty percent—I wouldn't have a chance.

The man on top of me is larger—bulkier, more muscled—but the bigger threat, I realize, is the trained man with the gun.

I stay still. I try to clear some of the cobwebs, but it really isn't happening. I feel lost, adrift.

Then the big man on top of me surprises me with a kidney punch.

The blow lands like an explosion, a bomb going off, shards of hot razors slicing through my internal organs. The pain paralyzes me for a moment. Every part of me hurts, wants to cover up and find relief.

The big man hops off me and lets me writhe in pain. I roll up against the divider between the front seats and the back. I look back toward my two abductors.

When they both take off their ski masks, two thoughts—both bad—hit me at once.

First, if they are letting me see their faces, they don't plan on letting me live.

Second—no doubt because I can see the resemblance—these are the brothers of Teddy "Big T" Lyons.

I try to stay put because every move is agony. I try not to breathe because, well, the same. I close my eyes and hope they think I've passed out. There is nothing to be done right now. What I need most is time. I need time without suffering further injury so as to recover enough to counter.

What that counter might be, I have no idea.

"End this," the larger brother, the one who'd straddled my back, tells his well-trained sibling with the gun.

The smaller brother nods and aims his gun at my head.

"Wait," I say.

"No."

I flash back to another time, when Myron was in the back of a van, similar to this, when he too asked someone assaulting him to wait. That man had also said no. I, however, was following them in a car and listening in via Myron's phone. When I heard that, when I heard the perpetrator say no and thus realized that Myron would not be able to talk his way out of it, I hit the accelerator and smashed my car into the back of the van.

Odd what memories come to you under duress.

"A million dollars for both of you," I blurt out.

That makes them pause.

The larger brother says in a semi-whine, "You hurt our brother."

"And he hurt my sister," I reply.

They share a quick glance. I am lying, of course, unless you are one of those Kumbaya types who believe that in a larger sense, we humans are all brothers and sisters. But my lie, like my million-dollars offer, makes them hesitate. That's all I want right now. To buy time.

It's the only option.

The larger brother says, "Sharyn's your sister?"

"No, Bobby," the gunman says with a sigh.

"She's in the hospital," I say. "Your brother has hurt a lot of women."

"Bullshit. They're just lying bitches."

Gun Brother says, "Bobby..."

"No, man, before he dies, he should know. It's bullshit. All these bitches, they come on to Teddy. He's a good-looking guy. They want to close the deal with him, you know what I'm saying? Lock him down, get married. But Teddy, he is— or he was before you blindsided him like a chickenshit—he's a player with the ladies. He doesn't want to settle down. When the bitches don't get the ring, suddenly they're all complaining about him. How come they don't complain right up front? How come they go out with him voluntarily?"

"I didn't blindside him," I say.

"What?"

"You said that I—and I quote—'blindsided him like a chickenshit.' I didn't. We went man-to-man. And he lost."

Big Bobby makes a scoffing sound. "Yeah, right. Look at you."

"We could settle it that way," I say.

"What?"

"We stop this van somewhere private. You know I'm un-armed. You and I go at it, Bobby. If I win, I go free. If you win, well, I die."

Muscled Bobby turns to Gun Brother. "Trey?"

"No."

"Aw, come on, Trey. Let me rip his head off and shit down his neck."

Trey's eyes stay on mine. He isn't fooled. He knows what I am. "No."

"Then how about that million dollars?" Bobby asks.

My vision is still blurry. I am dizzy and hurting. I am no better off than I was a few seconds ago.

"He's lying to us, Bobby. The million dollars isn't real."

"But—"

"He can't let us live," Trey says, "just as we can't let him live. Once he's free, he will hunt us down. Forget the police—we would have to spend the rest of our lives looking over our shoulder for him. He'll come after us, with all his resources."

"We can still try to get the money, can't we? Let him wire or some shit. Then we shoot him in the head?"

When Trey shakes his head, I realize that I am out of time and options.

"This was all decided the moment we grabbed him, Bobby. It's us or him."

Trey is, of course, correct. There is no way we can let the other side live. It is too much of an unknown. I will never trust that they won't come back for me. The same, Trey has realized, is true for them.

Someone has to die here.

We cross the George Washington Bridge and are now picking up speed where Route 80 meets up with Route 95.

I truly wish I had a better plan, something less guttural and primitive and ugly. The odds of this working are, I admit, slim, but I am seconds from death.

It's now or never.

I slump my shoulders as though defeated.

"Then let me just confess this to you," I say.

They relax just the slightest bit. I don't know whether that will help. But at this stage I have but one option.

If I go for Bobby, Trey will shoot me.

If I go for Trey, Trey will shoot me.

If I surprise them and go for the driver, I just may have a chance.

Out of nowhere, I let loose a bloodcurdling scream. It sends hot jolts of agony all through my skull.

I don't care.

They both, as I anticipated, startle back, expecting me to jump toward them.

But I don't.

I spin toward the driver.

My plan is crude and base and not very good. I am going to get hurt badly no matter what. I could bring out the broken-eggs-omelet metaphor again, but really, is there a point?

Trey still has the gun. It hasn't magically vanished. He's startled, yes, but he recovers fast. He pulls the trigger.

My hope is that the suddenness of my move will throw off his aim.

It does. But not enough.

The bullet hits me in the upper back below the shoulder.

I don't stop my spin. My momentum carries me through. I

keep a thin razor blade in the cuff of my right sleeve. Bobby didn't notice it as he searched me. Almost no one does. It shoots out now at the wrist and into my palm. I have the razor blade in my right hand, and while the driver is going at seventy-one miles per hour—yes, I see the numbers lit up large on the dashboard—I slice his throat to the point of near decapitation.

The van lurches hard to the side. Blood sprays from his artery, coating the inside of the windshield. I feel the warm contents of his neck—tissue, cartilage, more blood—empty out onto my hand. My left arm snakes through his seat belt harness so I can be somewhat braced for the upcoming collision.

I hear the gun go off again.

This bullet only grazes my shoulder before shattering the windshield. I grab the steering wheel and spin it. The van jerks off the road and teeters onto two wheels.

I close my eyes and hold on as the van flips, then flips again, then crashes hard into a pole.

And then, for me, there is only darkness.

CHAPTER 20

All superheroes have an origin story. All people do, when you think about it. So here is the abridged version of mine.

I grew up in privilege. You know that already. What you may consider relevant is that every human being is snap-judged by their looks. That's not exactly an earth-shattering observation and no, I'm not comparing or saying I had it worse than others. That would be what we call a "false equivalency." But the fact is, many people detest me on sight. They see the towheaded blond locks, the ruddy complexion, the porcelain features, my haughty resting face—they smell the inescapable stink of old money that comes off me in relentless waves—and they think smug, snob, elitist, lazy, judgmental, undeservedly wealthy ne'er-do-good who was born not only with a silver spoon in his mouth but with a forty-eight-piece silver place setting with a side of titanium steak knives.

I understand this. I, too, sometimes feel that way about those who inhabit my socioeconomic sphere.

You see me, and you think I look down on you. You feel resentment and envy toward me. All your own failures, both real and perceived, rise up and want to target me.

Even worse, I appear to be a soft, easy, pampered target.

Today's teenagers might dub my face "punch-worthy."

Inevitably, all of the above led to ugly incidents in my childhood. For the sake of brevity, I will talk about one. During a visit to the Philadelphia Zoo when I was ten years old, decked out in a blue blazer with my school crest sewn onto the chest pocket, I wandered away from my well-heeled pack. A group of inner-city students—yes, you can read into that as you might—surrounded me, mocked me, and then beat me. I ended up hospitalized, in a coma for a short time, and in a suddenly interesting life cycle, I nearly lost the same kidney Bobby Lyons had so recently pummeled.

The physical pain of that beating was bad. The shame that ten-year-old boy felt from cowering, from feeling helpless and terrified, was far worse.

In short, I never wanted to experience that again.

I had a choice then. I could, as my father urged, "stay amongst my own"—hide behind those wrought-iron gates and well-manicured hedges—or I could do something about it.

You know the rest. Or at least you think you do. Human beings, as Sadie noted, are complex. I had the financial means, the motivation, the past trauma, the innate skills, the disposition, and perhaps, when I am most honest with myself, some sort of loose screw (or primitive survival mechanism?) that allows me to not only thrive but take some pleasure from acts of violence.

Take all those components, puree them in a blender, and voilà. Here I am.

In a hospital bed. Unconscious.

I don't know how long I've been here. I don't know whether I dreamed this or not, but I may have opened my eyes and seen Myron sitting bedside. I did that for him when we scraped him off the pavement after our own government tortured him. Other times I hear voices—my father's, my biological daughter's, my deceased mother's—but since I know for certain that at least one of those voices cannot be real, perhaps I am imagining the rest.

I am, however, alive.

Per my "plan"—I use that word in the loosest sense possible—I'd managed to fold enough of my body across the driver's seat belt harness before the crash. It kept me strapped in during impact. I don't know the fate of Teddy's two brothers. I don't know what the authorities believed happened. I don't know how many hours or days it has been since the crash.

As I begin to swim up to the surface of awareness, I let my mind wander. I have begun piecing some of this case together, or at least it feels that way. Hard to know for certain. I am still mostly unconscious, if that's what you call this cusp, and thus many of my purported solutions—about the LLC, about the bank robbery, about the murder of Ry Strauss—seem plausible now but may, like many a dream, turn into utter nonsense when I awake.

I reach a stage where I can sense consciousness, yet I hesitate. I'm not sure why. Part is exhaustion, a weariness so heavy that even the act of opening my eyes would seem a task far too rigorous in my current condition. I feel as though I'm strapped down in one of the dreams where you're running through deep snow and thus moving too slowly. I'm also trying to listen and gather intel, but the voices are unintelligible, muffled, like Charlie Brown's parents or the audial equivalent of a shower curtain.

When I finally do blink my eyes open, it is not a family member nor Myron sitting bedside. It's Sadie Fisher. She bends toward me—close enough that I can smell her lilac shampoo—and whispers in my ear.

"Not a word to the police until we talk."

Then Sadie calls out, "I think he's awake," and moves to the side. Medical professionals—doctors and nurses, I assume—descend. They take vitals and give me ice chips for the thirst. It takes a minute or two, but I'm able to answer their simple, medically related questions. They tell me that I suffered head trauma, that the bullet missed my vital organs, that I will be fine. After some time passes, they ask me if I have any questions. I catch Sadie's eye. She gives the smallest shake of the head. I, in turn, shake mine.

Perhaps an hour later—time is hard to judge—I am upright in the bed. Sadie works hard to clear the room. The staff grudgingly obey. Once they are gone, Sadie takes a small speaker out of her purse, fiddles with her phone, and starts blasting music.

"In case someone is listening in," Sadie tells me when she moves closer.

"How long have I been here?" I ask.

"Four days." Sadie pulls a chair toward the bed. "Tell me what happened. All of it."

I do, though the pain medication is making me loopy. She listens without interrupting. I ask for more ice chips while I tell the tale. She pours them into my mouth.

When I finish, Sadie says, "The driver, as you already know, is dead. So is one of the two assailants, Robert Lyons. He flew through the windshield on impact. The other brother—he goes by Trey—suffered broken bones, but since there wasn't enough to hold him on, he's gone home to 'convalesce' in western Pennsylvania."

"What did Trey claim?"

"Mr. Lyons is choosing not to speak to the authorities at this time."

"What do the police think happened?"

"They aren't saying, except for the fact that they've pieced together that the driver had his throat slit by you. They have some forensics—the position of your body behind the corpse, the way the blade fit into your sleeve, the blood on your hands, stuff like that. It probably isn't court conclusive, but it's enough so that the cops know."

"Did you tell them about the brothers threatening you?" I ask.

"Not yet. I can always do that later. If I tell them now, they will want to know why they threatened me. Do you understand?"

I do.

"The cops are already connecting the dots between what happened to Teddy Lyons in Indiana and what happened in that van. For your sake, as my client, I don't want to help them."

Logical. "Advice?" I ask.

"The police are here. They want you to make a statement. I say we don't give them one."

"I already forget what happened anyway," I say. "Head trauma, you know."

"And you're still too weak to question," Sadie adds.

"I am, yes, though I still want to be released as soon as possible. I can recuperate better at home."

"I'll see whether I can arrange it."

Sadie rises.

"We kept this quiet, Win. Out of the papers."

"Thank you."

"There were other people who wanted to stay bedside. I advised against it because I wanted to make certain you spoke to me first. They all understood."

I nod. I don't ask who. It doesn't matter.

"Thank you," I say. "Now get me out of here."

———

But it isn't that easy.

Two days later I am moved out of the ICU into a private room. It is there, at three in the morning, while I am still blessedly riding the edge between the morphine highway and full slumber, that I sense more than hear my hospital room door open.

This is not uncommon, of course. Anyone who has endured a prolonged stay in a medical facility knows that you are prodded and probed at the strangest hours of the night, almost as though the intent is to keep you from any true REM sleep. Perhaps, to again use a superhero analogy, my Spidey senses were tingling, but I somehow know that whoever was broaching was not a nurse or physician or a member of the custodial crew.

I stay very still. I do not have a weapon on me, which is foolish. I also do not have my customary reflexes or strength or timing. I carefully open my eyes just a smidge, but between the drugs and the late hour, my vision is that of a man looking through gauze.

I do, however, see movement.

I could perhaps open my eyes a bit wider, but I don't want whoever is entering to know that I'm awake.

Still, I make out a man. My first thought is one that makes my pulse spike.

It's Trey Lyons.

But I can see now that this man is too large. He stays in the doorway. I can feel his eyes on me. I consider my next move.

The call button.

Every hospital room has one, of course, but being that I am not good about asking for help, I had paid little heed when the nurse explained it all to me. Hadn't she wrapped the cord about the bed railing? Yes. Had that been on my left or right?

Left.

With my body still under the covers, I try to snake my left hand toward the call button without being seen.

A male voice says, "Don't do that, Win."

So much for playing possum. I open my eyes all the way now. My vision is still murky, and the lights are low, but I can see the big man—and he's very big, I see now—standing by the door. I make out a long beard and a cap of some kind atop his head. Another man—swept-back gray hair, expensive suit—steps fully into the room. He is the one who warned me off the call button. He nods at the big guy. The big guy steps out of the room and closes the door behind him. Swept Back grabs a chair and pulls it up to me.

"You know who I am?" he asks me.

"The Tooth Fairy?"

It's not my best line, but Gray Hair still smiles. "My name is Leo Staunch."

I had guessed that.

"My men were following you."

"Yes, I know."

"You picked up the tail fast."

"Amateurish move," I reply. "Almost insulting."

"My apologies," Staunch says. "What's your involvement with Ry Strauss?"

"He had my painting."

"Yeah, we heard. What else?"

"That's it," I say.

"So all your snooping. It's just about an art heist?"

"It's just about an art heist," I repeat. "Also: Did you just use the word 'snooping'?"

He smiles, leans closer to me. "We all know your rep," he whispers.

"Do tell."

"People describe you as crazy, dangerous, a psycho."

"Nothing about my natural good looks or supernatural charisma?"

I realize my rather feeble attempts at humor may seem out of place. If you think these lines are cringeworthy, you really must meet Myron. But they do serve a purpose. You never show fear. Not ever. My reputation, which I've carefully cultivated, is to appear unhinged. That's intentional. Cracking wise during moments like this lets your opposition know that you will not be easily intimidated.

Staunch pulls the chair a little closer. "You're looking for Arlo Sugarman, aren't you?"

I don't answer. Instead I ask, "Did you kill Ry Strauss?"

And he predictably replies: "I'm the one asking questions."

"Can't we both?"

Staunch likes that one, though Lord knows why. "I had

nothing to do with Ry Strauss's murder, though I can't say I'm sorry."

I try to read his face. I can't.

Staunch says, "You know they murdered my sister, right?"

"I do, yes."

"So where is Arlo Sugarman?"

"Why?" I ask.

His eyes turn black. "You know why."

"And yet," I continue, "you want me to believe you had nothing to do with Ry Strauss?"

"Didn't you just tell me this is only about an art heist to you?"

"I did, yes."

Leo Staunch turns both palms to the sky and shrugs. "Then you don't give a shit who killed Strauss, do you?"

Staunch has me there.

We sit in silence for a moment. In the distance, I can hear a beeping noise. I wonder how they got in, but I imagine hospital security is nothing for a man like Leo Staunch.

When he speaks again, I can hear the anguish in his voice. "She was my only sister. You get that?"

I wait.

"Sophia, she had her whole life in front of her. And then, poof, gone. Our poor mother, happiest woman you ever met before that day, she cried every day for the rest of her life. Every. Single. Day. For thirty years. When Mom finally died, all everybody kept saying at the funeral was, 'At least, she's with her Sophia again.'" Staunch looks down at me. "You believe in that stuff? That my mom and my sister are reunited somewhere?"

"No," I say.

"Me neither. It's just the here and now." He straightens his back and puts his hand on my forearm. "So I'm going to ask you one more time. Do you know where Arlo Sugarman is?"

"No."

The door opens, and the big guy leans his head in. Leo Staunch nods at him and rises. "When you find him, you'll let me know first."

It wasn't a question.

"Why Sugarman?" I ask. "What about the others?"

Leo Staunch moves to the door. "Like I said before, I know your rep. If we go to war, you'll probably take a few of my men down. But I don't care about the casualties. You don't want to cross me, Win. The price will be too high."

CHAPTER 21

Three days later, I am transported by helicopter to Lockwood Manor.

I am better, of course, but I recognize that I am nowhere near one hundred percent. I would estimate that I am working somewhere between sixty-five and seventy percent capacity, and modesty prevents me from saying that I, at sixty-five percent, am still a potent force.

Nigel Duncan greets me by saying, "You look better than I thought."

"Charmed," I reply, and because I have no more time to waste: "Tell me about the Armitage LLC."

We stroll toward the house in silence.

"Nigel?"

"I heard you."

"And?"

"And I won't respond. I won't even bother responding whether I know what you're talking about or not."

"Loyal to the end."

"It isn't loyalty. It's legality."

"Attorney-client privilege?"

"Precisely."

"No, sorry, that doesn't play here. You are already listed as the attorney on the holding."

"Am I?"

"Duncan and Associates."

"There are probably other firms with that name."

"Do you know who benefits from Armitage LLC?" I ask.

The main house grows ominous as we draw closer. It has always been thus for me, since I was a young child. Every home is its own independent country. I stare at Nigel. I see his mouth is set. His jowls bounce with every step.

"Ry Strauss," I say. "It paid his bills."

Nigel's expression does not change.

"You need to tell me what's going on," I say.

"No, Win, I don't. Even if I knew—and again I won't confirm whether I have a clue what you're talking about—I don't need to tell you anything."

"It could be connected to Uncle Aldrich's murder. And Cousin Patricia's abduction. It could give us the answer to the Hut of Horrors. It could save lives."

He almost smiles. "Save lives," he repeats.

"Yes."

"You're usually not one for hyperbole."

"I'm still not."

"Ah, Win, I love you. I've loved you all your life." He stops and turns to me for the briefest of moments. "But if you want my advice, I would stay out of this."

"I don't."

"Don't what?"

"Want your advice."

Nigel lowers his head, smiles. "You want to right wrongs, Win. But you always seem to leave collateral damage in your wake."

"There is collateral damage in everything."

"That may be true. It's why in the end I stick to the rule of law."

"Even if that leads to greater collateral damage?"

"Even if."

"I could press my father on this."

"You could, yes."

"I assume Windsor Two was the one who set up the shell company."

"You can assume what you want, Win."

"Where is he?"

"He's on the practice facility."

"So he's feeling well."

Nigel doesn't bite. "I've set up the east wing suite for you. We have medical personnel and a physical therapist on call should you need it." His eyes are moist. "I'm glad you're okay after your ordeal, but if you insist on keeping this up, one of these days..."

With that he turns and leaves. I head up to my room and unpack. From the corner window I can see the practice facility. It is for golf—more specifically, the short game herein defined as shots within fifty yards of the hole. There is an oversized green with several cups to practice putting. There is a bunker so as to work on sand shots. The grass around the facility is cut to various lengths to duplicate chips and pitches from a multitude of lies.

I change into golf khakis and a polo shirt with the famed

logo of Merion Golf Club—a wicker basket atop a pin rather than a flag. I will let you in on a secret that most people don't know. Several of your most exclusive courses sell shirts and paraphernalia to visitors and guests—this is big business—but if the name of the club is written under the logo, it means that you are a tourist. If the name is not there, as it is not on mine, if there is only the logo and no words, that indicates that the wearer is a bona fide club member.

Class distinctions. They exist everywhere.

There is a pair of golf shoes in the closet. I slip them on and pad out to where my father is practicing pitch shots from thirty yards out. He turns and smiles as I approach. We don't bother with hello. This is golf. Words become superfluous. I grab a 60-degree Vokey wedge.

My father goes first in our endless rounds of Closest to the Cup. In his youth, Dad was a champion golfer. He won the Patterson Cup, Philadelphia's top amateur prize, when he was only twenty-one. A lot of his game has deteriorated with age, but he still has that feathery touch around the greens. He is using his old Callaway 52-degree pitching wedge. When he pitches, he keeps the ball flight low. The ball lands at the start of the green, follows the break, and curls up within two feet of the cup.

Merion Golf Club is down the road and around the corner. My father and I would walk there with our carry bags on our shoulder. That was where we played. My best childhood memories all revolve around being on the golf course, mostly with my father. We rarely spoke as we strolled. We didn't have to. Somehow my father and golf were able to convey life lessons to me—patience, failure, humility, dedication, sportsmanship, practice, small improvements, missteps, mental error, fate, doing everything right and still not getting the desired result—without words.

You may love the game, but as in life, no one—no one—gets out unscathed.

It is my turn. I open the clubface all the way so as to hit with a high-lofted trajectory with maximum spin—what is commonly called a flop shot. The ball sails into the sky and lands softly with minimal roll. My shot ends up six inches closer to the cup. My father smiles.

"Nice."

"Thank you."

"But the low roller is the higher percentage shot," he reminds me. "The flop is great on a practice facility. But on the course, when the pressure mounts, that shot is risky."

He doesn't ask me how I am, but then again, I'm not sure that he knows about my recent mishap in the van. Would Nigel have told him? I don't think so.

"Try another?" he asks.

"Sure." Then I say: "Per our last conversation, I asked Cousin Patricia why you and Uncle Aldrich became estranged."

The smile slides off his face. Using his pitching wedge, he scoops another ball forward and lines up for his chip. "What did she tell you?"

"About his Peeping Tom incident during her Sweet Sixteen."

Dad nods a little too slowly. "Tell me exactly what Cousin Patricia told you."

I do. We continue to chip. The practice green has six holes, so that he never hits the same shot twice. Dad doesn't believe in that. "You never hit the same shot twice in a row on the course," he would tell me. "Why would you do it on the range?"

"So," my father says when I finish, "Cousin Patricia told you that Ashley Wright's father came to see me."

"Yes."

"Carson Wright has been my friend since we were twelve," Dad says. "We played in the juniors together."

"I know."

"He's an honorable man."

I don't know whether he is or he isn't, but I say, "Okay," to keep the conversation flowing.

"It wasn't easy for Carson."

"What wasn't?"

"Coming here. To this house. Telling me the full story."

"Which was?"

"Your uncle did far more than merely peep." Dad held the follow-through on his next chip, checked his wrist position, and watched the ball roll. "I don't know what the term for it is now. Pedophilia. Rape. Inappropriate relationship. When it began, Aldrich was forty. Ashley was fifteen. And if you want to defend it—"

"I don't."

"Well, even if you did. People did in those days. 'You're sixteen, you're beautiful, you're mine.' 'Young girl, get out of my mind.' Songs like that."

"So Carson Wright came to you?" I prompt, trying to get him back on track.

"Yes."

"And said?"

"That a few months before the party, when your uncle wouldn't return her calls, his daughter Ashley swallowed pills. She had to have her stomach pumped."

"Yet she came to the Sweet Sixteen?"

"Yes."

"Why?"

"You don't know?"

I wait.

"Normalcy. That was the way it was, Win."

"Sweep it under the rug?"

My father scowls. "I always disdained that analogy. More like you get over it. You bury it so deep no one will ever unearth it."

"Except that didn't work."

"Not that night, no."

"So what did you do after Carson's visit?"

"I confronted Aldrich. The situation turned ugly."

"Did he deny it?"

"He always denied it."

"Always?"

"This wasn't his first time," my father says.

I wait. My father turns to me. He waits. This is a game we've both played before.

"How many others were there?" I ask.

"I couldn't give you a count. When a problem arose, we moved him around. That was why he didn't stay at Haverford like the rest of us."

"I thought he chose NYU to be different."

"No, your uncle started his collegiate life at Haverford. But there was an incident with a professor's fourteen-year-old daughter. No sex, but Aldrich took photographs of her scantily clothed. Money was exchanged—"

"Meaning her father was paid off."

"Fine, yes, if you wish to be crude about it. Payments were made, and Aldrich was sent off to New York City. That was one example."

"Can you give me another?"

"Your aunt Aline."

"What about her?"

But I knew already, didn't I?

"When Aldrich came back from Brazil with her, he told us she was twenty and a teacher in the school the family founded. We checked. She wasn't a teacher. She was a student. She wasn't the first he groomed, just the one he liked best. Our best guess? Aline was fourteen or fifteen when he brought her home—even our investigator couldn't say for certain."

I don't gasp. I don't bother with the inane why-didn't-anyone-report-him line of questioning. We are a powerful family. As my father said, "money was exchanged," often accompanied by threats both subtle and crude. It was also, as my father pointed out, a different era. That doesn't excuse it. It puts it in context. There is a difference.

"So how does the Armitage LLC fit into this?" I ask.

My father does not do coy well. He is not an actor nor a liar. When he looks genuinely baffled by my question, I am thrown. "I don't know what that is."

"A shell company set up by Nigel."

"And you think I set it up?"

"It stands to reason."

"I didn't."

There is no reason to follow this line. If he denies it, he denies it. "When was the last time you saw Uncle Aldrich?"

"I don't recall. There was a family function at Merion perhaps six or eight months before his murder. Perhaps then. But we didn't speak."

"How about the night before he was murdered?"

My father stops in his backswing. I have never seen him do

225

that. Never. Once he is committed to his swing, you'd have to shoot him to stop it.

"Pardon?"

"Cousin Patricia says you were at their house the night before he died."

"Did she?"

"Yes."

"But I just told you that I hadn't seen Aldrich for at least six to eight months before his murder."

"So you did."

"I would call that a conundrum."

"I would as well."

My father strolls back to the house. "Good luck with that."

CHAPTER 22

S ir Arthur Conan Doyle, through his legendary character
Sherlock Holmes, said, "Once you eliminate the impossible, whatever remains, no matter how improbable,
must be the truth."

I am thinking about this quote, even though it is not fully
apropos to the situation. Based upon what I am learning—and
assuming I believe that my father is telling the truth about not
setting up the shell company—the answer as to the creator of
Armitage LLC becomes rather obvious.

My grandparents.

Sexism has always ruled, of course, but whenever you see
a family like ours, a family that has managed to hang on to its
power and prestige across generations, the hoary, patronizing
chestnut of "Behind every successful man there is a woman"
doth usually apply. When my grandfather died, it wasn't
my father who stepped up, except perhaps in a ceremonial
manner.

My grandmother ran the show.

I wish I could talk to her. She would know what to do. Grandmama is still alive, but she is ninety-eight and hasn't spoken a word in a year. Still, I know where the answer lies— in the wine cellar.

As I start down the steps, I hear Nigel ask, "Where are you going?"

"You know where."

"I think it's best if you leave this alone, Win."

"Yes, I keep hearing that."

"Yet you don't listen."

I shrug and quote Myron: "Love me for all my faults."

Lockwood Manor's wine cellar is modeled on the original one at the Château Smith Haut Lafitte. The walls are stone, the ceiling arched. There are bottles and wooden barrels and oak shelves. The room is always kept at 56 degrees Fahrenheit and 60 percent relative humidity.

I head past the collection, some bottles worth thousands of dollars. In the far right-hand corner, I find a magnum of Krug Clos d'Ambonnay on the top shelf and pull it. A door opens, and I enter the back cellar. Yes, it is a secret room, if you will, and this cloak-and-dagger may seem a tad much, I suppose, but I think my grandmother just wanted a decent workspace away from prying eyes, yet still close to the grape.

All four walls are lined with six-foot-high file cabinets.

I am not intimidated by the sheer amount of paperwork. I am, in fact, at home here. One reason Myron and I make such a good team is that he is a big-picture guy whilst I am more detail oriented. He is a dreamer. I am a realist. He has an uncanny way of seeing the end game. I am more of a plodder. I don't take shortcuts. I do the grunt work. A huge part of my occupation involves looking at the minute details of various corporations with a fine eye, to study every facet of a business, to understand their pros and cons, their ins and outs, before making a buy or sell recommendation.

Despite what some masters of the universe claim, you can't do that on instinct.

I am thus big on due diligence.

Much of my family, especially my dear Grandmama, is the same. She has kept meticulous records on our family. Here, in her favorite sanctum, is every birth certificate, old passports, family trees, schedulers, calendars, bank statements, diaries, financial records, etc., dating back to 1958. There is a square table in the middle of the room with four chairs, legal pads, and sharpened Ticonderoga pencils. I start going through the files. I take fastidious notes. So much of this is in Grandmama's handwriting, and while I'm not a sentimental fellow—I don't display family photographs and you will rarely hear me waxing nostalgic—there is something so personal about penmanship, especially hers, the purity and consistency in her cursive, the beauty and the lost art and the individualism, that I cannot help but feel her presence.

I dig into my family's past. I get lost in it. My mind wants to jump to conclusions, but I resist the temptation. Again, that would be Myron's forte—spontaneous, disorganized, sloppy, brilliant. He can keep dozens of ideas in his head. I cannot. I slow myself. I need to have backing documentation. I need to see it visually, on the page, before it makes sense. I need a timetable and a map.

Still, as the hours pass, the pieces start coming together.

I hear footsteps behind me. I look up as Cousin Patricia steps into the room. "Nigel said you'd be down here."

"And so I am."

"Shouldn't you be resting?"

"No."

"You're okay then?"

"Yes, fine, can we move on now?"

"Sheesh, I was just being polite."

"Which you know I detest," I say. Then I ask, "Do you know how old your mother is?"

Patricia makes a face. "Come again?"

"When your parents came back from Brazil, the family didn't believe that Aline was, as he claimed, twenty. Nigel's father hired a detective firm in Fortaleza. Their best guess is that she was fourteen or fifteen."

Patricia just stands there.

"Did you know?" I ask.

"Yes."

I don't know whether that surprises me or not.

"It was the seventies, Win."

The same defense as my father. Interesting to hear it from his niece. "I'm not interested in judging your father. I don't care right now about the legality or ethics or morality."

"What are you interested in?"

"Getting the answers."

"What answers?"

"Who stole the paintings. Who killed your father. Who killed Ry Strauss. Who harmed you and the other girls."

"Why?"

It is an interesting question. My first thought is about PT and his five decades of guilt over his dead partner. "I promised a friend."

Patricia's face displays skepticism. In truth, I don't blame her for that. My answer sounds hollow in my own ears. I try again.

230

"It's a wrong that needs to be righted," I say.

"And you think the answers will do that?"

"Will do what?"

"Right the wrong?"

It's a fair point. "We will find out, won't we?"

Cousin Patricia tucks her hair behind an ear and starts toward me. "Show me what you have."

Perhaps I should warn Cousin Patricia that she will not like what I have to say.

Alas, no.

I would rather get her unguarded, unfiltered reaction. So I dive straight into the breakdown.

"Your father matriculated to Haverford College in September of 1971."

She arches an eyebrow. "Seriously?"

"What?"

"You're using the word 'matriculated' in casual conversation?"

I have to smile. "My most heartfelt apologies," I say. "Do you know your father originally attended Haverford?"

"I do. Like your father and their father and their father before them for however far we go back. So what? My father didn't want to go, but he didn't feel as though he had a choice. That's why he transferred."

"No."

"No what?"

"That's not why he transferred."

I produce the honor code report as well as the covering letter signed by the Dean's Disciplinary Panel. "These are dated January 16, 1972—the beginning of your father's second semester of his freshman year."

We are seated at the square table in the center of the room. Her purse is on the floor. Patricia reaches down and pulls out a pair of reading glasses. I wait for her to skim through the report.

"It's pretty vague," she says.

"Intentionally," I say. "Apparently your father took inappropriate photographs of the underage daughter of his biology professor named Gary Roberts." I hand her a canceled check. "On January 22, Professor Roberts deposited this check, made out from one of our shell companies, to his bank account."

She reads it. "Ten grand?"

I say nothing.

"Pretty cheap."

"It was the early seventies."

"Still."

"And I'm not sure he had a choice. Scandals like this never saw the light of day. If it did, Professor Roberts was probably convinced that his young daughter would be the one blamed and made worse for wear."

Patricia reads the letter again. "Do you have a photograph of her?"

"Of the daughter?"

"Yes."

"No. Why?"

"Dad liked young women," she says. "Girls even."

"Yes."

"But there is a difference between a physically mature fifteen-year-old and, say, a seven-year-old."

I stay silent. Patricia has asked me no question, so I see no reason to speak.

"I mean," she continues, "sorry to sound anti-me-too and I'm not defending him, but have you seen photographs of my mother at their wedding?"

"I have."

"She's . . . my mother was curvy."

I wait.

"She was built, right? What I'm saying is, I don't think my father was a pedophiliac or anything."

"You prefer ephebophilia," I say.

"I'm not sure what that is."

"Mid-to-late adolescents," I say.

"Maybe."

"Patricia?"

"Yes."

"Let's not get bogged down in definitions right now. It will only cloud the issue. He's dead. I see no reason to pursue his punishment at this moment."

She nods, sits back, and lets loose a deep breath. "Go on then."

I look down at my notes. "There isn't much mention of your father for the next few months in any of the diaries I've located so far, but my grandfather kept all of his scorecards from his rounds of golf."

"You're kidding."

"I'm not."

"He saved scorecards?"

"He did."

"So I assume my father's name is on some?"

"Yes. He played quite a bit starting in April. With my father, our grandfather, family members. I'm sure he played with his friends too, but of course, I wouldn't have those cards."

"What was his handicap?"

"Pardon?"

"I'm trying to lighten the mood, Win. What does that prove?"

"That he was in Philadelphia throughout the summer. Or at least, he golfed here. Then according to the calendar, a Lockwood staff member drove Aldrich to Lipton Hall, his residence housing on Washington Square, on September 3, 1972."

"Where he started at NYU."

"Yes."

"So then what?"

"For the most part, it seems everything is calm for a while. I need to go through the files more thoroughly, but as of now, nothing major pops out until your father arrives in São Paolo on April 14, 1973."

I show her the relevant stamp from Brazil in his old passport.

"Wait. Grandmama kept his old passport?"

"All of our old passports, yes."

Patricia shakes her head in disbelief. She turns to the photograph in the front and stares down at the image of her father. The passport was issued in 1971, when her father was nineteen years old. Her head tilts to the side as she stares at the black-and-white headshot. Her fingertip gently brushes her father's face. Aldrich was a handsome man. Most Lockwood men are.

"Dad told me he stayed in South America for three years," she says in a wistful voice.

"That seems right," I say. "If you page through the passport, you'll see that he traveled to Bolivia, Peru, Chile, Venezuela."

"It changed him," she says.

This too is not a question, so I see no reason to comment.

"He did good work down there. He founded a school."

"Seems he did, yes. According to the passport, he didn't return to the United States until December 18, 1976."

"December?"

"Yes."

"I was told earlier."

"Of course you were."

"So my mother was pregnant with me," Patricia says.

"You didn't know?"

"I didn't. But it doesn't make a difference." Patricia sighs and leans back in her chair. "Is there a point to all this, Win?"

"There is."

"Because we are now up to 1976. The paintings were stolen from Haverford in, what, the mid-1990s? I still don't see any connection here."

"I do."

"Tell me."

"The key is your father's departure from New York City to São Paolo."

"What about it?"

"Your father was still a student at New York University. He hadn't graduated. He seemed to be doing well enough. But suddenly, in April of that year, with the end of the semester less than two months away, he chose to travel on his overseas mission. I find that odd, don't you?"

She shrugs. "Dad was rich, impulsive. Maybe he wasn't doing great that semester. Maybe he just wanted out."

"Perhaps," I say.

"But?"

"But he departed April 14, 1973."

"So?"

I have the old newspaper article on my phone. Even I feel

a chill when I bring it up to show her. "So the Jane Street Six murders occurred two days earlier, on April 12, 1973."

Patricia is up and pacing. "I don't get what you're saying here, Win."

She does. I wait.

"It could be a coincidence."

I don't make a face. I don't frown. I just wait.

"Say something, Win."

"It can't be a coincidence."

"Why the hell not?"

"Your father runs off to Brazil almost immediately after the Jane Street Six murders go down. Twenty years later, valuable paintings of ours are stolen and end up in the hands of the leader of the Jane Street Six. Care for more? Fine. At Ry Strauss's murder scene, we find the suitcase you were made to pack when you were kidnapped after your father's murder. Oh, the icing: Nigel set up a shell account to purchase Ry Strauss's apartment—the murder scene—and to take care of his maintenance payments. Enough?"

Patricia stands and crosses the room. "So what are you saying? My father was part of the Jane Street Six?"

"I don't know. Right now, I'm still presenting the facts."

"Like what else?"

"I met a barmaid who works in a place called Malachy's. She had a relationship with Ry Strauss. She told me that Ry would often visit Philadelphia."

"So if I'm reading you right, you think my father was part of the Jane Street Six. He escaped. Our family paid off Ry

236

Strauss to keep quiet, I guess, about his role. Did we pay off the others?"

"I don't know."

"Didn't you tell me you talked to one? Lake something."

"Lake Davies."

"Wouldn't she know?"

"She might, but I'm not sure she would tell me, especially if she's been receiving payments. She also claims the women of Jane Street were low-level, so she may not know."

"But my father is dead," she says.

"Yes."

"So why would anyone still be paying to keep his reputation intact?"

Now I do make a face. "You just entered the gates of Lockwood Manor. Do you really need to ask that?"

She considers that. "Let's say you're right. Let's say my father was somehow part of the Jane Street Six."

I hadn't said or even concluded that yet, but I let it go for now.

"What does that have to do with stealing the Vermeer and Picasso all those years later? What does it have to do with my father's murder or . . ." Patricia stops. "Or what happened to me?"

"I don't know," I admit.

"Win?"

"Yes?"

"Maybe we know enough now."

"Come again?"

"I've built this charity on our family story. A large part of that is my father spending time helping the poor in South America and my desire to carry on his legacy. Suppose it comes out that the story is built on lies."

I think about that. She makes an excellent point. Suppose what I find ends up being damaging to the Lockwood name and, more specifically, Patricia's worthwhile cause.

"Win?"

"It's better if we are the ones to unearth the truth," I tell her.

"Why?"

"Because if it's bad," I say, "we can always bury it again."

CHAPTER 23

K abir hops off the helicopter, keeping one hand atop his turban so the slowing rotors don't blow it off his head. He wears a black silk shirt, a green puffy down vest, worn blue jeans, and bright-white throwback Keds. I look behind me and up, and I see my father at his window, predictably frowning down at what he sees as a foreign interloper.

I wave Kabir toward me and lead him down through the wine cellar to Grandmama's back room. When we arrive, Kabir takes it all in, nods, and says, "Bitchin'."

"Indeed."

When the press finally learned that Ry Strauss had been the murder victim found with the stolen Vermeer, the story, as you might imagine, generated enormous headlines. In the past, those headlines would have lasted for days, weeks, even months. Not today. Today our attention span is that of a child receiving a new toy. We play with it intensely for a day, maybe two, and then we grow bored and see another new toy and throw this one under the bed and forget all about it.

I spent most of the Ry Strauss media frenzy in the hospital. In the end, every news story, and yes, I'm moving if not mixing my metaphors, is a burning fire—if you don't feed it a new log, it dies out. So far, there was nothing new. A stolen painting, the Jane Street Six, a murder—all delicious in their own right and together forming an intoxicating brew—but that was eleven days ago.

The media had not yet learned about the suitcase with my initials found at the scene or the case's links to Cousin Patricia and the Hut of Horrors. That is good, in my view. That makes my investigation somewhat easier to navigate now.

Kabir carefully lays the file folders out on Grandmama's old table. The key to hiring a top assistant and working cooperatively is having a shared vision. Kabir understands that I am visual and that I like facts and evidence displayed in organized patterns. The folders are all the same size (legal, nine inches by fourteen) and the same color (bright yellow). His neat handwriting is on the tab of each.

"The Jane Street Six," Kabir says.

The six folders are in a neat row. I read the names in the tab from left to right: Lake Davies, Edie Parker, Billy Rowan, Ry Strauss, Arlo Sugarman, Lionel Underwood. Alphabetical order. To answer your question, I am not OCD, but much like the Kinsey Scale, I believe that we are all more on a spectrum than we care to admit.

"Okay if I start?" Kabir asks.

"Please."

"We know the fate of Ry Strauss and Lake Davies," he says, sweeping the two files away, leaving only four. "So let me update you on the others."

I wait.

"Beginning with Edie Parker. Her mother is still alive. She lives in Basking Ridge, New Jersey. She claims to have not seen or heard from her daughter since that night. She has also refused to talk to the media, but she will talk to you."

"Why me?"

"Because I told her it was your painting found with Ry Strauss. I may have also hinted that you know more about the Jane Street Six's whereabouts than reported."

"Tsk, tsk, Kabir."

"Yeah, you're a bad influence on me, Boss. Let's move now to Billy Rowan, okay?"

I nod.

"It seems that Billy and Edie were getting pretty serious, more so than people realized. Billy Rowan's father is still alive, the mother died twelve years ago. But here's the kicker: Ten years ago, Rowan's father retired and moved from Holyoke, Massachusetts, to an assisted living facility in Bernardsville, New Jersey."

I consider that. "Bernardsville is right next to Basking Ridge."

"Yes."

"So Mrs. Parker and Mr. Rowan now live within miles of one another."

"One point two miles, to be exact."

"That can't be a coincidence," I say.

"I don't think it is either," Kabir says. "Think they're doing the nasty?"

"The nasty?"

"The nasty, the ugly, knocking boots, boning, playing hide—"

"Yes," I say, "thank you for the thesaurus-like clarification."

"Of course, they both gotta be near nineties." Kabir makes a face as though he's gotten a whiff of Eurotrash cologne. He quickly shakes it off. "Anyway, I couldn't get William Rowan—that's his name—on the phone, but Mrs. Parker said that both she and Rowan's father would meet you at his assisted living facility tomorrow at one p.m., if you're up for it."

"I'm up for it. Anything else?"

"On Parker and Rowan? No."

He lifts the Parker and Rowan folders and places them in the same stack as the Strauss and Davies ones. That leaves only two.

"And if I can go out of order, I have nothing new on Lionel Underwood either."

He adds Underwood's folder to the pile. That leaves only one folder.

Arlo Sugarman.

I glance at Kabir. He is smiling.

"Paydirt," Kabir says.

"Go on."

"As you know, for years there has been zero sign of Arlo Sugarman—nothing since that FBI raid that killed an agent. But of course, you got new information from Lake Davies."

"That he was in Tulsa," I say.

"Exactly. More to the point, Lake told you that Arlo Sugarman was posing as a student at Oral Roberts University. You didn't tell PT about that, did you?"

I shake my head.

"Right, based on when Lake was still on the run, I figured that she and Ry would have had to have crossed paths with Arlo sometime between 1973 and 1975. To be on the safe side, I spread that timeline out until 1977 on the off chance that Arlo disguised himself as a freshman and stayed there for four years."

"And?"

"And then I started digging. Oral Roberts University has a pretty impressive alumni page. I started there." He tilts his head. "Did you know that Kathie Lee Gifford graduated from Oral Roberts?"

I say nothing.

"Anyway, I used a photoshop app to change photographs of Arlo Sugarman. In all the famous ones, he has long hair and a huge beard—kinda like me when you think about it, right?"

"As rain."

"Come to think of it, that would have been a good disguise."

"What would have been?"

"A turban. Except you guys are terrible at tying them. Anyway, using the software, I made Arlo look clean-shaven with short hair. I mean, Oral Roberts University. It isn't exactly a spot for campus radicals, right? Then I tried some alumni contacts from that era. Class officers. People like that. The groups are pretty active on Facebook. I got a fair amount of responses. Most were useless, but two people thought the image looked like a guy named Ralph."

"Ralph what?"

"That's the thing. They didn't know. It was all very vague, which, I thought, was what you'd want if you were kind of hiding out. Still, I had a first name. I had the years he may have been on campus. So my next step was, I had to get hold of the yearbooks from those years."

"Did you?"

"Yes."

"How?"

"E-Yearbook. It's a website. They have full scans of every page from tons of yearbooks. High schools and colleges. You can see them online if you pay a fee. If you pay a slightly higher fee, they'll send you a scan of your entire yearbook."

Kabir is trying my patience. "So you looked through them for the name Ralph?"

"Right, looked through the headshots. There were several Ralphs, but none that looked like Arlo Sugarman."

"He was probably smart enough to skip picture day."

"Probably, yeah. Am I taking too long telling you this?"

"I think it would be best to pick up the pace."

"Okay, cutting to the chase: This may sound a little complicated, but when I ran a facial recognition search through the yearbook scan pages, I came up with this."

Kabir opens Arlo Sugarman's folder and pulls out a black-and-white image.

"This is page 138 of the Oral Roberts University yearbook from 1974."

He hands me the page. The heading reads "Theater Moments." There are five photographs spread across two pages. One features a woman wearing angel wings. One features what looks like the balcony scene from *Romeo and Juliet*. One features four men dressed in medieval garb playing musical instruments and singing.

The second from the right, playing a mandolin, is Arlo Sugarman.

"Whoa," I say out loud.

In the old image, Sugarman wears black-framed glasses, which he hadn't in any previous photographs I had seen. He is clean-shaven. The curly locks are cut shorter. You wouldn't recognize him unless you were looking closely, which, it seems, the facial recognition software had been.

"Long story short, I located the student who directed that

show. His name is Fran Shovlin. He works at a megachurch in Houston. Nice guy. He remembers Ralph as Ralph Lewis. What's interesting is, there was a Ralph Lewis in that class, but he was sick and didn't seem to attend any classes. So I think Arlo just used his name."

"Makes sense."

"According to Shovlin, the only thing he really remembers about Ralph was that he dated a woman named Elena. I looked her up. She's Elena Randolph now. She's divorced and owns a beauty salon in Rochester, New York. I called her, but as soon as I mentioned the name Ralph Lewis, she hung up on me. I've called back, but she refuses to talk."

"Interesting," I say. "And I assume you've done every kind of search under the name Ralph Lewis?"

Kabir nods. "Nothing pops up."

Not surprising. Sugarman probably changed identities several times over the years. There was a chance that Ralph Lewis was never an identity, that he just used that name knowing the confusion with the real Ralph Lewis would keep him off the radar. It would be hard to pull off that stunt today—colleges keep track of students, have greater security concerns—but back in the seventies, anyone could have probably walked onto a campus and sat in on classes and not been questioned.

Kabir and I agree on a schedule. I will visit Parker's mother and Rowan's father at the Crestmont Assisted Living Village tomorrow at one p.m. It will be easiest to drive there—the ride would only be about ninety minutes—and then if I decide it would help, I can grab a private plane at nearby Morristown Airport and fly to Rochester to confront Elena Randolph. Kabir will take care of all the details.

"You know what to do with Elena Randolph," I say.

"On it," Kabir says, rising from the chair.

"Do you want to stay for dinner?" I ask.

"Nah. Got a hot date."

"How hot?" I ask.

"I like her, man."

"You can keep the copter for the night," I say.

"Huh?"

"Keep the copter. Take her to my beach club on Fishers Island. I can arrange a table on the ocean."

Kabir does not reply. He instead points to the files stacked on the table. "Should I leave these here for you?"

"Yes."

"Thanks for the generous offer, Boss. But I think I'll pass."

I wait a beat. Then I say, "May I inquire why?"

"If I do something this grand on our fourth date," Kabir replies with a shrug, "what will I do for the fifth?"

"Wise," I say.

My mobile vibrates. When I see the caller is Angelica Wyatt, I feel the spike of fear and hit the green button with dizzying speed. Before I can skip my customary "Articulate," Angelica says, "Ema is fine."

Amazing how well Angelica knows me, especially considering how little she knows me. And yes, this is Angelica Wyatt. *The* Angelica Wyatt, the movie star.

"What's up?" I ask.

"Ema has been asking for you."

Ema is a high school senior. She is also my biological daughter.

"I brought her to the hospital to see you," Angelica tells me.

This displeases me. "You shouldn't have." I glare at Kabir,

but I'm still talking to Ema's mother. "How did she even know I was—?"

"You were supposed to have breakfast with her that morning," Angelica replies.

"Oh," I say. "Right."

"She's worried, Win."

I don't say anything. I don't like this.

"When can she see you?" Angelica asks.

"Would tomorrow work?"

"Your place?" Angelica asks. "Dinner?"

"Yes."

"I'll drop her off."

"You can come too, if you'd like."

"That's not how we do this, Win."

Angelica is right, of course. We agree on a time. I hang up and continue to glare at Kabir.

"Ema called looking for you," Kabir explains, "and I know you wouldn't want me to lie to her."

I frown because he is correct, and I don't like it. "How much does she know?"

"Just that you were hospitalized. I told her you'd be okay. She didn't believe me. She wanted to stay in your room."

I am not sure how to react to this. I am often left adrift and unsure when it comes to Ema. This new relationship, if that is what we want to call it, often leaves me teetering and unbalanced.

Which reminds me.

"Trey Lyons," I say.

"What about him?"

"Sadie said he went home to convalesce."

"In western Pennsylvania," Kabir says. "To some ranch or something."

"I want eyes on him, twenty-four seven."

"Got it."

"Two men. I want to know where he is at all times. Run a background check too."

Sometime later, with Kabir on the copter and heading back to Manhattan for his hot albeit serious date, I am back at the practice green, working on my putting, trying to clear my head, when I spot Cousin Patricia coming over the hill. She strides toward me with her shoulders back, her face set on grim, and one does not need to be a body-language expert to see that something is amiss.

Because I'm quick on the uptake, I say, "Something amiss?"

"You let me be a cowardly chickenshit," she tells me.

"Redundant," I say.

"What?"

"A chickenshit by definition is cowardly. Either call yourself a coward or a chickenshit. But a cowardly chickenshit?"

She crosses her arms. "Really, Win?"

I consider telling her to love me for all my faults, but I refrain.

Patricia picks up a club—a nine iron for those keeping track—and starts pacing. "So after we talked, I go back to the shelter where we help abused teens. That's what I do, Win. You know this, right?"

There is a bit of a rant in her voice. I don't reply.

"I mean, lately, it feels as though all I'm doing is executive bullshit—raising funds—but at the end of the day it is about those teens that we rescue because they have no one and that's Abeona's mission. We help kids in trouble. You get that, right?"

"I do, yes."

"And you know what started me down that path?"

"Yes," I say, "I've read your brochure."

She is still pacing, but the word "brochure" makes her pull up. "What?"

"You went through a severe and brutal ordeal. It made you recognize the need."

"Yes."

"Despite all the horrors you experienced, you felt lucky. You had the resources and support to put your tragedy behind you. Now your mission is to provide the same for those less fortunate."

"Yes," Patricia says again.

I spread my hands as if to say, *Well then.*

"So what was that crap about reading the brochure?"

"I don't think that's the full story," I say.

"Meaning?"

"It was more than your recognizing a need."

"Like?"

"Like survivor's guilt," I say. "You escaped from that hut. The other girls did not."

She does not reply. I continue.

"You believe now that you owe those girls something. Simply put, those girls haunt you because you had the audacity to live. That's the part that really drives you, Patricia. It's not so much that you had resources and others do not. It's that you survived, and irrational as it is, you blame yourself for that."

Patricia frowns at me. "That Duke psychology major didn't go to waste."

I wait.

"Do you know why I'm upset right now?" she asks.

"I can make an assumption."

"Go ahead."

"After we talked, you went back to the Abeona Shelter. Rather than hang upstairs in your executive office, you rolled up your sleeves and went into the field because you felt the need to connect or get to your roots or some similar banality. Perhaps you took the van out on rescue missions. Perhaps you counseled a young girl who was recently assaulted. At some point, you raised your head and took a good look around at this rather impressive shelter you, Patricia, built. And then you got misty-eyed and marveled to yourself something akin to: 'These girls are all so brave, while I'm not going to the FBI because I'm a redundantly cowardly chickenshit.'"

Patricia almost laughs at that. "Not bad."

"Am I close?"

"Close enough. I have to come forward, Win. You get that, right?"

"It doesn't matter what I get. I'm here to support you."

"Good, but you're wrong about one thing," she adds.

"Oh, do tell."

"Those girls who never came home?" she says. "They don't haunt me. They just expect me to do right by them."

CHAPTER 24

W e see no reason to wait. I call PT and tell him that
      Patricia is ready to talk.
          "Glad you chose to call us," PT says.
"Why's that?"

"Because we were coming to you. See you in an hour."

He hangs up, but I didn't like his tone. An hour later—PT is
nothing if not prompt—an FBI helicopter lands at Lockwood.
We exchange pleasantries before convening in the parlor, where
the Vermeer's empty frame looms larger than normal. PT has
brought a young agent he introduces as Special Agent Max.
Special Agent Max wears hip neon-blue-framed glasses. I don't
know whether Max is his first name or last, but I don't care either.

PT and Max sit on the couch. Patricia takes our grandfather's
old chair. I stand and coolly lean against the fireplace mantel
like Sinatra against a lamppost. The word you are looking for is
"debonair."

PT cuts right to it. "Win told me that the suitcase we found
at the murder scene belonged to you. Is that correct?"

Patricia says, "Yes."

"You know about the murder, of course."

"Of course."

"Did you know the victim, Ry Strauss?"

"No."

"Never met him?"

"Not as far as I know."

"Ever been to his apartment at the Beresford?"

"No, of course not."

"Ever been to the Beresford at all?"

"No, I don't think so."

"Don't think so?"

"I guess at some point I may have been there for a function of some kind."

"A function?"

"A fundraiser, a party, some kind of social event."

"So you were at the Beresford for something like that?"

I don't like this.

"No," Patricia says, seeing it too, "I don't think so. I don't remember. But it's possible. I've attended fundraisers in many apartment buildings on the Upper West Side, but I don't specifically recall one in the Beresford."

PT nods as though he's totally okay with that answer. "Where were you on April fifth?"

That is the day of the murder. I do not like the way this is going—more of a tat-tat-tat interrogation than a cooperative coming forward. I decide to break up the rhythm. "What exactly is going on here?" I ask.

PT knows what I'm doing, so he ignores my question. "Ms. Lockwood?"

"Call me Patricia."

"Patricia, where were you April fifth?"

"It's no secret," she says.

"I didn't say it was a secret. I asked where you were."

I say, "Stop."

PT now turns to me. "I'm asking questions, Win."

"It's okay," Patricia says. "It's public knowledge. I was at Cipriani that night for a fundraiser."

I confess that this information surprises me.

"The Cipriani in midtown?" PT asks.

"On Forty-Second Street. By Grand Central station."

"So you were in New York City?"

"If Grand Central station and Forty-Second Street are still considered New York City," Patricia replies with a hint of irritation, "then the answer is yes."

"When did you arrive in New York City?"

She sits back and looks in the air. "I spent two nights at the Grand Central Hyatt. I arrived by Amtrak on Friday and departed Sunday."

The room grows silent from the obvious implication. Patricia breaks it.

"Oh please. We've recently opened an Abeona Shelter in East Harlem, so I would venture to guess that over the past six months, I've been in New York City almost as much as Philadelphia. I can get you my work calendar if that will help."

"That would be nice," PT says.

I stick my nose in again. "Is there a point to this?"

"Win," Patricia says. The edge in her voice is there but blunted. "Let me handle this."

She is right, of course.

Patricia turns her attention to both PT and Max. "So what

is your theory here? A quarter century after my father was murdered and I was kidnapped, I...what...found out that the perpetrator was living as a recluse in New York City, so I killed him?"

"No need to get defensive," PT says.

"I'm not defensive."

"You sure sound defensive. Your suitcase connects you to the murder scene. I would be remiss if I didn't explore every avenue. Which leads me back to the night of your father's murder and your abduction."

"What about it?" she asks.

Special Agent Max takes out a binder and hands it to PT.

"I've gone over all the statements from that time period, and there are a few things I would like to clarify."

Patricia offers up a *what gives?* look. I reply with a small shrug.

"Your mother, Aline Lockwood, found your father's body when she came home from shopping. She then called the police."

PT stops. Here again he leaves a little uncomfortable pause to see whether his suspect dives in. Patricia does not.

"Why wasn't your mother at home with you and your father?" PT asks.

Patricia lets loose an aggravated sigh. "The report says, doesn't it?"

"It says she was at a supermarket."

We wait.

"It was almost ten p.m.," he continues.

"Agent..." Patricia pauses. "Do I call you Agent PT?"

"PT is fine."

"No, that doesn't feel right. Agent PT, when my mother

returned, I was tied up in the trunk of a car and blindfolded. I really couldn't speak to what my mother was doing."

"I'm simply asking whether your mother often went supermarket shopping at that hour."

"Often? No. Sometimes? Yes. The FBI checked my mother's alibi, didn't they?"

"They did."

"And she had been supermarket shopping, right?"

"Yes." PT shifts in his seat. "Did you ever find that odd? I mean, she goes supermarket shopping. It takes under an hour. That's a pretty narrow window—yet that's when the killers show up. Convenient, don't you think?"

Patricia shakes her head. "Wow."

"Wow?"

"You don't think I read up on my own case over the years?" she says, still keeping her temper in check, but the mercury is rising. "My mother, I mean, with all the crap you guys threw at her, she never complained. Of course, you guys thought it was her. You grilled her. You searched through her financials. You questioned everyone she ever knew. They found nothing."

"Back then maybe."

"What does that mean?"

"Were you supposed to be home, Patricia?"

"What do you mean?"

"When the killers arrived. You were a popular and attractive eighteen-year-old girl. It was a Friday night. My guess is, you were supposed to be out. My guess is, your dad was supposed to be home alone. According to the file, you were in your bedroom. You heard noises and then a gunshot. You came out of your room and you saw two masked men and your father dead on the ground."

"Point being?" Patricia snaps.

"Point being, if it was a hit, how would the killers have known you were home? It was a Friday night. You didn't have a car, did you?"

"No," she says.

"So it's not like they could have seen your car in the driveway. The hitmen come. They see only your father's car. Your mother's car is gone. They break in, they kill him right away, and then—*bam*—you surprise them. That's all possible, right?"

"Possible," Patricia allows.

"So then what happened?"

"You know. It's in the file. I ran into my bedroom."

"They kicked down the door?"

"Yes."

"And then?"

"They told me to pack a bag and come with them."

"Why pack a bag?"

"I don't know."

"But they specifically told you to pack a bag?"

"Yes."

"And you did?"

Patricia nods numbly.

"This is the part we in the FBI"—PT nods toward Special Agent Max—"have never understood. We didn't understand it back when your father was murdered. We don't understand now, over twenty years later."

Patricia waits.

"This whole suitcase thing. I don't want to cast aspersions or anything, but it has never quite added up. Do you know what my colleagues back then concluded? I mean, once they found out about the suitcase being packed. Oh, and your mom didn't tell them. Seems she didn't notice. One of the agents went through your room. Saw clothes missing from a hanger."

Patricia does not move.

"We don't understand the suitcase, Patricia, do you?"

Her eyes well up. I debate calling a stop to this, but she gives me a strong side-eye that screams, *Don't you dare*.

"Do you?" PT asks again.

"I do, yes."

"Tell me then. Why would they ask you to pack a suitcase?"

Patricia leans a little forward and keeps her voice soft. "They wanted to give me hope."

No one replies to that. The grandfather clock chimes. In the distance, a landscaper turns on a lawn mower.

"What do you mean, hope?" PT finally asks.

"The one guy," Patricia continues, "the leader, he's in my bedroom. His voice is almost kind. He tells me I'm going to stay in a nice cabin by a lake. That he wanted me to have my own clothes—'Don't forget a bathing suit,' he actually said that—so I would be comfortable, he said. He said I would only be gone a few days, a week at the most. He did that a lot."

PT leans further forward. "Did what a lot?"

"Gave me hope. I think he got off on it. Sometimes, after he raped me in that hut, he would tell me, 'Oh, Patricia, you're going to go home soon.' He would say that my family was finally ready to pay the ransom. One day, he told me he finally got the money. He tossed a pair of handcuffs and a blindfold into the shed. Said to put them on for the ride. 'You're finally going home, Patricia,' he tells me. He led me to a car. Helped me into the backseat. He put his hand on top of my head. 'Don't bump your head, Patricia.' I remember how gentle he was, putting the seat belt across me. Like suddenly he was too modest a man to touch me. Then he got in next to me. In the back. Someone else—maybe the guy from the first night, I don't know—he drove us. 'You're going home,' my rapist kept telling me. 'What are you going to do first when you're free? What food are you craving?' Like that. On and on. You can't imagine. For hours . . . and then at last, the car stopped. Both of them took me by the elbow. They march me to what I hoped was freedom. I can't see anything, of course. I'm still blindfolded and handcuffed. 'Your mom is right up ahead,' he whispers. 'I can see her.' But now I know."

For a moment, no one moves.

"Know what?" PT asks.

But Patricia doesn't seem to hear him. "They lead me through a door."

The room is completely silent, as though even the walls are holding their breath.

"And I know for sure," she says.

"Know what?" PT asks again.

"That familiar stench."

"I don't understand."

"You don't forget that stench." Patricia raises her head and meets his gaze. "I was back in that same shed. They just drove me around in circles. I can hear them both laughing now. I'm back in the hut and I'm handcuffed and blindfolded, so they both come in . . ."

She wipes her eyes, shrugs, forces up a smile.

For a while no one says anything. Even the creaks of this old home stay respectfully silent. After some time passes, PT gestures at Max, and Max pulls out a sheet of paper.

"Could this be the man who raped you?" PT asks in his gentlest voice.

He slides a sheet with six different images of Ry Strauss. The

first was a closeup of the famed Jane Street Six image. The last
was Ry Strauss in death. The four between them had probably
been created using age-progression software. One image would
theoretically be Ry Strauss at thirty, another at forty, at fifty, at
sixty. In some, Strauss had facial hair. In others he did not.

Patricia stares at the photographs. Her eyes are dry now.
I am still trying to sort the possibilities in my head. Did Ry
Strauss know my uncle Aldrich? I'm assuming so. Did Ry
Strauss coerce or blackmail Aldrich or my family into giving
him substantial financial assistance? Again I'll assume that it
was an affirmative. So what happened next? Why the art heist?
Why kill Aldrich? Why kidnap Patricia?

What am I missing?

"I don't know," Patricia says with a shake of her head. "I
could have seen this man years ago. The kidnapper always wore
a mask, but this could be him."

PT puts the images away. "After you escaped, you found a
way to turn your personal tragedy into some good."

It is a compliment, of course. The words, that is. The tone,
however, tells a different story. We seem to be at this interrogation's conclusion, but there is still something hanging in the air. I
have found that in these circumstances, it is best not to force it.

"To be clear," PT says, "I'm talking about your creating the
Abeona Shelter."

She wants to move this along, so she says, "Thank you."

"May I ask how you came up with the name?"

"The name?"

"Abeona."

I snap, "Why, PT?"

I instantly regret it. PT is no fool. He doesn't ask dumb or
pointless questions. I cannot see how the name of her shelters

259

could possibly matter, but I know that his interrogatory here is not a casual one.

"Abeona is the Roman Goddess of Safe Passage," Patricia explains. "When a child first leaves from home, Abeona is there to protect and guide them."

PT nods. "And your logo, the butterfly with what looks like eyes on the wing."

"A *Tisiphone abeona*," Patricia says, as though she has answered this question a thousand times, which she probably has.

"Yes," PT says. "But how did you come up with it?"

"Come up with what?"

"The idea of using the Roman goddess Abeona and the *Tisiphone abeona* butterfly logo. Was it your idea?"

"It was."

"Did you study ancient Roman religions? Were you, I don't know, a collector of butterflies?" PT leans forward, and suddenly his tone is inviting, kind. "What inspired you?"

I am trying to read Patricia's expression right now, but the signals are mixed. Her face has lost color. I see confusion. I see fear. I see what might be some sort of dawning realization, but really, who can tell?

"I don't know," Patricia says in a distant tone I don't think I've ever heard come from her.

PT nods as though he understands. With his eyes still on Patricia, he stretches his hand toward Max. Max is ready and drops the sheet into his hand. PT slowly and almost tenderly hands it to her. I look over his shoulder. It's a photograph of a forearm. And on the forearm is a tattoo of that logo—a *Tisiphone abeona* butterfly.

"This is Ry Strauss's arm," PT says. "It's the only tattoo we found on him."

CHAPTER 25

It is much later in the evening—one-too-many-cognacs o'clock, to be more precise—when Patricia finally says, "I remember the tattoo."

We are alone in Granddad's parlor. I am sprawled on the couch, my head tilted back, staring up at the art deco inlaid-tile ceiling. Patricia sits in Granddad's chair. I wait for her to say more.

"It's funny what you forget," she continues, and I hear the slur of the cognac in her voice. "Or what you make yourself forget. Except, I guess, you never totally forget, do you? You want to forget, and you even do forget, but you don't. Am I making sense?"

"Not yet," I say, "but keep going."

I hear the clink of ice being dropped in her snifter. It is something of a crime to drink this particular lineage on the rocks, but I'm not in the judging business. I stare up at the ceiling and wait. When Patricia is settled back in Granddad's chair, she says, "You push the memories away. You force them down. You block. It's like..." The slur seems to be growing. "It's like there's a basement in my brain and what I did was, I packed that awful shit into a suitcase, kind of like that damned monogrammed suitcase you gave me, and then I dragged that suitcase down the basement stairs and I jammed it into a dank back corner, and then I rushed back upstairs and locked the door behind me and hoped I'd never see that suitcase again."

"And now," I say, "to keep within your colorful analogy, that suitcase is upstairs and open."

"Yes," she says. Then she asks, "Wait, was that analogy or a metaphor?"

"An analogy."

"I'm terrible with that stuff."

I want to reach out and put a hand on my cousin's arm or do something innocuously comforting, but I'm very comfortable on the couch, enjoying the buzz, and I'm too far from her perch in Granddad's chair, so I don't bother.

"Win?"

"Yes?"

"The shed had a dirt floor."

I wait.

"So I remember when he was on top of me. In the beginning, he would pin my arms down. I would close my eyes and just try to ride it out. After a while...I mean, you can't keep your eyes closed forever. You can try, but you can't. I would look up. He wore the ski mask, so I could only see his eyes. And I didn't want to. I didn't want to look at his eyes. So I would turn my head to one side. Just trying to ride it out. And he'd be holding himself, on top of me, and I remember his arm, and there...there was that butterfly."

She stops now. I try to sit up, but it isn't happening.

"So I would stare at it. You know? Like focus on its wing. And when he'd thrust and his arm would jiggle, I could imagine the butterfly's wings were beating and it was going to fly away."

We stay in the dark. We sip some more cognac. I am drunk so I start thinking about existential nonsense, about the human condition, perhaps, like Patricia, trying to block what I just heard. I don't really know Patricia, do I? She doesn't really know me. Do we all ever know one another? Man, am I drunk. I'm enjoying this silence. Too many people don't get the beauty of silence. It is bonding. I bonded with my father when we would golf in silence. I bonded with Myron when we would watch old movies or television shows in silence.

Still, I feel compelled to break it: "You were in New York City the day Ry Strauss was murdered."

Patricia says, "I was, yes."

I wait.

"I told your friend PT the truth, Win. I go to New York City all the time."

"You don't call me."

"Sometimes I do. You are one of the shelters' biggest supporters. But you wouldn't want me calling you every time I come to town."

"That's true," I say.

"Do you think I killed Ry Strauss?"

I've been mulling that over for the past few hours. "I don't see how."

"What a ringing endorsement."

I sit up a little. The liquor hits me, and I feel the head rush. "May I speak bluntly?"

"Do you ever speak any other way?"

"Hypothetically, if you did kill Ry Strauss—"

263

"I didn't."

"Ergo my use of the term 'hypothetically.'"

"Ah. Go on."

"If you killed him, hypothetically or otherwise, I would not blame you in the slightest. I might, in fact, want to know, so that we could get in front of it."

"Get in front of it?"

"Make sure that it would never trace back to you."

Patricia smiles again and raises her glass. She is fairly wasted too.

"Win?"

"Yes?"

"I didn't kill him."

I believe her. I also believe she isn't telling me everything. Then again, I could be wrong on both counts.

"May I ask a hypothetical now?" Patricia asks.

"But of course."

"If you were me and you had the chance to kill Ry Strauss, would you?"

"Yes."

"Not much hesitation there," she says.

"None."

"Almost like you've been in that situation before."

I see no reason to reply. Like I said before, I don't really know Patricia, and she doesn't really know me.

———

Years ago, I was at a private weekend "retreat" with a number of Washington, DC, politico types, including Senator Ted Kennedy. The location of said retreat is confidential, so the most I can tell you is that it was held in the Philadelphia area. On the final night, there was a party where—I kid you not— the United States senators took turns performing a karaoke number. I admired it, truth be told. The senators looked like fools, as we all do when we perform karaoke, and they didn't care.

But back to Ted Kennedy.

I forget what song Ted—even though we had just met, he insisted I call him that—chose. It was something from the Motown family. It may have been "Ain't No Mountain High Enough." Or was that Barbara Boxer? Or did Ted and Barbara do it as a duet like Marvin Gaye and Tammi Terrell? I can't remember. Anyway, even though we disagreed on many issues, Ted was ridiculously charming and fun. He drank at the party. A lot. He started to stumble-dance, and if he didn't put a lamp- shade on his head, it was only because he was too drunk. By the end of the night, Ted needed to lean on a loved one to get through the door and find his room.

Why am I telling you this?

Because the next morning, I had to depart the retreat early. I woke up at 5:30 a.m. and hit the breakfast room at six. When I arrived, only one person was up. You guessed it.

"Good morning, Win!" Ted called out to me. "Sit with me."

He was reading the *Washington Post* with a cup of coffee, a mountain of food on the plate in front of him. Ted was clear-eyed and showered and wide awake. We had a spirited discussion on a variety of topics, but the gist is this: I have never seen someone handle spirits quite like that, and I don't know whether that was a positive or negative.

My guess is, it was a negative.

The long and short of my name-dropping tale? I am very

good at handling spirits. But I'm no Ted Kennedy. My head aches when I wake up. I let out a low groan and as though on cue, there is a knock on my door.

"Good morning!"

It is Nigel. I groan again.

"How are we this morning?"

"Your voice," I manage.

"What about it?"

"It soothes like a jackhammer against a cranial nerve."

"Are we hungover, Master Win? Be grateful. I brought you my top-secret cure."

He drops two pills into my palm and hands me a glass.

"It looks like aspirin and orange juice," I say.

"Shh, I'm thinking of applying for a patent. Should I open the curtains?"

"Only if you want to get shot."

"Cousin Patricia is getting dressed."

Nigel leaves the room. I shower for a very long time and get dressed. Patricia is gone by the time I get downstairs. I down a quick breakfast with my father. The conversation is stilted, but that's not a surprise. When I'm done, I head out to see Edie Parker's mother and Billy Rowan's father at the Crestmont Assisted Living Village in New Jersey.

Mrs. Parker gave me her first name, but I don't recall what it was. I like to use titles, such as Mr. or Mrs., when I converse with my elders. It is how I was raised. The three of us are in Mr. Rowan's room, which has all the warmth of a dermatologist's office. The colors are beyond-bland beige and golf-club green. The décor is Contemporary Evangelical— plain wooden crosses, tranquil religious canvas prints of Jesus, wooden signs with biblical quotes like PUT GOD FIRST, which is cited as Matthew 6:33, and one that really catches my eye from Micah 7:18:

FORGIVE AND FORGET

An interesting choice, no? Does Mr. Rowan really believe that, or does he need the daily reminder? Does he look up on that wall every day and think about his son? Has he come to terms with it? Or is it more the flip side? Does Mr. Rowan embrace this particular passage in the hope that the victims of the Jane Street Six will pay heed?

Mr. Rowan is in a wheelchair. Mrs. Parker sits next to him. They hold hands.

"He can't speak," Mrs. Parker tells me. "But we still communicate."

I assume that I am supposed to ask how, but I'm not all that interested.

"He squeezes my hand," she tells me anyway.

"I see," I say, though I don't. How does squeezing a hand lead to genuine communication? Does he squeeze once for yes and two for no? Does he squeeze out some kind of Morse code? I would ask, but again I can't see the relevance for me or what I'm after here. I soldier on.

"How did you and Mr. Rowan meet?" I ask.

"Through my Edie and his Billy."

"May I ask when?"

"When..." She makes a fist and puts it up to her mouth. We both look at Mr. Rowan. He stares at me. I don't know what, if anything, he sees. Oxygen cannulas run from his nostrils to a tank attached to the right side of his wheelchair. "When Edie and Billy disappeared."

"Billy and Edie were dating though, yes?"

"Oh, more than that," Mrs. Parker says. "They were engaged."

She hands me a framed photograph. Sun and time have faded the colors, but there were college students Billy Rowan and Edie Parker, cheek to cheek. They were on a beach, the ocean behind them, their smiles as bright as the sun, the sweat leaving a sheen on their deliriously happy (or so it appeared) faces.

Mrs. Parker says, "They look so in love, don't they?"

And the truth is, they do. They look young and in love and untroubled.

"They're beautiful, aren't they?"

I let myself nod.

"They were just dumb kids, Mr. Lockwood. That's what William here always says, don't you, William?"

William doesn't blink.

"Idealistic, sure. Who isn't when they're young? Billy was a big lovable goofball, and my Edie wouldn't hurt a fly. She just watched the news every night and saw those boys coming back in body bags. Her brother, my Aiden, served in Vietnam. Did you know that?"

"I did not, no."

"No, they never talked about that on the news, did they?" Her tone is bitter now. "To them, my Edie was just a crazy terrorist, like one of those Manson girls."

I try my best to look sympathetic, but this is where having "haughty resting face" becomes an issue. Myron is so good at this. He would put on a display of empathy that would make Pacino take notes.

"When was the last time you heard from Edie or Billy?"

Mrs. Parker seems taken aback by my query. "Why would you ask that?"

"I just—"

"Never. I mean, not since that night."

"Not once?"

"Not once. I don't understand. Why are you here, Mr. Lockwood? We were told you could help us."

"Help you?"

"Find our children. You were the one who found Ry Strauss."

I nod. It's not true, but alas, I go with it.

"When William and I saw Ry's picture on the news, I mean...do you want to hear something strange?"

I try to look open and accepting.

"When you found Ry Strauss..." Again she turns to look at Mr. Rowan. He doesn't turn or even react. I don't know whether he hears us or not. He may have aphasia, or he may be totally out of it, or he may have a great poker face. I simply don't know. "Do you know what the weirdest part was?"

"Tell me," I say.

"Ry was an old man now. Do you understand what I'm saying? Not old like William and me, of course. We are in our nineties, but for some reason, even though we knew better, of course, we still think of Edie and Billy as being young. Like time froze when they disappeared. Like they still look exactly like this." Mrs. Parker takes the frame back from me. Her finger touches down on her daughter's image, and her head tilts tenderly as it does so. "Do you think that's strange, Mr. Lockwood?"

"No."

She taps Mr. Rowan's hand. "William here, he was a golfer. Do you play?" she asks me.

"I do, yes."

"Then you'll get this. William used to joke that he and I were on the 'back nine' of life—now he says the two of us are

269

walking up the fairway on the eighteenth hole. See, we still call Edie and Billy 'our children.' But his Billy would have just turned sixty-five years old. My Edie would be sixty-four."

She shakes her head in disbelief.

Normally I would find all of this tedious and beside the point, but in truth, this is why I am here. I don't suspect that I will get any useful information from Mr. Rowan or Mrs. Parker. That's not really the point. What I want to do is cause a stir and see what happens. Let me explain.

If Edie Parker and Billy Rowan have been alive this whole time, chances are they would have reached out to their families at some point. Perhaps not the first year or two when the heat was on them. But it has now been over forty-five years since the Jane Street Six went on the run. If "her" Edie and "his" Billy were alive, it is reasonable to assume that at some point they would have been in touch.

That doesn't mean, of course, that Mrs. Parker (let's leave the silent Mr. Rowan out of this for now) would tell me. Just the opposite. She would do all in her power to persuade me that she has not seen her daughter in all these years, even if she had. So—is Mrs. Parker telling me the truth or is she playing me?

That's what I am trying to discern.

"How did you first hear about the"—what is the tactful word to use here?—"incident involving the Jane Street Six?"

"Do you mind if we don't call them that?"

"Sorry?"

"The Jane Street Six," Mrs. Parker says. "It makes them sound, well, like the Manson Family."

"Yes, of course." So much for my attempt at tact. "How did you hear about the incident?"

"A bunch of FBI agents crashed into my house. You'd have

thought they were looking for Al Capone the way they busted in. Scared me and Barney half to death."

I know this already. I've looked at the file. Again I'm not trying to gather information. I'm trying to gauge truthfulness and perhaps, as you'll see in a bit, cause a reaction.

I try to make my voice properly solemn. "And you never saw your daughter again?"

She nods once. No words. Not much emotion. Just a nod.

"And you never spoke to her either?"

"I spoke to her," she says.

I wait.

"That night. An hour before the FBI came."

"What did she say?"

"Edie was crying." She looks over at Mr. Rowan. He still doesn't move, but his eyes start to water. "She said something went terribly wrong."

"Did she say what?"

Mrs. Parker shakes her head.

"What else did she say?"

"That she and Billy would have to go away, maybe for a long time, maybe forever."

A single tear runs down Mr. Rowan's face. I glance at their hands. They are gripping one another's so tightly, their skin is transforming from parchment to white.

"And then?"

"That's it, Mr. Lockwood."

"Edie hung up?"

"Edie hung up."

"And?"

"And I never heard from her again. And William, he never heard from Billy."

"What do you think happened to them?" I ask.

"We are the parents. We are the worst to ask."

"I'm asking anyway."

"We thought they were dead." Mrs. Parker bites down on her lip for a moment. "I think that's why William and me got together. After our spouses died, of course. We would never before that. But it was like our relationship was an echo of our children's, like a tiny sliver of their love lived on and brought the two of us together." Then Mrs. Parker echoed my very thoughts: "If my Edie and his Billy were alive all this time, they'd have found a way to let us know. That's what we used to believe anyway."

"You don't believe that now?"

She shakes her head. "Now we don't know what to believe, Mr. Lockwood. Because we also thought Ry Strauss was dead this whole time. So now, well, that's why you're here."

With her free hand, Mrs. Parker reaches out for mine. I want to pull away—gut impulse, sorry—but I make myself stay still. Now her left hand holds my hand, her right hand holds Mr. Rowan's. We probably stay that way for a second, maybe two or three, but it feels much longer.

"Now William and I have hope again," she says, choked up. "If Ry Strauss survived all these years, maybe our children did too. Maybe Edie and Billy ran off somewhere and got married. Maybe they have children and even grandchildren of their own, and maybe, just maybe, we can all be reunited before, well, before William and me finish that eighteenth hole."

I am not sure what to say.

"Mr. Lockwood," she continues, "do you think Edie and Billy are alive?"

272

I choose my lie carefully. "I don't know. But if they are, I will find them."

She looks into my eyes. "I believe you."

I wait.

"Will you contact us when you learn the truth?" Mrs. Parker asks. "Either way. We've been waiting a long time for closure. Do you know what that's like?"

"I don't," I admit.

"Promise us you'll tell us when you learn the truth. No matter how awful. Promise us both."

And so I do.

CHAPTER 26

I sit in the passenger seat of a parked tow truck driven by a man named Gino. I know his name because the name is sewn in red cursive on his work shirt.

"So now what?" Gino asks me.

I am watching Elena Randolph, the woman who purportedly dated Arlo Sugarman at Oral Roberts University, through her storefront window at the CityGate Plaza in Rochester, New York. The other strip mall tenants include a psychic, a tax service, a Dollar Palace (cue my shudder), and a Subway (cue my double shudder). According to the flashing neon sign, Elena Randolph's beauty parlor or hair salon or whatever terminology they now use for such establishments is called Shear Lock Combs. I don't know whether to applaud or put a bullet through the sign.

Elena Randolph's 2013 Honda Odyssey has the vanity plate DO-OR-DYE. I frown. I wish Myron were here. He enjoys these sorts of puns. He and Ms. Randolph would, no doubt, get along.

"We just gonna sit here?" Gino asks.

My phone rings. It's Kabir.

"Articulate," I say.

"No calls," he says.

I am not surprised. We'd been monitoring Mrs. Parker and Mr. Rowan since I'd left a little more than an hour ago. My hope was that they were lying to me and once I left, they would reach out and warn Edie and Billy that I was searching for them. But alas, that didn't happen. Onward.

"Anything else?"

"I did some research on Trey Lyons. You were right. Ex-military. Works security in a variety of countries."

I consider that. "Put two more men on him."

Trey Lyons will be a festering problem if I don't take care of it soon. How had he put it in the van? He can't let me live, and I can't let him.

I check my watch. It's half past three p.m. and Shear Lock Combs—the name is growing on me—doesn't close until five. Enticing as the prospect of chilling with Gino for the next ninety minutes may be, I choose to forgo the pleasure and get moving.

"Wait for my signal," I tell Gino.

"You're the boss."

I step out of the tow truck and head toward the salon's door. When I enter, all eyes turn to me, though some do so via mirrors. There are three chairs, all in use. Three women clients in black chairs, three women beauticians. Two more women lounge in a waiting area. The coffee table is blanketed with gossip magazines, but both waiting women prefer their phones.

The ladies all smile at the male interloper, save one. Elena

Randolph is tall and slender. Despite being sixty-five years old, she wears tight slacks and a sleeveless top, and it works well enough on her. Her hair is gray and spiky, her face birdlike, her expression harsh. Reading glasses hang from a chain around her neck.

"Can I help you?" she asks.

"We need to talk," I say.

"I'm with a client right now."

"It's important."

"We close at five."

"No, sorry, that won't do for me."

There is what some might call an uncomfortable silence, but as I think we've established by now, I find no silences uncomfortable.

The fleshy redheaded beautician working the chair next to Elena's says, "Uh, I can finish Gertie for you."

Elena Randolph just stares at me.

The redhead bends down to an old woman whose hair is covered in tinfoil. "I can finish you up, can't I, Gertie?"

Gertie shouts, "Huh?"

Elena Randolph slowly puts down a comb and scissors, places both hands on Gertie's shoulders, bends down, and says, "I'll be right back, Gertie."

"Huh?"

Elena's eyes shoot daggers at me. I deflect them with a smile that could best be described as disarming. She marches out the door so that we are now both in front of the window of her salon. All eyes stay on us. No one goes back to work.

"And you are?" Elena asks.

"Windsor Horne Lockwood the Third," I say.

"Am I supposed to know you?"

"I believe you spoke to my assistant Kabir on the telephone."

She nods as though she expected this. "I have nothing to say to you."

"It would be wonderful if we could just skip this part," I say.

"Pardon?"

"The part where you say you won't talk to me and then I start my barrage. It really is such a waste, and in the end, you will cave."

She puts her hands on her narrow hips. "Are you a cop?"

I frown. "In these threads?"

That almost makes her smile.

"Tell me about Ralph Lewis." I hand her the scan from the yearbook with the medieval band. "You two dated at Oral Roberts University."

Elena doesn't so much as glance at the page. "I don't know what you're talking about."

I sigh dramatically. I had hoped to avoid this, but my patience is wearing thin. I raise my hand and snap my fingers. Two seconds later, the tow truck pulls into the lot and stops behind her Honda Odyssey. Gino jumps out, slips on a thick pair of gloves, and pulls a lever to start lowering the flatbed.

"Hey," Elena shouts. "What do you think you're doing?"

"That's my main man Gino," I say. "He's repossessing your car."

"He can't—"

I hand her the orders. "You are in heavy debt, Ms. Randolph. On your vehicle. On your house." I point to the salon. "On your place of business."

"I've made arrangements," she says.

"Yes, with the old collection agency. But I've purchased your debt, and so now you owe me. I've examined your financial situation and feel that you are a bad risk, ergo, per my rights, I'm foreclosing on your assets as of right now. Gino here will take the Honda. I have two men who are at this moment pad-locking the front door of your home. In ten seconds, I will open the door to your business and inform your customers that they will have to vacate the premises immediately."

Elena Randolph's wide eyes scan down the first page. "You can't do this."

I sigh, though this time with a tad less spectacle. "Your denials are tiresome." I reach for the salon's door. Elena shifts her body to block me.

"I don't know where Ralph is, I swear."

"I didn't say you did."

"So what do you want from me?"

"I would put my hand on my chest and say, 'The truth,' but I feel it would be over the top, don't you?"

Elena is not in the mood. I don't blame her. I'm not naturally a needler, but this is something else I learned from Myron. Needling keeps your adversary off-balance. "And if I don't co-operate?" she asks.

"Really? Have I not made this obvious? Your car, your house, your business will all be mine. By the way, what's the redhead's name? I'm going to fire her first."

"There are laws."

"Yes, I'm aware. They favor me."

"I know my rights. I don't have to tell you anything."

"That's correct."

The flatbed reaches the ground. Gino looks at me. I nod for him to go ahead.

"You can't..." Tears spring to Elena's eyes. "This is bullying. You just can't..."

"Of course, I can."

I don't enjoy this, but I don't mind much either. People used to buy the "everyone is equal" rationale we Americans brilliantly sold throughout our esteemed history, though lately more and more get what has always been obvious: Money tilts all scales. Money is power. This isn't a John Grisham man-against-the-system novel—in reality, the little man can't stand up to it. As I warned Elena Randolph at the get-go, she will eventually cave.

I'm not sounding like the hero of this story, am I?

Is it right that the wealthy can wield this power over you? Of course not. The system isn't fair. Reality is a bothersome thing. I have no interest in hurting Elena Randolph, but I won't lose sleep over this either. She may be harboring a fugitive. At the very least, she has information that I require. The sooner I get it, the sooner she goes back to her own life.

"You won't quit, will you?" she says.

My disarming smile returns.

"Let's go sit in the Subway."

"Subway?" I am appropriately aghast. "I'd rather have my kidney removed with a grapefruit spoon. We can talk here, so let's get to it, shall we? You knew Ralph Lewis at Oral Roberts University, correct?"

Elena wipes her eyes and nods.

"When did you last see him?"

"More than forty years ago."

"If we skip the lies—"

"I'm not lying. Let me ask you something before we get into this."

I don't like it, but it may take longer to express that point. "Go on."

"You're not a cop."

"We've already established that."

"So why are you after Ralph?"

Sometimes you play vague. Sometimes you go right for the throat. Right now, I choose the throat. "You mean Arlo Sugarman, don't you?"

The remark draws blood. Conclusion: Elena Randolph knew that Ralph Lewis was really Arlo Sugarman.

"How did you—?" She stops, sees that there's no point, shakes her head. "Never mind. He didn't do anything, you know."

I wait.

"Why are you after him? After all these years."

"You heard about Ry Strauss being found."

"Of course." She narrows her eyes. "Wait, I saw your picture on the news. You owned that painting."

"Own," I correct. "Present tense."

"I don't get why you'd be looking for Arlo."

"The art heist was not a solo job," I say.

"And you think, what, that Arlo has your other missing painting?"

"Perhaps."

"He doesn't."

"You haven't seen him in over forty years."

"Still. Arlo would not be involved in something like that."

I try dropping the bomb: "Would he be involved in the abduction and murder of young girls?"

Her mouth drops open.

"In all likelihood," I say, "Ry Strauss and an accomplice murdered my uncle and kidnapped my cousin."

"You can't think—"

"Did you meet Ry Strauss when he came to campus?"

"Listen to me," Elena says. "Arlo was a good man. He was the best man I ever knew."

"Cool," I say. "So where is he?"

"I told you. I don't know. Look, Ralph...I mean Arlo...we dated for two years at Oral Roberts. I came from a rough background. As a child, I was..." The tears start coming to her eyes, but she works hard to shake them off. "You don't want to hear my whole life story."

"Heavens, no."

She manages a chuckle at that, though I hadn't meant to be funny. "Ralph—that's what I always called him—Ralph was kind."

"When did you learn his real identity?"

"Before we dated."

That surprises me. "He confided in you?"

"I was his campus contact in the underground. I helped him get settled, found the pseudonym, whatever he needed."

"And, what, you two grew close?"

She moves close to me. "Arlo wasn't there that night."

"When you say 'that night'—"

"The night with the Molotov cocktails and all those deaths."

"Arlo Sugarman told you that?" I give her my best skeptical eyebrow arch, which is, modesty aside, a work of art. "You've seen the photograph of the Jane Street Six?"

"The famous one in the basement? Sure. But that was his last time with them. He thought it was just a prank, that they'd never really fill the bottles with kerosene. When he saw they were serious, he backed out."

"Arlo told you this?"

"He told me Ry had turned crazy. He didn't go that night."

"There are photographs from that night."

"None of him. There are six people, yes. But you don't see his face, do you?"

I give this a moment. "So how come Arlo Sugarman never told the police?" I ask.

"He did. Do you think anyone believed him?"

"It could be he was lying to you."

"He had no reason to lie to me. I was on his side anyway."

"And I suppose he didn't shoot Special Agent Patrick O'Malley either."

Elena Randolph blinks and looks toward her Honda.

"Do you know about Special Agent O'Malley?" I ask.

"Of course."

"Did you ask him about it?"

"Yes."

"And?"

"First tell that asshole to step away from my car."

I turn toward Gino and tilt my head. He backs off.

"Arlo would never talk about that shooting. He'd just shut down."

I frown, try to get back on track. "You and Arlo started dating?"

"Yes."

"Did you love him?"

Elena smiles. "What difference does that make?"

Touché.

"Where is he now?"

"I told you. I don't know."

"When was the last time you saw Arlo?"

"At graduation."

"Were you two still a couple?"

She shakes her head. "We broke up."

"May I ask why?"

"He found someone else."

I feel as though I'm supposed to say I'm sorry, but I don't.

"So you saw him at graduation?"

"Yes."

"And that was the last time?"

"That was the last time."

"Did you hear where he went after graduation?"

"No. Those are the rules with the underground. The fewer people who know, the safer he is. My part in his life was over."

Dead end.

Except it didn't feel like a dead end.

"I have no interest in hurting him," I say.

Elena glances inside the salon. Everyone is still staring at us. "How were you able to buy my debt so fast?" she asks.

"It's not hard."

"You own a Vermeer."

"My family does."

She meets my eyes and holds them. "You're superrich."

I see no reason to reply.

"I told you that Arlo left me for someone else."

"You did indeed."

"I'll give you the name under two conditions."

I steeple my fingers. "I'm listening."

"First, you promise if you find him to hear him out. If he convinces you he didn't do anything, you let him go."

"Done," I say.

It isn't as though this promise is binding. I believe in certain degrees of loyalty and "my word is my bond" stuff. I don't believe in all of it. I am bound by what I believe is best, not some false promise or faux loyalty. Either way, it is easy to say, "Done," mean it or not.

"What's the second condition?"

"You forgive all my debts."

Confession: I'm impressed. "Your debts," I say, "total more than a hundred thousand dollars."

Elena shrugs. "You're superrich."

I have to say. I like it. I like it a lot.

"If the name you give me ends up being a lie—" I begin.

"It's not."

"Do you think there is any chance they are still together?"

"I do. They seemed very much in love. Do we have a deal?"

It's going to cost me six figures, but I lose and gain that amount every minute when the markets are open. I am also philanthropic, mostly because I can afford to be. Elena Randolph and her salon seem like a worthy cause.

"We have a deal," I say.

"Mind if we orally confirm that?"

"Sorry?"

She takes out her phone and makes me record my promise. "Just putting it on the record," Elena says.

I almost tell her that my word is my bond, but we both know that's nonsense. I like her more and more. When we finish the recording, she puts the phone back in her purse.

"Okay," I say. "So who did Arlo Sugarman leave you for?"

"I didn't understand at the time," she says.

"Sorry?"

"It was the seventies. We were at an evangelical school. It just wasn't..."

"Wasn't what?" I ask. "Who did he leave you for?"

Elena Randolph picks up the photocopied image of the

medieval group from her old yearbook. She points—but not at Arlo. She points instead at the lead singer on the far left. I squint to see the blurry black-and-white image better.

"Calvin Sinclair," she says.

I look up at her.

"That's why we broke up. Arlo realized he was gay."

CHAPTER 27

I hate that I care about Ema so much.

I never wanted children because I never wanted this feeling, this feeling of horrendous vulnerability, where someone else's welfare has the ability to destroy me. I can't really be harmed, except via my biological daughter Ema. To have her in my life now—she sits across from me as we dine in my apartment overlooking Central Park—is to know worry and pain. Some would say this feeling, this parental worry, makes me more human. Whatever. Who wants to be more human? It's awful.

I had no children because I wanted no fears. I had no children because attachment is a hindrance. I worked this out analytically, so let me explain: I list the possible positives of having Ema in my life—love, companionship, someone to care for, all that—and I list the negatives—suppose something happens to her?

When I review this equation, the negatives win out.

I don't want to live in fear.

"You okay?" Ema asks me.

"Groovy," I say.

She rolls her eyes.

Her real name is Emma, but she always wears black clothes and black lipsticks and silver jewelry, and in middle school some dumb kid noted that she looked goth or "Emo" and so her classmates started calling her "Ema" and thought they were being clever and perhaps mean, but Ema turned the tables on them and embraced it. Ema is a high school senior now, but she's also taking classes in art and design in the city.

When Ema's mother, Angelica Wyatt, became pregnant, she didn't inform me. She didn't inform me upon Ema's birth. I wasn't angry or the slightest bit annoyed when Angelica finally told me. She understood how I felt about kids and respected it, but a few years back, she came clean, so to speak, for three reasons. One, she figured that enough time had passed (meh reason); two, I deserved to know the truth (ugh reason—I don't deserve anything); and three, if something happened to Angelica—she had a breast cancer scare at the time—I would be there should Ema need me (decent reason).

What's my point in telling you this?

I don't deserve this relationship with Ema. I wasn't there when it mattered, and if I had been given the choice, I wouldn't have been. That is why I call her, even in my head, my "biological" daughter. Ema is magnificent in every way, and I can take no credit for that. I do not have the right to bask in the parental glow of her greatness.

I didn't ask for this relationship. I don't really want it either—I explained to you the pros and cons—but for now, this is Ema's choice, and I need to respect that.

So, like it or not, we do meals like this.

Addendum: Ema gets me.

"I have a boyfriend," she says.

"I don't want to know."

"Don't be like that."

"It's what I'm like."

"No advice?"

I put down my fork. "Boys," I say, "and by boys I mean 'all boys'—boys are creepy."

"Duh, like who doesn't know that. What's your take on teenage sex?"

"Please stop."

Ema stifles a laugh. She likes teasing me. I don't know how to behave around her because I feel like the blood is leaving my head sometimes. At some point, Angelica decided to tell Ema about me. No great plan on Angelica's part. Perhaps Ema had reached an age. Perhaps Ema had simply asked who her father was. I don't know and it's not my place to ask.

Angelica is some mother.

You hear the following a lot: When your child is born, your life changes forever. That's why I avoided fatherhood. I don't want something in my life I care about more than me. Is that wrong? When Ema finally told me she knew—when she asked me to dance at Myron's wedding—I was knocked off-balance. It was hard to breathe. When Ema and I stopped dancing, the feeling didn't totally go away.

It still hasn't.

In the vernacular of a teenager: That suuucks.

I think about my own parents now, especially my mother, what she must have gone through when I cut her out of my life, but dwelling on past mistakes is not good for anyone, so I move on. Ema puts her fork down and looks at me, and while this is obviously some kind of projection, I swear that I see my mother's eyes.

"Win?"

"Yes?"

"Why were you in the hospital?"

"No big deal."

Ema makes a face. "Really?"

"Really."

"You're going to lie to me?" She stares at me hard. When I don't say anything, she adds, "Mom says you never wanted to be a father, right?"

"That's true."

"So don't start being one now."

"I'm not following."

"You're lying to protect me, Win."

I say nothing.

"That's what a father does."

I nod. "True."

"You never know how to act with me, Win."

"Also true."

"So cut it out. I don't need a father, you don't need a daughter. Just tell me: Why were you in the hospital?"

"Three men tried to kill me."

If I'd expected her to recoil in horror, I would have been disappointed.

Ema leans forward. Her eyes—my mother's eyes—light up. "Tell me everything."

———

And so I do.

I start with my attacking Teddy Lyons after the NCAA Final Four and my rationale for doing so. I move on to the Ry Strauss murder, the Jane Street Six, the recovery of the Vermeer, the monogrammed suitcase, Uncle Aldrich, Cousin Patricia, the Hut of Horrors, being attacked by Trey and Bobby Lyons. I talk for a full hour. Ema sits rapt through all of it. I confess that I am not this good a listener. I lose focus after a while and drift off. I get bored easily, and people see it on my face. Ema is the opposite. She is a great listener. I don't know how much I planned to tell her—I do want to be honest because, well, why not?—but something in her mannerisms, in her eyes, in her body language, makes me more open than I intended.

Come to think of it, her mother is a bit like that.

When I finish, Ema asks, "Do you have paper and anything to write with?"

"In the rolling desk, why?"

She rises and heads toward it. "I want to go through all this again in more detail and write stuff down. It helps me to see it on paper." She opens the rolling desk. When she spots the legal pads and the number-two pencils, her face lights up.

"Whoa, sweet," Ema says, grabbing a pad and three exquisitely sharpened pencils. She heads back toward me and pulls up. "What?"

"Nothing."

"Why are you smiling at me like a dork?"

"Am I?"

"Stop it, Win. It's creepy."

We go through it again. She takes notes, just like, well, you know. She tears off sheets. She slides them around the table. We lose track of time. Her mother calls. It's getting late, Angelica says. She is ready to pick Ema up.

"Not now, Mom."

I say, "Tell her I'll get you home."

Ema relays the message and hangs up. We continue. After a while, Ema says, "We need to have a more structured plan."

"What do you have in mind?" I ask.

"Let's talk about Ry Strauss first."

I sit back and look at her.

"What?" she asks.

"You've done this before."

Ema sits back too. And—I kid you not—she steeples her fingers.

"When Myron found his brother," I say. "With your relationship with Mickey. I wasn't really around for all that. I'm sorry about that."

"Win?"

"Yes?"

"Let's focus on you right now. We can deal with my past some other time."

I hesitate, pulse a-flutter, but then I acquiesce. "Okay."

"Back to Ry Strauss."

"Okay."

"We need to focus on who killed him." Ema releases the finger-steeple and starts sorting through her notes. "The CCTV picked up Ry Strauss in the basement with a bald guy."

"Yes."

"And the FBI techs can't get more details than that?"

"No. Bad pixels or something. Plus he kept his head down."

Ema thinks about it. "Interesting he'd show us he's bald."

"Pardon?"

"Why not wear a baseball cap?" she asks. "Maybe he's not really bald. Last year, at the talent show, a bunch of guys pretended they were the Blue Man Group."

"Who?"

"Not important. But they bought these skin caps that make you look bald. So maybe it's just a disguise. Maybe he wants us to look for someone bald."

I think about that.

"Also"—Ema starts shuffling through the legal pad—"that barmaid from Malachy's . . ."

"Kathleen," I say.

Quick clarification: While I did tell Ema about my conversation with Kathleen in Central Park, I did not tell her about Kathleen returning with me to this very apartment. There is being honest—and there is being ew-gross.

"Right. Kathleen." Ema has found the applicable section in her notes. "So Kathleen tells you that Ry was panicked about a robbery at his bank."

"Correct."

"Except we know that Ry didn't have any money there. His money came from that LLC your grandmother—"

"Your great-grandmother," I add.

"Hey." Ema stops and smiles at me. "That's right."

I smile too.

"Anyway"—the smile drops and Ema is all business again—"let's get back to your conversation with Kathleen. Ry, we know, never leaves his apartment except at night to meet Kathleen in the park, but suddenly he goes out in the middle of the day."

"And," I add, "on the day he gets murdered."

"Exactly. So you"—Ema grabs a yellow sheet from the upper right-hand corner of the table—"use your contacts as Mr.

Super-Rich Guy and visit the bank. The manager tells you that the robbers broke into safe deposit boxes."

"Yes."

"Which is odd, don't you think?"

I shrug. "There are a lot of valuables in those boxes."

"Yeah, I guess that could be it..." Ema says slowly.

"But?"

"But I have another theory."

I sit back and spread my hands, indicating I would like her to continue.

"Ry Strauss rented out a safe deposit box at the bank, probably under a pseudonym."

"That makes sense," I say, not yet letting on that I had figured out that much already. "Any theories on what was in it?"

"Something that identified him in some way," Ema says, tapping the pencil eraser against the tabletop. "Look, Ry Strauss probably used several identities over the years, agreed?"

"Agreed."

"So he probably needed a safe place to keep the various IDs and, who knows, maybe his real passport and birth certificate too. You wouldn't throw those things out."

"No," I say, "you wouldn't." I mull this over. "Are you saying that the bank robbers weren't really after money—that they broke into those boxes because they wanted to find Ry Strauss?"

"Possible," Ema says.

"But unlikely?"

"Unlikely," Ema repeats. "I have another theory."

I confess that I am enjoying this conversation tremendously. "I'm listening."

"Your FBI mentor, PT."

"What about him?"

Ema checks her phone for the time. "Is it too late to call him?"

"It's never too late to call him. Tell me why."

"PT said they caught one of the robbers."

"Right."

"Can you get to him?"

"Get to him?"

"Ask him questions," Ema says. "Interrogate him. Can you use your Mr. Super-Rich Guy persona to get access to this bank robber?"

I frown. "I'll pretend you didn't ask."

"Then that's our first step, Win." Her face breaks into a smile that reaches deep into my chest. "Call PT and set up the meet."

CHAPTER 28

I f you'd expect an FBI interrogation room to look like what you see on TV, you would be correct. We are in a tight windowless/airless room with a generic table in the middle. There are four generic metal chairs of which three are taken. I sit alone on one side of the table. Steve, the captured robber, and his attorney Fred are across from me.

"My client has already cut a deal in respect to the alleged bank robbery," Fred begins.

"I don't get it," Steve says. Steve is petite and small boned with the hands of a pianist or perhaps a safecracker, who's to say? His enormous bushy mustache dominates his diminutive face and monopolizes your attention. "Who the hell is this guy?"

Fred puts a hand on his forearm. "It's okay, Steve."

Steve glares down at the hand. "You mind?"

Fred's hand slides off his arm.

"What do you want?"

"Information."

"You don't look like no prosecutor." His accent is a thick combination of the Bronx and dese-and-dose.

"I'm not," I say. "I also don't care whether you're guilty or innocent or any of that. I just care about one thing."

Steve's eyes narrow. He has almost no eyebrows, which appears strange on a man with such a prominent mustache. "What's that?"

"The contents of a certain safe deposit box."

I watch closely as I say this and see immediately that he knows precisely to what I'm referring.

"I don't know what you're talking about," he says.

"You don't play much poker, do you, Steve?"

"Huh?"

"I really don't have time for any of this, so let me make an offer. You can then say 'accept' or 'decline.'" Ema had been the one to put most of it together. If I am able to get the information from this, she will feel justifiably pleased. "I want you to tell me all about the contents of that one particular safe deposit box. That is all. Just the one. In return, I will give you five thousand dollars and not blow up your immunity deal."

"The immunity deal is set in stone," Fred says. "You can't just"—air quotes—"'blow it up.'"

I just look at him and smile.

"Can he do that?" Steve's mustache bounces up and down when he speaks, like Yosemite Sam's.

"Yes, Steve, I can. Accept or decline?"

"Decline," he says, and there is fear in his voice. "I don't want the money."

He starts to pet the mustache as though it's a lapdog.

I'd expected this to go easier. "Of course you do."

"It's healthier for me if I stay quiet."

"I see."

"If it gets out I said anything, I'm a dead man."

"But it will get out," I say, "if you don't say anything."

Steve frowns. "What's that?"

"Yes," Lawyer Fred says, sitting up. "What are you talking about?"

"Simple." I lean back and steeple my fingers. "If Steve chooses not to talk to me, I will inform everyone that he did."

This confuses them both for a beat.

Then Steve snaps, "But you don't know anything."

"I know enough."

"If you know what I'm going to say, why are you trying to get me to talk?"

I sigh. "Got me there, Steve. I have a theory. Do you want to hear it?"

Fred says, "I don't like this. We agreed to see you as a courtesy and now you're throwing threats around. I don't like it. I don't like it one bit."

I look at him and put a finger to my lips. "Shhh."

Steve sits back and continues to stroke his mustache; it looks as though he and the mustache are conferring. "Okay, pretty boy, let's hear your theory."

"Well, it's not really my theory. It's—" I almost say "my daughter's," but I don't want Ema brought into this dank room in any way. I also decide to dive right into it: "When you broke into the safe deposit boxes, you came across information on the current whereabouts of one Ry Strauss."

The mustache twitch tells me I struck gold.

"Wait," Fred says, eyes widening. "*The* Ry Strauss? If this is about—"

"Shh," I say to him again, keeping my eyes on Steve. "You

then gave or sold that information, I'm not yet sure which, to an individual who killed Mr. Strauss. That, my facially hirsute friend, makes you an accessory to murder."

"What?" Steve and his mustache are appropriately still, but Fred is ready to do faux battle for his client.

"You can't prove—"

"Steve, right now, I alone know this. I won't say a word to the authorities. Not ever. I won't make it public. I won't let it get back to whomever you so dreadfully fear. You will tell me what you know, and then we will all continue our lives as though this never happened. The only change in your life? You'll be five thousand dollars richer."

No reply.

"If you choose to decline my offer or lie to me or claim you don't know what I'm talking about, I will walk down the corridor to my friends in law enforcement and tell them that you are an accessory to murder. Fred here can tell you that I have friends. Lots of friends. You don't get the chance to come in here and chitchat alone with a bank robber in custody if you don't have friends. Am I right, Fred?"

"You can't—"

"Shh." I look over at Steve.

Steve shifts in his chair. "What exactly do you want to know?"

"I want to know the contents of the safe deposit box. I want to know who else knows about the contents."

Steve looks at Fred. Fred shrugs. Steve turns his attention back to the mustache. "How about ten grand?"

I can easily afford it, but what fun would that be? "I take that as a 'no deal' then." I put two fists on the table as though to push myself to a stand. "Have a good day, gentlemen."

Steve waves his tiny hands at me. "Just . . . stop that, okay?

You promise it doesn't leave this room? I mean, forget the cops. If it gets out I talked—"

"It won't," I say.

"Promise?"

I mime crossing my heart.

Fred looks as though he's going to argue, but Steve shakes him off.

"Yeah, okay, we broke in. We all know this. And the cash in the safe is light. One of our guys got it wrong. He thought the pickup...never mind, that doesn't matter. So we are already in there, that's the hard part, so I suggest we go for the boxes. We have the tools. You interested in the technical details?"

"Of how you broke into the boxes?"

"Yeah."

"Not in the slightest," I say. "Skip ahead."

"Okay, right, so anyway, we get the stuff back to our safe house. It's in Millbrook. You ever been? Gorgeous place. Not far from Poughkeepsie."

I stare at him.

"Right, right, not important. Anyway, we get a lot of good stuff. People keep all kinds of great stuff in those boxes. Watches, diamonds."

I gesture for him to speed up with my hand. "And Ry Strauss?"

"Right, sorry. Yeah, I find this birth certificate. All official-like. I'm about to throw it out, but then I figure maybe one of the forgers can use the paper stock. It's got a raised seal too. So I hand it to Randy, that's my brother-in-law. Anyway, Randy reads it and is like 'Holy shit, let me see the rest of his stuff.' And it's just more paperwork, fake IDs, a deed on an apartment, stuff like that. I say, 'What's the big deal? Who is Ryker Strauss?'

See, that was the name on the certificate. Ryker. So Randy, he says, 'Dummy, it's Ry Strauss,' and I'm like, 'Who?' and then he explains about how famous he is and that he's been missing and all that. You want to know what our first thought was?"

I'm not sure, but I reply, "I would, yes."

"We could sell this stuff to, like, a TV station."

"A TV station?"

"You know, like one of those magazine shows or cable news shows. *60 Minutes* or *48 Hours*. It could be a huge story. But I'm thinking Geraldo too."

"Geraldo?"

"Geraldo Rivera? You know who he is?"

I let him know that I do.

Steve looks wistful. "I always liked Geraldo. Tells it like it is. And I think he got a bum rap on that whole Al Capone vault thing, do you remember that?"

I let him know that I do.

"So I'm picturing a bidding war for this information, or maybe, I don't know, like I said, I really admire Geraldo, so maybe we just make the deal with him. I bet I could meet him too. Geraldo seems like a regular guy. Tells it like it is."

"And you two have the mustache in common," I say, because I can't help myself.

"Right?" He's animated now. "See? And maybe, who knows, but maybe I can even get my picture taken with Geraldo or something. I mean, look what I'm bringing him. Geraldo, he's a regular guy. He'd be grateful. And talk about redemption. If he's the one who finds Ry Strauss, I mean, wow, people forget that stupid Capone vault was empty, am I right?"

I look at Fred. Fred shrugs.

"But Randy, he slaps me in the head. Not hard. Gentle like.

Randy and me, we're close. It's why you have to keep his name out of it. Anyway, Randy says we can't sell it to a TV show because it'll be a huge story and draw a lot of attention. The cops will be all over the place, and they'll pressure the TV network or whatever and then it'll be over for us. I argue that Geraldo would never sell us out. He wouldn't. He's not the type. But Randy, he says that even if he doesn't sell us out, there'll be so much heat on us, something will crack. I'm disappointed— I mean, I really figured Geraldo could use this—so I start defending Geraldo, but then Randy says it's too dangerous for another reason."

"That reason being?"

"Look, it's pretty well known in certain circles that the Staunch family has been after this Ry Strauss for a long time. That's what Randy tells me. The whole group of them. Rumor is, they found one of the guys years back and the old man, well, Nero skinned him alive. Literally. Like, it took weeks for the guy to die. Scary stuff. That's why. That's why you can't talk, okay?"

Steve is stroking the mustache like a long-lost lover.

"Okay," I say. "I won't talk."

"Now my crew, we don't work for the Staunches. We steer clear, you know what I'm saying? We don't want no trouble. But Randy, he sees a chance to do them a favor and maybe make a few dollars too."

"So Randy sold it to the Staunches?"

"That was the plan, yeah."

"The plan?"

"I mean, I assume it all went okay, but I got picked up a month ago. It's not like I'm going to ask Randy about it."

CHAPTER 29

The Staunch Craft Brewery was packed with—I shouldn't stereotype—annoying hipsters. Located in a tony warehouse in Williamsburg, the epicenter of the hipster, the bar drew a crowd in their twenties, maybe early thirties, who were trying so hard not to appear mainstream that they simply redefined the mainstream. The men had hipster glasses (you know what they are); asymmetrical facial hair; flimsy scarfs draped loosely around their necks; suspenders on strategically ripped jeans; retro concert tees that struggled to be ironic; man buns or a potpourri of awful hats, such as the cable-knit slouchy beanie, the Newsie flat cap, and of course, the carefully tilted fedora (unwritten hipster rule: Only one guy per table can wear the fedora at a time); and of course, boots that could be high or low or any hue but somehow you'd still label them hipster boots. The female of the species offered up a wider range—second-hand vintage pickups, flannels, cardigans, unmatching layers, acid wash, fishnets—the rule being nothing mainstream, which again makes them just mainstream with a desperation stench.

I'm being too harsh.

The many, many beers on tap—IPAs, stout, lager, pilsner, porter, autumnal, winter, summer (beers now have seasons), orange, pumpkin, watermelon, chocolate (I almost looked for a Cap'n Crunch artisanal)—are being served in mason jars rather than glasses or mugs. One entrance has a sign saying BREWERY TOUR. The other reads TASTING ROOM, the crowd of which had spilled outside to the sticky picnic tables. As I pass through them, I hear a swirl of the following terminology: bro, bae, edible, gluten, FOMO, kale, sesh, self-care, fleek, screenplay, kombucha, I can't even, the struggle is real.

Clarification: I do not literally hear all those terms, but I think I do.

In the old days, gangsters hung out in bars or restaurants or strip joints. Times, they do a-change. As I duck inside, a pretty young barmaid with pigtails in cutoff shorts approaches me.

"Oh man, you have to be Win," she says. "Follow me."

The floors are concrete, the lighting low. In the right-hand corner, someone spins vinyl records. Eco-friendly yoga mats that appear to be as comfortable as tweed undergarments are laid out to the left; a flexible man with a beard the approximate dimensions of a lobster bib leads the mildly inebriated through a sun salutation. The barmaid takes me down a corridor lined with beer kegs and for-sale merchandise until we reach a big metal door. The barmaid knocks and says to me, "Stay here."

She saunters away before I can offer a tip. The door opens. It is, I think, the big man who accompanied Leo Staunch to my hospital room, but it is hard to say. I can only tell you that he is north of six six with wide shoulders and a hairline so thick and low that it seems to start at his eyebrows. He, too, sports the prerequisite facial hair and a fedora that looks too small on his head, like one of those baseball-shape-headed mascots with a tiny cap.

"Come in," he says.

I do. He closes the door behind me. There are four other hipsters in the room, all offering up tough hipster glares behind hipster glasses.

"I'll need your weapons," says the big hipster who opened the door.

"I left them in the car."

"All of them?"

"All of them."

"How about that razor you got tucked up your sleeve?"

Big Hipster grins at me. I grin back.

"All of them," I repeat.

The big hipster asks for my phone. I make sure the passcode is locked and hand it over. He then nods toward another hipster. This second hipster produces a handheld metal detector and starts to run it over my body until a voice says, "Let it go. If he does something stupid, all of you shoot him, okay?"

I recognize Leo Staunch from his hospital visit. He waves for me to join him, and I enter an office that if I read up more about the subjects, I would probably describe as "Zen" or "feng shui." It's white with orbs and a huge window with a view of a fountain in a courtyard. There are also, I note, handicap railings and a wheelchair ramp.

When the door closes, I can no longer hear the sounds from the brewery. It is as though we've entered another realm. He asks me to sit. I do. He goes around a see-through Plexiglas desk and takes the chair across from me. His chair is a few inches higher than mine, and I want to roll my eyes at the weak attempt at intimidation, except for one thing:

Leo Staunch was right about one thing when he visited me. I am not bulletproof. I am also not suicidal, and while I have taken way too many chances with my personal safety, I like to think that I do so with a modicum of discretion.

In short, I need to be careful here.

"So," Leo Staunch begins, "you know where Arlo Sugarman is?"

"Not yet."

Leo Staunch frowns. "But on the phone—"

"Yes, I lied. Alas, I'm not the only one."

He takes his time with that. "Tread carefully, Mr. Lockwood."

"Why?"

"What?"

"Come now, you don't hit me as the type who wants things sugarcoated, so let me state this plainly. When you visited me at the hospital, you assured me that you had nothing to do with Ry Strauss's death."

I don't know what reaction I'm expecting from Leo Staunch. Denial perhaps. Faux surprise possibly. But instead he waits me out.

I add, "That wasn't true, was it?"

"What makes you say that?"

"I've come across some new information."

"I see," Staunch says, spreading his hands. "Let's hear it."

"Did you kill Ry Strauss?"

"That's a question," he says, "not new information."

"Did you?"

"No."

"Did you know Ry Strauss lived in the Beresford before his death?"

"Again no." He runs his hand through his hair to slick it back

305

down. Leo Staunch has that kind of waxy skin that suggests something in the cosmetic/Botox family. "What is your new information, Mr. Lockwood?"

"Not long before the murder," I say, "you were told that Ry Strauss lived in the Beresford."

He crosses his legs and starts tapping his chin with his index finger. "Is that a fact?"

I wait.

"Tell me how you know this."

"The how is irrelevant."

"Not to me." Leo Staunch tries to give me the hard eyes now, but the spark won't flame. "You come into my place of work under false pretenses. You call me a liar. I think I'm owed an explanation, don't you?"

I do not wish to get Steve in trouble, but here we are. "There was a bank robbery," I say.

His expression is unreadable, cold stone. I spend the next minute or two explaining about the bank robbery and the safe deposit box belonging to Ry Strauss. I keep names out of it, but really, how difficult would it be for a man like Leo Staunch to find out who my source is?

"So your contact," Leo Staunch says when I finish. "He claims that he sold the information on Ry Strauss to me."

"Or gave."

"Or gave." Staunch nods as though this suddenly makes sense to him. "So what do you want from me?"

The question throws me. "I want to know whether you killed Ry Strauss."

"Why?"

"Pardon?"

"What difference does it make?" Staunch continues, but I

can feel a shift in the air. "Let's pretend your source is telling you the truth. Suppose he gave us this information. Suppose, hypothetically, I decided to use it to avenge my sister. So what? Are you going to arrest me?"

I thought the question was rhetorical, so I wait. He does the same. After a few seconds pass, I finally say, "No."

"Are you going to tell the cops on me?"

My turn again: "No."

"So you and I, we need to focus on what's important here."

"And what might that be?" I ask.

"Finding Arlo Sugarman." His voice is odd now, faraway. Something in the room has definitely changed, but I am not sure what to make of it. Staunch suddenly spins his chair, so his back is to me. Then, in a low voice, he adds, "What difference does it make if I killed Ry Strauss?"

I find this disconcerting. I am not sure how to proceed. I decide to heed his earlier warning and thus tread carefully. "There is more to this."

"More to Ry Strauss's death?"

"Yes."

"You mean, like the art heist?"

"For one."

"What else?"

Do I want to get into Cousin Patricia and the Hut of Horrors with him? No, I do not.

"It would help me," I say with as much care as I can muster, "to know the full truth. You went to avenge your sister. I understand that."

I hear a chuckle. "You don't understand at all."

There is a heaviness in his tone, a profound and unexpected sadness. Leo Staunch stands now, still not facing me, and moves to the floor-to-ceiling window. "You think that I want you to find Arlo Sugarman so I can kill him."

It was not a question, so I choose not to answer.

"That's not the case at all."

His back is still to me. I wait and stay silent.

"I'm going to tell you something now that will never leave this room," he says. He finally turns around and faces me. "Do I have your word?"

So many promises made today. Two of our biggest delusions are that "loyalty" and "keeping promises" are admirable qualities. They are not. They are oft an excuse to do the wrong thing and to protect the wrong person because you are supposed to be "a man of your word" or have a bond with or allegiance to someone who deserves neither. Loyalty is too often used as a replacement for morality or ethics, and yes, I know how strange it may sound to hear me lecture you thusly, but there you go.

"Of course," I say, lying with ease (but not immorally). And then, because words are so very, very cheap, I thicken it with, "You have my word."

Leo Staunch is facing the window. "Where to begin?"

I do not say, "At the beginning," because that would (a) be a cliché and (b) really, I would rather he just get to it quickly.

"I was sixteen years old when Sophia was killed."

Sigh. So much for getting to it quickly.

"She was twenty-four. It was just the two of us—me and Soph. After my mother had her, the doctors told my mom that she couldn't have any more kids, but eight years later, surprise, there I was." I see him smile via the reflection in the window. "You can't believe how much they all spoiled me." Leo Staunch shakes his head. "I don't know why I'm telling you this."

I see no reason to interject here, so I stay quiet.

"You know who we are, right?"

Curious question. "You mean, your family?"

"Exactly. The Staunch family. Let me give you some quick background. Uncle Nero and my dad were brothers. They were super close. With these kinds of, shall we say, enterprises, you need one leader. Uncle Nero was older and nastier, and my dad, who everyone tells me was a gentle soul, was happy to stay behind the scenes. Still that didn't save him. When my dad got whacked back in 1967, well, maybe you know about the outcome."

I do a bit. There was a mob war. The Staunches won.

"So Uncle Nero, he became like a father to me. Still is. You know he comes in here a few times a week? At his age, amazing. He had a stroke so it's hard for him. He uses a wheelchair."

I look at the handicap railings. I remember the ramp at the door.

"Let me skip ahead, okay?" he says.

"Please."

"When those college kids killed my sister, no one had to say anything because we all understood: The family was going to avenge Sophia's death. In Uncle Nero's eyes, this was worse than what happened to my father. That, at least, was business. The Jane Street Six to us were a bunch of spoiled, overeducated, anti-war, draft-dodging, leftist pinkos. It made Sophia's death, in our eyes, even more senseless."

I could see that. Someone like Nero Staunch would see these rich, pampered kids—students who would look down at someone like him, make him feel inferior—and feel even more enraged.

"So Uncle Nero put out the word. He started searching for them. He made it very clear that anyone who gave us

309

information on any of the Jane Street Six—or heck, could prove he killed one—would be richly rewarded."

"I bet you received some leads," I say.

"We did. But you want to know something surprising?"

"Sure."

"None panned out. For two years, we got nothing."

"And then?"

"And then Lake Davies got caught or turned herself in, I don't even know which. Lake understood the score. Once she got into the prison system, we would be able to get to her. And if by some chance we couldn't—if they put her in protective custody, for example—we would get her when she got out. So her lawyer came to us to deal."

"Davies gave you information," I say.

"Yes."

This all made sense to me. Lake Davies would make a deal with the Staunches so as to protect herself. When she was released from prison, she then changed identities and, in short, went back undercover just in case the Staunches chose to no longer honor their deal.

I remembered what Lake Davies had said to me when we met up at her pet hotel, the Ritz Snarl-Fun. I asked her whether she'd gone into hiding in West Virginia because she feared Ry Strauss would find her. Her reply:

"Not just Ry."

"So who did Davies give you?" I ask.

A shadow crosses his face. "Lionel Underwood."

The room falls silent.

I ask, "Where was he?"

"Does it matter?"

"No, not really."

"I always figured they were hiding on hippie communes or something. But Lionel, maybe because he was Black or something, I don't know, he was living under the name Bennett Leifer in Cleveland, Ohio. He worked as a trucker. He was married. His wife was pregnant."

"Did the wife know who he really was?"

"I don't know. Doesn't matter, does it?"

"No," I say. "I guess not."

"You can probably guess the rest."

"You killed him?"

Leo Staunch says nothing, which says everything. He collapses back into the chair hard, as though someone had taken out his knees. For a few moments, we just sit there in silence. When Leo speaks again, his voice is low.

"We own the entire row of warehouses on this side of the street. There is a building two doors down. It's a muffler shop now, but back then..." His eyes close. "It took three days."

"You were there?"

His eyes are still closed. He nods his head. I am not sure what to make of it, so for now, I go with the obvious. Lionel Underwood is dead. Of the Jane Street Six, I now know the fate of three—Ry Strauss is dead, Lionel Underwood is dead, Lake Davies is alive. I still have three to go—Arlo Sugarman, Billy Rowan, Edie Parker.

There is another issue, a bigger issue, ablaze right now: Why has Leo Staunch decided to tell me this? Some may believe that this is a very bad sign for me, that now that I know the truth, Leo Staunch will have no choice but to kill me. I don't believe that. Even if I was foolhardy enough to run to the feds, what could they do after all these years? What could they prove?

Moreover, if Leo Staunch's plans include killing me, there would be no reason for the confession first.

"I assume," I continue, "that you or your uncle asked Mr. Underwood about the whereabouts of the other Jane Street Six."

He stares off behind me, unseeing. His eyes are shattered marbles. "We did more than ask."

"And?"

"And he didn't know."

"Did he tell you anything else?"

"By the end," Leo Staunch says in a hollow voice, "Lionel Underwood told us everything."

He is flashing back to that time in the now-muffler shop. His face is losing color.

"Like what?"

"He didn't throw a Molotov cocktail."

"You believe him?"

"I do. He broke. Entirely. By the second day, he begged for death." His eyes have tears; he blinks them away. "You want to know why I'm telling you this."

I wait.

"For a while, I convinced myself I was okay with it. I got revenge for my sister. Maybe Lionel Underwood didn't throw this explosive, but as my uncle reminded me, he's still guilty. But I couldn't sleep. Even now, all these years later, I still hear Lionel's screams at night. I see his contorted face." His eyes find mine. "I'm not afraid of violence, Mr. Lockwood. But this kind of, I don't know, vigilantism, I guess..." He wipes one eye with a forefinger. "You want to know why I'm telling you this? Because I don't want the same thing to happen to Arlo Sugarman. Whatever his sins, I want him captured and brought to trial. I lost my taste for revenge." He leans closer to me. "The reason why I am asking you to find Arlo Sugarman is, so I can protect him."

Do I believe this?

I do.

"One problem," I say.

"Oh, there are more than one," Leo says with the sad chuckle.

"My bank robber source was adamant. He sold you the information on Ry Strauss's whereabouts."

"You believe him?"

"I do."

Leo Staunch considers this. "Did your source say that he sold the information to me—or did he say he sold it to a Staunch?"

I am about to reply when my gaze gets snagged on those handicap railings. I stare at them a second before I turn back to Leo. "You think he sold it to Uncle Nero?"

"I don't know."

"Your uncle had a stroke. He's in a wheelchair."

"Yes."

"But that doesn't mean he couldn't hire someone to do the job."

"I don't think he did."

"Then what?" I ask.

"Just find Arlo Sugarman."

"What about the others?"

"When you find Arlo Sugarman," Leo Staunch says, heading toward the door, "you'll find all the answers."

CHAPTER 30

T he Reverend Calvin Sinclair, graduate of Oral Roberts University and, if Elena Randolph is to be believed, onetime lover of Ralph Lewis aka Arlo Sugarman, exits the front door to St. Timothy's Episcopal Church. He walks a British bulldog on a ropy leash. They say that pet owners oft look like their pets, and that seems to be the case here. Both Calvin Sinclair and his bulldog companion are squat, portly-yet-powerful, with a wrinkled face and a pushed-in nose.

St. Timothy's Episcopal Church is located on a surprisingly large plot of land in Creve Coeur, Missouri, part of Greater St. Louis. The sign out front tells me that services are Saturday at 5:00 p.m., Sunday at 7:45—9:00—10:45 a.m. In smaller print, it notes that prayer services will be led by "Father Calvin" or "Mother Sally."

The Reverend Sinclair spots me as I get out of the back of a black car. With his free hand, he shields his eyes. He looks to be his age—sixty-five—with thin wisps of hair on his scalp. When he'd opened the church door, he wore a practiced wide smile, the kind of thing you put on just in case someone is around and you want to appear kind and friendly, which—who am I to judge yet?—Calvin Sinclair may very well be. When he sees me, however, the smile crumbles to dust. He adjusts his wire spectacles.

I start toward him. "My name is—"

"I know who you are."

I arch one eyebrow to register my surprise. Calvin Sinclair's voice has a nice timbre to it. I am sure that it sounds celestial coming from a pulpit. I did not call beforehand or announce my arrival. Kabir had contacted a local private investigator who assured us that Sinclair was at the church. Had Sinclair traveled somewhere else whilst I was in the air, said private detective would have followed him so I could have confronted him wherever I saw fit.

The British bulldog waddles toward me.

"Who's this?" I ask.

"Reginald."

Reginald stops and regards me with suspicion. I bend down and scratch behind his ears. Reginald closes his eyes and takes it in.

"Why are you here, Mr. Lockwood?"

"Call me Win."

"Why are you here, Win?"

"I assume you know why."

He nods with great reluctance. "I suppose I do."

"How do you know my name?" I ask.

"When Ry Strauss was found murdered," he begins, "I knew that would mean renewed interest in..." Calvin Sinclair stops and squints up at either the sun or his version of God. "You were on the news a lot."

"Ah," I say.

"Ry Strauss stole your paintings."

"Seems so."

"Naturally, I followed the story with interest."

"With personal interest?"

"Yes."

I was glad that the Reverend Sinclair was not going to give me a giant song-n-dance pretending that he had no idea why I was here, had never heard of Arlo Sugarman—all the verbal red tape I had feared having to waste time slicing through.

"Come along, Reginald."

He gives the leash a gentle snap. I stop scratching Reginald behind the ears. They start walking. I stay with them.

"How did you find me?" he asks.

"Long story," I say.

"You're a very rich man, from what I've read. My guess is, you are used to getting what you want."

I don't bother to reply.

Reginald stops by a tree and urinates.

"Still," Sinclair continues. "I'm curious. What part of our life gave us away?"

I see no reason not to tell him. "Oral Roberts University."

"Ah. Our start. We were more careless then. You found Ralph Lewis?"

"Yes."

He smiles. "That was three aliases ago. Ralph Lewis became Richard Landers and then Roscoe Lemmon."

"Same initials," I say.

"Perceptive."

We are behind the church now, heading toward a path in the woods. I wonder about that. I wonder where we are going, whether there is a destination or whether the Reverend Sinclair is just taking his mighty Reginald on their daily walk. I don't bother asking. He is talking, and that, after all, is what I want.

"After we graduated," Sinclair says, "Ralph and I went on a missionary trip to what was then known as Rhodesia. It was supposed to be a one-year deal, but with the heat still on him, we ended up staying on the continent for the next twelve years. He and I had different interests. I was religiously focused, albeit in a much more liberal way than what we'd learned at Oral Roberts. Ralph despised religion. He had no interest in conversions. He wanted to work the classics: feed and clothe the poor, get them access to clean water and medical care." He looks at me. "Are you a religious man, Win?"

"No," I tell him.

"May I ask what you believe?"

I tell him the same thing I tell any religious worshipper—be they Christian, Jew, Muslim, Hindu: "All religions are superstitious nonsense, except, of course, yours."

He chuckles. "Good one."

"Reverend," I begin.

"Oh, don't call me that," Sinclair says. "In the Episcopal tradition we say 'the reverend' as an adjective, a descriptive. It's not a title."

"Where is Arlo Sugarman?" I ask.

We are in the woods now. If we look straight up, we can see the sun, but the trees are thick anywhere off this path. "There is no way I can convince you to just go home and let this go, is there?"

"None."

"I figured as much." He nods, resigned. "That's why I'm taking you to him."

"To Arlo?"

"To Roscoe," he corrects. "You know something funny? I've never called him Arlo. Not once in the more than four decades we've been together. Not even in private. I think it's because I was always scared that I would mess up and call him that in front of other people. This was always our big fear, of course—that this day would come."

We are getting deeper into the woods now. The path narrows and veers down a steep incline. Reginald the Bulldog stops in his tracks. Sinclair sighs and lifts the dog with a huge grunt. He carries Reginald to the landing below.

"Where are we going?" I ask.

"He didn't do it, you know. Arlo—yes, I'm going to call him that—backed out. He wanted to draw attention to the war by throwing what appeared to be Molotov cocktails, but in reality, the bottles would only be filled with water dyed red to look like blood. Just something symbolic. When Arlo realized that Ry meant to really firebomb the place, they had a falling-out."

"Yet," I say, "he ran and hid anyway."

"Who would have believed him?" Sinclair counters. "Do you know how scary-crazy it was those first few days?"

"Curious," I say.

"What's that?"

"Are you also going to claim that he didn't kill a federal agent?"

Sinclair's jowly jaw is set, but he doesn't stop walking. "Patrick O'Malley."

I wait.

"No, I won't claim that. Arlo shot Special Agent O'Malley."

There is a clearing up ahead. I can see a lake.

"We're almost there," he tells me.

The lake is gorgeous, serene, still, almost too still, not the slightest ripple. The blue sky reflects off it in a perfect mirror. Calvin Sinclair stops for a moment, sucks in a deep breath, and then says, "Over here."

There is a wooden bench so rustic that it still has bark on it. It faces the lake, but more to the point, it faces a small tombstone. I approach it and read the carving:

IN MEMORY OF

R.L.

"LIFE IS NOT FOREVER. LOVE IS."

BORN JANUARY 8, 1952—DIED JUNE 15, 2011

"Lung cancer," Calvin Sinclair tells me. "And no, he never smoked. We found out in March of that year. He was dead less than three months later."

I stare at the tombstone. "He's buried here?"

"No. This is where I spread his ashes. The congregation built the bench and memorial."

"Did the congregation know you two were lovers?"

"It's not like we made a big thing of it," he says. "You have to understand. When we fell in love in the seventies, being gay wasn't accepted in the slightest. Between hiding his real identity and our orientation, we were used to being deceptive. We lived our whole lives that way." Calvin Sinclair puts his hand to his chin, his eyes gazing upward. "But by the end, yes, I think a lot of the congregation knew. Or maybe that's wishful thinking."

I look at the lake. I try to picture it—Arlo Sugarman starting his life as a Jewish kid from Brooklyn and ending up here, in the woods behind this church. I almost see it as a film montage complete with melodramatic score.

"Why didn't you ever say anything?" I ask.

"I thought about it. I mean, he was dead. No one could hurt him anymore."

"So?"

"So I'm not dead. I harbored a fugitive. You tell me: How do you think the FBI would feel about that?"

He has a point.

"There is one more thing," Sinclair says, "but I doubt you'll believe me."

I turn to him. "Try me."

"Arlo didn't want to kill that agent."

"Well, yes, I'm sure that's true."

"But that agent," he continues. "He shot first."

A cold trickle slithers down my back. I want to ask for him to elaborate, but I don't want to lead him either. So I wait.

"Special Agent O'Malley came in through the back door. Alone. Without a partner. Without backup. He didn't give Arlo a chance to surrender. He just fired." He tilts his head. "Have you ever seen old photographs of Arlo?"

I nod numbly.

"He had that huge Afro back then. The bullet, Arlo told me, traveled right through it. Literally parted his hair. Then—and only then—did Arlo fire back."

Two conversations echo and then ricochet through my head.

First, Leo Staunch's words about his uncle came back to me:

"He made it very clear that anyone who gave us information on any of the Jane Street Six—or heck, could prove he killed one—would be richly rewarded."

Second, my conversation with PT when this all began:

"We only sent two agents to the brownstone."
"No backup?"
"No."
"Should have waited."

Why hadn't they waited for backup?

The answer seems fairly clear now.

Without another word, I turn and start back down the path.

I know it all now. Leo Staunch had hinted as much to me. He told me when I found Arlo Sugarman, I would find all my answers. He was right, I realize. In terms of the Jane Street Six, there is still a bit of cleanup work to do, but I came here for answers and now I have them.

Calvin Sinclair calls after me. "Win?"

I don't stop.

"Are you going to tell?" he calls out.

But I still don't stop.

CHAPTER 31

B ack on the jet, I get three calls.

The first I see incoming is from PT. I don't want to talk to him quite yet, not when I'm so close to the end game, and so I let it go into the voicemail. This will no doubt displease PT, who will quickly deduce that I am avoiding him, but I can live with that.

The second call is from Kabir.

"Articulate," I say, opening up the browser on my laptop. Kabir will normally email me all relevant backing documentation because, again, like my daughter, I am visual.

But his reply catches me off guard: "I have Pierre-Emmanuel Claux on the line. He sounds upset."

It takes me a second to remember the name of the art curator and restorer whom I had insisted the FBI use to authenticate and tenderly care for the family's Vermeer. I tell Kabir to patch the call through.

"Mr. Lockwood?"

"Speaking?"

"This is Pierre-Emmanuel Claux at the Institute of Fine Arts at NYU." I hear the muffled panic in his tone. "You asked me to look into a painting the FBI recently located for authentication and condition purposes—*The Girl at the Piano* by Johannes Vermeer."

"Yes, of course."

"When can you get to the institute, Mr. Lockwood?"

"Is this urgent?"

"It is, yes."

"Is there an issue with the Vermeer?"

"I think it's better if we discuss this in person." I hear the quake in his voice. "As soon as possible, please."

I check the time. Depending on traffic, it should take about three hours in total.

"Will you still be there?" I ask him.

"The institute will be closed, but I won't leave until you arrive."

The third call is from Ema.

After I offer up my customary greeting, Ema asks, "Any updates?"

I fill her in on the day's happenings. I don't hold back. I don't sugarcoat. I do feel my heart swell, but alas, so what? As Ema might say, "Get over it." I finish by telling her I'm heading straight to New York University Institute of Fine Arts' Conservation Center across Central Park from the Dakota.

"Oh good," Ema says. "That's why I called."

"Go on."

"I'm going over the FBI witness transcripts for the art heist at Haverford," she continues.

"And?"

"And the early investigators seemed convinced that it was

an inside job, most notably the night guard, Ian Cornwell. In the end, they had no proof so they dropped it."

I tell her I know all this.

Ema says, "You questioned Cornwell, right?"

"I did. He's a political science professor at Haverford now."

"Yeah, I saw that. What did you think of him?"

I do not want to prejudice her reaction. "What do you think of him?"

"I think the original investigators got it right. There is just no way it could have worked the way Ian Cornwell claims."

"Yet," I say, "those investigators couldn't make the case."

"Doesn't mean he didn't do it."

"Doesn't mean that at all," I agree. I hear street noise. "Where are you?"

"I'm heading into the subway, so I can catch the train home."

"I'll have someone drive you."

"I'd rather do it this way, Win. Anyway, I don't know how, but we need to get Ian Cornwell to talk. He's the key. Oh, and let me know what the art conservator tells you."

Ema hangs up. I replay the conversation in my head, and I know that as I do, I have a smile on my face. I close my eyes and try to nap for the duration of the flight. That won't happen. I am feeling itchy, antsy, and I know why. I take out my phone and find my favorite app. I set up a rendezvous for tonight at midnight with username "Helena." Midnight is later than I normally do, but it seems today will be a hectic day.

NYU's Institute of Fine Arts is located on Fifth Avenue in the French-styled James B. Duke House, one of the few surviving "millionaire mansions" from New York's Gilded Age. James Duke—yes, my beloved alma mater, Duke University, is named for his father—made his fortune as a founding partner

in the American Tobacco Company, modernizing the manufac-
turing and marketing of cigarettes. The old adage is that behind
every great fortune there is a great crime—or, as in this case,
if not a great crime, the fortune was certainly built on a pile of
dead bodies.

The institute has a boatload of security for obvious reasons.
I pass through it all and find Pierre-Emmanuel Claux pacing
alone in the second-floor conservatory. He wears a white lab
coat and latex gloves. When he turns toward me, I can see
something akin to terror on his face.

"Thank God you're here."

The conservatory is a hybrid of the old-school mansion and
a state-of-the-art research center. There are long tables and
special lighting and tapestries and paintbrushes and scalpels
and what look like microscopes and dental tools and medical
testing equipment.

"I'm sorry for the dramatics, but I think..."

His voice fades out. I don't see the Vermeer, that image of
the girl at the piano. The longest table holds but one item, a
possible painting facedown, and it is approximately the correct
size of the Vermeer. Next to it sits a Phillips-head screwdriver
and several screws.

Pierre-Emmanuel walks toward it. I follow.

"First of all," he says, his tone steadier now, "the painting is
authentic. This is indeed *The Girl at the Piano* by Vermeer, most
likely painted in 1656." There is a hushed awe in his voice. "I
can't tell you what an honor it is to be in its presence."

I give him this moment of silence, as though this is a
religious service, which, for him, may be apropos. When I meet
his eyes, Pierre-Emmanuel clears his throat. "Let me get to
why I so urgently needed to see you." He points to the back

of the painting. "First off, there was a Masonite backing board covering the entire reverse of your Vermeer. It's not original obviously, but Masonite backings are not uncommon. They protect the painting from dust and physical impact."

He glances over at me. I nod to show that I am listening.

"The backing board is screwed in, so I carefully took out the screws and removed the Masonite in order to inspect the painting more thoroughly. That's the backing board over there."

He points to what looks like a thin school blackboard. On it, I can see the faded Lockwood family crest. Pierre-Emmanuel turns his attention back to the flip side of the Vermeer. "You can see here the stretcher up against the back of the canvas. That's not uncommon either, but the thing is, first you need to remove the backing. Then you need to look under the stretcher. It's not easy to do. But that's where someone hid them—under a screwed-in backing board and taped between the stretcher and the canvas."

"Hid what?" I ask.

He has it in his gloved hand. "This envelope."

It had probably started life as white, but it is now yellowed to the point of being near manila.

"At first," he continues, his words a rushed babble now, "I was so excited. I thought maybe it was a letter of historical importance. Oh, and it wasn't sealed. I wouldn't have slit it open or looked inside, if that was the case. I would have just put it to the side."

"So what was inside?" I ask.

Pierre-Emmanuel leads me over to a desk and points. "These."

I look down at the brown yet transparent images.

"They're film negatives," Pierre-Emmanuel continues. "I

don't know how old they are, but most people take digital pictures nowadays. And those screws hadn't been removed in years."

The shape of the negatives appears odd to my layman's eyes. You usually think of negatives as being rectangular. These, however, are perfect squares.

I look at Pierre-Emmanuel. His lip is now trembling.

"I assume you looked at them."

His voice is a terrified whisper. "Only three," he manages to tell me. "That's all I could handle."

He offers me a set of latex gloves. I snap them on and turn on his lamp. I carefully lift one of the negatives with the pads of my thumb and forefinger. I raise it to the light. Pierre-Emmanuel has taken a step back, but I know that he is watching my face. I show nothing, but I feel the jolt everywhere. I gently put the negative back and move to a second. Then a third. Then a fourth. I still show nothing, but there is an eruption going on inside. I won't lose control. Not yet.

But the rage is coming. I will need a way to channel it.

After I view ten of the negatives, I say to him, "I'm sorry you had to see these."

"Do you know who those girls are?"

I do. More than that, I know where the photographs were taken.

In the Hut of Horrors.

CHAPTER 32

It is dark by the time I arrive at the faculty housing area of Haverford College.

I drove myself from the airport because I want no one around. I drive fast. I drive with a fury. When Ian Cornwell sees me at his door at this late hour, he is unsure how to react. Part of him still fears my name and how important my family is to this institution—but more of him, I have come to believe, wants nothing to do with me or the awful past I keep dragging back to his doorstep.

"It's late," Ian Cornwell tells me as I stand on his stoop. He blocks the door so that I cannot enter. "I already told you everything I know."

I nod. Then without warning, I punch him hard in the stomach. He folds at the waist as though it has hinges. I shove him inside and close the door behind me. The punch was well placed, so as to knock the wind out of him. His eyes are wide with fear as he retches, seeking air. I know that I should feel bad, but as I explained previously, violence gives me a rush. It would be dumb to lie and pretend otherwise.

He drops to the ground. Having the wind knocked out of you just means the impact to your celiac plexus causes a temporary diaphragmatic spasm. It doesn't last. I pull over a chair and sit next to him. I wait until he can breathe.

Through gritted teeth, Cornwell says, "Get out."

"Look at these."

Pierre-Emmanuel helped me make rudimentary reproductions of two of the negatives. I drop them next to him. He looks at them and then he looks back at me in abject horror.

"These were hidden in the frame of the Vermeer," I say.

"I don't understand."

"These girls," I continue, "are victims from the Hut of Horrors."

His eyes go wide again, a mixture of fear and total confusion. It doesn't compute for him. Not yet. "What does that have to do—?"

"I don't have time for this, Ian, so I'll ask you one more time. What really happened the night of the heist?"

He puts his hand on his stomach and rolls into a sit. The stomach will be sore tomorrow. I can see his mind searching for a way out, and what that tells me, with very little doubt, is that Ian Cornwell knows more than he is saying. I say "very little doubt" rather than "no doubt" because, of course, I can be fooled as easily as anyone. The stupidest men are the ones who think they can't be wrong. The stupidest men are the ones who are most sure. The stupidest men are the ones who don't know what they don't know.

But right now, if I were to hypothesize, Professor Ian Cornwell is stalling so that he can rummage through all the possibilities. Showing him two sickening images of the fifteen-year-old victim we will call Jane Doe—in both she is naked,

329

on her stomach, and trussed with barbed wire—was, of course, designed to shock him into revealing the truth. Now, however, I wonder whether I went too far, if the images will cause paralysis rather than openness. My concern now is that his brain is working thusly: Suppose, he may be wondering, he does confess to something involving the art heist—will that now link him to these unspeakable crimes? Could he end up being charged as an accessory? Silence has worked for him so far. Silence eventually got the FBI to leave him be. Silence has kept him out of prison.

His wheels are churning. I give him another second, perhaps two, and then he looks up at me with pleading eyes.

"I wish I could help you," Ian Cornwell predictably begins, "but I'm telling the truth. I don't know anything."

Many martial arts specialize in what we commonly call pressure points—that is, pressing or striking sensitive nerve clusters in order to cause pain. I would not advise using them in a real fight. In a real fight, you are in constant motion, and your opponent is in constant motion. That is two moving targets, thereby making strikes with the pinpoint accuracy these techniques rely upon unrealistic. Pressure points, when done well, can cause excruciating pain, though you never know your opponent's pain threshold. Opponents often react by squirming away from such a grip with suddenly alarming strength.

My—pardon the pun—(pressure) point?

Pressure points work best in more passive situations. They are, if you will, pain-compliance techniques. If you want to safely but effectively escort a drunk patron out of a pub, for example, or break a hold, they can be useful. If, for a more vivid and immediate example, you want to cause enough distress to induce someone to cooperate, pressure points can be frighteningly efficient.

I won't go into much technical detail, but I grab his hair

with one hand to hold him in place. Using my opposing thumb, I dig deep into his neck, more specifically, the upper trunk of the brachial plexus above the clavicle known as Erb's point. Ian Cornwell's body convulses as though I had hit him with a stun gun, which, come to think of it, I should have brought. He tries to let out a gnarled scream. I pull back my thumb suddenly, giving him a second of relief, but I don't stop there. I move quickly to another spot on the underside of the bicep, squeeze hard, cover his mouth. Then I go back to Erb's point, pushing down on the nerve bundle even harder. Ian Cornwell thrashes impotently, like a freshly caught fish dropped on a dock. I straddle him now, pin him down, and go after the pressure point on the underside of the jaw. His body stiffens. Then I move up to the temples, then back to the neck. I put my fingers together, forming two spears, and shove those spears deep into that hollow beneath both ears. When I jerk up hard on his skull, his head jerks and his eyes roll back.

Of course, I could be wrong. We have established that already. Ian Cornwell may have been telling the truth from the get-go—that he didn't know anything, that he is innocent, that he was indeed tied up by two masked men. If that is the case, we will soon know for certain. And yes, I will feel bad for what I've done to him. Violence is a high, but I am not a sadist. That may sound like I'm threading an awfully thin needle, but I do experience empathy, and if I hurt an innocent man, I will feel bad about it. But life is a series of close calls, of weighing pros and cons, and if both Ema and I (not to mention the original FBI investigators) believe that Ian Cornwell has not been truthful, the pros of crossing this particular line win out.

And so I continue my assault, methodically, expressionless, until he cracks and tells me everything.

Well, that was interesting.

Here is what Professor Ian Cornwell told me:

Three months before the Vermeer and Picasso theft, young Ian Cornwell, a Haverford research assistant one year removed from graduating, met a lovely lass named Belinda Evans at a local pizzeria. Belinda was, according to Ian Cornwell, a "knock-out" with long blonde hair and sun-kissed skin. He fell hard.

At first, Belinda claimed to be a junior attending Villanova University, but as their relationship progressed, she admitted to her new beau that she still attended nearby Radnor High School as a sophomore. Her parents, she said, were very strict, so they would have to keep their relationship a secret. Ian Cornwell concurred. He did not want his relationship with a high school girl, a sophomore at that, to be made public, thereby harming his chances for academic and career advancement.

This, of course, presented a problem for a budding romance— simply put, where to hook up. Her home with the strict parents was a no-no, as was Ian's campus suite, which he shared with three other research assistants who would definitely gossip.

Belinda suggested a solution.

Ian worked nights alone as a security guard in Founders Hall. The work was, to put it mildly, uneventful. Haverford was a sleepy campus. Ian spent most nights alone at the security desk, reading and studying. What if, Belinda proposed, he could sneak her into Founders Hall, where they could spend hours late at night alone?

Ian readily and excitedly agreed.

The young lovebirds met up this way, Ian estimated, approximately ten times over a three-month period. Ian fell harder and harder for Belinda. The routine was a simple one: Belinda would go to the locked back entrance. There was a primitive security camera back there. Ian would see her via the monitor at his desk. She would wave and smile. He would come back, let her in, and you can guess the rest.

But on one special night—the night of the heist obviously—when Ian unlocked that back door after seeing Belinda on the monitor, a man burst in wearing a ski mask and brandishing a handgun. At first, Ian thought the man had forced Belinda at gunpoint, but it soon became apparent that that wasn't the case. They were working together, Belinda and this man in the ski mask. He held the gun on Ian while Belinda explained in the calmest voice, one Ian had never heard her use before, the situation—how they would tie Ian up, how Ian would tell the authorities that two men had fooled him by pretending to be policemen, how the MO would appear similar to the Gardner Museum heist in Boston so as to throw them off. Belinda did all the talking. The man in the ski mask just held the gun.

Belinda told Ian Cornwell that if he ever talked, she would tell the authorities that the heist had been Ian's idea. Ian was, after all, the inside source. She also reminded Ian that there was not much he could offer the police anyway. He couldn't identify the man in the ski mask, and as for Belinda herself, nothing she had told him was the truth. She did not attend Radnor High School. Her name was not Belinda. After tonight, he would never see her again. Even if he told the police the truth, the leads would be scant; Ian would only be incriminating himself, she reminded him. He had, after all, sneaked a high school girl into Founders Hall over a three-month period. At best, Ian would be expelled for that indiscretion and academically tarnished.

To further emphasize her seriousness, Belinda told Ian that if he did talk, they would come back and kill him. As she gave him that final warning, the man in the ski mask grabbed Ian by the scruff of the neck and pushed the muzzle of the gun into his eye.

The morning after the art heist, when Ian was found tied up, he debated coming clean and telling the truth. But the FBI agents were so aggressive, so sure that he was involved, Ian feared that everything Belinda told him would come to pass would. He would take the fall. Suppose, after he spilled his guts, they never found Belinda or the man in the ski mask. Would the FBI be satisfied—or would they need a convenient fall guy, a guy who, at best, showed poor enough judgment to let one of the two thieves repeatedly trespass?

It was clear to Ian that he had to remain silent and ride it out. As long as he didn't trip himself up, the FBI had nothing on him—because, alas, he was innocent. That was the delicious irony: The only way they would be able to nail Ian for anything was if he told the truth about the fact that he didn't do anything.

I asked Ian: "Did you ever see Belinda Evans again?"

When he hesitated, I made the spear shape with my fingers.

Yes, he said. Many years later. He couldn't be sure it was Belinda, he said, though I think that's a lie.

He was sure.

———

The late-night sex with Username Helena is not very good.

After I leave Ian Cornwell, it is too late to do more sleuthing. I am not sure that I need to do more immediate work anyway.

I know it all now.

There are a few loose ends, but if I let all this evidence

settle for a few hours—plus having Kabir and my team spend the night nailing down a few additional details—I firmly believe all will become clear in the morning.

So, with that rationale in my mind, I keep my sex app appointment with Username Helena. She is willing and enthusiastic, and I am disappointed and surprised that I do not respond in kind. I find myself distracted. I know it appears that I am casual with sex, but the truth is very much the opposite. Sex is sacred to me. It is the closest thing I will ever know to religious euphoria. Many people feel like this in church or on a runner's high or, in Myron's case, when Springsteen plays "Meeting Across the River" followed by "Jungleland" in concert. For me, it only happens during sex. Sex is the excellent adventure, the grand voyage from which we completely disembark the moment we slip out of this bed. For me, sex is best when you have a—to use a business phrase I absolutely detest—"shared vision." Tonight, there was simply too much static for a connection; it was merely a release, not all that different from masturbation.

As we lie back in silence, catching our breaths, eyes on the ceiling, Username Helena says, "That was nice."

I say nothing. I debate a Round Two—perhaps that will put me more in the zone—but I'm not as young as I used to be, and it is getting late. I am idly wondering how we two will transition to exiting when my phone rings.

It is Kabir. The time is two a.m.

This can't be good news. "Articulate," I say.

"We have a big problem."

CHAPTER 33

"Y ou found Arlo Sugarman."

It has been twelve hours since Kabir's phone call. My adrenaline spike has subsided, the crash thus imminent. I have not slept, and I can feel myself fraying at the edges. Stamina is a large part of my training, but genetically I am not predisposed to it. I am also aging, which obviously hampers stamina, and I have very little real-world experience in needing it. I have rarely had to stay up all night on patrol, as one might in the military, or been forced to go days on end with no sleep. I do battle—and then I rest.

The old woman speaking to me now is Vanessa Hogan.

I am back at her house in Kings Point. We are alone. Jessica set this up for me. At first, Vanessa Hogan was reluctant to consent to a second meeting. The enticement that pushed her over the edge, as I suspected it would, was that she and I would meet alone, only the two of us, and I would tell her the whereabouts of Arlo Sugarman.

"Could we start with you?" I ask her.

Vanessa Hogan is propped up via pillows on the same couch. Her skin tone is rosier than at our last meeting. She appears less frail. A scarf still covers her head. The house is empty. She'd sent her son Stuart to the grocery store.

"I really don't know what you mean."

"I recently visited Billy Rowan's father," I say. "Do you know he and Edie Parker's mother are something of an item?"

"I did not," Vanessa says, her voice dripping something overly sticky. "How nice for them."

"Yes. William Rowan is in assisted living. His room is filled with Christian imagery. There are framed Bible quotes on the wall. I found the contrast striking."

"What contrast?"

"With your home," I say, lifting both hands in the air. "I don't even see a single cross."

She shrugs. "That's show religion," Vanessa replies with a tinge of bitterness. "That doesn't mean anything."

"Alone, you're correct, it wouldn't. But I have done some digging. You've never been associated with a church, as far as I can see. You've never given money to any religious institution. In fact, before Frederick was killed—"

"Murdered," Vanessa Hogan interrupts, a sticky-sweet smile plastered to her face. "My son wasn't killed. He was murdered."

I try to mirror the smile. "We are getting to it now, Ms. Hogan, aren't we?"

"What does that mean?"

"My best friend was robbed of a pro basketball career because a man named Burt Wesson intentionally injured him. Destroyed his knee. One day, I paid Burt a visit. He hasn't been the same since. There are men who have crossed my path who have done great wrongs. Over the years, I've conducted 'night tours.' Some survived, some didn't, but none were ever the same. Most recently, right before Ry Strauss's body was found, I made sure a bullying abuser would never harm anyone else again."

Vanessa Hogan studies my face. "Do you have your phone with you, Mr. Lockwood?"

"I do."

"Take it out and hand it to me."

I do as she asks. She looks at the screen.

"Do you mind if I power it off?"

I signal for her to suit herself.

Vanessa Hogan presses the button on the side and holds it. The phone goes dark. She leaves it on the coffee table. "What are you trying to say, Mr. Lockwood?"

"You know," I say. "We both felt it that first meeting. All of our talk about vengeance."

"I told you that vengeance should be the Lord's."

"But you didn't mean it. You were testing me, gauging my re-action. I could see it in your face. The bullying abuser I injured last week? He was an active danger. Now he isn't. Simple. He was neutralized by me because the law wouldn't stop him."

She nods. "You said you wanted to do the same to the men who killed your uncle."

"Yes."

"And killed the poor girls."

I nod. "You understood," I say. "You sympathized."

"Of course."

"Because you've done the same."

I lean back. I put a hand into my pocket.

"Where is Arlo Sugarman?" she asks.

"I could just turn him in," I say.

"You could, yes."

"But you'd rather I not."

The room falls silent. We are right on that edge now.

I say, "You know what happened to Lionel Underwood, don't you?"

She doesn't reply.

"It was too much for Leo Staunch. He didn't want anyone else to endure what Lionel Underwood had. So he asked me to help him protect Arlo Sugarman. I found that odd."

"As do I," she says.

"No, not that he didn't want to hurt Arlo—I got that." I lean closer and lower my voice. "But why did Leo only ask about Arlo?"

"I'm not following."

"Why," I continue, "didn't he ask me about Billy Rowan and Edie Parker?" I sit back. "It kept nagging at me, but the answer was obvious."

"What's that?"

"Leo Staunch didn't ask about Billy and Edie," I say, "because he knew they were already dead."

Silence again fills the room, pushes out, suffocates.

"It is funny how so many of the early theories ended up being the correct ones," I say. "Take the Jane Street Six. After Lake Davies turned herself in, there were only five. How, everyone wondered, could the remaining members have managed to stay hidden all these years? One person? Okay. Two? Unlikely, but perhaps. But all five of them alive and unseen for all these years? Now we know the answer, don't we? Lionel Underwood has been dead for more than forty years. Nero Staunch took care of that. And Billy and Edie have been dead even longer. You saw to that, Ms. Hogan."

Vanessa doesn't reply. She just sits there with the sickly-sweet smile.

"You are eighty-three years old," I say. "You are ill. You want to tell someone the truth, and you see me as a kindred spirit. You have my phone—I would have no proof anyway. Do you fear I will report what you say to the FBI?"

Vanessa Hogan's eyes lock hard on mine. "I don't fear anything, Mr. Lockwood."

Of this I have no doubt.

"They stole my life." Her voice is a pained and harsh whisper. She takes in a deep breath. I watch her chest rise and fall, taking in oxygen, gaining strength. "My only son, my Frederick . . . When I first heard he was dead, it felt like somebody had whacked me with a baseball bat. I dropped to the floor. I couldn't breathe. I couldn't move. My life ended. Just like that. All that love I had for that boy, the precious beautiful boy, it didn't die. It turned to rage. Right there." She shakes her head, her eyes dry. "Without that rage, I don't think I would have ever stood up."

There is a water bottle next to her with a straw. She lifts it to her lips, and her eyes close.

"I became consumed with justice. You, Mr. Lockwood, you worry about stopping bad people before they commit more crimes. What you do is admirable and even practical—you stop crimes. You prevent more people from having to go through the horror of what happened to Frederick and me. But that wasn't my motivation. I didn't think or even care if the Jane Street Six did it again. I had that rage. I had that rage—and I had to put it somewhere."

"Tell me what you did next," I say.

"Research," she replies. "Do you research your enemies, Mr. Lockwood?"

"I do."

"I learned that three of the six came from religious families—Billy Rowan, Lake Davies, and Lionel Underwood. I also figured that they were scared, trying to find a way to come in from the cold. So I made that pitiful religious appeal on television. And I prayed—no joke—that one of them would call me."

"And one did call you," I say.

"Billy Rowan. That part was true, just like I told everyone. He came in the kitchen door."

"What happened next?"

"That baseball bat. A literal one rather than figurative. I hid it next to the refrigerator. Billy was sitting at my kitchen table. I asked if he wanted a Coke. He said yes, please. So polite. Hands folded in his lap. Crying. Telling me how sorry he was. But I had planned this. He had his back to me. I took the bat and whacked him in the skull. Billy's whole body shuddered. I hit him again. He teetered on the chair and then fell to the linoleum. I hit him again and again. That rage. That burning rage. It was finally being fed—you've felt that?"

I nod.

"Billy was on the floor. Bleeding. Eyes closed. I raised the bat over my head again. Like an axe. It felt so good, Mr. Lockwood. You know. Beforehand I'd worry that the actual act would make me queasy. But my God, it was the opposite. I was enjoying myself. I was idly wondering how many more blows it would take to kill him when I suddenly had a better idea."

"That being?"

Vanessa Hogan smiles again. "Find out what he knows."

"Makes sense," I agree.

"I called Nero Staunch. We had met in Lower Manhattan at a meeting for the victims' families. I asked him to come alone.

The two of us dragged Billy down into my basement. We tied him to a table, then we woke him. Nero used a power drill with a narrow bit. He started on Billy's toes. Then he moved to his ankles. At first, Billy claimed he didn't know where the others were—they had all split up. Nero didn't buy it. It took some time. Billy loved Edie Parker. Did you know they were engaged?"

"I did, yes."

"So Billy tried to hang on, which only made it worse. Inevitably, the truth came out. He didn't know about the others, but he and Edie were hiding together. They planned on turning themselves in. And you're correct, Mr. Lockwood—those two didn't throw cocktails that night. They'd planned to, he admitted, but when the bus went over the railing, they all just ran. Billy and Edie's hope was that if they surrendered early, they'd be spared the worst of it, especially if one of the parents was willing to forgive them."

Vanessa Hogan ups the sickly-sweet smile.

"That parent," I say, "being you, of course."

"Of course. To be on the safe side, Billy had come alone to feel out the situation, leaving Edie hiding alone at a lake cabin owned by an English professor at SUNY in Binghamton. Nero and I drove up with Billy in the trunk. We found Edie Parker. We made sure she didn't know anything more—which enraged me. I wanted to find them all, but obviously that wasn't going to happen quite yet. Then we finished with Edie and Billy."

"What did you do with the bodies?" I ask.

"Why would you want to know?"

"Idle curiosity, I guess."

Vanessa Hogan's eyes are on mine now, probing. A few seconds later, she waves her hand and says, "Oh, why not?"

in a too-cheerful tone. "Nero had an alliance with a mob boss named Richie B who lived in Livingston. Richie B had a furnace on the back of this huge estate. We brought the bodies there. That was the end of that."

Her story is pretty much what I had expected, and she relishes the telling of it.

"So two are dead almost immediately," I say. "A few years later, Lake Davies turns herself in. She goes to Nero Staunch and makes a deal for Lionel Underwood. Were you aware of that?"

Vanessa frowns. "Nero told me—but after the fact. I wasn't happy about it."

"You wanted to get both of them?"

"Of course. But Nero said it wasn't as easy as you see on TV to kill her in prison. For one thing, Lake Davies was being held in a federal facility. That makes it harder, he said. But between you and me? I think Nero was just an old-world sexist. Killing men? No problem. But his stomach couldn't handle Edie Parker. I took the lead in that."

I nod slowly, trying to put it together as she speaks. "So that's four of the six accounted for," I say.

"Yes."

"And then, what, you heard nothing?"

"For over forty years," she says.

"And then someone—maybe a man named Randy—comes to Nero Staunch with information on Ry Strauss's whereabouts," I say. "Nero is too old and sick to do anything about it anymore. He's in a wheelchair. His power is all ceremonial. His nephew Leo is the boss now, and Leo's against this kind of vigilantism. So Nero calls you. I can show you three calls coming from the Staunch family craft brewery to your home. Landlines, which, if you don't mind me saying, is old-school."

"That's not proof of anything."

"Not in the slightest," I agree. "But I don't need proof. This isn't a court of law. It's just you and I having a chat. And I still need answers."

"Why?"

"I told you."

"Oh right." Vanessa nods, remembering. "The Hut of Horrors. Your uncle and your cousin."

"Yes."

"So go on," she says. "Tell me the rest of your theory."

I hesitate—I want her to say it—but then I dive in. "I don't know if the information came to you directly from Nero Staunch or if Staunch sent this Randy to you. That doesn't really matter. You ended up getting the contents of Ry Strauss's safe deposit box. That told you what name he was using, where he lived, perhaps a phone number. Ry was understandably panicked about the robbery. You called him and pretended to be someone from the bank. What did you tell him exactly?"

She narrows her eyes, tries to look wily. "What makes you so sure it was me?"

I open the file I've brought with me and pull out the first still from the CCTV camera in the basement. "We thought the perpetrator was a small, bald man. But once I realized that the killer could be a woman, one who perhaps lost her hair because of chemotherapy, well, that's you, isn't it?"

She says nothing.

I pull out the second still and hand it to her. On it, a man with jet-black hair and a brunette are exiting via the front door.

"This is the CCTV from the lobby of the Beresford. It was taken six hours after the one I just showed you from the basement. The man"—I point—"is a building resident named

Seymour Rappaport. He lives on the sixteenth floor. The woman with him, however, is not his wife. No one knows who she is. Seymour didn't know either. He said the woman was in the elevator when he got in, so she had to have come from a higher floor. We checked pretty thoroughly. There is no sign of this woman entering the building. You were very clever. You wore an overcoat on the way in via the basement. You dumped it in the middle of Ry's apartment. No one would notice it unless they specifically looked. When you put on that wig, the bald man vanished for good. Then you took the elevator down and exited with another resident. Genius really."

Vanessa Hogan just keeps smiling.

"You did make one small mistake though."

That makes the smile falter. "What's that?"

I point to the left shoe in one photograph, then the other.

"Same footwear."

Vanessa Hogan squints at one image, then the next. "Looks like a white sneaker. Common enough."

"True. Nothing that would hold up in a court."

"And come now, Mr. Lockwood. Aren't I too old to pull this off?"

"You'd think so," I say, "but no. You had a gun. You kept it against his back. I could, of course, ask the FBI to pull all the nearby street camera footage from the day. I'm sure we would find the bald man holding a gun on him. We might even get a clearer shot of your face."

Vanessa is loving this. "You don't think I would have disguised my face too? Nothing much, just a little stage makeup?"

"More genius," I say.

"I wonder though."

"Wonder what?"

"I never realized the painting over his bed was so valuable."

"And if you had?"

Vanessa Hogan shrugs. "I wonder if I would have taken it."

"You don't know?"

"I don't, no."

So there we are. I now know the fate of all six of the Jane Street Six. It occurs to me, as I sit there with Vanessa Hogan, that I am the only person in the world who does.

As if she could read my thoughts, Vanessa Hogan says, "Now it's your turn, Mr. Lockwood. Where is Arlo Sugarman?"

I ponder how to answer this question. There is still one more thing I want to know. "You interrogated Billy Rowan and Edie Parker."

"We went over that."

"They told you that they didn't throw Molotov cocktails."

"Yes. So?"

"And what about Arlo Sugarman?"

"What about him?"

"What did they say about his role in all this?"

The smile is back. "I'm impressed, Mr. Lockwood."

I say nothing.

"You think that makes Arlo guiltless?"

"What did Billy and Edie tell you?"

"Do you promise that you'll still tell me where Arlo Sugarman is?"

"I do, yes."

Vanessa settles back. "You seem to know already, but okay, I'll confirm it for you. Arlo wasn't there—but he was still the one who planned it. The fact that he ended up being too gutless to show doesn't make him any less guilty."

"Fair enough," I say. "One final question."

"No," Vanessa Hogan says, and I hear steel in her voice. "First, you tell me where Arlo Sugarman is."

It is indeed time. So I just say it: "He's dead."

Her face drops.

I produce a photograph of the tombstone. I tell her what Calvin Sinclair had told me. It takes a while for Vanessa Hogan to accept all of this. I take my time. I explain all I know about Arlo Sugarman, how he spent time in Oklahoma and overseas, how he seemed to do good in his life and try to right whatever wrong he'd committed.

After some time, Vanessa Hogan says, "So it's over. It's really over."

It was for her. It wasn't for me.

"One more thing," I say, as I rise to leave. "If Billy and Edie didn't throw the explosives, did they say who did?"

"Yes."

"Who?"

"Ry Strauss, for one."

"And for the other?"

"You've seen the grainy images," she says. "There were still six people there. Ry Strauss got someone else to take Arlo Sugarman's place. He threw the second one."

"And his name?"

"Billy and Edie didn't know him before that night," she says. "But everyone called him Rich." She sits up a little straighter. "Do you have any idea who that is?"

Rich, I say to myself.

Short, of course, for Aldrich.

"No," I tell her. "No idea at all."

CHAPTER 34

When I take the helicopter to my familial home of Lockwood, I customarily don't appreciate the views. Human beings adapt, one aspect of which is that when something becomes common, we lose the sense of awe. We take the everyday for granted. I am not saying this is a negative. Too much is made of "live every moment to its fullest." It is an unrealistic goal, one that leads to more stress than satisfaction. The secret to fulfillment is not about exciting adventures or living out loud—no one can maintain that kind of pace—but in welcoming and even relishing the quiet and familiar.

My father is on the putting green. I stop twenty yards away and watch him. His stroke is a perfect metronome. Golfers will disagree, but to be great at the game, you have to be a little OCD. Who else can stand over the same putts for hours on end and work on their stroke? Who else can spend three hours straight in the same bunker in order to perfect spin and trajectory?

"Hello, Win," my father says.

"Hello, Dad."

He is still eyeing up his putt. He has a routine. He does it every time, no matter what, no matter how many putts in a row he practices. His theory, which is the same one I apply to martial arts, is that you practice the same way as you play.

"Penny for your thoughts," he says.

"I was thinking that to be great at golf, you have to be a little OCD."

"Elaborate, please."

I explain briefly about obsessive-compulsive disorder.

He listens patiently, and when I finish, he says, "Sounds like an excuse not to practice."

"That could be."

"You're a very good player," he says, "but you never wanted it enough."

That is true.

"Now Myron," Dad continues. "He seems sweet and nice, and he is. But on the basketball court? He's barely sane. He wants to win that badly. You can't teach that kind of competitive spirit. And it's not always a healthy thing either."

He stands up now and turns to me. "So what's wrong?"

"Uncle Aldrich."

He sighs. "He's been dead for more than twenty years."

"Did you know about his problems?"

"Problems," he repeats, and shakes his head. "Your grand-parents preferred the term 'predilections.'"

"When did you know?"

"Always, I guess. There were incidents when he was still in middle school."

"Like what?"

"Oh, what difference does it make, Win?"

"Please."

He sighs. "Peeping Tom to start. He would also get too aggressive with girls. You have to remember. This was the sixties. There was no such thing as date rape."

"So your parents moved him around," I say. "Or they paid people to let it go. He changed high schools twice. He started at Haverford and then the family shipped him to school in New York."

"If you know all this, why are you asking?"

"Something happened in New York," I say. "What?"

"I don't know. Your grandparents never told me. I assume it was another incident with another girl. They sent him to Brazil."

I shake my head. "It wasn't a girl," I say.

"Oh?".

"Aldrich was one of the Jane Street Six."

I wanted to see if he knew. I can see from his face that he didn't.

"Uncle Aldrich was there that night. He threw a Molotov cocktail. A few days later, your parents sent him to Brazil. Kept him in hiding, just in case. They set up that shell company to keep Ry Strauss quiet."

"What is the point of this, Win?"

"The point is," I say, "that didn't stop Aldrich. Men like him don't get better."

My father's eyes close as though in pain. "Which is why I broke off with him," he says. "Cut him off and never spoke to him again."

There is anger in his voice—anger and deep sadness.

"He was my baby brother. I loved him. But after that

incident with Ashley Wright, I knew that he would never change. Perhaps, I don't know, perhaps if our parents hadn't always facilitated him, perhaps if they had made Aldrich get help or face some consequences, it wouldn't have come to that. But it was too late. Granddad was dead, so it was up to me. I did what I thought best."

"You cut ties."

He nods. "I didn't know what else to do."

I nod and move closer to him. He is a simple man, my father. He has chosen to live behind these hedges, safe, protected. He has chosen to be passive. Has that worked for him? I don't know. I am my father's son, but I am not my father. He did what he thought best, and I love him for it.

"What?" he asks. "Is there something else?"

I shake my head, not trusting myself to speak.

"What is it?" he asks.

"Nothing," I assure him.

He searches my face for a few moments. Again I show nothing.

I do not want to break his heart.

After a few moments pass, he points to the rack on his left. "Grab a club," he says, as he lines up the balls for our favorite backyard game.

I want to stay with him. I want to stay and play Closest to the Cup with my father until the sun sets, like we used to when I was a child.

"I can't right now," I tell him.

"Okay." He looks down at a golf ball, as though he's trying to read the logo on it. "Later maybe?"

"Maybe," I say.

I want to tell him the truth. But I never will. It would only hurt him. There would be no upside, no positive change. I stay silent and wait until he turns his attention back to the small white ball on the green. His eyes focus on it, only it, and I know, because I've seen him doing it many times, he is escaping into this simple, habitual activity. I try to do the same sometimes. I even get there once in a while.

But it's not really who I am.

CHAPTER 35

The sound of tires crunching on the gravel awakens me. I'd fallen asleep on the couch, which is a surprise. Exhaustion alas trumped keyed-up. I wouldn't have guessed. I am still lying on the couch when the front door opens and Cousin Patricia walks in carrying a bag of groceries.

The first thing she sees is me on the couch.

"Win? What the hell?"

I stretch and check my watch. It's 7:15 p.m.

"How did you get in? I locked the doors and set the alarm."

"Oh yes," I say with all the droll I can muster. "It's really impossible for me to get past a Medeco lock and an ADT alarm system."

When Patricia looks past me, when her gaze reaches the dining room table, she stumbles a step back. I wait. She doesn't speak. She just stares. I slowly stand, still stretching.

"Cat got your tongue, Cousin?" I ask.

"You broke into my home."

"Nice deflection," I say. "But if we must go there, yes." Then

353

I point to the dining room table and mimicking her voice, I add, "You stole my Picasso."

It's not my Picasso, of course. But I liked the repetitiveness of the phrasing.

"I expected a more arduous search for it," I tell her. "I can't believe you just hung it in your bedroom."

Cousin Patricia gives a small shrug. "I don't let anyone go in there."

"And that's where it's been this whole time?"

"Pretty much."

"Ballsy," I say.

She shrugs. "Not really. If anyone asked, I would say it was a replica."

I nod. "People would buy that."

She starts toward the dining room table. "Why did you screw off the back?"

"You know why," I reply. "What did you do with the negatives?"

"How do you know about them?"

"Our art authenticator found a set in the back of the Vermeer. The negatives were square shaped—six centimeters by six—unusual by today's standards. It didn't take long to realize that they were very likely to have come from an old camera"—I glance at the shelf—"like your father's Rolleiflex. Anyway, I figured that if your father had hidden some in the Vermeer, maybe he also hid some in the family's only other masterpiece—the Picasso."

Patricia stands over the painting now. "So you checked?"

"Yes."

"And you didn't find anything."

I sigh. "Do we have to play this game, dear Cousin? Yes, the negatives are gone. You removed them. I did, however, notice a certain stickiness on the stretcher—from Scotch tape perhaps. In the Vermeer, the negatives were taped to the stretcher. It would stand to reason that the same applies to the Picasso."

She closes her eyes and tilts her head back. I see her swallow and I wonder whether tears will follow. This is probably a time to offer a word or two of comfort, but I don't think that will play here.

"Can we skip the denials, Patricia?"

Her eyes blink open. "So what do you want, Win?"

"You could tell me what really happened."

"The whole story?" She shakes her head. "I wouldn't know where to start."

"Perhaps," I say, "with your father befriending Ry Strauss in New York City."

"You know about that?"

"I do. I also know about the Jane Street Six."

"Wow," she says. "I'm impressed."

I wait.

"This is years after that night though," she continues. "He would visit us from New York City. Ry, I mean. Dad introduced him as Uncle Ryker. He said Uncle Ryker was CIA, so I couldn't tell anyone about him. I think I first met him when I was fifteen. He took an interest in me, but, I mean, yes, he was very good-looking and almost supernaturally charismatic. But I was fifteen. Nothing happened. It was never like that. I realized later that Ry was periodically coming to my father for money or a place to crash..."

She stops and shakes her head. "I don't know where to go with this."

"Jump ahead," I tell her.

"To?"

"To when you and Ry Strauss decided to steal the paintings."

Patricia almost smiles at that. "Okay, why not? So this is after Ashley Wright. Your father had already thrown my father out of the family, but my dad would still sneak into Lockwood to see Grandmama. She was, after all, his mother. She could never say no to him. One day, my father comes back furious and frantic because the family—your father—had agreed to loan the two paintings to Haverford for an upcoming exhibit. I couldn't figure out why he was so angry about this. When I asked him, he started ranting about how your father had cut him off and taken what was rightfully his. A lie, of course. I'm now sure it was about the negatives. Anyway, I was a senior in high school. We were in this small house while you all lived it up in the grand Lockwood Manor. I was looked down upon at school, the subject of whispers and innuendo. You know how it was. A few days later, Uncle Ryker came to visit again. I'll be honest. I wanted him. I really did. I think we would have, but once he heard me talk about the paintings, he hatched the plan." She looks up at me, baffled. "How did you figure it out?"

"Ian Cornwell."

"Ah. Poor sweet Ian."

"You seduced him," I say. "Slept with him to gain his trust."

"Don't be a sexist, Win. If you were eighteen and needed to sleep with a female guard to pull off a heist, you wouldn't have given it a second thought."

"Fair point," I agree. "More than fair, actually. I assume that Ry Strauss was the man with the ski mask."

"Yes."

"He saw you once years later. Ian Cornwell, I mean. You were on *The Today Show* promoting the Abeona Shelter."

"I had long hair when I was with him," she says. "Dyed it

blonde for those three months. After the robbery, I cut it and never let it grow back again."

"Cornwell claims that he still wasn't certain you were his Belinda—but even if he was, what could he prove?"

"Exactly."

"And you didn't tell Aldrich about the robbery?"

"No. By then, I knew Ryker was really Ry Strauss. He confided in me. We grew close. We even got the tattoos together."

She turns to the side and pulls down on the back of her top, revealing a tattoo—the same *Tisiphone abeona* butterfly that I'd seen on the photographs of Ry Strauss's corpse.

"What's the significance of that butterfly?" I ask.

"Beats me. That was all Ry. He ranted about the goddess Abeona, of rescuing the young, I don't know. Ry was always full of such passion. When you're young, you don't realize how thin the line is between colorful and crazy. But the planning and execution of the heist was"—her face breaks into a wide grin— "it was such a high, Win. Think about it. We got away with stealing two masterpieces. It was the best thing I'd ever done in my life."

"Until," I say, arching an eyebrow for effect, "it turned into the worst."

"You're such a drama queen sometimes, Win."

"Again: Fair. When did you find the negatives?"

"Six, seven months later. I dropped the Picasso in the basement, believe it or not. The back of the frame broke. When I tried to fix it . . ."

"You found them," I finish for her.

Patricia nods slowly.

When I ask my next question, I hear the catch in my throat. "Did you shoot Aldrich or did Aline?"

"I did," she says. "My mother wasn't home. That part was true. I sent her out. I wanted to confront him alone. I still hoped for an explanation. But he just snapped. I had never seen him like that. It was like...I had a friend with a really bad drinking problem. It wasn't just that she would fly into a rage—it was that she would look straight at me and not know who I was."

"And that's what happened with your father?"

She nods, but her voice is oddly calm. "He slapped me across the face. He punched me in the nose and ribs. He grabbed the negatives and threw them in the fireplace."

"The broken bones," I say. "Those were the old injuries the police found on you."

"I begged him to stop. But it was like he didn't see me. He didn't deny it. Said he did all this and worse. And I mean, those negatives, the images on them..."

"You now knew what he was capable of," I say.

"I ran into his bedroom." Her eyes are far away now. "He kept the gun in his night table drawer."

She stops and looks at me. I help her out.

"You shot him."

"I shot him," she repeats. "I couldn't move. I just stood over his body. I didn't know what to do. I just felt, I don't know, confused. Unmoored. I knew I couldn't go to the police. They'd figure out I stole the paintings. They'd learn about Ry for sure—he would go to prison for life. The negatives were ashes in the fire, so where was my proof? I also thought—I know this will sound weird—but I worried about the family too. The Lockwood name, even after we'd been kicked to the curb. I guess it's ingrained in us, isn't it?"

"It is," I agree. "You said my father came to see yours the night before he was murdered. That wasn't true."

"I was just trying to throw smoke at you. I'm sorry."

"And the part about two assailants kidnapping you?"

"Made it up. Same with that story about the kidnappers giving me hope and letting me think I was being let go. Some of the rape and abuse stories I told came straight off those negatives, but none of that happened to me."

"You just wanted to muddy the investigation."

"Yes."

I want to get her back to her story: "So you'd just shot your father and you felt confused. What happened next?"

"I was in shock, I guess. My mother came home. When she saw what happened, she totally freaked out too. Started ranting in Portuguese. She said the police would lock me away forever. She told me to run and hide somewhere, that she would call 911 and say she found my father dead. Blame it on intruders. I just reacted. I grabbed my suitcase—well, your suitcase—and I packed it and I ran."

"I'm guessing," I say, "that you ran to Ry Strauss?"

"I knew he lived at the Beresford. I was the only one he trusted with that, I think. I don't know. But when I got there, Ry was in bad shape. Mentally, I mean. He was hoarding. He hadn't shaved or even showered. The place was disgusting. I woke up the second night, and Ry had a knife against my throat. He thought some guy named Staunch had sent me."

"You left."

"In a hurry. I didn't think twice about the suitcase."

I can't help but note that in both cases—the murder of my uncle and the theft of my family's paintings—the investigators' first instincts had been correct. With the art heist, they suspected some involvement on the part of Ian Cornwell. That was correct. In the case of Uncle Aldrich's murder, one of the first theories was that Cousin Patricia had shot her own father, packed a suitcase, and then she'd run away.

That too had been correct.

"This is going to sound crazy," she says, her voice barely a whisper, "but I was with my dad when he bought that shed at a hardware store. We drove up not far from the site, and he dropped it off." She looks at me, and I feel the temperature in the room drop ten degrees. "I was in the car, Win. Think about that. I look back now, and I wonder if one of the girls was tied up in the trunk. How messed up is that?"

"Very," I say.

"I don't know what was on your negatives, but there were some outdoor shots, so I had some idea of where the shed might be. When I was ten or eleven, Dad used to take me camping up there."

"How long did it take you to find it?"

"The shed? Nearly a month. That's how well he hid it. I must have walked by it ten times."

"Did you ever actually stay in the shed?"

"Just that last night. Before I faked my escape."

"I see," I say, because I don't. Something isn't adding up. "And you came up with this plan?"

Patricia's eyes narrow. "What do you mean?"

"You're eighteen years old. You shot and killed your own father. It was clearly traumatic. So traumatic, in fact, you still keep his photographs on the wall." I point behind her. "You made your father a big part of your story. Aldrich was, you claim, what inspired your good works."

"That's not a lie," she counters. "What I did...my dad...it haunted me. He was my father. He loved me, and I loved him.

That's the truth." She moves close to me. "Win, I committed patricide. It shaped everything else in my life."

"Which brings me back to my point."

"Which is?"

"You, a confused eighteen-year-old girl, came up with the idea of pretending to be a victim. Because if that's true, kudos. It was brilliant. I bought it completely. I never for a moment questioned it. You were able to bring closure to those girls' families. You were able to 'expose,' if you will, the Hut of Horrors, but not your own father. You gained attention and used it to launch the Abeona Shelter. To do good. To try to make up for what your father had done. I'm amazed you thought of it on your own."

We stare at one another.

"But I'm guessing," I say, "that you didn't think of it on your own, did you?"

She says nothing.

"You were on the run. Your one ally, Ry Strauss, is crazy. You couldn't call your mother. You probably didn't count on the police suspecting her too—but now they had eyes on her." I steeple my fingers. "I'm putting myself in your place—trapped, alone, young, confused. Who would I call for help?"

Her weight shifts from one foot to the other. She doesn't say it, so I do.

"Grandmama."

Three reasons why this made sense to me. One, she loved Cousin Patricia. Two, she had the resources to hide her. Three, Grandmama would do anything to protect the family from the scandal this revelation would bring forth.

Cousin Patricia nods. "Grandmama."

Before you judge, it isn't just a Lockwood thing. Families

361

protect their own. That's what we do. And not just families. In a sense, we all circle the wagons, don't we? We use the excuse about the "greater good." Churches cover up their clergy's crimes and hide them in new locations. Charitable organizations and ruthless businesses are all adept in the art of covering up indiscretions, at self-protection, at rationalizing with some configuration of the ends justifying the means.

Why would it surprise anyone that a family would do the same?

From the time he was young, my uncle Aldrich committed bad acts and never paid a price. He never got help, though to be fair, you can't really help someone like that.

You can only put them down.

"So what next, Win?"

How did I put it before? There is no bond like blood, but there is no compound as volatile either. I think about that common blood coursing through both of us. Do I have some of what Uncle Aldrich had? Is that what makes me prone to violence? Does Patricia? Is it genetic? Did Uncle Aldrich just have a damaged chromosome or chemical imbalance or could some kind of major therapy have helped?

I don't know and I don't much care.

I have all the answers now. I'm just not sure what to do with them.

CHAPTER 36

Life is lived in the grays.

That is a problem for most people. It is so much easier to see the world in black and white. Someone is all good or all bad. I try sometimes to glance online, at Twitter or social media— at the outrage real, imagined, and faux. Extremism and outrage are simple, relentless, attention-seeking. Rationality and prudence are difficult, exhausting, mundane.

Occam's razor works in reverse when it comes to answers: If the answer is easy, it is wrong.

I warn you now. You'll disagree with some of the choices I make. Don't fret about it. I don't know whether I made the right ones either. If I was certain, per my personal axiom, I would probably be wrong.

When I arrive back at the Dakota, PT is waiting for me. I bring him up to my apartment. I pour us both cognac in snifters.

"Arlo Sugarman is dead," I tell him.

PT is my friend. I don't really believe in mentors, but if I did, PT would be one. He has been good to me. He has been fair.

"You're sure?" he asks.

"I had my people call the crematorium that works with St. Timothy's to look into their records for on and around June 15, 2011. They also looked into death certificates for the Greater St. Louis area for that date."

PT sits back in the leather wing chair. "Damn."

I wait.

He shakes his head. "I wanted him, Win. I wanted to bring him to justice."

"I know."

PT raises the cognac. "To Patrick O'Malley."

"To Patrick," I say.

We clink glasses. PT collapses back into the chair.

"I really wanted to right that wrong," he says.

With the glass near my lips, I add, "If you did anything wrong."

PT makes a face. "What does that mean?"

"You were the junior agent," I say.

"So?"

"So those were his calls, weren't they?"

PT carefully puts down his glass on the coaster. He watches me. "What calls?"

"To not wait for backup," I say. "To go in through the back door on his own."

"What are you trying to say, Win?"

"You blame yourself. You've blamed yourself for almost fifty years."

"Wouldn't you?"

I shrug. "Who called that tip in?" I ask him.

"It was anonymous."

"Who told you that?" I ask. "Never mind, it's not important. You both drove to the house, but when you got there, Special Agent O'Malley made the decision not to wait for backup."

PT looks at me over his snifter. "He thought time was of the essence."

"Still," I say, "he broke protocol."

"Well, technically, yes."

"He kicked in the back door on his own. Who fired the first shot, PT?"

"What difference does it make?"

"You didn't mention it to me. Who fired first?"

"We don't know for sure."

"But Special Agent O'Malley did discharge his weapon, correct?"

PT stares at me hard for a few long seconds. Then he tilts his head back on the leather and closes his eyes. I wait for him to say more. He doesn't. He just sits with his head tilted back and his eyes closed. PT looks old and tired. I stay silent. I've said enough. Perhaps Special Agent Patrick O'Malley was just overzealous. Perhaps he wanted to catch Arlo Sugarman and make himself the hero, even if it meant shattering standard FBI procedure. Or perhaps O'Malley, a father financially stretched with six kids, had heard that Nero Staunch had put a bounty on the Jane Street Six, and really, they were killers anyway and so what if one of them got shot trying to escape?

I don't know the answer.

I don't want to push it.

Life is lived in the grays.

"Win?"

"Yes?"

"Don't say another word, okay?"

I don't. I just sit there with my drink and my friend and let the night close in around us.

———————

The next morning, I drive out to Bernardsville, New Jersey, and I visit Mrs. Parker and Mr. Rowan again.

This for me is the grayest of the gray.

They made me promise to tell them what I learned about their children.

So do I? Do I tell these two elderly parents that their children are dead—or do I let them go on believing that maybe Billy and Edie survived and have children and possibly grandchildren? What good will knowing the truth at their age do for them? Should I let them live with their harmless fantasy? Will the truth cause too much stress at their age? Do I have the right to make that call?

I warned you that you may disagree with some of the calls I make.

Here is one.

Mrs. Parker and Mr. Rowan have waited nearly fifty years to learn the truth. I know the truth. I promised that I would tell them the truth.

And so I do.

I don't go into gruesome detail, and mercifully they don't ask.

When I finish, Mrs. Parker takes my hand in hers.

"Thank you."

I nod. We sit there. They cry for a bit. Then I make my excuses and leave.

They'd wanted to know who killed their children.

Here again I am making a call you may not like.

I tell them it was Vanessa Hogan.

As I leave the assisted living village, I take out my phone and hit the send button on my email. I am emailing an audio file to PT. Of course, I realized that Vanessa Hogan might ask for my phone in order to confess—and of course, I carry a spare.

I cut out the opening—my words about my own unlawful acts—but the FBI will have her full confession on tape. Vanessa Hogan crossed the line in my view. You hear me say this, and you think me a hypocrite. You counter about my "night tours" and my beating of Teddy "Big T" Lyons in the beginning of this tale. Teddy did me no harm. On the other hand, Vanessa Hogan's victims—Billy Rowan and Edie Parker—were responsible for the death of Vanessa Hogan's only son.

I understand that. None of these are easy calls.

We live in the grays.

But Billy Rowan and Edie Parker were young with no record. They didn't throw the explosives. They were remorseful and willing to surrender. They would not have continued to kill and harm people. Should Vanessa Hogan pay for what she did?

I'll leave that to the courts.

Am I threading too thin a needle again?

Well, we aren't done yet.

―――――――――

My jet awaits. We fly back out to St. Louis. When we land, I take the drive myself. The address is already in my phone navigation. I arrive at the farm and park on the road. I trek through the high grass. There are signs warning me about trespassing. I don't much care. The farm has been in the Sinclair family for three generations. The Reverend was born in that farmhouse. But I am more interested in the caretaker.

I didn't buy Reverend Calvin Sinclair's reasons for not letting the world know who "R.L." was once Arlo Sugarman died. He could say he had just learned his identity. There was no real danger in the truth anymore. The Reverend was also so ready for my arrival at his church, and thus I suspected that he had been warned, which, it turns out, he had been. Elena Randolph had called him within minutes of our confrontation.

With all that in mind, I did, as I told PT, have my people call not just the crematorium St. Timothy's normally uses but all the local ones. I also had them check the county death records. In both cases, they found nothing matching anyone with the initials RL who died on June 15, 2011. In fact, there were no male deaths matching Arlo Sugarman's description—age and height anyway—at all during that time.

When I walk up through the farm's gate, I turn right. A man steps into view. He looks to be his age—sixty-six years old—with a shaved head. He is also the right height.

"Can I help you?" the man asks.

I can still hear the slightest hint of a Brooklyn accent.

Arlo Sugarman didn't show up the night they tried to firebomb the Freedom Hall because he didn't believe in that kind of destruction. He ended up caught up in something beyond his control and spent his life on the run. If I told PT the truth, would he have wanted to take Arlo in and bring him to trial? Or would he have seen it the way I do?

I don't know. It isn't PT's call anyway. It's mine.

"It isn't over," I tell him. "You need to run again."

"Pardon?"

The back door of the farmhouse slams open. Calvin Sinclair hurries out. When he sees me, he starts to rush, obviously concerned by my intrusion, but the man with the Brooklyn accent puts up his palm to stop him.

"I figured out you're still alive," I say. "Someone else could too."

The man looks as though he's about to make denials or arguments, but instead he nods at me and says, "Thank you."

My gaze moves to Calvin Sinclair, then back to Arlo Sugarman. I almost ask what they are going to do now. But I don't. I have done my part. The rest is up to them. I turn and head back down the hill.

I still have one more stop to make.

———————

As I pull off Hickory Place and up the long driveway, I see the old baronial mansion in the distance. I am back in New Jersey. Ema lives here with her movie star mother, Angelica Wyatt. I soon spot them both waiting for me by the front door.

I think by now you've guessed that I've told no one about Cousin Patricia. She gunned down a monster—a monster, per my own justification with Teddy "Big T" Lyons, who would have continued to maim and kill. There is no reason for Cousin Patricia, who ended up doing so much good, to pay any sort of price for that. I admit that I may be slightly biased because this decision also neatly fits into both my personal narrative and my own self-interest.

I don't want my father and my family scandalized.

But regardless, I think this decision is just. You may disagree. Too bad.

When I park and get out of the car, Ema runs from the door

369

to greet me. She doesn't break stride as she wraps her arms around me, holding me tight, and I feel something in my chest crack open.

"Are you okay?"

"I'm groovy," I say.

"Win?"

Ema buries her face in my chest. I let her.

"What?"

"Don't ever use the word 'groovy' again, okay?"

"Okay."

I look over her shoulder and see her mother watching us. Angelica is not happy to see me. I meet her eye and try to give her a reassuring smile, but that does little to placate her. She does not want me here. I understand.

Angelica spins away and heads inside.

Ema pulls back and looks at me. "You'll tell me everything?"

"Everything," I reply.

But I'm not sure that's true.

As I look at my daughter's face, I flash back to the night before.

I'm in bed with Username Helena. My phone rings. It's Kabir.

"We have a big problem."

"What is it?"

"We lost Trey Lyons."

I snap up fast, startling Helena. "Details," I say.

But you don't need the details. You don't need the details of how my men lost Trey Lyons's SUV on Eisenhower Parkway. You don't need the details of how I surmised that Trey Lyons had eyes on the Dakota, how those eyes must have spotted Ema, how they followed her back, how stupid I felt not to have realized that earlier. You don't need the details on my call to

Angelica at two a.m., how I told her to hide in the basement with Ema. You don't need the details on how fast I rushed out here, how I parked on Hickory Place, how I ran up the drive wearing night goggles with a Desert Eagle .50 cal semi-automatic in my hand. You don't need to know how I spotted Trey Lyons breaking in through a back window. You don't need to know that I didn't call out to him, didn't tell him to put his hands up, didn't give him a chance to surrender.

This one may seem to be another gray to you. But it is not.

This one was easy. This one was black and white.

He came for my daughter. My. Daughter.

"Come on," Ema says. "Let's go inside."

I nod. It's a warm, sun-kissed day. The sky is the kind of blue only something celestial could have painted. Ema leads the way. She is wearing a top with spaghetti straps, so I can see her upper back. As we get closer to the door, I spot what looks like a familiar tattoo peeking out from between her shoulder blades . . .

A *Tisiphone abeona* perhaps?

I almost stop, almost ask, but when my daughter turns and looks at me, all those grays suddenly vanish in the bright of her smile. For perhaps the first time in my life, I only see the white.

Am I being hackneyed? Perhaps.

But since when have I cared what you thought?

ACKNOWLEDGMENTS

I am an expert in very little and thus rely on the kindness of strangers and friends. With that in mind, I would like to thank in alphabetical order James Bradbeer, Fred Friedman, Larry Gagosian, Gurbir Grewal, Shan Kuang, and Beowulf Sheehan. These people are top specialists in a variety of fields, and so if mistakes are found in this text, I feel comfortable throwing them under the bus.

Ben Sevier has been my editor/publisher for a dozen books now. The rest of the team includes Michael Pietsch, Beth de Guzman (reuniting with my editor on *Tell No One* after a lot of years), Karen Kosztolnyik, Elizabeth Kulhanek, Rachael Kelly, Jonathan Valuckas, Matthew Ballast, Brian McLendon, Staci Burt, Andrew Duncan, Alexis Gilbert, Joe Benincase, Albert Tang, Liz Connor, Flamur Tonuzi, Kristen Lemire, Mari Okuda, Kamrun Nesa, Selina Walker (heading up the UK team), Charlotte Bush, Glenn O'Neill, Lisa Erbach Vance, Diane Discepolo, Charlotte Coben, Anne Armstrong-Coben and, perhaps most important, Person I'm Forgetting Who Is Very Forgiving.

I'd also like to give a quick shout-out to Jill Garrity, Elena Randolph, Karen Young, Pierre-Emmanuel Claux, and Don Quest. These people (or their loved ones) made generous contributions to charities of my choosing in return for having their name appear in this novel. If you'd like to participate in the future, email giving@harlancoben.com for details.

Win is telling me that I've gone on long enough, but I know that he'd cut me some slack to thank you for requesting this book and taking the journey with us. You, dear reader, rock out loud. Articulate.

ABOUT THE AUTHOR

Harlan Coben is a #1 *New York Times* bestselling author and one of the world's leading storytellers. His suspense novels are published in forty-five languages and have been number one bestsellers in more than a dozen countries, with seventy-five million books in print worldwide. His Myron Bolitar series has earned the Edgar, Shamus, and Anthony Awards, and many of his books have been developed into Netflix series, including his adaptation of *The Stranger*, headlined by Richard Armitage, and *The Woods*. He lives in New Jersey.

For more information you can visit:
    HarlanCoben.com
    Twitter: @HarlanCoben
    Facebook.com/HarlanCobenBooks
    Netflix.com/HarlanCoben

D - 4/2

8/2

14/2

10/22

9/23

9/23